MONTROSE: THE CAPTAIN-GENERAL

James Graham steadied himself against the thrumming cordage as the vessel rolled and pitched, and stared back at the receding land. Already the features and details of the coastline, dramatic as it was, were fading, levelling out, and the great mass of the inland mountains seemed to grow, to come closer to the shore, to dominate all, in their blue, shadow-slashed infinity – those mountains which for so long had been both his sure ally and his continuing challenge, his refuge and yet his constant problem. Would he ever look on them again, he wondered?

**Also by the same author,
and available in Coronet Books:**

Robert the Bruce:
Book 1 The Steps to the Empty Throne
Book 2 The Path of the Hero King
Book 3 The Price of the King's Peace
Black Douglas
Montrose: The Young Montrose
The Clansman
Gold for Prince Charlie
The Wallace
Lords of Misrule
A Folly of Princes
The Wisest Fool

Montrose: The Captain-General

Nigel Tranter

CORONET BOOKS
Hodder and Stoughton

Copyright © 1973 by Nigel Tranter

First published by
Hodder and Stoughton Ltd 1973

Coronet edition 1974
Third impression 1980

Set, printed and bound in Great Britain for Hodder and
Stoughton Paperbacks, a division of Hodder and Stoughton
Ltd, Mill Road, Dunton Green, Sevenoaks, Kent
(Editorial Office: 47 Bedford Square, London, WC1 3DP)
by Cox & Wyman Ltd, Reading

ISBN 0 340 18619 4

CONTENTS

Part One   11

Part Two   191

Part Three   319

MONTROSE: THE CAPTAIN-GENERAL

PRINCIPAL CHARACTERS
In Order of Appearance

JAMES GRAHAM, 5th EARL and 1st MARQUIS OF MONTROSE: twenty-third chief of the Grahams, Viceroy and Captain-General of Scotland.

PATRICK GRAHAM, YOUNGER OF INCHBRAKIE: known as Black Pate, friend and kinsman of Montrose.

GEORGE MACKENZIE OF KINTAIL, 2nd EARL OF SEAFORTH: Chief of Clan Kenneth, doubtful royalist.

JAMES OGILVY, 1st EARL OF AIRLIE: Chief of the Ogilvys, staunch royalist.

GEORGE, LORD GORDON: eldest son of Marquis of Huntly.

ALISTAIR MACDONALD, YOUNGER OF COLONSAY: nicknamed Colkitto, Major-General to Montrose.

SIR JOHN HURRY OF PITFICHIE: Covenant Major-General.

DAVID CARNEGIE, 1st EARL OF SOUTHESK: father-in-law of Montrose.

MAGDALEN CARNEGIE, MARCHIONESS OF MONTROSE.

WILLIAM BAILLIE OF LETHAM: Covenant General.

COLONEL MAGNUS O'CAHAN: Irish commander of gallow-glasses.

LORD LEWIS GORDON: third son of Huntly.

SIR DAVID OGILVY: second son of Airlie.

COLONEL NATHANIEL GORDON: soldier of fortune.

JAMES GORDON, VISCOUNT ABOYNE: second son of Huntly.

ARCHIBALD, MASTER OF NAPIER: Montrose's nephew.

JOHN MACDONALD OF MOIDART, CAPTAIN OF CLANRANALD: great Highland chief.

ALEXANDER OGILVY OF INVERQUHARITY: young lieutenant.

PROVOST JAMES BELL: chief magistrate of Glasgow.

ARCHIBALD, 1st LORD NAPIER OF MERCHISTON: statesman, brother-in-law of Montrose.

JAMES, LORD OGILVY: eldest son of Airlie.

REVEREND DR. GEORGE WISHART: Montrose's chaplain and secretary.

WILLIAM, 1st MARQUIS OF DOUGLAS: Chief of that great house.

LUDOVICK LINDSAY, 16th EARL OF CRAWFORD: royalist Major-General.

GEORGE GORDON, 2nd MARQUIS OF HUNTLY: Chief of Clan Gordon.

KING CHRISTIAN IV OF DENMARK: warrior, and uncle of Charles I.

QUEEN ELIZABETH OF BOHEMIA: daughter of James VI and I, sister of Charles; known as The Winter Queen, and Queen of Hearts.

PRINCESS SOPHIA: daughter of Elizabeth.

PRINCESS LOUISE: daughter of Elizabeth.

PRINCESS ELIZA: daughter of Elizabeth.

ARCHDUKE LEOPOLD: brother of Emperor Ferdinand III, Governor of the Spanish Netherlands.

JOHN ASHBURNHAM: Gentleman-in-Waiting to Queen Henrietta Maria.

HARRY, LORD JERMYN: Master of the Household to Queen Henrietta Maria.

QUEEN HENRIETTA MARIA: wife of Charles I, and Princess of France.

JEAN FRANCOIS DE RETZ: Archbishop-Coadjutor of Paris.

EMPEROR FERDINAND III.

WILLIAM HAY, 3rd EARL OF KINNOUL: royalist officer.

SIR EDWARD HYDE: Chancellor of the Exchequer, adviser to Charles II.

KING CHARLES II: aged eighteen.

JOHN KENNEDY, 6th EARL OF CASSILLIS: Covenant representative.

JOHN MAITLAND, 2nd EARL OF LAUDERDALE: Scots statesman.

JAMES CRICHTON, VISCOUNT FRENDRAUGHT: royalist officer.

SIR EDWARD SINCLAIR: Orkney laird.

MAJOR ALEAXANDER SINCLAIR OF BRIMS: royalist officer.

NEIL MACLEOD OF ASSYNT: Highland laird.

MAJOR-GENERAL HOLBOURN: Covenant officer.

GENERAL DAVID LESLIE: Covenant commander-in-chief, later Lord Newark.

SIR JAMES STEWART OF COLTNESS: Provost of Edinburgh.

ARCHIBALD JOHNSTON, LORD WARRISTON: Covenant lawyer and judge.

JOHN CAMPBELL, 1st EARL OF LOUDOUN: Chancellor of Scotland.

ROBERT GORDON: an Edinburgh boy.

PART ONE

CHAPTER ONE

The thin slanting sunlight of a March forenoon was sore on eyes
that had not closed all night, and James Graham frowned. Some
ridiculous corner of the man's mind was even grateful that he
could so frown and narrow his eyes unashamedly; it might not
be perceived that the King's Lieutenant-General and representative in Scotland was in fact fighting to keep the tears from
spilling from those narrowed eyes, the firm lips from quivering
under the luxuriant moustache and above the trim little pointed
under-lip beard. Bare head high, frowning straight into that
level dazzlement, and seeing nothing at all, he sought not to
hear either, hear the dread words of the Gordon minister of this
remote northern parish of Bellie where mighty Spey spreads
itself over wide marshlands before reaching the sea; those words,
of dust unto dust and ashes to ashes, that signified the end of the
earthly journey of one who had barely started along it. Somewhere in the same numbed mind, the man was trying to pray,
seeking to assure himself that this was indeed but the beginning,
the start of an infinitely fuller and finer and more rewarding
journey, for Johnnie Graham, a journey on which, one day, his
father would join him again and they would continue together
towards a goal of unimagined fulfilment. For himself, that day
could not come sufficiently soon.

James Graham was not aware of it, but there were many eyes,
other than his own, damp and strained and narrowed, that
March morning of 1645, hundreds, it might be thousands, the
eyes of harder, fiercer men than he, tough Irish kerns, proud
Islesmen, bare-shanked West Highland clansmen, veteran
Athollmen, Grahams and Drummonds from Strathearn,
Ogilvys from Strathmore. If the serried ranks of Gordon
cavalry were dry-eyed enough, it had to be remembered that
they had but newly joined the royalist army, and had neither
known Johnnie Graham nor yet come to love the father whose
slender and so upright figure in the black, rusty half-armour,
thigh-length, mud-stained riding-boots and tartan plaid, stood
alone beside the open grave – and all but broke other men's

hearts. John, Lord Graham, titular Earl of Kincardine, aged fourteen, had served with his sire, and these others, all through the most savagely taxing winter campaign of Scottish military history, and choked to death in his own blood, in his father's arms, the day before, worn out by his privations. Now he lay there in the new-dug earth, beside the little parish kirk, wrapped in the same Royal Standard which had flown over the stupendous victory at Inverlochy a month before, and which he and his father had taken it in turns to carry, wrapped round their persons, in snow and rain and mist, across flooded rivers and ice-bound passes, through screaming storms and freezing nights in the heather. Now they would lie together, the thin, great-eyed boy and the King's banner both, on the curlew-haunted flats of Speymouth; and father and army would march away and leave them there, to win Scotland back for its feckless, high-souled monarch, without his flag.

As the minister's harshly vibrant voice died away, the darkly swarthy hatchet-faced man who stood a little way behind the Marquis, and was his aide, kinsman and closest friend, Black Pate, Colonel Patrick Graham, Younger of Inchbrakie, raised a hand to the trumpeter near by, who lifted his instrument and blew a simple high reveille, clear, sweet, a little tremulous, its last pure note long-maintained, almost insupportable.

In the quivering silence that followed, Montrose took a single hesitant step forward to the very lip of the grave, his upright carriage drooping suddenly. He stared down into it, lips moving. So he stood for long moments, while, ranked outside and around the little riverside kirkyard, 3,000 men waited motionless, hushed. Then, turning his back on his son, the man straightened up, squared his shoulders and swung round to face the vast array, sun behind him also now. Head high, he raised his hand.

'Pate – have the March sounded. We have work to do,' he called, clear for all to hear. 'Advance in column.'

Even as the trumpet rang out again, this time in the stirring, cheerful bugle-notes that commanded forward in order of march, Montrose paced briskly between the table-stones to the group of officers who stood near the long, low thatched-roofed church of St. Ninian, a motley group, some in the extravagant magnificence of Lowland cavaliers, some in the tartans and calfskins of Highland chieftains, some in sober broadcloth, some in dented and dulled breastplates and ragged nondescript captured clothing – the veterans, these.

14

'My friends,' he said, and sought to keep his too expressive voice even, businesslike. 'Time we were amove. To your stations of march, if you please. My lord of Gordon – you will ride with me. The Master of Madderty and Sir David Ogilvy command the rearguard.' He held out his hand. 'My lord of Seaforth – I bid you a good day and God-speed. May you find your lady fully recovered, at Brahan Castle.' That was James Graham, Marquis of Montrose, *An Greumach Mor*, gentleman, to the man who less than a month before had led an army against him.

George Mackenzie of Kintail, chief of the name and 2nd Earl of Seaforth, blinked little pale eyes, and bowed low. 'My lord Marquis – you may rely on me to hold the North secure for you . . .'

'For His Grace, King Charles,' the Graham amended, but courteously – even though, at his back, somebody muttered 'Treacherous Hielant tod!' sufficiently loud to be heard by all.

Seaforth elected not to hear it. He was not in a position to do anything about it, having come in from the North with only one or two of his chieftains two days before, to submit himself to the King's Lieutenant – but leaving his army of Mackenzies, Macleods, MacRaes and Rosses safely behind, unblooded, in his own glens. Inverlochy had convinced him that he was temporarily on the wrong side. But an equivalent defeat would as swiftly detach him again.

Montrose turned to the old Earl of Airlie, who was sitting on a tombstone, wrapped in a borrowed ragged plaid. 'My good lord,' he said, in a very different tone, 'we part, for a space. You have been beyond all men faithful, splendid. It is my pride to have served and striven at your side. You will regain your strength at Strathbogie. There to act my recruiter, to send me more Gordon horse. And when you are fully well, to come to me again.'

The Ogilvy chief shook his grey head. 'It grieves me sore, James. To leave you thus. With so much still to win. But, God pity me, I but hold you back. I am a done auld carle, and by with it. But – come the good summer days and I'll be with you again, lad. And . . . and meantime, you have my sons.'

The other spread his hands. Sir David Ogilvy had already taken leave of his father to go with Madderty to command the rearguard. Sir Thomas lay dead in Inverlochy Moss. And the eldest, the Lord Ogilvy, lay rotting in Edinburgh Tolbooth's

15

darkest pit, there long months, bought from Cromwell for gold by Argyll, to humiliate and use as weapon against his father. The old earl had indeed served his King to the full, and broken his own health in winter campaigning in the process.

'I will lift Jamie out of Argyll's pit for you, my friend, never fear,' the Graham assured. 'And I will look to Davie's safety – if I may. God knows you have paid sufficient price. My thanks – and we shall meet again, with the King's cause triumphant . . .'

So they went their ways, Seaforth north, Airlie west to the Gordon hills, and Montrose and his ragged army east by south, with a kingdom to conquer.

*   *   *

Through South Moray, Banff and the uplands of Buchan they went, in predominantly hostile country. This was the land where the Committee of Estate's General, the Lord Balfour of Burleigh, had been lurking for many months, hiding his Covenanting army out of harm's way. They had been safe, if inactive, supported by the majority of the local lords and lairds. Now it fell to the King's Lieutenant to teach these Northern gentry that it did not pay to forsake their allegiance to their monarch and maintain His Grace's enemies. Montrose was in stern mood, as well he might be, and forced himself to unrelenting severity in spelling out this lesson, burning many a laird's-house and tower and granary, levying fines, requisitioning food, horses, gear, in a wide swathe south-eastwards. None put up more than token resistance. He was, however, equally stern with his own people, that there should be no bloodshed, rapine, savagery. He was a mild, almost gentle man for a great captain, but only deceptively so where principle was concerned. He had hanged men in the past for such conduct, and assured that he would do so again, be they heroes or none. His army was a wild one, mixed, of Irish kerns, Islesmen, Highland clansmen, Gordons, Angus lairds, few loving the other; under a less sure hand they would undoubtedly have run riot. But in coming to love this handsome, courteous, warm-eyed man, tested and tested again in the fiercest fire, who never asked his men to do anything that he would not, or could not do himself – they accepted this firm hand surprisingly well, with even the ungovernable giant major-general, Alastair MacDonald, Younger of Colonsay, showing a sort of reluctant respect. The Gordon cavalry was new, and less biddable; but they obeyed their young chief; and the Lord

Gordon, now that he had at last made up his mind where his allegiance lay, was attentive to James Graham's word.

They reached Turriff on the 9th of March, without any major clash of arms, with no word of Burleigh, or where he might now be hiding himself. It was six years since Montrose had last been at Turriff, when as Covenant lieutenant-general himself he had thrown down the gauntlet before Huntly and his Gordons. It would have been a bold prophet who would have forecast the changes and realignments which had taken place since then, and that King Charles's throne should now be tottering in England and Scotland both.

At Turriff further proof of Inverlochy's profound effects was demonstrated in the arrival of a deputation from the city of Aberdeen, no less, seeking the Marquis of Montrose and pleading that he would not again descend upon their much-fought-over town. Burleigh was not in Aberdeen, they declared, and all Covenant forces had been sent away. The citizens were at heart still loyal to King Charles, and all they wanted was to be left in peace.

James Graham was only moderately responsive. Although an honorary burgess of the city, Aberdeen had latterly shown him little but ill-will. They had cherished his and the King's enemies, had welcomed Argyll and accepted a Covenant garrison for long months. Why should they expect clemency from the King's Lieutenant?

The Irish, they quavered – the Irish . . . ! Like so many Lowland Scots, the Aberdonians conceived Colkitto's Catholic Irish – and the West Highlanders and Islesman likewise – to be little better than barbarian savages and fiends of hell. Their descent upon the city after the Battle of the Bridge of Dee, six months before, was being called the Sack of Aberdeen, and ever becoming, in retrospect a greater nightmare.

Montrose yielded so far as to assure that he would not let Colkitto's men nearer than Kinellar, nine miles from the city. He himself, however, must and would take over Aberdeen, in the name of King Charles. He required that the Provost and magistrates had the keys of the city ready to hand over, with all cannon, weapons and ammunition, and the citizenry orderly and well-behaved for his entrance in, say, four days' time. With this the emissaries had to be content. The Graham sent them away hoping that they did not really recognise how tiny and ill-equipped was his force, and that the train-bands and burghers of Aberdeen could overwhelm them by sheer numbers – if they plucked up the courage for the attempt.

Three days later, at the little grey town of Kintore on the lower Don, Montrose encamped, and ordered forward an advance party of Gordon cavalry, some eighty strong, to show the King's standard and make due arrangements for the entry of the royal representative on the morrow. He would have sent them under their own chief, the Lord Gordon; but that young man was not a little self-conscious about his change of sides – for the last time that he had been in Aberdeen it was as leading a cavalry brigade *against* Montrose; moreover, he was very well known in the town. So he asked to be excused. Instead, Colonel Nathaniel Gordon was sent. But Nat was something of a wild character, and liable to do rash things. So the reliable and level-headed Donald Farquharson of Braemar, whom all men respected, and was also a familiar figure in Aberdeen, was chosen to accompany him.

That evening, in the Manse of Kintore, with most of his officers happy to seek what amenities and facilities even a little town had to offer those starved of such modest delights for long, James Graham found himself alone with George Gordon for almost the first time since their reunion. Armies on the march offer little opportunity for private converse. His back to the minister's well-doing log fire, he considered the younger man thoughtfully.

'You are less than happy, I think, my friend, over your change of allegiance ? You still are anxious about your father ?' he asked. 'That he will be much angered. It distresses you ?'

'My father ? No – I have won past that. I have known for long that my esteemed sire is blessed with but poor judgment. For himself, or his family, that might be of little consequence. But as wielder of the Gordon power, it is of great account. I *had* to take decision of myself – since he has washed his hands of all leadership. No – it is not my father's frowns that trouble me now.'

'What then, George ?'

The other leaned forward, slight, dark, still-featured, but with deep-set glowing eyes. 'You will not understand, my lord. But . . . I fear to hear men call me turncoat !'

'Turncoat ! And you think *I* will not understand ? I, whom so many have called that same. Have I not grieved over it ?' Montrose shook his head. 'Too well I know your trouble, friend. But a man is no man, a poor creature indeed, who cannot

18

change his mind. When issues change, when he gains new light, when he learns better. The man who truly uses the wits God gave him, *must* change his mind. Frequently. All men err. If they never may change, they are of God's creatures the most pitiable.'

'Aye – but to lead men, on one side, in a great cause. And then so soon, to lead them on the other! I see the fingers pointed at me, too clearly. You did, yes. But you are Montrose. Of the stuff of greatness. I – I am but one of Huntly's brood, who has now changed sides twice ...'

'And both times on my account! At my pleading.' Montrose nodded. 'I know it, lad. And recognise my responsibility in this, as in so much else. *I* changed – but I did not change lightly. Nor lightly besought others to do so. Mine was the first signature on the National Covenant. I helped set up the Tables and the Committee of Estates. I was the Covenant's lieutenant-general. And believed that I did well, in the sight of God and of honest men. And then, when we had won what we sought, the freedom to worship as we believed right, the reform of government in Scotland – when I learned that many of those with me were not content, that they fought indeed for other ends, to pull down the King's Grace and set themselves up to rule in his stead ... this I could by no means stomach. To seek to dethrone the Lord's Anointed! Charles Stewart made errors amany, and had to be shown it. As one of the earls of Scotland it was no less than my duty to show him the error. But I am the King's loyal subject, always was and always will be. When the ministers turned against the King, in their overbearing spiritual arrogance, I could no longer walk with them. And when they allowed Archibald Campbell of Argyll to use their cause, and mine, for his own evil ends, and make himself master of this kingdom in place of his liege lord – then I had to draw my sword against them, and him. And to urge others to do likewise. As their simple duty. You, George, have done so. If this is to be turncoat, would God there were more of the breed!'

'You speak truth,' the Gordon admitted. 'All this I know. Have told myself many times. But ... I have not your strength. I am weak, foolish. Too concerned with how men think of me ...'

'*I* would not think that! Of George, Lord Gordon? With a mind of his own. When I remember the long months when my chiefest thought was how to change that mind of yours! On King Charles's behalf ...'

'And I in a misery of remorse, indecision, hating myself! You have won a sorry lieutenant, my lord Marquis.'

'I have won the man I wanted most to win,' the other declared simply. 'And not merely on account of the Gordon cavalry.'

Almost hungrily the younger man stared at him. 'If I could believe that . . . !' he said.

'It is plain truth, man. Since the day we first met, at Strathbogie, I have known that one day we would be brought together. It was fated.' James Graham smiled faintly, ruefully. 'Although I near cursed you thereafter. For you it was who made *me* first to doubt. Really doubt. Doubt my Covenant cause. You who asked if religious freedom meant freedom for all – or only for the King's Protestant subjects. Forced me to admit that a Catholic is equally entitled to a conscience. And then, later, at Inverurie, not five miles from this place, told me that you had decided that I was on the wrong side in this conflict. I, and the Covenant both. Do you remember? George Gordon's well-considered opinion!'

'And you were!'

'And I was.'

They considered each other, these two, so dissimilar, the assured, nobly-handsome man of thirty-three, looking older, thin, worn with fierce campaigning and personal sorrow, yet with an air almost of gaiety in the high purpose he emanated; and the twenty-seven year old, looking so much younger, diffident, slight, lacking poise but with a great sincerity.

Slowly, wordlessly, the Gordon nodded, rather as though a binding agreement had been contracted.

'You ride at my side into Aberdeen tomorrow, then?' the other asked.

'Yes.'

'Praise be for Gordon!'

George Gordon drew a long breath. 'Before you say thanks for Gordon, I would warn you. To my sorrow, I fear that you cannot altogether trust my brother. Lewis. He has his virtues. He will make a better captain of horse than ever will I. But . . . he has much of our father in him. Although more fierce. He is not wholly your man, I think. As I am. Do not rely on him too heavily, my lord.'

'You say so? I have never esteemed the Lord Lewis to be of *your* calibre, friend. Headstrong – but spirited. He would never betray us?'

'Not betray, I think. But he might fail you. In a pinch.'

'In a pinch, I might fail myself! But – would he let *you* down, and the Gordons likewise?'

'He might see it otherwise. His mind works differently from mine. And he might carry some of the Gordons with him. He has done, before.'

'You think that your father might work on him?'

'I do not know. It is a sorry business when a man cannot trust father or brothers.'

'We live in sorry days, with house divided against house. Civil war is of all evils the most grievous, I believe.' Montrose quelled a sigh. 'But you trust Aboyne, at least.' The Viscount Aboyne, second of Huntly's sons, had been fighting for the King for years, since his late teens, and was even now beleaguered in Carlisle, besieged by General David Leslie.

'Aboyne always gangs his ain gait. So long as *you* go that gait...'

The calm acceptance in the younger man's estimation of his family's failings was somehow moving. Huntly had eleven children, and had let them grow up wild, professing more interest in his dogs. Lady Huntly, with the last of them, had gone to her reward.

Montrose, whose own family life held its problems, changed the subject to that of logistics for the morrow's entry into the third city of the kingdom. With man-power so low, all would have to be most carefully stage-managed.

In the event, it was not stage-management that was called for, but something sterner. In the early morning Nat Gordon came back to Kintore at the gallop – but with only some thirty of his eighty troopers. And minus Donald Farquharson.

The roused royalist camp heard with mixed sorrow and fury what had transpired. The advance-guard had been well enough received by the city fathers, and suitably entertained, arrangements for the next day being agreed upon with every appearance of amity. But while this proceeded, couriers had been sent hurriedly southwards into the Mearns – whether with official knowledge or no was not clear. The Earl of Balcarres, Master of Horse to the new Covenant commander-in-chief General Baillie, was in the Mearns, protecting the flanks of Baillie's army, which was based on Perth. And with Balcarres was Sir John Hurry, or Urrie, of Pitfichie, an Aberdeenshire laird turned professional soldier, impartial as to his loyalties and methods, but effective and swift in their execution. Hurry, with a couple of squadrons of cavalry, had made a dash northwards from Conveth, reached Aberdeen that same evening, and fallen upon the unsuspecting Gordons – or such as were not bedded down with the ladies of the town. No quarter had been given. Donald Farquharson had been cut down where he stood, along with most of the advance party. Where Nat Gordon had been during this interlude was not specified – but he had managed to gather together what remained of his company and escape from the city, northwards, even as Hurry and his dragoons dashed away southwards again.

Montrose's heart sank within him at the news. Aberdeen seemed fated to destroy his good reputation and character. The major stain on his name hitherto had been its so-called sack, when after the treacherous killing of his Irish drummer-boy, under a white flag mission, he had allowed his angry troops to teach the city a lesson. He had never ceased, since, to regret that relaxation of discipline – even though probably he could not have prevented it in any case. The trouble was, he was not really a soldier at all, however successful at times he appeared at the business; he was a partisan, an enthusiast, a strategist and tactician, a would-be righter of wrongs, God forgive him – and he could not bring himself to accept the inevitable concomitants and horrors of war.

George Gordon took the blow hard, conceiving the blame as in some measure his own, since he had brought these men out but had failed to accompany them into the city. But he did not rant and rave like his brother Lewis, who immediately demanded that he should be given the rest of the horse to descend upon Aberdeen and demonstrate the price to be paid for assailing Gordon. Refusal of this demand was not well received.

Montrose laid down his programme in more assured and certain terms than he felt. He would enter Aberdeen as planned, swords sheathed. He would take steps to discover who was responsible for sending for Hurry, and deal with them. He would recover the bodies of the slain, and give them due and proper burial, with military honours. He would ensure that the city paid their dependants an ample sufficiency. And he would impose a collective fine for the King's cause, on account of Aberdeen's harbouring of the King's enemies. But there would be no reprisals, no looting, no savagery. This was no conquered city, but one yielding to the King's peace.

The growls of dissent were undisguised and general amongst his officers. Here was no way to deal with rebels and traitors. The blood of slain men demanded better than this, he was told. The King's cause must be vindicated.

'It is the King's cause that I am concerned with,' James Graham asserted, though reasonably. 'Aberdeen is a large city. We cannot garrison it, or hold it. When we pass on southwards, as we must, on the King's behalf, I would have behind us a city thinking well of us rather than hating us. To ride through its streets, shooting and slaying and burning might draw some of the hurt out of *you*. But it would serve King Charles nothing, for these are his subjects, as are we. Until I have five times so many men as I have today, I will not make Aberdeen more my enemy than it is now.'

Only a few agreed with him. It was ironic that one of those who could have been relied on to support him in this was Donald Farquarson of Braemar. George Gordon's support was dutiful rather than whole-hearted.

'I could use this evil circumstance to clear me of my promise to keep the Irish at a distance,' Montrose went on. 'But I shall not. No good would come of it, and much ill might. But you, Alastair, and you, Magnus, and some of your officers, should come with me, I think. You the citizenry will not fail to recognise – and so perhaps also recognise what they are escaping!'

His gigantic major-general snorted. 'A God's name – I'd have Aberdeen praying on its stiff knees that it would never see me or mine again! They would recognise me, to be sure!'

'No doubt, my friend – if afterwards you survived, with a great and hostile city at your rear, and the rest of Scotland to conquer!'

'I'd take my chance on that, whatever!' Colkitto shrugged bull-like shoulders. 'Soldiering, I'd sooner be feared than loved!'

A murmur of approval ran through the company.

'But more than soldiering is required of the King's Lieutenant, Alastair, I'd mind you of it. All of you . . .'

And so, that March afternoon, only a token force of about five hundred marched by Bucksburn and the Forest of Stocket, into Aberdeen, watchful, wary, grim, but with swords in their scabbards and at least a superficial aspect of peace. They were met at the city gates by the Provost and his anxious-looking magistrates and chief burgesses – but with no ministers, it was to be noted – with the keys, and urgent protestations that they had had nothing to do with General Hurry's attack, had no knowledge that he was coming, and greatly deplored the blood-shed and slaying. They prayed that the Lord Marquis would not hold the city in any way responsible . . .

'You may not have been responsible, gentlemen, but you did nothing, I think, to halt this shameful killing in your streets. Nor to detain Hurry thereafter,' the Graham replied, at his sternest. 'You have train-bands, guildry, thousands of able-bodied citizens. Yet you interfered nothing. You cannot escape responsibility, sirs. Keep your keys. I prefer to hold this town, in the King's name, by my own strength than by your leave.' And, as the municipal eyes were busy counting the numbers of men he had behind him, added, 'Major-General MacDonald's Irish and Highland Brigades are rather nearer than the nine miles I spoke of to you. But they will remain outwith the city, as promised, unless there is occasion to call them in.'

'One blast on my horn, and they will be here, by the Mass!' Colkitto roared, coming in on his cue. 'And Donald Farquharson shall be avenged!'

Hastily, fervently, the city fathers assured that that would not be necessary, that Aberdeen was the King's loyalest town in Scotland, or England either, that all was at the disposal of the Lord Marquis and his officers, every soul and stick and stone.

'Very well. I will hold you to that. I accept this city in King Charles's name, and require its due adherence to His Grace's rightful cause. So long as this is forthcoming, the citizens may go about their lawful occasions in peace. Now – I want dis-covered to me the identity of those who sent for Hurry. And I want the bodies of my friends slain . . .'

There was little or no trouble thereafter, on either side. They buried Hurry's victims at the great church of St. Nicholas next day, with an impressive and dignified service unflawed by incident – although there were one or two tense moments in the kirkyard. It was almost unbearably poignant for James Graham, who read the Lesson, so soon after that other funeral at the little kirk of Bellie; he realised that every such that he attended hereafter would amount to a re-burial of his own son. He had to remind himself that it was the souls of Donald Farquharson and forty or fifty Gordon troopers that he was praying for, not Johnnie Graham's.

Any sad preoccupation with Johnnie's present situation was

rudely shattered that evening, when a rider arrived hot-foot from Kinnaird and the Marchioness of Montrose. John Hurry had not halted again at Conveth on his southward flight, it seemed, but had gone on to Kinnaird, on his way apparently to Dundee. And from there he had forcibly taken Jamie, the new Lord Graham and Earl of Kincardine, despite his mother's, and the Earl of Southesk's entreaties, declaring him necessary hostage for his father's better behaviour, and moreover in need of proper upbringing and schooling. The boy was now aged twelve.

Montrose had been learning, for long now, how to control his passions, hurts and angers, learning the hard way. But this latest blow taxed all his resources of will-power and enforced calm. No doubt Hurry, a plain soldier, was acting under orders from Argyll, for he would be unlikely to make war on women and children. And no violence was beyond the godly Archibald Campbell. What would they do with the boy? Where would they take him? Would Hurry and the military keep him? Or hand him over to the Campbell and the Estates? What would *he* do, to aid Jamie? Could he do anything at all . . . ?

As well as the news itself, another thought came to prey on the man's mind. The courier brought only the grim news from Kinnaird, no letter, no message from Magdalen. Questioned, the man declared that her ladyship had given him no other instructions to carry than the bare tidings. Her husband found the implications ominous. He had written to her, at length, over the death of Johnnie, detailing, commiserating, seeking to comfort, as best he could. She would have received this letter days ago, and had ample time to reply. She had not done so. And now this. He feared, he greatly feared, for Magdalen's state of mind.

Private fears, however, were no more permissible for commanders to show than were hot anger and reprisals. Two days later they marched out of the city, for Stonehaven and Angus. Old Montrose, his own house, and Kinnaird Castle where Magdalen had returned to stay with her father, lay but two score of miles to the south.

CHAPTER TWO

William Keith, 7th Earl Marischal, next to Gordon was the most powerful man in the North-East. He was a cheerful, unsubtle individual, younger than Montrose a little, undistinguished as to features and apt to have a wide grin for most occasions. He had been James Graham's lieutenant once, and they were good enough friends; but he had not changed sides when Montrose did. Not particularly able as a soldier he nevertheless could muster large numbers of men, a considerable proportion of them cavalry – and for this reason had been Argyll's Master of Horse for a while. But Montrose's prowess at the Battle of Fyvie had damped his ardour, and his brother's death there, plus many of his trooper's, had made him less active in the Covenant support. But he had not succumbed to appeals to join the King's cause. And so Stonehaven burned.

Stonehaven, fifteen miles south of Aberdeen, was the Marischal's town, and head burgh of the Mearns, a pleasant place in a sheltered bay between headlands, with offshore the great rock which gave the place its name. Its houses were close huddled together and mainly thatched, and it was this that Montrose burned, and of a set purpose. There was no killing allowed, no raping and a minimum of looting – two of his men hanging at the Mercat Cross helped to ensure that; and the fired reed thatch could be readily replaced and no great harm done. But it all made a most impressive smoke, guaranteed to be seen at Dunnottar, the Earl Marischal's mighty fortress-castle on its sea-girt rock two miles to the south. Will Keith was safe in his eyrie, even from cannon – it was said, in the company of the Reverend Andrew Cant, third in the Covenant hierarchy of ministers, who had slipped out of Aberdeen hereto at Montrose's arrival. But the sight of the billowing smoke, and that of other and lesser properties of his along that seaboard, might convince the earl that he was in fact on the wrong side in this business – where letters from James Graham had gone unheeded.

No evident response had been evoked when operations had

to be called off. Scouts brought alarming news. Hurry, whether or no he had gone to Dundee as the Kinnaird courier reported, was back at Conveth, not much more than a dozen miles away – but now with 600 cavalry. As Montrose's horse were reduced to 150-odd, the situation was perilous in the extreme – especially with great black smoke-clouds rising 500 feet in the spring air to shout aloud their whereabouts. Something had to be done, and quickly, for 2,000 infantry, however bold and experienced, could not prevail against 600 cavalry save in a strongly defensive position. And Stonehaven was far from that – a trap, rather, in its deep hollow, cut off by the sea.

Typically, Montrose decided on advance towards the enemy, as the tactic least to be expected. But he did not do it directly. Conveth was on the rising ground at the south side of the wide, level Howe of the Mearns, with much bare and open country in between. He ordered his march due westwards, by Fetteresso and the high ground of the Braes of Glenbervie, the foothills of the Grampians, which here came fairly close to the sea; and once amongst them, turned south by Glen Farquhar and Strathfinella; closed, hidden ways, to emerge at length at the southern end of the Cairn o' Mount pass, at the mouth of the Howe indeed, but from the north-west, not the north-east where Hurry's scouts might have looked for them. Conveth lay across the levels no more than five miles away, as the crow flies. They camped in the wooded foothills just north of Fettercairn, which they reached in the dusk.

Montrose was up with the dawn next morning, to make his way, with Black Pate, to make survey of the spreading levels of the Howe of the Mearns from the high viewpoint of the old ruined royal castle of Kincardine, a mile or so to the north-east. Presently he sent Pate back for George Gordon, while he himself quartered every acre of the land spread before him with his calculating retard. He knew it well, had hunted over it, hawked and fished, not ten miles north of his old home.

He put it to George Gordon – would he be so kind as to take his Gordon horse and act decoy? In due course, let them ride openly forward from hereabouts, as though unaware of Hurry's presence at Conveth – which could be seen smoking blue against the green of Garvock Hill, in the new-risen sunlight. There was nowhere between where a body of cavalry could remain hidden. Hurry's look-outs would be bound to see them. If they were to ride, openly, unhurriedly, towards the House of Halkerton, there, two-thirds of the way across the Howe, then turn west-wards along that slight ridge. They could see it from here. The chances were that Hurry would not resist the chance to make a sally out to deal with them, 600 against 150.

'Decoy, you said ?'

'Yes. You would get plenty of warning, see you – for Hurry will have as little cover to approach you, as you to hide from him. You would pretend not to observe him, at first. Let him get within half a mile, perhaps. Then turn and spur back in seeming panic, north by west, as though direct for this Kincardine. Not the way you had come – but direct. It is important. You are not to know it, but there is the deep and mud-lined Ducal Water in the way, a wide and evil stank draining the marshlands of Halkerton. You do not know of it, see you – but Hurry could not fail to. And to know that horse cannot cross it. Hawking, I have often cursed it. Now it must serve us. He will conceive you trapped by it.'

'And I am *not* trapped?' the other wondered, without enthusiasm.

'Think you I do not value you, and your cavalry, too highly for that, man ? You will turn due westwards along it, as in alarm, and dash with all speed, seeking a crossing. There is none for miles He will believe he has you. See – you can trace the line of the Ducal from here – alders and willows. You will gallop along its southern lip. And just over that lip, I will have every musketeer and archer I possess, in a long line, hidden in the dip of the stank. Lining the bank, all my infantry. We shall let Hurry pursue you. He will seek to cut you off, but must himself follow that river-bank, strung out. And so we shall have him!'

Pate Graham slapped his thigh. 'Glory be!' he exclaimed simply.

'Mmm. But supposing Hurry thinks better of it ? Senses a trap ? Does not follow . . . ?'

'Then no harm done. But why should he ? I will keep my infantry hidden. I promise you. From now on. No fires, no movement. Hurry will see only your cavalry, on a reconnais-sance. When you flee north by west, you will seem to heading for this gap in the hills behind us, the entry to the Cairn o' Mount pass, whence you have come. A natural retiral. What would *you* do, Pate ? In Hurry's place ?'

'If I knew that I was dealing with James Graham of Montrose, I'd turn and ride for Dundee as though Auld Nick was at my tail!' that dark man declared, grinning. 'Otherwise, I'd chase Gordon, to be sure. The more so if I knew about that Ducal stank.'

'Hurry has been in this Conveth area for ten days at least. He cannot fail to know of it. He is a professional cavalry captain. Knowledge of the ground around him will be ever in his mind. He will know. And will not fail to know, likewise, that Gordon's 150 is all the cavalry that I have.'

'My men will not relish fleeing from Hurry,' the Lord Gordon pointed out. 'After he slew their comrades at Aberdeen.'

'Their chance will come. Once the trap is sprung. Tell them so, George . . .'

And so, that sunny first day of April, the royalist infantry spent an uncomfortable forenoon bent double much of the time, Colkitto leading in stupendous if breathless swearing, as they crawled down burn-channels, ditches and marshy hollows of the wide flats south-east of Kincardine, dodging, scuttling, creeping, in most undignified and unsuitable fashion for veteran warriors. It was not until nearly noon, when almost all were in position, that Gordon rode openly out at the head of his squadron.

From a carefully chosen spot midway along the line, Montrose scanned the wide prospect, dividing his attention between the Gordon's progress, plainly visible, and the distant Conveth. Assuming Hurry was there, he knew what he would do were he in his place.

And presently, keen eyes could discern Hurry doing exactly that. What looked like a dark cloud shadow moved out from the scattered housing below Garvock Hill and its woodland – but since the morning was bright, it could be only a tight-knit body of horse, a large body. Gordon would not see it yet, for the shadow was keeping to the east of the Halkerton woodland which would screen it from the north.

Owing to the watchers' angle of vision, however lowly, they could see exactly when the two sides came into mutual view. Suddenly the smaller Gordon group changed direction – and speed. Now they were coming directly northwards, across the marshy flats, at the gallop, spraying up mud and water, towards the hidden burn-channel and the line of waiting men. Gone was any neat formation, as the horsemen spread out to find their driest and swiftest way across the wet lands. From his low-set position, Montrose now could not see beyond them, to what

Hurry might be doing. But obviously the Gordons were fleeing in a major and sustained fashion, so that the enemy could be taken to be not far behind. All along the line the infantry readied themselves, tense now.

From the Halkerton woodland to their stretch of the Ducal Water was a good mile; but at the speed of the flight, it took only two or three minutes for the Gordons to cover the distance. As they approached the waterside area they tended to do so at an angle, as it were cutting the corner. And now behind them, could be seen the masses of Hurry's dragoons, spread wide across the levels, between quarter and half a mile away, a daunting sight even though they were being deliberately coaxed hither.

'Gordon is going to strike us midways,' Black Pate objected. 'Coming in where he will, he'll waste half our men. Those to the left will not be able to engage.'

'A hard thing for Gordon to judge. With those devils at his tail! But, no matter, We have enough . . .'

Presently the Gordon horse were thundering up the burnside track not a stone's throw from the crouching infantry, divots and stones from urgent hooves coming raining over on the watchers. The Gordons were strung out now, and the drumming of hooves, the snort and pant of the horses' breath, the creak of saddlery and the clank of steel beat a tattoo of excitement that set men's fingers itching at triggers and bowstrings.

But they had to be patient yet awhile. With the Gordons all streamed past, it was not long until the first of the Covenant troopers came pounding up, Major-General Hurry well to the fore, lashing his foaming beast with the flat of his drawn sword, a gallant figure dressed as cavalier rather than Covenanter. His men were all armoured in steel jacks and peaked-and-necked helmets, riding notably heavier mounts than the Gordon garrons, low-country beasts from Fife and Lothian. Montrose had given the strictest orders – no shooting until he gave the signal, on pain of dire penalty.

'Pray George Gordon remembers his instructions,' he murmured to the Master of Madderty, who was cursing steadily, monotonously, beneath his breath. 'If he goes too far . . . !'

But the Gordons did not overshoot their mark, which was a slight rise half a mile to the north-west, where Montrose, even from his lowly position, could see them. Here, as though realising that there was no crossing of the Ducal Water, they all abruptly turned to swing away at right angles south by west again, leaving the burn-side for the open levels. And, seeing it, James Graham gave them a few moments, and then raised a horse-pistol and fired a deliberate shot at the nearest of Hurry's horse, in front of him.

Immediately pandemonium erupted along that line of the burn. Every musket and pistol in the royalist army blazed out – at least, save for those too far to the east to have any targets. Every bowstring twanged. And even the poorest marksman could scarcely miss – for the enemy rode within fifty yards of them in the main, totally unaware of their presence.

More complete surprise could not have been achieved. Horses went down like ninepins in lashing ruin – for they made a surer mark than did the riders – and many that escaped the shooting tripped and crashed over the fallen, men being hurled in all directions. A fair proportion survived that first assault, of course, and most of these turned to face the unexpected attackers. But even so they were at a hopeless disadvantage. For the mud-splattered infantry were protected by the steepish bank which dropped to the water, a bank no horseman could cope with. Some who attempted to ride down the shooters, as they reloaded, slithered and fell in screaming, flailing disaster down into the stream. More drew over and swerved along the bank waving swords or firing pistols – but to little effect. None dismounted to come to grips. These were professional cavalrymen, and never considered fighting on foot.

At this stage the Gordon horse wheeled round and came dashing back, decoys no longer, swords drawn.

Hurry, up at the front, and so far unharmed, was no fool. Recognising a quite impossible situation, he shouted to his trumpeter to sound the retiral. He and those about him clearly preferred to take their chances with the Gordon cavalry than to run the gauntlet again of that grim river-bank, and swung off to the south-east, back towards Halkerton, forthwith. But others took retiral literally and merely reined round to spur back whence they had come – and these largely fell victims to Montrose's men before they perceived their error and pulled out desperately, anyway, eastwards, The Gordons got most of them.

It was all over in ten minutes – not a battle, nothing like a battle, since there was no fighting, as such, but only killing, with no royalist casualties at all save one Gordon whose horse pecked at a ditch and threw him, and one Irishman who toppled to fall into the burn and was fished out half-drowned. But it was a victory, undoubtedly, cheaply won. There were many more horses killed than men, but even so they captured eighty good mounts. The nearly 200 prisoners were something of an embarrassment; but thirty of them offered to change sides and serve with Montrose – indeed some had already done so – and the rest were sent under guard to Aberdeen. But the morale victory was much more important than the actual, Hurry made to look a fool, his Aberdeen raid avenged, and yet another infantry triumph over cavalry chalked up for all Scotland to consider, to enhance the legend of Montrose.

Always meticulous about such matters, James Graham held a burial service for the enemy dead, using the prisoners as gravediggers. And in the evening, when his scouts brought word that Hurry and his remaining dragoons had evacuated Conveth and were heading south fast, Montrose handed over command temporarily to Major-General Alastair, and taking no companion, despite protests, rode off southwards himself, public duty yielding at last to private.

*　　　*　　　*

It was only ten miles from Fettercairn to Kinnaird, in its great parks at the head of the vast landlocked bay of Montrose, and he came to the castle before dark. Even so the drawbridge was up and the gates locked against troubled times, and the caller had to wait some time at the moat-side before the porter obtained instructions to let him in.

David Carnegie, 1st Earl of Southesk, received his son-in-law in the Great Hall, an irascible, florid, heavy man, with a shock of white hair, white beard and choleric eye. He had his brother John with him, from nearby Ethie Castle, created Lord Lour in 1639 and since Montrose had last seen him, a less strong character but perhaps with a nimbler brain. No women were present.

'I hear that you have been showing that knave Hurry his business!' Southesk greeted, without preamble. 'Not before time. If you had done it a mite sooner, we'd all have reason to be the better pleased, by God!'

James Graham did not specifically answer that. His father-in-law had never loved him, even though he had been one of his guardians – which was why he had been married off to Magdalen Carnegie at the age of seventeen.

'I have come as soon as I might, sir,' he said, bowing. 'I hope I see you well? And you, my lord? May I offer my belated congratulations on your advancement?'

John Carnegie began to reply, but his brother interrupted brusquely. 'He came here, to Kinnaird, with hundreds of his bullyrooks. Hurry. To Kinnaird. Insulting me in my own house – me, Southesk! Declaring that he came in the name of the Estates. The Estates in which *I* sit! To browbeat my daughter. And remove my grandson. For *your* faults, sirrah! On your account. I hope that you are proud of yourself!'

'I have no reason to be proud, sir. But nor have I reason to reproach myself in this, I think. I conceive it to be Argyll's doing. Only *he* makes war on women and bairns. And Argyll is now a friend of yours, I am told?'

The other spluttered. 'Friend – no! We work together, on occasion. That is all. For the realm's weal. No more.'

'The King's greatest enemy, sir. An ill man to work with, I would think.'

'Not so. Be not so insolent, man. I'd mind you to whom you speak. Old enough to be your father . . .'

'And the King's former friend!'

'The King's friend still, damn you! If he had but taken my advice! Can I help it if Charles Stewart acts the fool? I am his loyalest subject. Nor is Argyll his enemy. He but cherishes the realm, until His Grace comes to his senses.'

'Cherishes, you say? Dear God, sir – do we speak the same language, you and I? Argyll cherishing Scotland, with sword and dagger and hangman's rope! Ask you Archie Napier how Argyll cherishes Scotland – your old colleague and fellow Lord of Session. Or ask Airlie. Or George Stirling of Keir. These will tell you, from Edinburgh's dungeons!'

'Cha! Men who rise against the lawful authority must be prepared to pay the price.'

'Perhaps these believed the *King* to be the lawful authority in this realm! As did once yourself, my lord. In whose name are you Earl of Southesk? Or Lord of Session Extraordinary?'

'Do not lecture *me*, on my duty, young man! His Grace rules Scotland through a lawful parliament of the Estates . . .'

'Of which Argyll is but one member! As indeed am I! Not even President, Convener or Chairman. Not Chancellor – he leaves that to his minion Loudoun. Yet do you deny that King Campbell rules in Scotland today? Who did Hurry obey? You, or Argyll? From whom does Sandy Leslie take his orders? Or this General Baillie? Or Callendar, Balcarres and the rest?' The younger man paused, drawing deep breath. 'But I did not come, sir, to reproach or suffer reproach. We choose our own paths, as we see best. Have you any word of my son? Of Jamie?'

'Only that he has been sent to Edinburgh. To the care of the Estates.'

'The care of Argyll! Where is he kept? How treated? Is he well . . . ?'

'I know not. He was well enough when Hurry took him. How can I tell? You should look to your own bairns, James Graham . . .' Even David Carnegie paused there, no doubt recollecting the other bairn, whom James Graham had looked to, and taken with him on his campaigns. He coughed.

Hurriedly his brother intervened. 'I go to Edinburgh in two days, my lord Marquis,' Lour said. 'On affairs. I shall make it my business to discover how Jamie does. And to aid him if I may. I have promised Magdalen . . .'

'Aye, Magdalen,' Montrose echoed 'I thank you, sir. I shall be your debtor. Magdalen? She . . . she is . . . well?'

Her father produced something between a sniff and a snort. Her uncle spread his hands. Neither spoke.

'I will go to her. With your permission.' And not waiting therefore, Montrose bowed briefly and left them.

The Grahams, in their early married life, had been allotted a flanking-tower of the great courtyard castle, and thither the man hurried now, his heart leaden. This house of Kinnaird had always depressed him, its influence on his marriage not to his taste. Well he knew that his wife had always looked on it as home, rather than on any house he had provided for her. Not her fault, but there it was.

He climbed the twisting turnpike stair to her little sitting-room on the first floor; but only a dying fire was there. He climbed higher – and would have gone still farther to the third floor, but stayed himself. Up there would be his two remaining children. Robert aged five and Jean three. In their beds, no doubt. That he had to steel himself to knock at the other, second-floor door, was the measure of his failure as a husband.

There was no response, and quietly he opened the door. The room was unlighted, and beyond the great canopied bed a woman sat, staring out of the north-facing window at the last of the

34

day's dying on the distant Grampians. Hunched, she sat, silent – and did not turn as he came in.

'Magdalen! My dear!' he said, his voice tight, choking.

'Yes,' she answered, flatly. She did not so much as glance behind her.

He moved over to her, but almost hesitantly for that assured and positive man. 'Lassie,' he murmured, 'it is I – James.'

'Yes,' she repeated, after a moment, and with no more emphasis.

He looked down at her hunched shoulders and drooping head, and knew a great pity. She had always been a plump, big-made girl, comely enough, however shy and retiring. Now she was almost fat, flabby, slumped there, a picture of dispirited dejection, of letting go. Was this his doing? She was younger than he was, only thirty-one.

'Magdalen, girl – I am sorry. Desperately sorry.' He put hand to her shoulder – and felt her shrink away. 'You are sore hurt. And I – I am much to blame.'

'Aye, you are to blame,' she agreed, but lifelessly, an acceptance rather than an accusation, challenge.

'My sorrow – what can I say? I am desolated, as you are. It is hard, grievously hard. But . . . Jamie will be well enough, never fear. They will not harm him. We will get him back. He is but hostage . . .'

'And Johnnie? Shall we get him back? My Johnnie. Whom you stole from me. And killed.'

Shocked, the man gripped her. 'Magdalen! How can you say such a thing!'

'You took him. In your pride and folly. A child. And where is he now? My fine Johnnie. Where is he now?' She turned, for the first time, to look up at him. 'Tell me, James Graham – where is my Johnnie now?'

Now that he saw her full face, he was shaken by the change in her, the puffiness of flesh, the sag at the corners of her mouth, the lack-lustre eyes and the heavy droop of eyelids. This was not just sorrow and pain. Here was sickness of the mind.

'Johnnie is, I think, better off than are we, my dear,' he said, slowly. 'His troubles are by with. We still have ours to thole. Johnnie was tested, tested hard. And proved a man, whatever his years. He will fare none so ill on the next stage of his journey – of that I am sure. What do we have to take to the hereafter with us? Only the character we have fought to forge on earth.

35

This must be our charter and warrant in the next world – only that, and God's infinite mercy. So – I do not fear for our Johnnie. We shall see him again, one day – and know him well blessed, I think.'

'Words!' the woman declared. 'Fine words, meaning nothing. Johnnie is dead – *dead*, do you hear? Because you took him to the wars, a child.'

He sighed. 'Dead, yes. But I believe that there are worse states than to be dead. More especially for those who have lived well. Struggled. Striven. And died well. As did Johnnie. He ... he was fine. Courageous. Cheerful. To the end. A son to be proud of. He died in my arms ...'

She put her hands over her ears. 'Stop! Stop, I say. I do not want to hear. Enough! Enough that he is dead. And gone. You may keep your fine swelling words, James. You always had them, in plenty. I have less faith in them.'

'You do not wish to hear how it was? With him? What I could not tell you in my letter ...?'

'No.'

'There could be comfort in it.'

'There is no comfort for me. Comfort! I am done with comfort. Save it for those who know no better.' She turned away again.

'Magdalen – this will not do. You torture yourself. You *need* comfort. As do I, God knows! We are husband and wife. We should cherish each other ...'

'*You* say that! When are you with me, to cherish me and mine? You cherish only James Graham. And need nothing from me. Nor ever have.'

If that had been said vehemently, harshly, with any spurt of feeling, it might have been less hard to bear, in that it could have engendered retort, perhaps indignation. But it was said levelly, hopelessly, and the man knew only sorrow, pain, guilt.

'I have come, now, at least. I would have come sooner, if I could,' he said, on a sigh. 'But Hurry lay between. He is gone now – but only to Dundee, I think. I must follow him, before he raises that city against us; against the King. I must be back with my little army by dawn. We have not long together, lass. Do not let us squander it, in this fashion.'

'Together?' she asked, simply.

He swallowed 'It was for that I came.'

'If it is the bed that you want, I cannot say you nay, my lord.' That was a whisper.

36

Biting his lip, he shook his head. 'No. Not so. I came only in love. Seeking to give, and receive, comfort, affection, help.'

'Then you came too late, James. Too late, by years. I am your wedded wife, and you may do with me as you will. But you are too late for these things – love, affection, comfort. They are dead, James. Like . . . like Johnnie; I am sorry.'

'No! I will not accept that, Magdalen. I cannot. But . . .' He touched her shoulder again, lightly, and changed the subject. 'I would see the children, my dear. Let us go up-stairs to see young Robert. And Jean. They will have grown much . . .'

'Go, yes,' she said.

'And you. Surely you also . . . ?'

His wife shook his head.

Sighing, he turned and left her.

They had had five children. David, the third, had died in infancy. Robert and Jean were asleep in cots in the room directly above their mother's. Their father did not disturb them, al-though he longed to take them in his arms, especially the cherubic, pink-faced little girl. He scarcely knew them, having been but little at home these last five years and more – con-firmation of Magdalen's indictment. Was he grievously at fault? Had he done altogether wrongly in choosing to concern himself with the affairs of the realm and the King, instead of those of his own family, his wife and children? He need not have done so. Nobody forced him to it. But . . . he was one of the earls of Scotland – he never thought of himself by this new-fangled title of marquis – one of the lesser kings, whose traditional duty was to advise, guide and support the monarch – *Ard Righ*, the Great King. Others admittedly had not taken this duty so seriously. But he was not one of the new men. He was *An Greumach Mor*, head of the house and line of Graham, which had been a sure support of the Crown since Celtic days. The land where he stood, although it was Carnegie's now, had been given to his ancestor Sir David the Graham by the Bruce himself, 320 years before. And that David was far down the long line. Should *he* have shrugged that heritage away? How could he have done – the Graham – and continued to respect himself? Yet – what sort of a father had he been to these sleeping innocents? What sort of a husband to that unhappy woman downstairs? Was it all selfishness of a sort, crass pride? Had he indeed taken the wrong turning, years ago? And now bairns were paying for it? What was duty? Where did it lie? To a man's country, heritage and liege lord? Or to wife and bairns?

Stooping over those cots, suddenly he was aware that Magdalen was standing just outside the door, looking in. He turned to her – and at once, like a shadow, she was gone.

He took a step or two after her, and then halted. What use? But at least she had come so far ..

He stayed there with the children for some time, perhaps half an hour, just sitting, watching, even after the last of the light was quite gone. He would not do better in this house. And it might give time for Magdalen to think, to reconsider.

At length, he reached out lightly to stroke those small heads and whisper something incoherent. In present circumstances, he had little assurance that he would ever see them again.

Downstairs, he was disappointed. Though the lamps were unlit. Magdalen still sat at the window, as before, silent, with-drawn. She had nothing to say to him, no comment to make. Clearly she now inhabited some sad, grey world of her own – and, try as he would, he could by no means penetrate to it. Presently he gave up the attempt, and stooped to kiss the heavy coils of her hair.

'Goodbye, my dear,' he said. 'God keep you until I come again. God have mercy upon us both. For we need it. Perhaps, when next I come, things will be better, kinder, for us. I pray that it is so. You must try to forgive me, Magdalen – for all our sakes. I have failed you grievously. But I must follow the road I have taken. There can be no turning back for me, now. Thousands depend on me – God pity me! But ... we will have decision soon. And then – we will do better. Do not despair, lass. Time will heal much – and we are young enough yet. Try to pray for me.'

She made no response. But nor did she round on him.

He left her then, and made his way back to the main keep, to take leave of her father. The old man sat still at the head of the dais-table in the hall, a great wine-flagon before him, his brother sprawled over the board and snoring.

'Well, man – you have seen what you have done to my daughter,' Southesk growled. 'Are you satisfied?'

'I am sore at heart,' the younger man told him. 'How long has she been thus?'

'Too long. Months. Do you wonder?'

'It was before ... before Johnnie died?'

'Long before. That worsened it. She has pined for you too long, man. Now all is gone sour in her.' The old man took a great draught from the flagon, and then banged it down on the table. 'God's curse on it!' he cried. 'My lassie!'

'I should have taken her with me,' his son-in-law said, slowly.

'Eh . . . ? Taken her ? To the wars ?'

'Yes. She asked it, once. After Tippermuir. At Perth. Pleaded with me. When I took Johnnie. He pleading also. She said she would be a camp-follower. I said that it was impossible, not to be considered . . .'

'I should say not! What folly! *My* daughter, trailing at the heels of an army, like any Irish drab . . .!'

'*That* was not my concern. It was the hardship, the danger, the rough living. But . . . it might have saved her from . . . this.'

'Nonsense, man. If you think that, you are an even greater fool than I took you for!'

'There are fools and fools!' his son-in-law observed, sombrely.

In that spirit he left Kinnaird.

CHAPTER THREE

With Hurry gone and no Covenant forces remaining in the neighbourhood, the countryside hastened to make at least its provisional peace with Montrose. Deputations arrived at Fettercairn from Brechin, Forfar and Montrose itself, announcing these towns' welcome to the King's Lieutenant. But James Graham, what with one thing and another, was not in forthcoming mood. He sent Colkitto to Brechin, which had shown active hostility, and Madderty to Forfar, permitting them to requisition, with a little plunder – but not to harry or ravage, making clear distinction. For old times' sake, he himself went to Montrose, where he had spent much of his boyhood. It was the best port north of Forth until Aberdeen, and its merchants prosperous, its warehouses well-stocked. There was much his ragged army required which Montrose town could supply – but here he would pay for his purchases, on the principle that it is a dirty bird which fouls its own nest. And he had hopes that he might raise a troop of cavalry from the local lairds.

At Montrose, however, messages from his advance scouts informed him that General Baillie, spurred on by Hurry's discomfiture, had at last moved out of his comfortable quarters in Perth and was heading north against the royalists, evidently directly, via Strathmore. James Graham knew Baillie, another professional, who, like Leslie had trained under the great Gustavus Adolphus, and had much respect for his abilities as a soldier. Especially as he now was reinforced by 3,000 of Leslie's seasoned infantry sent up from England and withdrawn from Ireland, as a result of the Invergarry affair, in addition to his own local forces and Balcarres's horse. But Montrose was not going to forfeit his valuable image as a bold and victorious general by avoiding the superior enemy. He sent out hurried couriers to his scattered units, and headed south to meet William Baillie.

Next afternoon the two armies met near Coupar Angus – or almost met. For the winding but major River Isla lay between them, and it was in fairly high spate with the melting snows from the mountains. There was no bridge across it all the way from where it emerged from the hills of Glen Isla to its confluence with Tay, nearly twenty miles, only fords. The best of these, for any large body of men, was just north of Coupar, at Couttie – part of the reason for the town's existence indeed. Baillie having arrived first, had taken possession of this ford. But he had not brought his army across.

Halting on a low rolling ridge of the Strathmore plain called the Hill of Bendochy – hill being an exaggeration – Montrose had the Covenant army in full view before him, four times the size of his own, gay with flags and banners, a fitful sunlight glinting on steel, a stirring sight.

Drawing up his own force extended along the ridge – so that it might appear as large as possible, and that there might well be more behind – Montrose sent mounted gallopers dashing hither and thither with great urgency on mainly mythical errands, to give the impression of great activity and marshalling, he himself scanning the terrain intently the while. It was highly significant, of course, that Baillie had not crossed the Isla when he had opportunity. It showed, as well as caution, probable doubts as to the royalist strength – a state of affairs to be fostered and exploited, if possible. It would be strange, of course, if Hurry had not given an exaggerated report of the force which had so humiliated him.

But how to exploit the situation, in the face of that impassable river, taxed even Montrose's fertile imagination. No flanking or encircling move was feasible, no feint or gesture was of any validity that did not involve crossing the water; and that could be attempted only at the guarded ford. Admittedly the same applied to Baillie – but he had clearly *chosen* to remain where he was. It looked like tactical stalemate.

James Graham made up his mind, and quite quickly. It was vital that he retained the initiative, or seemed to. He hoisted a white flag alongside the new royal standard he had had made, and ordered his trumpeter to blow a fanfare. Then, with a few of his officers, he rode down to the river-side. Swiftly Covenant officers appeared on the other bank, cantering over the green haughland.

After another trumpet flourish, Montrose spoke. 'The King's Lieutenant and Viceroy, James, Marquis of Montrose, requests the courtesy of speech with Lieutenant-General William Baillie of Letham,' he called.

'To what end? Are you surrendering?' somebody called back.

'I would speak as one gentleman with another. That is all. Kindly convey my request to your general.'

The horsemen spurred off.

Montrose sat his mount, patiently waiting.

Presently a little stout cherub of a man, mounted on a horse much too big for him, came unhurriedly down, surrounded by aides, lordlings and black-robed ministers. James Graham recognised many faces amongst them, including the sardonically handsome Hurry, the Earl of Balcarres, Master of Horse and the young Earl of Lauderdale.

'You desired speech with me, my lord?' Baillie shouted across, in a surprisingly deep and strong voice to emerge from so small a man.

'I do, sir. I greet you kindly. And since you come into my country with a large host, I wish to ask whether you come to submit yourself, and it, to the King's peace, as is your duty? Or whether you remain in shameful rebellion to that peace, as creature of my lord Argyll?'

'I come as commander of the forces of the Estates of Scotland, my lord marquis. With warrant for your arrest and trial on a charge of high treason.'

'Ah! And whose signature is on that warrant, sir, I pray you? A Campbell's, I swear!'

'Hmmm. It is my lord Earl of Loudoun's, Chancellor of this realm.'

'Aye – a Campbell's, as I thought. And how can he be Chancellor, when the realm's lord and master, King Charles, no longer recognises him?'

'Did you call me here to barter words, my lord?'

'No, sir. I did not. Since you come in declared enmity, I crave your co-operation that we may come to a fair decision, on the matter which divides us, like gentlemen. That is why I sought your presence. At present we cannot do so because of this river. Either, will you stand your force back while we cross over unassailed, so that we meet in fair fight? Or shall I do so, that *you* may cross unhindered? The choice is yours, sir.'

There was a brief pause, and then Baillie answered, more roughly than hitherto. 'There is no choice in it, man. For I will do neither. I will fight my battles at my own pleasure and convenience – not yours!'

'You hesitate to put the matter to the test in fair fight, then? Perhaps you are wise, sir.'

'Enough of this!' The other jerked his horse's head round. 'Good day to you. But – I will have you in Edinburgh Tolbooth before long, never fear!'

'But not today, General? You prefer to leave it till an occasion when you feel that you might win?'

Without another word, Baillie and his suite rode off.

'Are you disappointed, my lord?' Colonel O'Cahan asked.

'I am not, Magnus. Relieved, rather. Since we are in no state to fight four times our numbers, and without advantage of surprise or site, I am well content.'

'You expected it thus, b'God?'

'Indeed, yes. Given a man of cautious temper, like Baillie, he was all but bound so to choose. Now *we* can choose our course, and declare aloud that Baillie refused to fight.'

'If the King had even one more general like yourself, James,' the Lord Gordon declared, 'he would sit secure on his throne.'

Back at the main force, Montrose gave orders to remain drawn up, there on the rise, but for the infantry to seem to make camp. And to endeavour to give the impression that there were many more of them behind the ridge. The Covenant army likewise remained where it was. And all that afternoon and evening they watched each other at a mile's distance.

As night came down and cooking-fires were lit, Montrose gradually withdrew his regiments and squadrons behind the rise. But he left a small working-party of Gordon cavalry to keep these fires lit and replenished all night, with whatever they could find to burn, and only to follow after the rest at dawn. And he left an advanced picket, with its own fire, down not far from the ford at Couttie, to discourage any night ventures. Thereafter, he commanded fast, silent marching – and when James Graham said fast marching, he meant fast indeed.

They went north-eastwards now, as steadily so as the land would allow with tributaries of the Isla to cross and marshland to circumnavigate, difficult in the darkness. But these were all Airlie lands, and Sir David Ogilvy, with some of his men, made excellent guides. It was nine or ten miles before they could cross Isla, at Inverqueich Mill ford; but this they avoided, Montrose giving Baillie credit for having pickets as far out as this, to prevent his flank being turned. In another four miles, however, they were well into the Grampian foothills, and mounted scouts

43

reported that the ford at Kilry was not held. Cheered but wary still, they pressed forward into the deep den where, below rapids, was a shingly stretch passable for determined men.

If many of the company now expected their general to swing back, southward to bear down on the Covenant left, they were surprised. For Montrose led his force on almost due westwards, against the grain of the land, over rather than through the billowing skirts of the hills, taxing, trying work. But at least here they were safe from observation, with only cattle lumbering off into the night affrighted, and they could march openly and less silently. They went behind the Hill of Alyth, avoiding the Ramsay castle of Banff, and on across the high desolation of weird Drimmie Muir with the eerie stone-circles looming up like giants in the darkness. The deep valley of the swift-running Ericht then fell to be crossed, which they managed at Strone of Cally, to start climbing again, but now swinging directly south-wards over Cochrage Muir to the long remote valley of the Lornty Water, amongst more ancient burial-cairns and the constant reminders of long-dead races. Finally, having circled all the populous area of Rattray and Blairgowrie, they came down to the east-west Stormonth road at Drumellie Loch, an hour short of dawn. Even then there was only a brief rest, with Montrose not satisfied, for security reasons. There were still eight miles to Dunkeld, in the throat of Atholl, but now easy going, with a drove-road all the way. What was another eight miles to his heroes?

He had his way, and three hours later the royalist army limped into the haughs of Tay across from Birnam Wood, just short of Dunkeld, weary and spent – but having transformed the entire strategic position. Now Baillie was left islanded in Strathmore, friendly Atholl and the Central Highlands were at Montrose's back, and the great Tay valley open in front, the way to the south, unguarded. Perth was theirs for the taking, Strathearn and Strathallan, Graham and Drummond country, beyond. Argyll, in Edinburgh, would feel the cold draught from the north, with nothing but miles between him and his enemy.

But James Graham, in his strategic brilliance, had forgotten something – the great weakness of any Celtic army, the pull of home ties and families. Even before he wakened, around noon that day, men were slipping away. After the Ulstermen and Isles-men, the bulk of his infantry were Athollmen – and now, after long absence, they were within smelling distance of their own

44

hearths and peat-reek. It was not desertion, for they would come back in due course. But meantime, the call was too strong for them. The Stewarts, Murrays and Robertsons faded away. The Drummonds likewise, heading southwards, even some Grahams. Up Strathbraan, down the Sma' Glen, and they were into Strathearn. The exodus from Dunkeld began. Montrose, in his heart, could not blame them, disappointed as he was.

Waiting, fretting, at Dunkeld, while he sent out officers all around to try to raise more men from lairds and lords who *should* be friendly, Montrose learned that Baillie also had wasted no time, that he was now hurrying southwards diagonally across Angus, for Fife, undoubtedly to defend the Forth crossings. It was going to be too late for any descent on the capital.

Then further trouble developed at Dunkeld. The Lord Lewis Gordon declared, out of the blue, that he for one had not come all this way just to skulk and hide and twiddle his thumbs, awaiting the pleasure of a wheen Hielant barbarians. He could do better than this for King Charles back in Aberdeenshire. Unless Montrose led them on to Perth and Stirling, at least, he personally was going back home – and he did not doubt but that he would take not a few of the Gordon horse home with him.

After an angry scene, his brother managed to persuade him to stay his hand. But things said could not be unsaid, and there was bad blood now between the brothers and amongst the Gordon ranks. The fact was, Gordon as a power had always acted for itself, never made a satisfactory *part* of any force under the controls of others.

Not only the Gordons were demanding action. It was another weakness of the Celtic host that it did not find waiting easy. None bolder, braver, more gallant when the clash came, the Gaelic warrior had little gift for patient restraint and inaction. Colkitto did not join the Lord Lewis in threats; but he urged action, any action. Otherwise his Islesmen would be the next to head for home.

Since keeping his force in being was, after all, the first priority, and since the south was now barred and Perth warned, Montrose decided to make a strike at Dundee. It was twenty-five miles back to the east. and would never anticipate an attack; but it was a major city, and in royalist hands would support a claim that all the North was the King's. In a war which was being waged for the soul of a nation, that sort of claim could be important.

That night of the 3rd of April, he sent off his baggage, sick and less able men, to march by easy stages for Brechin, towards the north-east end of Strathmore, whilst with some 600 infantry and such horse as remained he himself slipped out of Dunkeld as suddenly and discreetly as he had come. At the last moment Lewis Gordon decided that Dundee was an insufficient target for Gordon. It was the flimsiest of excuse – but the break had to come. Montrose did not seek to hold him, or those who felt like him, despite the Lord Gordon's protests, but requested that they escort the baggage-train as far as Brechin, on their way home. It was a grievously reduced host, then, which set out for the coast and Dundee.

Since his men had wanted action, they got it now. They had twenty-five miles to cover, and it was necessary that any descent on Dundee should be a surprise. This time they followed Tay directly down through the lower Stormonth to Meikleour, by level lands, comparatively easy going, to cross the Isla at the same spot near Coupar Angus formerly held by Baillie and now deserted. Then they slipped through the green range of the Sidlaws by the easy Tullybaccart pass, just as the grey dawn was breaking; and in an hour or so saw the walled town of Dundee before them, between the towering law and the dazzlement of the sun's rising over the Tay estuary. Scouts sent word that the gates of the city were being opened for the new day. The necessary surprise would be achieved.

But it could only be a limited surprise, sufficient to ensure that there could be no reinforcement of the town's small permanent garrison. For there was no way of hiding the little army's final two miles of approach. Inevitably the gates would be shut again, and the walls beginning to be manned.

Montrose had two small cannon, which he had borrowed from the Earl of Atholl's castle at Dunkeld. These he had dismantled and slung in panniers on garrons, with a limited supply of ball. Dundee's garrison would have many and much larger cannon – but they would be distributed at various points round the perimeter of the walls, and it would take time to assemble them at any given point of assault. Therefore time, now, was of the essence – despite the weariness of men who had marched twenty-five miles. Also the point of attack was vital. The town walls were substantial and high, and Montrose had no illusions about his chances of taking them. But he had a precious item of information, obtained when he lay at Fettercairn, that there had been a collapse of the wall, where a burn flowed beneath, near the north-east corner, and his scouts confirmed that this point was still under repair. He planned his tactics accordingly.

His main force marched forward, swiftly and openly, towards the main west gate, where the road from Perth entered. But secretly he sent a small party, with those cannon, by devious hidden ways, with bales of hay on the horses' backs to hide their burdens, the men looking as like ordinary countrymen as they might, arms not in evidence. These, under Magnus O'Cahan, were to get into position near the broken portion of the walling, set up the cannon, but to remain quiescent meantime.

As expected, they found the West Port shut and barred against them – and Montrose could imagine the panic and frenzied activity within the city. And, he hoped, the hasty dragging of heavy defensive cannon to this threatened western area. There was an eminence here, just within the walls, ideally situated for artillery defence, called the Corbie Hill. Montrose knew it well, and knew that any commander would use it. To give time for a concentration of the city's artillery here, he sent a trumpeter and a Gordon laird, under a flag of truce, as emissary to the Provost and magistrates, requesting the city gates to be opened to him in the King's name, and assuring that no harm would befall Dundee if all was done peaceably and without delay.

'What hope have you of submission?' George Gordon asked.

'None,' he was told. 'The city is much too strong to consider it, I think. They can see that we are but a small force – we cannot hide it. If I know them, they will parley with our messenger, delay, while they get their cannon assembled and into position on yonder Corbie Hill. These will be scattered round the town. Then we shall have our answer – in the shape of powder-and-ball. Watch you that hill-top.'

'You will let them get so far? Into position on the hill?'

'We cannot stop them. But we are out of range, here. They will do us no harm. We wait, with what patience we can summon...'

Sure enough, after the best part of an hour, waiting, they could discern much activity on the top of Corbie Hill. It was only a gentle eminence, and the city walls were too high to allow the watchers to see all but a small hummock on it. But men's heads and shoulders could be observed, and presently the upper parts of straining horses – undoubtedly dragging cannon up the slope. Montrose was satisfied. But their envoys did not return.

Another trumpeter was sent forward, to the foot of the walls, to announce to the gate-keepers that the King's Lieutenant's patience had run out. Unless the authorities threw open the gates to him in ten minutes, he would take it that they were in rebellion against His Grace, denying his Lieutenant entry. He would take the city by force.

At the same time, he sent another runner racing round to the north, to the party opposite the broken portion of walling. Open fire five minutes after receiving the message, he directed.

No reply came from Dundee's leaders. Nor did the Gordon and the trumpeter return. Everyone waited, tensely now.

Then the crash of cannon sounded from the north. Immediately, all was transformed. As yells and shooting rose from the walls and within, the royalist ranks swung around in disciplined units, and went off at the double northwards, following the perimeter. There was some delay before the city's cannon on Corbie Hill thundered raggedly – but their ball did no damage to the running regiments.

Another two shots boomed from the pieces at the north-west angle. Magnus O'Cahan had much experience as a cannoneer.

By the time that Montrose got round to the point of bombardment, there was little need for further preparation. The collapsed wall had by no means been fully rebuilt, and at point-blank range the cannon had battered a sizeable gap in it already. There was no sign of defenders, as yet – certainly no artillery reply in this sector.

Montrose's trumpeter sounded the advance, breathlessly, and the Irish infantry poured through.

There was no real opposition, at this stage. The guns on Corbie Hill were masked from here, useless. Citizens wisely stayed indoors, and such few armed men as were about faded rapidly away. One troop did come rushing down a narrow side-street, from the south, saw that they were too late to prevent entry, also much outnumbered, and turned to bolt back whence they had come.

Montrose and Colkitto kept their men very closely under control – for nothing is so dangerous as for a comparatively small force to take a town and to become dispersed therein. They led them back in roughly the direction they had come, only inside the walls, a swift-racing silent band of 600, the cavalry left outside. It would have been a brave train-band commander who attempted to stem that Celtic flood.

Montrose, in front, took them directly to Corbie Hill, approaching it from the north-west side now. When it came into view, there was again great activity on the crest, a dragging round of cannon, a milling of horsemen and shouting of orders. When the hill-top cannoneers suddenly saw the Irish regiments breasting the hill at the run, in grim, panting silence, they were scarcely to be blamed that they bolted also, to a man. There was no fighting, no resistance. The cannon, and horses harnessed to them, were left as they stood.

'O'Cahan!' James Graham shouted, and pointed eastwards, into the city centre. 'These pieces to face there. Down Overgate and Nethergate, to Market Gate. Do not fire until I give word.'

The situation was now almost laughably reversed. Corbie Hill commanded all the centre of the town, the principal streets, the Tolbooth and Town House, the high tower of St. Mary's Church, all spread conveniently below. Their own cannon now held Dundee at their mercy.

When O'Cahan's men had the pieces turned and trained – they were already loaded and primed – Montrose said, 'Two shots, Magnus, if you please. Where they will do least hurt. The graveyard perhaps, if you can. The Howff, there. Two only.'

The first two cannon-balls produced no recognisable reaction. Montrose was loth to order a bombardment of the city. He waited, his men impatient now. Presently he sent another four shots down into the Market Gate. Thereafter, fairly quickly, a white flag was hoisted from the top of St. Mary's tower. The magistrates could see, as well as anyone else, that the heart of their city could be pounded to pieces by the artillery.

It was a practically bloodless victory.

But all was not over yet. As the victors marched down the Nethergate, there was sniping at them from side-streets and wynds. Angered, the Irish infantry turned hunters, and Montrose now had to use all his powers of command and persuasion to prevent savage reprisals. He did not want a sack of Dundee on his conscience, to add to that of Aberdeen. But at least this behaviour gave him excuse to allow a certain amount of pillage, taking of food, forage, clothing, footwear and other gear, which the ragged army so desperately required, without payment. James Graham's personal fortune which, for so long had borne most of the cost of the King's campaign, was by now in shaky condition indeed.

When he had accepted the surrender of the city, and warned

what would happen if guerrilla resistance continued, he went back to the Corbie Hill, partly to maintain the threat of those cannon – for 600 men in a city of thousands were vulnerable indeed – and partly because it was the best look-out point within the walls.

It was as well that he did. Two galloping horsemen caught his eye almost at once, heading from the district of Invergowrie, for the West Port. Their haste and urgency was eloquent, as of men chased. Raising his gaze, he scanned the area to the west, behind, screwing up his eyes in the slanting late afternoon sun. And there, a dark shadow was spilling out from the wide dip which was the valley of the Gowrie Burn. It could only be men in large numbers, an army . . .

His trumpeter was blaring the Recall, with three blasts for urgency, within seconds, and messengers were racing off.

Montrose waited there only long enough for his galloping Gordon scouts to reach him, their horses lathered in spume. Baillie had turned back from Fife, they panted. He had ferried his men across Tay, farther up, Hurry's cavalry first. Now they, the cavalry, were not two miles behind.

'How many ?'

'God knows! A great force. All Balcarres's horse, by the looks o' it . . .'

James Graham was shouting orders before the words were out. The cannon to be slewed round again, to face and fire westwards. The West Port to be manned by musketeers. It would not take Hurry long to find the gap in the walls, to the north – but the delay might be just sufficient. He would send cavalry to pick up the cannoneers and musketeers, as soon as he might. Start the gunfire right away, without ball – it would serve to warn their own people that there was trouble, and might make Hurry cautious, slow him down.

Jumping on a horse, he dashed down to the Market Gate.

Gathering together 600 men in a city, especially when they have been given a licence to pillage, and where there are women available by the score, is no swift and simple task. The trumpeting and resumed cannonade helped; but even so it was an infuriatingly slow and involved process. When a different note in the cannon-fire indicated that it was now ball being fired, in earnest, Montrose sent Nathaniel Gordon and a troop of horse back, to evacuate the cannoneers by pillion. He decided that he had no option but to cut his losses. He had no illusions as to what a large force of cavalry could do to a smaller scattered infantry force shut up inside a town. Almost a hundred men short, he commanded immediate and speedy retiral by the Seagate and East Port, himself waiting for Nat Gordon. It was ignominious, heart-breaking. Little or nothing of their pillage could be taken with them. But it was necessary if the force was to be preserved as a weapon of war.

They were only just in time. Had Hurry known the full circumstances, of the Athollmen's absence, Lewis Gordon's defection, and the fact that there could be no real attempt to hold the town against him, undoubtedly he would have pressed on faster, rushed the gates, and thereafter foregone the checking of side-streets and lanes. As it was, Montrose, with his cavalry as rearguard, were clattering down the Seagate to the East Port as Hurry moved heedfully down the Nethergate.

It was the measure of Hurry's respect for Montrose as a tactician that, with the evening descending and the light beginning to fade, out in the open country with room to manoeuvre, skirmish and ambush, he did not attempt any brash riding down of the retiring royalists. He followed on, but with care, scouts and pickets testing every yard of the way. Only that, a beneficial result of the Ducal Water affair, saved the Irish infantry – for the cavalry of course *could* have made good their escape – as they hastened along the Angus coast, eastwards.

Sundry delaying tactics Montrose did attempt. He lit the whins behind them near Broughty Castle which, with the evening breeze, made a swift-running moorland blaze calculated to alarm and puzzle following cavalry. At the ford of the Dichty Water, short of Monifeith, he left two more fires, like beacons, with the same purpose. And he sent a picket of swift horsemen, under Nat Gordon to ride round and back, in the darkness, to fire a fusillade of pistol- and musket-shots *behind* Hurry's ever more preoccupied force.

The cumulative effect was satisfactory in so far as it prevented the Covenant cavalry from finally catching up with the hard-pressed Irish and Islesmen regiments. And about midnight, having crossed the wide sandy wastes of Barry, at West Haven just beyond Carnoustie, Montrose swung his desperately weary marchers abruptly north-westwards, away from the coast, at right angles to their line of retreat hitherto, to slip up the shadowy and hidden winding den of the Monikie Burn, passing close to the Kirkton of Panbride, and on beyond. The cavalry he ordered to continue on their former course meantime, to disguise if possible the sudden change of route of the foot, and draw Hurry after them. They could rejoin them later, in the Guthrie area, on their joint way to Brechin, where they would rendezvous with the baggage-train, and all detachments and stragglers.

The ruse worked. Scouts came to report that the large force of Covenant horse had not so much as paused at the Monikie ford, but splashed, across and on heedfully, towards Arbroath.

They were climbing up from the coastal plain now, by cattle pastures and thin-dotted moorland. In the Carmylie vicinity, at Guynd, Montrose reckoned that he could allow his panting, weary men a rest. Many of them, tough as they were, were in a bad way, liquor too hastily consumed at Dundee having its effect. Hurry would never find them again tonight. Two hours they could have, he declared. Then on to Guthrie and Brechin.

But before they made a move, the scouts that Black Pate Graham never failed to have out, front, flanks and rear, brought reports of a new threat. Another large force was in front of them, heading fast through the night north-easterly up Strathmore's southern flank, diagonally across their own line of march. It could only be Baillie, seeking to cut them off from their safe refuge in the Angus glens and the mountains beyond. Someone must have talked, told him of the Brechin rendezvous. It looked as though they had underestimated their enemy. Baillie must have been closer behind Hurry than they had thought, and proving that he could move fast when he put his mind to it.

Montrose was in no position to challenge Baillie any more than Hurry. He could only take avoiding action. He sent fast horsemen off to warn the people at Brechin to disperse northwards and make for Strathfinella and the entrace to the Cairn o' Mount pass. Others to try to find the Gordon cavalry at all costs, in the region between Arbroath and Brechin, watching out for Hurry meantime, and order them to flee at their fastest up the Howe of the Mearns to Glenbervie, and there turn south and west again, through the Glen of Drumtochty, to reach Strathfinella from the north – this to avoid the risk of bringing Hurry in pursuit, down on the infantry again. They would all meet at the mouth of the pass. God willing.

The main body resumed its northwards march cautiously, swinging somewhat to the west now, across the scrub birch, pines, whins and marshes of Montreathmont Moor, hoping to strike the levels of Strathmore well behind their foes.

At Markhouse, with still two hours to dawn, they reached the wide plain, scouts assuring that the way was clear and that Baillie's rearguard was fully three miles ahead. Thankfully, Montrose led his desperately tired men across the ford of the South Esk and out into the levels, Brechin seven miles on their right, Forfar the same distance to the left. Nothing was likely to hold them up now, except sheer fatigue.

The sun was up long before they reached Strathfinella, in the throat of the mountains; but this was Ogilvy and Lindsay country, where they were relatively safe. They found both the Gordons and the Brechin party already there, awaiting them, having had no contact with the enemy. All moved on a mile or so up into the steeply climbing gut of the Cairn o' Mount pass. They were out of Baillie's or Hurry's clutches now; none could trap them in such a place, none would venture to follow them, mountain-warfare veterans, into these lonely barren heights. They might go hungry, but they would not die.

Montrose had saved his pathetic remnant of an army from disaster. But he was not proud of himself. He had acted against his better judgment, taken grave risks for insufficient purpose, taken for granted enemy dispositions which he should have more closely checked, and not given Baillie and Hurry credit for being the professionals they were. He could blame none but himself. He was the commander, and the responsibility was his.

James Graham was not to know that, with the military historians of the future, this retiral from Dundee was to rank with his greatest victories, outshining some of them indeed, as a feat of arms. Not for him to evaluate the worth of a general who could take a walled and warned city almost without a drop of blood shed; halt what amounted to a sacking of that city in a matter of minutes; collect, marshal and extricate an army of half-starved, part-drunken and notoriously independent Irish and Gaelic irregular infantry from a major cavalry assault; and thereafter, already weary with great marching, get them over thirty desperate miles in the darkness, avoiding one army in pursuit and another intent on heading them off. Such a man was, by any standards, no ordinary commander.

They rested all that day and the next night – and their scouts sent no word of enemy approach. The day following they marched northwards, unhurriedly now, into the mighty mountain spine of Scotland.

CHAPTER FOUR

The valley of the Feugh made as good a place as any to halt, to lick their wounds, to consider the future. It lay at the northern end of the long Cairn o' Mount pass, a hidden side-glen of the great valley of Dee, populous enough with Gordons and Farquharsons to provide food and forage for this modest army, yet sufficiently remote and inaccessible to be secure. Amongst the green mountains, with their pine-forested lower slopes, dark Lochnagar itself dominating the scene to the west, Montrose settled for a space, to rest his troops and rack his wits.

Here in the Forest of Birse three days later a courier found them, disguised as a packman, after a month on the road seeking Montrose. Despite his lowly and undistinguished appearance, this was a very special visitor, an Irish Colonel Small, from King Charles himself no less at Oxford, the first link James Graham had had with his liege lord for many a long month. The colonel carried brief despatches, but longer and fuller message by word of mouth – even Charles Stewart was learning discretion, it seemed. The verbal royal commands would be backed by written authority as soon as it was practicable.

Small's tidings were to this effect. His Majesty had received Montrose's letter, after Inverlochy, and was highly delighted and encouraged by that great victory. His well-beloved and trusted friend was now Captain-General in Scotland, endowed with every power to act in the King's name in all matters, supreme – royal warrants to follow. The King intended to act on Montrose's advice, and come to Scotland in person, just so soon as it could be arranged. It was his royal intention that he should advance over the border from Cumberland and that Montrose should strike southwards, and they would trap the King's rebels between two fires. Meantime, recognising his friend's great need for cavalry, His Majesty would send north a body of horse, to be entirely under Montrose's command.

James Graham reacted to these tidings in entirely positive fashion. The fact was that, for once, Charles had given him what he needed. Not the Captain-Generalship, which he had once refused and which, as a mere title, was unimportant. But the feeling that he was not, after all, alone, forgotten, a man chasing cloud-shadows; that his so strenuous efforts were not just a beating of the air but part of a great and noble purpose. Desperately, indeed, he was requiring such assurance.

He was sufficiently moved, therefore, almost elated, to shake hands with the colonel a second time. 'My friend – I cannot sufficiently thank you for risking your life to bring me these tidings,' he said. 'And His Grace for sending them. It is long since I had any news of his cause and progress. I am like a man in a dark room, to whom you have brought a gleam of light. To let me see my way ahead, again. To know that I am not forgotten is, in itself, as good as a regiment of cavalry!'

'Sakes – you are not forgotten, my lord!' Small assured, grinning. He was a cheerful, devil-may-care Ulsterman, stocky, blunt-featured and with a slight cast in one eye, dirty, unshaven and clad in ragged clothes that stank. 'Forgotten is the last state of the Marquis of Montrose, b'God! Though some might wish that you were! For the King builds you up before all, no less. As a shining exemplar, see you. The only one of his generals who can win battles! Your name is seldom off the royal lips these days. And not all loving the sound o' it!'

'Mm.' James Graham looked perturbed. 'That is unfortunate. I do not merit such acclaim, besides. I have won some few encounters, yes – but am almost as far from winning Scotland for the King as ever I was, I fear.'

'You say so? I will not tell His majesty that, by the Powers – however much it might please some close to him!'

'Close? How close?'

'Of the closest, sir.'

'You mean – the Queen?'

The other glanced about him, at the Lord Gordon, Sir David Ogilvy, Pate Graham and other officers who listened interestedly. 'I did not say that, my lord Marquis,' he observed, after a moment.

'No, sir – you did not. All witness it. But . . . I have my enemies at that Court, I know well. To my sorrow. Two close to His Grace will support me, however, I believe. His nephews, the Prince Rupert and Maurice.'

'No doubt, sir. But Rupert is not in the highest favour, these days, see you. And his brother with him. The King is led to believe him too rash. They are scarce in the royal confidence . . .'

55

'But – these are his own kin. His sister's sons. And, moreover, his best commanders . . .'

'No doubt. But *Her* Majesty no longer finds them altogether to her taste, my lord.'

'I see. It is that way?' Montrose took a turn across the greensward before the cot-house which presently was his head-quarters. 'Tell me, Colonel – how goes the cause in England?'

'Ill,' the other said, baldly.

'So! How ill, man?'

'Ill enough to cause His Majesty consider coming to Scotland!'

Montrose's colleagues exchanged grim glances. But, though he himself stared thoughtfully at the speaker, the Graham was not surprised. Deep within him, he had guessed as much, recognised that the war *could* not be prospering in England, or the reactions of the hard-headed realists of the Estates of Parliament would have been very different from what it was. And even though it was desperation that was to bring Charles to Scotland, that might be none so ill a contingency.

'You mean, it will be flight rather than policy which brings him here?'

'You could say so, yes. The man Cromwell has the King's high-born generals trussed like fowls for market! There is not one of the noble lords who can face him. If *you* were to come south, now, sir . . .'

'No – I am well content that it should be His Grace who comes north. Whatever the reason. This I have long urged upon him. The Stewarts, I believe, made their greatest mistake when they forsook their own Scotland for England. They represented a thousand years of rule in Scotland. But what in England? The English have no *Ard Righ*, nor ever had. Their kings were always conquerors – and if they could not conquer, they fell. The idea of kingship, as of government and religion, is quite different in the two realms. And James Stewart threw his Scots heritage away – for what? A poorer, lesser, uncertain thing. And, to be sure, vaults of English gold!'

'That was forty years ago, my lord.'

'True. But the situation remains. Charles, I fear, has lost England, at least for the present. But there is no reason why he should lose Scotland, his ancient inheritance, also. He should have come back, long ere this. Come back, to bide. Let England take its own course, meantime. Let them choose King Cromwell, if they will. Charles is still, and will always be, King of Scots.'

'Yet the Scots seem to love the King little more than the English do. Or the Irish! Was it not here that revolt started? With your Covenant?'

'You mistake, my friend. That was not revolt. Protest, yes. A plea for reform. But with no thought of putting the King from his throne. Putting down some of the King's ill-advisers, yes – but never the King. Scotland lacking a King of Scots is inconceivable. It is the oldest kingdom in Christendom, old when there was no England, only warring German tribes. Charles should return home, prepared to make concessions, call a true parliament – and summon Argyll before it. If he stayed away, the Campbell would be forfeited, outlawed. If he came, he would be voted down – nothing surer. He is the best-hated man in the kingdom. King Charles, if he relied on honest men, not on Hamilton, Lanark, Lauderdale and the like, could put down King Campbell.'

'And Leslie? Baillie? Callendar? The armies of the Estates?'

'These are paid soldiers. Mercenaries. Not Callendar, but the others, the important ones. Able, but venial. They serve who pays highest, who seem to win.'

'That, then, is your advice for His Majesty, my lord? To abandon England and come to Scotland. So soon as may be. With his armies . . . ?'

'With his English armies – no! The King must not bring English troops against his Scottish subjects. Or very few, and officered by Scots. We are a prickly race, sir, the thistle not our emblem for nothing! But there are many Scots serving in England with His Grace. A corps of these, coming over the West March with the King, would draw much support in Dumfriesshire and Galloway. To threaten the Earl of Callendar from the south. I would move down from the north, and we would have them between two fires. Callendar is no rash hero. He would temporise, and then slip away, if he might, I do believe. Leslie would be forced to come home from Yorkshire. Before he could do so, we would be secure in Edinburgh, calling a parliament. Leslie would wait at the border, to see how the cat jumped. And his men, so near home, would not all wait with him! I know! Scotland would be the King's within a month.'

'A fair dream, my lord Marquis. But a dream, nevertheless, I fear.'

'I do not content myself with dreaming, Colonel,' Montrose said briefly – and his friends smiled.

The Irishman made hasty amendment. 'I meant nothing such, on my soul!' he assured. 'All the world knows your lordship's prowess as a general. None esteems it more than I do. I meant only that such a campaign would be more easily planned than carried out. So much might go awry . . .'

'No doubt. But that could apply to both sides. The King would start with advantage, because he *is* the King. And takes the initiative.'

'And because *you* are Montrose!' Colkitto, who had just come up, declared from behind

'That is as may be. But at least I have the most seasoned and renowned infantry in Europe, to strike terror into more humdrum forces!'

'Very well, my lord. That message I will carry to His Majesty. Whether he will heed it is another matter! For few at Court will agree that England should be abandoned . . .'

'That is for His Grace's ear alone, man – of a mercy! Do not stress it, even so. Just the seed to be sown. What is important is to hasten the King's coming to Scotland. How soon was he minding to?'

'That I cannot tell. You know His Majesty! Time is of small account to him . . .'

'But it is of large account to his cause! To me, and mine, it is vital. You must impress it upon him, sir. It is now April. All must be done by August, or it will be too late. With harvest, the clansmen go home. Request His Grace to come in June, if he can. And I will come to meet him.'

It was left so, and that night Colonel Small took his departure southwards.

Now, spurred on with new drive and purpose, Montrose was all energy again. He had to build up his army once more, and swiftly. He sent George Gordon back to Strathbogie to recruit more cavalry and counter any ill influences of his brother Lewis. Colkitto was despatched westwards to the MacDonald country of the Hebridean seaboard, to seek to involve Clanranald, Glengarry and Keppoch once more, with others of the Western clans. Black Pate and the Master of Madderty went south, by Glen Shee and Kirkmichael to Atholl, Strathtay and Strathearn, seeking Stewarts, Robertsons, Murrays, Drummonds, Hays and Grahams. Other emissaries went elsewhere. They were all to rendezvous at Skene, some fifteen miles down the Dee, by the end of the month or thereabouts.

James Graham was not the man to sit idly waiting while others were busy. Moreover, his Celtic troops were not the sort who improved with inactivity. When, two days after his messengers had left, his scouts brought intelligence that Baillie had retired to his former quarters at Perth, while Hurry, with 1,200 foot and an unspecified number of horse was pushing northwards for Aberdeenshire, he decided on an interim ploy of his own. He asked for volunteers, and when practically every man raised hand, selected the 500 fittest. He had only a small number of horse left, so he took fifty of these, warning all concerned that they were in for an exercise in swift movement. Let any who had second thoughts say so now, and stay comfortably at Feughside. Needless to say not a man resiled, however many may have wondered what they were letting themselves in for.

Leaving Magnus O'Cahan, despite pleas to be taken along, in command of the residue, they set out up the Feugh, through the Forest of Birse and over the skirts of the great hills to Loch Muick. Then southwards by the high passes of the Capel Mounth, at well over 2,000 feet, to the head of Glen Clova. By nightfall, after a tremendous day, they were in wild Glen Doll, Montrose pointing out that this was a mere flexing of muscles. They must do better hereafter.

Next day they crossed the shoulder of mighty Mayar, at a height of nearer 3,000 than 2,000 feet, to the head of Isla, and down that fair glen to Airlie's burned castle of Forter, where Argyll had played the savage five years before. Then, through a short side-glen below Mount Blair they reached Glen Shee, which when crossed brought them down past the lonely Spalding castle of Ashintully into Strathardle, at Kirkmichael. They were, of course, travelling wholly against the grain of the land, crossing the vast ridge-and-valley system all the way, desperately difficult going that only notably fit, active and determined men could maintain for long. Montrose treated it as an exercise and a challenge, to himself as much as to the rest. Any force which could swiftly and unexpectedly move about Highland Scotland like this would possess an enormous advantage and set at naught all the accepted strategies.

The third day they crossed from Strathardle, by remote Loch Broom, to Tulliemet and the Tay above Dunkeld, safely into Atholl again. But they did not pause there, save to eat mightily of the young Earl of Atholl's provision. They had word of Black Pate nearby, recruiting, but did not seek him out meantime. *They* were not really recruiting. They struck off up Strath Braan, to Amulree, and then down the Sma' Glen. That night they lay at the head of lower Glen Almond, and Lowland Scotland stretched before them, Perth itself no more than fifteen miles away, and to the *east*. They had covered nearly eighty miles of mountain territory in three days' mighty marching, and were where no one in the land could have expected them to be. James Graham was bone-weary, but satisfied – meantime. With such an army he could tie his enemies in knots.

In the morning they marched, openly and leisurely, down to the town of Crieff, near the head of Strathearn, to proclaim the King there and summon all loyal subjects to his service. Montrose reckoned two hours, at the most, for General Baillie to learn of it at Perth.

William Baillie was not a rash or impetuous man, but even he, after his first surprise had worn off, could not resist the challenge of this impudent handful at Crieff. He waited until nightfall, and then moved out in force, westwards up the Earn. Montrose's skilfully placed Drummond scouts, knowing every yard of this their own country, swiftly brought him word. Between 5,000 and 6,000 men were on the march. But Balcarres's horse, such as were not with Hurry in the north, were in Fife, and could not be involved for at least three days.

Well content, the Graham marched his rested men out of Crieff and over the Earn, to the south. Then turned westwards again, along the river-side, the three miles or so to where the fairly wide strath narrowed suddenly with the steep, intrusive wooded hills of Torlum and Lennoch. Here, beyond Strowan, he turned his force around, and settled to wait.

In due course, with the early sun behind him, Baillie found them there, blocking his path. Obviously it was a strong position, a narrow, thickly-wooded pass, and even with ten times the opposition's number, the Covenant general was not going to risk an assault. Which was entirely as Montrose had anticipated.

So now he commenced his drag-wing progress. Leaving a screen of men to guard the narrows, he quite openly withdrew his main force westwards, to take up another defensive position about three miles on, beyond Dalginross, where the Romans had done the like before him. There was no lack of such sites in the upper Earn valley, with the mountains shouldering close. Settled there, he called back his rearguard.

Soon Baillie was before this position also.

It was no more of a practical proposition to attack here than had been the other. Soon Montrose made another strategic withdrawal. In the process even David Ogilvy observed that this was an undignified proceeding and singularly lacking in profit, in his view. What was the object?

'The object, my good friend, is that of any commander in the field – to defeat the enemy. With our small numbers, and lacking cavalry, we cannot now defeat Baillie by force of arms. But we can, I believe, bring low his name and credit, which means much in this sort of warfare. He has come out against us with ten times our numbers. Now, he must either follow us thus, until we choose to fight – which will be on ground of *my* choosing. Or he must give up, stop following, turn back. He has no other choice. In which case, we blazon it to all Scotland. For the second time, the Covenant commander-in-chief has refused battle with a vastly smaller army. He cannot win, today, see you.'

'This was your intention . . . ?'

'If I could coax him to it, yes. Another four miles, and we are at the foot of Loch Earn. We must take one side of the water, or the other. So must he – if he comes at all. We shall take the south shore, the longer by a little, with more headlands to circle. It is my hope that Baillie will choose to take the north shore, to hurry along at all speed, so as to turn the head of the loch before us – try to bring us to battle on the open flats there, where his numbers would tell.'

'Your hope . . . ?'

'We would turn up the glen of Arvorlich. Where the mad major is laird,' Nathaniel Gordon intervened. 'Climb the hill over into Glen Artney. And so mock them.'

'You are wrong, Nat. We would turn *back*. Back whence we have come. Down Strathearn again, and fast. Twice so fast as Baillie can move. Nor halt at Crieff.'

'You mean . . . ?'

'Aye. Perth lies undefended. We could take it this night. All Baillie's stores, ammunition, cannon, will be there. It is the key to Fife and the South, down to Stirling. To my own Graham lands. If Baillie lost Perth, his credit would scarce recover.'

'Dear God in heaven . . . !'

But, tremendous as was this conception, for a few hundred

men, it was not to be. Baillie, whether he saw the trap, or merely tired of this fruitless stop-and-go procedure, called a halt. At St. Fillans, at the foot of Loch Earn, where Montrose took the southern shore, he neither followed nor took the northern but remained where he was. Probably he did not guess at the sheer bold extravagance of Montrose's design on Perth; but he would recognise that the royalist commander was seeking to lure him farther into the mountains for some purpose which could scarcely be to his advantage. Wary, as ever, he halted while he still had options open to him, room for at least some manoeuvre, and a clear line of retiral to his base.

When, half-way down the seven mile long loch, this became clear to Montrose, he was disappointed but in no way cast down. He still held the initiative, still could go where he would, and could declare that he had won a moral victory over the Estates commander who was abandoning the fight. It was as much as he had set out to achieve, in this exercise.

They passed Arvorlich where his former officer, Major James Stewart, was laird, Stewart who had murdered Montrose's kinsman, lieutenant and friend, the Lord Kilpont, in a fit of mad anger – but Stewart was from home, indeed acting turncoat with Balcarres's cavalry in Fife, and the Graham did not wage war against women and bairns. They marched on to St. Blane's Chapel at the head of the loch, and then turned south for Balquhidder, to camp in an excellent defensive position in the jaws of that valley.

It would be interesting to see what Baillie would do.

But in due course scouts reported that the Covenant army had in fact turned back, and was in steady retiral down Strathearn, pride swallowed in the interest of good sense. The royalists were on their own again.

From Balquhidder they crossed the passes above Glen Gyle and down to Loch Katrine-side. The Gregarach, Children of the Mist, were out-of-love with the Crown – Charles's father, King James, having persecuted them sorely and even denied them their name. But they had as little love for the Covenant, judging the Campbells as worse than the Devil. Donald of Glengyle supplied food and forage for Montrose's gold, and even contributed a token force of fifty clansmen – pointing out that this was as good as any 200 ordinary mortals. More interesting he disclosed that there was a little group of royalist refugees hiding, by his good offices, at Portanellan, along the lochshore, where there was an island nearby to offer sanctuary if necessary. Some were wounded, including their leader – who would not give his name but had a lordly way with him, though young.

Intrigued, Montrose went on ahead of his people, with only two companions to avoid alarming the fugitives, to investigate.

They were spied from afar, and could perceive men scattering off into the birchwoods and junipers from the lonely reed-thatched house of Portanellan. A little group of four, however, got into a boat and pulled a few yards from the shore, to await the arrival of the visitors in safety.

Coming down to the pebbly strand, Montrose doffed his Highland bonnet, and raised his hand. 'Friends,' he called, 'have no fear. I am James Graham of Montrose, your King's Lieutenant. Glengyle told me of you . . .'

There was a great shout, out in the boat, and a hasty and far from co-ordinated splashing of oars to bring the craft back to the beach. Out into the shallows jumped one of the young men, arm in a grubby sling, to come running in a splatter of water.

'My lord! My lord James!' he cried. 'God's mercy – it's yourself! Here's joy. It is I, James Gordon. Aboyne . . .'

'Aboyne! You – of all men! My dear lad – I believed you beleagured in Carlisle . . . ?'

It was the Viscount Aboyne, second son of Huntly, next brother to the Lord Gordon. Montrose had left him, a year before, when he had made his secret and unauthorised dash back to Scotland from Cumberland, and Aboyne, with the Lord Ogilvy and other Scots of Montrose's English army had remained in the King's service in the south. Ogilvy had been captured by Leslie's Covenanting force and sold for gold to Argyll, at Edinburgh; but Aboyne had been with the remnant driven back on Carlisle, where they had been besieged and shut up for long months.

'I escaped,' the younger man cried, a slight, sharp-featured redhead, hot-eyed like his brother Lewis but with less wolflike an expression. 'I contrived to bolt. One night. A sally, with a score of troopers. From the Scots Gate postern. I wearied for home. Had enough of Carlisle, by God! And the English, too! One night, we slipped out. Unknown to any. We cut our way through Callender's lines. Lost two. My horse shot under me. My shoulder put out.' He patted his slung arm. 'Came north by Annandale and Douglasdale. At the ford of Frew, near to Stirling, we fell in with these . . .'

Montrose had raised his glance to the other two young men who were disembarking more conventionally. 'Archie!' he exclaimed. 'Young Archie! I did not know you – my own sister's son! Dear God – *you* I thought deep in Edinburgh's Tolbooth!'

'Aye, Uncle, and so I was. But Sandy here and I got out; Sandy Alexander you will know, son to the late Earl of Stirling? We bribed a gaoler to let us in with the women – strumpets, slit-purses, thieves – and there changed clothing with two of them. Lord – you should have seen us! And so won out, offering our favours to drunken guards! Only *we* did the poking, not them – with dirks! We were on our way north, to join you . . .'

'And your father? My good lord?'

'He rots there still. With Ogilvy, Stirling of Keir, your chaplain Wishart. And many another. Argyll's prisoners. Held below ground. In worse case than the cut-throats and pickpockets . . .'

'Aye!' That was almost a groan. 'The price of being friend to James Graham!'

'The privilege, sir!' his nephew declared, proudly. He was a delicately good-looking youth, just twenty, Archibald, Master of Napier, son of the late Lady Margaret Graham and of Montrose's friend and former curator, the first Lord Napier of Merchiston. His companion, even younger, was Alexander, a son of the poet 1st Earl of Stirling, from Menstrie Castle.

Montrose was greatly enheartened by this encounter. Apart from his pleasure in the company of friends long-parted, he had a great sense of kinship, of community. Moreover, he badly needed lieutenants, officers on whom he could rely. He did not know much about young Alexander, although his father certainly had been a man of great initiative, inventor of the new-fangled degree of baronet of Nova Scotia. But his nephew Archie was sound, steady and less delicate than he looked. As for Aboyne, despite his youth he was a proved leader of light cavalry, with a flair for hit-and-run tactics. He had not the sober worth of his brother George – but he had far more dash and vigour, yet without Lewis Gordon's moody fickleness. They were a strange family, admittedly, their father Huntly little short of an oddity and their mother, of course, a Campbell.

That night Montrose moved to Cardross, amongst the extensive marshlands of the Flanders Moss in the wide vale of the upper Forth, in an effort to coax Baillie southwards and to alarm the Convenant leadership – for here he was only a dozen miles from Stirling, less than fifty from Edinburgh itself, and moreover with the barrier of the Forth turned. They dared not press on, of course, with so small a force and without cavalry; but the threat was there, and the lower Forth crossings which Balcarres was so heedfully guarding, were outflanked. But at Cardross, in Graham country now, a courier from the north found them, from George Gordon. Hurry was pressing him hard, and devastating the lower Gordon lands on Deeside and Donside. If Montrose wanted to raise a Gordon cavalry force, he had better come quickly.

Once more strategy had to yield to immediate necessity. They left the wildfowl-haunted marshes of Forth that same night, on one of Montrose's major cross-country marathons. But at least they were reinforced in numbers – although the newcomers were liable to hold them up in their prodigious marching.

It took them three strenuous days and nights to win slantwise back across Scotland to Aberdeenshire. At the Skene rendezvous they found Black Pate and the Master of Madderty just arrived. with Atholl and Strathearn recruits. But Colkitto was not yet back from the Highland West; and George Gordon was still in Strathbogie, for it seemed that Hurry had now moved on northeastwards to threaten the Gordon lands from the territories of their hereditary foes on Speyside and the Deveron, the Crichtons, Forbses, Frasers and Inneses.

James Graham decided to wait for Colkitto. Hurry was alleged to have 4,000 foot now, and over 400 horse – a major army, for the foot included the regular line regiments of Loudoun's, Lawers's, Buchanan's and Lothian's – although the last seemed to have been in some sort of mutiny, details unclear. Hurry was playing a waiting game too, it appeared, for recruits were flocking in from Moray and Nairn, mainly from hatred of the Gordons – this was the price Montrose must pay for the essential cavalry. And worse, that turncoat, the Mackenzie Earl of Seaforth, had changed sides once more, only two months after parting from Montrose at the graveside at Bellie, and was now marching from the far North-West, with the Earl of Sutherland and a large force of clansmen. Hurry would wait for that.

Fretting, Montrose marked time.

As usual, his light-foot host was short of supplies and ammunition, a chronic state for an army which refused to lumber itself with a baggage-train and commissariat. Yet Aberdeen was close and comparatively undefended. Montrose refused to saddle himself with the responsibility of the city which could only hold him up and fritter away his energies. But the Viscount Aboyne came to plead and urge that he give him such cavalry as there were – these were mainly Gordons anyway – and let him make a swift raid on the town, while they waited. He promised that he would bring back all the supplies they required.

James Graham knew him well enough to recognise that this was a necessary Gordon gesture, the signal to Scotland that Aboyne was back on his native heath, and the Gordon power no longer in wavering hands. There were only some eighty horse, all told – but skilfully led, eighty determined Gordons descending on Aberdeen might achieve much, given surprise. Besides, it was the sort of thing Montrose himself would have liked to have done. He gave permission.

Aboyne's raid, essayed in broad daylight, was astonishingly successful. He suffered no single casualty and even included ships in the harbour in the assault. His eighty came back not only richer than they went, but more numerous, with an extra score of laden horses and a dozen volunteers to ride them. Also with twenty kegs of gunpowder, from one of the ships, and food enough to solve their problems meantime. With May upon them, forage was now no difficulty.

When, two days later, Major-General Alastair turned up from the west, he proved to have been worth waiting for, bringing 1,100 MacDonalds, Camerons and Macleans, under the Captain of Clanranald – who had led them at Inverlochy. This made the royalist army just over 2,000 strong, with some of the best infantry in the world. Once they had their Gordon cavalry ...

There was no waiting now. With all speed they marched north for Strathbogie.

Montrose found George Gordon in something of a stew. His brother Lewis had got home before him and had sent out emissaries to all the main Gordon lairds urging them not to get involved with Montrose, saying that he spoke in his father's name. Since all knew that this indeed was Huntly's attitude, wherever he was hiding himself, they were all more prepared to listen. And when Hurry's troops were menacing Gordon lands, it was reasonable for able-bodied men to stay near their homes and guard their hearthstones. When the Lord Gordon arrived, then, recruiting, he met with a distinctly cool reception, by and large, and now had less than 250 men assembled. His delight at finding his brother James with Montrose was in fact as much relief as fraternal affection, and he thankfully handed over responsibility for things military to Aboyne, his junior by a year but who had always taken the lead in that young family – a situation which was oddly reflected in their titles, for James was the Viscount Aboyne whereas the elder George was merely the Lord Gordon. This was explained by the fact that James was Huntly's favourite; he could not make him his heir, but he himself had been created Viscount Aboyne before he succeeded his father as 2nd Marquis of Huntly, and he had passed on his personal title to his second son. Aboyne lacked the depth of character of his elder brother, but he was a born leader.

Leaving him at Strathbogie to get on with the business of countering Lewis and his father's influence, and enlisting somehow or other the essential cavalry, Montrose pressed on northwards with George and his 250 horse. Despite the disparity in numbers, he was anxious to bring Hurry to battle before the large Seaforth and Sutherland reinforcements could reach him.

But Hurry was not going to be rushed. He retired before the advancing royalists, backing away from the Spey through the laigh lands of Moray, towards Nairn. The faster he fell back, the sooner he would link up with the oncoming North-West Highland contingent. Baillie was now said to be in Atholl, burning his way northwards also, punishing that mountain province for its continuing support of Montrose. No doubt he intended to join up with Hurry, perhaps at Inverness.

Montrose was in something of a quandary. He was anxious to keep Hurry isolated, but, with only half his numbers, was in no position to force attack, in any but very favourable conditions. And he would have preferred to wait for Aboyne and maximum cavalry support. He followed Hurry on, by Avon and Spey, not pushing, with scouts out far and wide. Hurry and Baillie had to be defeated before he could strike south again to meet King Charles. But he himself must not be defeated, at this stage, or the King's cause was lost. He must play this very heedfully.

It was hardly James Graham's normal procedure. And he had a spirited team to hold in. Oddly enough, and to his own surprise, when decision at last came, it was not he who made it.

CHAPTER FIVE

The village of Auldearn lay in the Moray plain not much more than two miles east of Nairn town, a poor place and small. When the royalist army reached it, on the wet, chill evening of the 8th of May, Hurry was declared by scouts to be no more than an equal distance the other side of Nairn, and still retiring. Montrose called a halt here, for it was in a fair defensive position, on a low U-shaped ridge, with much marshy land around. They had been as near to Hurry as this before – but James Graham always took due precautions. He found the village deserted, no doubt horror tales of the barbarous Irish having preceded them; but though it was a wet and miserable night, he had his troops camp in the open, and himself with them. There were not enough roofs to shelter a quarter of his people; also, once men got settled in houses they were less readily turned out swiftly in an emergency.

Montrose had information that the Earls of Seaforth and Sutherland had indeed at last reached Hurry, but not with their full strength, having merely come on ahead on horseback, their trudging main body still in the vicinity of Inverness. Strangely enough, almost the same position applied with himself, for though Aboyne had now come on, it was only with some fifty more horse, the larger body he had assembled, almost 300, still being equipped and given elementary training by Nat Gordon at Strathbogie. They would come on in a few days. Montrose decided, however, that if at all possible he must bring the enemy to a stand the next day, before the main Highland host reached them. A swift circuit west-about, by Geddes and Cawdor, fording the River Nairn at Kilravock, to trap them between that river, the lochy swampland of Flemington and the sea, perhaps ? An early start, while it was yet dark . . .

As well that they did make that early start. For they were just moving out of Auldearn, at dawn, when racing scouts arrived to announce that Hurry was almost upon them. He had apparently changed to the attack, slipped round behind Nairn in the darkness, with his whole force, and was heading this way. Undoubtedly he knew that the Marquis was at Auldearn . . .

Taken by surprise, for once, James Graham reacted swiftly and without panic. He had little time, and little choice of manoeuvre. But at least their present position was a good defensive one, and might be utilised to advantage.

Much depended on Hurry's intentions. If he was planning an immediate dawn attack, though it gave little time for dispositions, it meant that the fighting would be on ground that Montrose knew, an immense advantage. It must be his objective, then, to *make* Hurry fight here, if he did not already intend to.

With this in view, Montrose divided his force into four groups. Five hundred of the Irish and Islesmen infantry he sent forward, under Colkitto, to hide in scrubland at the northward approaches of the village. The slight ridge on which it was built ended here in a knoll called Castle Hill. A sluggish burn found its way round this from the south-west, and because the ridge was shaped like a wide U, the burn had spread itself as bog in the central basin. The road from the north, therefore, shouldered the Castle Hill and kept to the higher ground, and on down the village street; and to the east of it the ground sloped down through scrub-birch and whins to more marshland, the saltmarsh of the sea nearby.

The cavalry, about 370 strong, under Aboyne, were sent to the extreme south-west horn of the ridge, to wait there on the crest, in view, as a threat – though the soft ground before them was far from ideal for cavalry. But then, the same would apply to the enemy. Magnus O'Cahan was given the best of the musketeers and bowmen, some 300 all told, with most of the powder and shot, to man the yards, back-gardens, pig-sties and cattle-sheds of the village itself. Most of the houses, stretched along the ridge, had long riggs of cultivable strips reaching down to the bogland on the west, with dry-stone dykes to keep the beasts out; and at the foot were the sties and byres, where the animals could be herded on to the common land. These, in the hands of skilful marksmen, could serve as so many strong points. The main body, about half the total infantry, Montrose himself took, to hide, as it were hull-down, behind the ridge to the south and east.

Hurry did not keep them waiting long. A mounted picket appeared on the skyline of the shoulder of Castle Hill, and there halted, scanning the scene. The rain had stopped, but it was a grey chill morning. Presently they were joined by a small group of mounted men. Hurry and his officers, almost certainly, gazing across the half-mile and more of the village, the bogs and the U-shaped ridge.

'Pray that he does not move 200 yards to his left, from that road,' Montrose almost whispered. 'Or he might glimpse Colkitto's men in the scrub. However low they lie.' He shrugged. 'But – why should he?'

Hurry had learned not to be rash in dealing with James Graham. He sent his mounted picket forward, to canter along the deserted village street. This was of no danger, so long as they did not proceed much farther along than the last of the houses, where Montrose's own main body would come into view. To counter any threat of this, Aboyne sent a small detachment spurring to intercept – a perfectly natural-seeming gesture. The picket did not wait for them, but turned and hurried back. O'Cahan's musketeers and bowmen lay low.

Satisfied, Hurry waved on his hidden columns.

It was a nerve-racking business for the watchers to contemplate, inactive, as the seemingly endless files of men, the four regiments first, disciplined, confident, then the local Moray and Nairn volunteers, hundred upon hundred, then the spreading, teeming multitudes of the northern clans.

'His cavalry? Where is his cavalry?' Pate Graham growled. 'He is not sending them forward.'

Montrose was frowning. 'Either he keeps them in reserve. Or he has sent them off west-about. To win behind us. Cut off our retiral. Perhaps both.'

'He has 500 horse, they say. This could hit us sorely,' Gordon exclaimed.

'Could. But not necessarily. It could be a blessing. Pate – you scouted the area last evening. How far west does this bogland reach?'

'Two miles, perhaps. Or three. Broken, sour land. It has been a loch, in part, once. I think . . .'

'And as wide? Bad ground for cavalry, then. A long circuit. This might serve us none so ill. So be it that the battle is short! Much of his cavalry out of action the whole . . .' Montrose paused, and pointed. 'Ha – see. We spoke too soon.'

Mounted men were now appearing to the west of the marching infantry columns.

'Thank God they are on the right!' Gordon said. 'On the left they would mask Colkitto.'

'Wait, you,' Montrose murmured.

'It is Colkitto who will not wait – if I know him . . .!'

'I told him to. Till most of the host was well past. Into the village.'

'That is not all Hurry's cavalry,' Pate declared. 'Here is but a squadron. A plague on it – are the rest behind, in reserve ? Or riding west, circling the bogs ?'

'Pray the latter . . .' Montrose began, when he was interrupted. A great shout arose, and maintained, over there on the right front, as Alastair and his Irish, tired of waiting indeed, leapt up from their cover amongst the scrub and flung themselves, forward in a wild charge, to cross the 300 yards of rising ground between them and the enemy's flank.

'Too soon!' Montrose groaned. 'Half Hurry's infantry is not yet into sight. And if his main cavalry is still behind there . . .' He left the rest unsaid.

'It may be that he can see more than we can . . .'

'Shall we advance now ?' David Ogilvy demanded.

'No!' That was a bark. 'Colkitto has struck too soon. But he will not force my hand! All depends on the next minutes. Wait.'

Colkitto, if he had failed to contain his impatience, at least had not forgotten some of his general's commands. He had the proud Royal Standard fluttering above him as he flung himself onwards at the head of his warriors – calculated, of course, to give the impression that here was the King's Lieutenant himself, and the main host. Whether Hurry in fact so interpreted it, there was no knowing; but if he did, it could have a major influence on the proceedings.

The sudden Irish eruption on the scene was as dramatic in its effects as in its appearance. The Covenant force was marching in column, naturally, and though not wholly confining itself to the muddy roadway was nevertheless strung out along and alongside it in very extended order. Abruptly assailed on its left flank, it was easy enough for its columns to turn and face eastwards. But then they represented a very thin and elongated front, and one very difficult for any unified control. Colkitto had let the four regular regiments past before he struck, so that these now represented the enemy's nearly half-mile-long right wing, with Buchanan's regiment just right of centre. The local volunteers of Moray and Nairn and Speyside formed the actual centre and immediate left – and it was at these that the Irish and Islesmen hurled themselves directly, no doubt considering them to be the weakest link in the chain. The mass of Mackenzies, Sutherlands and northern clans were still streaming over into sight from the north, in no sort of formation. And the cavalry, or such squadron as had shown itself, was islanded on the west, behind all.

There was a great confusion, officers bellowing commands, trumpets blowing, slogans being shouted, and the blood-curdling, ululating roar of a Celtic host in a life-and-death charge.

'God in Heaven, hear them!' Pate cried. 'Four hundred against five thousand! Look at them! What folly – but glorious folly!'

'And we stand here watching, idle!' young Napier exclaimed.

'Where, now, is Sir John Hurry?' Montrose asked, voice calm, steady, almost conversational – even though he had to steel himself to keep it so. 'I see no banner. And his position is of some importance in this.'

The sound of the clash, as the charge struck home on the Moraymen, was like the clanging of hammer on anvil, a metallic crash ringing through and above the rest of the din, a frightening noise indeed for men whose own flesh shrank momentarily from the impact, in sympathy.

But there was no real fighting, at this stage. No fairly narrow cordon of men, however brave and experienced, could have withstood that first furious onslaught – and some of the Moray-men had not waited to try. In seconds only, the yelling Irish had surged right through, sweeping away the entire middle section of the enemy column, like chaff. Hurry's army, in those brief moments, was cut in two.

'Pray the good Lord he remembers!' Montrose all but croaked, forgetting his own nonchalant pose. 'Remembers his orders. To turn left. *Left !* Or he is lost . . .'

But Major-General Alastair MacDonald, Younger of Colonsay, was a most able commander of his kind, if impetuous and no strategist. He was not so busy wielding his great sword like a windmill as to be unaware of the squadron of enemy cavalry standing waiting on the ridge to his right. Now that he was through the infantry line, those horsemen could plunge down upon him if he continued to pursue the broken remnants he had smashed; or equally, if he swung right to roll up the enemy's left wing. Whether he recollected his leader's prior instructions or no – and he was no slavish obeyer of orders – he could see his dire danger staring him in the face. Urgently he waved and yelled his screaming cohorts round to the left, southwards into a dip of the ridge.

'Holy Mother of God be praised!' George Gordon, whose Reformed state was only politic, breathed. 'Now, shall we move?'

'No. Not yet. Let them be.'

Colkitto was now facing the four regular regiments detached from Leslie's Yorkshire army and sent north to aid Baillie on Argyll's instructions. They represented a vastly greater challenge than did the Moray levies, and between them added up to almost 1,800 disciplined men, well-equipped and officered. But they were meantime at a disadvantage, caught unprepared in no defensive posture, and now their flank turned. Given a few minutes, they undoubtedly would have marshalled themselves into a state in which they could have cut Colkitto and his people into ribbons. But those minutes were denied them. Moreover, there was no coherent command – for it appeared that wherever Hurry was, he was not with them. He was a cavalryman always, of course, a master of horse not of foot, and was unlikely to march with the line regiments.

The Irish charge, although it had lost some of its impetus, was by no means spent; and now, in renewed fury if less than any coherent line, flung itself upon the hastily turned columns of Buchanan's regiment, while the shattered ranks of Moray and Nairn were left to stream away north and westwards in flight, masking their own cavalry for the time being. The Buchanans did not break, but began what was intended to be an orderly retiral up towards the village, where the houses would offer the cover they needed for regrouping and a stand. The other regiments' lieutenant-colonels were of the same mind, obviously, and a general falling back on the line of the village ensued, standard tactics indeed for such a situation.

It was then that Colkitto seemed to remember Montrose's orders. The sort of commander who always led from three or four paces in front of all others, he abruptly left off the direct attack, and swung his swordsmen on to follow him, racing along the east flank of the enemy regiments, southwards, parallel with the road. Shots began to crack out now, as the Covenant musketeers had time to bring their weapons into action. Men fell. But racing men, crossing a front, do not make good targets, and there was no major hold up.

'Bless him!' James Graham whispered. 'I wager O'Cahan is blessing him likewise! Alastair remembered him, at last!'

Colkitto was concerned now not merely to get parallel with the enemy, but to get beyond him, as it were to head him off, like a sheepdog might do with a flock. That he was able to achieve this in any degree was thanks to various factors; the waiting and obvious Gordon horse in the distance, for one – the columns would not want to be driven towards that. Also, their natural tendency would be to move back northwards, to rejoin the rest of their army. Moreover, without uniform command, they were scarcely in a position to take sudden and unified aggressive action. They drifted to a halt, and remained more or less stationary, uncertain, content with musket-fire meantime.

'Can he do it ?' Gordon demanded. 'Force four times as many back. On the village ? Now there is no surprise ?'

'I will go aid him.' Clanranald had moved up to where Montrose and his aides lay peering over the grassy crest of the ridge, amongst the whins. He was anxious for his fellow-MacDonald. 'We will roll up the Sassenach between us. As we did at Inverlochy.'

'Bide you, friend, if you please,' Montrose told him. 'No doubt you *would* roll them up. But those four regiments do not represent half Hurry's infantry. And he has still 400 cavalry somewhere. Since I can see no sign of him, I guess that he is commanding this himself, a cavalryman always. He is saving them for something.'

'But, Alastair . . .! By the Mass, Alastair could be cut to pieces there, whatever!'

'Alastair knows what he is doing. He will not be trapped. He has miles of marsh behind him. But, see you – those Lowland regiments with their mercenary officers – they will not wish to stand there in the open, facing an Irish charge, when there are houses behind to give them cover. It is against all their training. Those village houses will be drawing them as water does a thirsty man! For a wager, in a little, they will retire on the houses – safety. Which is what we want . . .'

'O'Cahan is there ? He lies low, I say!'

'On my orders. O'Cahan is perhaps the best infantry officer I have. He is not in the houses, but down in the pig-sties and byres at the garden-ends. He will do nothing to warn the enemy away from those houses. But once they are in, he will keep them engaged. And Hurry's best weapon will be bottled up, wasted . . .

Sure enough, as Colkitto's 500 began to get into a position to charge again, the regiments began a steady and orderly withdrawal, by platoons, towards the long single-sided street of

74

houses – although it was hardly a retiral, since they were, in fact, advancing in relation, to their main army. But they moved back from the Irish threat meantime. And Colkitto, for once, restrained his fierce companies, so that they edged forward instead of charging. It was probably one of the hardest things that he had ever had to do, for the platoons which covered the withdrawal of the others were now using their muskets to better effect, and on good slow-moving targets. Montrose gnawed his lip as he watched his Irish fall. But he did not give the sign his agitated and impatient officers waited for.

It was O'Cahan who came to his fellow-countrymen's aid, then – but did it heedfully, so as not to invalidate his orders. He sent a number of his musketeers and bowmen out from their hiding amongst the pig-sties, to race to the north end of the village gardens and riggs, and from there to open fire on the rear of the retiring regiments. At the sight and sound of it, Colkitto's men let out one of their terrifying yells, as though to commence their charge indeed. It was sufficient. The Covenant infantry decided to forget orderly and planned withdrawal meantime, and turning, made a run for the shelter of the houses.

Presumably somewhere Hurry was watching, and deemed this the moment to throw in his counter-attack. Or it may have been that he was only now ready with it, for all the action hitherto had taken place swiftly, in much less time than it takes to tell. At any rate, over the Castle Hill's northern shoulder came the hordes of irregular infantry, in their thousands, shouting, to bear down upon Colkitto's right. The squadron of cavalry on the ridge began to move down on the flank.

Hastily the Irish reformed to face this new threat. But Alastair was not the man to await any attack in a passive posture. Leaving a screen of some scores to preoccupy the regiments in the village, he turned and plunged forward with the rest of his people, towards the oncoming, shouting host, their own fierce war-cry ringing high above all. At the same time, all O'Cahan's musketeers from the line of the village gardens, opened up on the backs of the houses, further to surprise and perplex the infantrymen milling there.

'That Colkitto is a hero!' Archie Napier declared. 'Look at him! Numbers mean nothing to him. One in a thousand!'

His uncle nodded. 'Ten thousand, rather. I told him that, if this day should be ours, the victory would be his. We see him earning it.' He had been scanning the entire scene keenly, as he spoke. He turned abruptly to the Lord Gordon. 'Off with you now, George. To your brother. My compliments. And my thanks for his patience. So long. He may charge now. Destroy that squadron. And assail the foot's flank. But . . . to watch for Hurry's main cavalry. Away, now – and God be with you.'

'We go now?' Clanranald asked, urgent.

'A little longer, friend. Until I am sure that Hurry's main force is engaged. We are dealing with a veteran fighter, see you.'

Again the clash of headlong collision. But this time the odds were hopelessly against Colkitto, and he must be forced back and overwhelmed. The cavalry squadron had not yet been able to engage, with a stretch of soft bog to cross. But it was only a question of time.

The blaring of Aboyne's trumpeter sounding the charge whinnied high, and like a coiled spring released the horsed ranks plunged forward and downhill at last, slogans of 'Strathbogie!' and 'A Gordon! A Gordon!' bursting from nearly 400 pairs of lungs. They had marsh to get over, likewise, but would skirt the worst of it.

'Now we should learn what Hurry has in reserve!' Montrose said.

The enemy squadron did not fail to perceive its danger, and pulled away hastily in its descent upon Colkitto's hard-pressed flank.

O'Cahan's musketeers were keeping up a constant fusillade against the village and the close-huddled regiments therein.

Even Pate Graham, loyalest of the loyal, was uneasy now at his chief's inaction, with all the detachments of the army engaged – save only for the main body. The Irish foot and the Islesmen were in extreme danger. If the regular regiments should sally out from their cover, it would be the end of Colkitto.

James Graham was no steely calm imperturbable, however straight he sought to keep his face. His knuckles gleamed a tell-tale white now, as he watched and waited. Then, with a great exhalation of breath, he pointed.

'There! There, at last, is Hurry! His standard. Cavalry only. Aye – and no great numbers, by the Powers! Thank God! He must have sent his main horse to the west. To encircle us. As I hope. There is no more than another squadron there. Praise be!'

On the ridge of Castle Hill, behind the forces locked in battle, had appeared a new fringe of horsemen, with three banners fluttering above them, one of them very large. But it was no large force – one hundred perhaps. And no further masses of foot had moved up, to support them.

At last, Montrose was satisfied. 'To your commands, gentlemen,' he cried. 'Clanranald – you will lead the van. With Glengarry. No trumpet-calls. No shouting, until we are in plain view. Forward, my friends – in the King's name!'

That they achieved complete and demoralising surprise was obvious. With over a thousand fresh men, mainly MacDonald swordsmen at that, hurled into the fray unexpectedly, the enemy quailed and faltered. Even though they still greatly outnumbered their attackers. They were badly split up, and, by a masterly piece of psychologically inspired manoeuvring, their best units, the four southern regiments, were cooped up in the village, secure but almost useless. Long before Clanranald and his kilted, half-naked van reached them, Hurry's main infantry were hurriedly breaking off their assault upon Colkitto and streaming back whence they had come.

And now the Gordons had their revenge for all the humiliations they had had to suffer of late. Ignoring the two squadrons of Covenant horse altogether, they thundered up the slope from the waterlogged ground in the central basin of the great U, to fling themselves upon the retiring enemy infantry, in sabre-slashing fury. Almost immediately retiral became a rout, every man for himself. The first Covenant cavalry squadron, instead of turning to attack the Gordon's flank, turned the other way altogether, and actually rode down many of their own fleeing foot, either by mistake or blind panic. Hurry, on the ridge, saw all disintegrating before his eyes, and though he himself rode forward, to rescue what he could, his reserve cavalry turned and disappeared sensibly northwards.

Montrose and most of his main body had not so much as blooded their swords. But it was not time yet for cheering. The regular regiments which O'Cahan had been keeping preoccupied were still unbeaten, in their cottages and out-houses and gardens. If they chose to sit tight there, as in a strong point, the royalists were unlikely to be able to dislodge them lacking artillery, and short of powder and ball as they were. And to sit down around them, in a sort of siege, would be to give Hurry time to halt and reassemble his fleeing irregulars, and possibly return to the attack. Moreover there was the main Covenant cavalry force still to consider – for the two squadrons they had seen could represent little more than a third of it. Presumably it was somewhere to the west, circling the marshlands. But it could be highly dangerous still.

Montrose sent Black Pate and a horsed picket to go look for it; and word for the Lord Gordon and half his Gordon horse to keep up the pursuit of the fleeing enemy, to prevent any rallying. Aboyne and the remainder to round up stragglers near at hand, and hold themselves in readiness to deal with a sudden enemy cavalry attack.

When opportunity offered, he strode forward to grip the panting and slightly wounded Colkitto by the hand, wordlessly, and led him along to consult Magnus O'Cahan, amongst the pig-sties.

'Here's the hero of Auldearn, Magnus!' he declared. 'Alastair has done his part. Now, I require *your* aid. How are we to dislodge these coneys from their warren ?'

'A charge – and a plague on their muskets!' the irrepressible Colkitto jerked. 'Then cold steel. House to house.'

'No, Alastair. Not that. So we lose many, many men. Enough of your fine fellows have fallen this day. The main battle is won. I will not sacrifice more brave men than I must. Rather would I march away and leave these . . .'

'If the weather had been dry we might have burned them out, my lord. Or smoked,' O'Cahan suggested. 'Flaming arrows to the thatches. But I fear they would not catch, so wet it has been.'

'Whins pulled, and set alight ? And a charge through the smoke ? Shrouding their musket-fire. There's a notion . . .'

Montrose was interrupted by a great rattle of musketry from the north end of the village – which was strange, for though the entire perimeter was now surrounded, there was no particular target there for the enemy marksmen. Then, as this died away, out from the same northern extremity of the houses sallied a company of men, orderly, close-knit, but running hard.

'Sainted Mary! A bolt . . .!' Alastair cried. 'They flee, the fools!'

'They were safe there,' O'Cahan muttered. 'If they all come out . . .!' He left the rest unsaid, and ran off to his command again.

Whoever was responsible for the decision, it seemed that the Covenant regulars had elected to leave their security and make a dash to regain the retreating and defeated army – possibly with the object of rallying it. Whatever the reason, it was folly as unexpected as it was desperate – and doomed to failure. For heavily accoutred Lowland foot to pit themselves to outrun light-footed and half-naked Highland and Irish sworders was hopeless beyond all telling. Although the companies emerged in planned order, in a leap-frogging procession, intermittently running and halting to cover the escape of their fellows, such disciplined tactics could not be kept up in the circumstances, and over broken ground, with no central control. Not with Colkitto, Clanranald, Glengarry and O'Cahan leading their veterans against them. Even so, had they accepted the fact, and bunched together in schiltrom formation, hedgehogs, squares, they might have saved much from the wreck, even against Aboyne's horse. But no such refinement developed, and the flight quickly deteriorated into a prolonged shambles, just an endless killing, one-sided, terrible, shameful. Indubitably the Lowland foot fought gallantly enough; but leadership was almost non-existent and they fell by the score, the hundred, almost the thousand, without profit.

When Montrose could stand it no longer, he called off his dogs of war – but with difficulty. The enemy, imbued with the spirit of that Covenant hymn of hate, 'Jesus and No Quarter!', seemed to prefer to die rather than surrender – perhaps Argyll's tales that the Catholic Irish tortured, even flayed and ate their prisoners, conditioned them. At any rate, prisoners were few, and the killing took a deal of stopping. Loudoun's, Lothian's, Lawers's and Buchanan's regiments came to a bloody and complete end there at Auldearn's ridge and bogs, in the name of God and Archibald Campbell. That two of the regiments were Campbell-officered, Loudoun's and Lawers's, made the MacDonalds especially difficult to draw off. Sir Mungo Campbell of Lawers himself was one of the last to die, on a heap of his own dead. No fewer than nine kinsmen of Douglas of Cavers fell, in the Lothian ranks.

With Black Pate's scouts returning to report that a fairly large body of enemy cavalry had been spotted, but had suddenly turned back, inland in the Kinsteary area, it could be accepted that all was over. Hurry was not only outmanoeuvred and beaten, but destroyed as a force, Seaforth taught a lesson. And Baillie was isolated, and in the Highlands, where he was at a disadvantage.

Baillie was a better general than Hurry, and would have to be tackled with care.

Montrose, assured that Hurry and the remnants of his force were in full flight for Inverness and beyond, turned back for Elgin, to rest his troops, treat his wounded, bury his dead, and consider how to trap William Baillie.

CHAPTER SIX

It was a curious reversal of roles. James Graham sat in the castle hall, and waited for David Carnegie, suppliant. It could be only as suppliant that old Southesk came all this way to see his son-in-law, eighty miles from Kinnaird by the shortest route, over the Cairn o' Mount, by Deeside and up Don, to Corgarff, at the very head of Strathdon, amongst the high mountains. Admittedly Corgarff was a small and stark castle, nothing like great Kinnaird, and not even Montrose's own to sit in, but forcibly taken from the hostile Forbeses; but at least he sat in authority here, and his father-in-law must be well aware of it. Not that Southesk was liable to be obsequious, or even mildly respectful, under any circumstances. But he must want something strongly to have travelled all this way.

Nevertheless the younger man rose courteously to his feet, as Pate Graham knocked and came in, to announce impressively, 'My lord Earl of Southesk craves audience with the King's Captain-General, the Most Honourable the Lord Marquis of Montrose.'

'Damn you, man – I crave nothing!' the older man snorted, stamping into the small bleak stone-walled hall, reeking with peat smoke. 'I am here to see my good-son, James Graham – that is all.'

'Then greetings, sir,' Montrose said. 'You are the more welcome in that visits from you are . . . unusual. I see you well – or you could scarce be here. I hope that you bring me fair tidings from Kinnaird ?'

'Are there any fair tidings in all Scotland, these ill days ?' the other demanded. 'Or England either! The world's awry, and an honest man knows not which way to turn, on my soul!'

'Ha! Can it be that you are unsure of your course, my lord ? You – Southesk ? That, surely, is for lesser men!'

Balefully the earl glared, tugging at his bristling white beard. '*My* course is not in doubt, man. It is others' courses that gar me grue.'

'Mine, I take it, sir ?'

'Aye, yours. Man – do you care naught for the hurt you cause others? Those akin to you, and who have done no harm to any? Have you no heart?'

'I esteem myself to have a heart, my lord. Indeed, it causes me a deal of trouble! But – what are you at? My family? Is there trouble there? Or since *you* have come all this way seeking me, is the trouble yours?'

'Hm. There is a guard put on my house, sir! Day and night. Quartered on me. A company of wretched soldiery. At my cost! On your account . . .'

'Mine?'

'Aye, yours. Since Auldearn. My house is in ward, by God! Mine! Your son Robin in custody . . .!'

'Little Robert? But six years? I'll not believe it!'

'It is true. In Magdalen's custody. So she is in ward also. My daughter, in my own house! She may not leave it. A prisoner. Because of you, sir.'

'But why? How will this serve Argyll?'

'I know not. But I will not be treated so. I am Sheriff of Angus. A Lord of Session . . .'

'Argyll is your friend, is he not? Your colleague . . .?'

'No longer, 'fore God! This is too much. Has the man lost his wits? He'll no treat David Carnegie so!'

His son-in-law smiled faintly. 'And Magdalen? How is she? How does she take it?'

Southesk snorted. 'She . . . she isna caring. No' in her right mind. You have seen her. She seldom speaks. But she is sore about Jamie – that I can tell you . . .'

'Jamie? What of Jamie?'

'He's been put in close ward. In Edinburgh. In the damned Tolbooth, they say. With the others.'

'The Tolbooth! A twelve year old! God – no! A mere lad . . .'

'But your *heir*.'

'Was holding him not enough? They are monsters.'

'Just angry men. You shouldna fight battles against them, if you canna look after your own wife and bairns! Aye, and your friends, too. You've young Napier with you now, I hear? Cocking a snook as a soldier, eh? Well – tell him his new bit wife's flung into the Tolbooth too! His sister, forby. It was as a wench that he made his escape, they say. So they've filled his bit cell wi' wenches! Besides his father . . .'

Montrose turned to pace the stone-flagged hall, his features

82

set. He found no words to express his hurt, resentment, shame.

'You'll no' lie down under it, I'm thinking?' the other observed, in a different tone of voice.

James Graham looked at his father-in-law sharply. 'Is not that what you wanted me to do?'

'If you hadna started this folly, aye. But, now, the situation is . . . changed a mite.'

'You mean, I have defeated Hurry. And Baillie is intent on avoiding battle, these eight weeks since Auldearn.'

'Aye, well. Maybe.'

'What is it that you want, sir? You have not come all this way, to Donside, just to give me ill tidings. Out with it, of a mercy!'

Southesk came to tap him on the shoulder. 'Come you to Kinnaird, James,' he said. 'With your army. Rid me o' these insolent knaves. Then I'll ride with you to Dundee. I warrant that they'll no' hold out against you in *my* company. With Dundee and Aberdeen, you'll have the whole North-East. Come you to Kinnaird, I say.'

It took Montrose some moments to grasp the message, to realise what the older man was proclaiming. It was a complete *volte-face*. Battles won did produce results, after all. Southesk was changing sides. Or, at least, was proposing to commit himself. Presumably, therefore, he now conceived the King's cause as likely to prevail.

'You surprise me, sir,' he said. 'You wish to be identified with *my* campaign?'

'His Grace's campaign, is it not?'

'To be sure. But the King has now made me Captain-General, with fullest vice-regal powers in Scotland.'

'Aye. But he will soon be here, himself, to take command. Will he not?'

Montrose drew a quick breath. 'You . . . you know of that?'

'Aye.'

'Dear God – how? How could you have heard it? Who told you? This was the strictest secret . . . !'

'All the Council knows it. A courier was captured. On his way from you to the King. Small, by name. Irish. Calling himself a colonel. They hanged him, anyway . . .'

'Damnation! Small captured. And *hanged*? God rest his soul. And . . . and he talked? He had little in writing . . .'

The other shrugged. 'Men can be made to talk.'

'Yes. With the shame on the makers, rather than the talker!'

So that was it! Why Southesk had turned. And come all this way. Montrose's own victories and the King's coming, together. Charles must not be displeased with the man whom he had built up, made lord, then earl and judge.

'When do you look to see the King?'

'Did not Small tell you? Or the Council?'

'Only that it was to be soon. How soon?'

His son-in-law did not answer. He was thinking hard. If Small had never reached the King, Charles would not have received his own message. Urging haste. And he was notoriously dilatory, never doing today which might be put off till the morrow. There would be no June or July rendzevous, then. He must get off another messenger, forthwith.

'Does Charles seek to bring an army with him?' Southesk went on.

The younger man was wary. He did not altogether trust such sudden conversions. 'That remains to be seen,' he said.

'He'd be wiser not to, man,' the other declared. 'Leslie's been ordered from York. To Westmorland and Cumberland. To cut off any descent on Scotland, on the West. That's the way he was to come, was it not? And the other Leslie, David, is still besieging Carlisle. Charles will not have an easy road home. If he tries to bring an army. No' that he's got that much of an army left, since Naseby, by all accounts.'

'Naseby? What is this?'

'You havena' heard? Guidsakes, man — has none told you? There was a mighty defeat of the King's host, at this Naseby. In Northamptonshire, it is. By the man Cromwell. In mid-month. They had near double the numbers, mind — Cromwell and Fairfax. Rupert's horse broken quite, the foot annihilated. The King's greatest disaster. Small wonder he comes to Scotland...'

'Defeat in England! Rupert beaten again, by Cromwell! My sorrow — these are ill tidings to bring me. But... but it will serve to bring the King the sooner, yes. To let him see that his first duty was to be King of Scots. The ancient kingdom of his race. The lesson I have been trying to teach him, for long. Let Cromwell and Fairfax and their friends have England — which never has owed the Stewarts true allegiance. Scotland, their true heritage, the most ancient kingdom in Christendom, may correct but will never do without its king.'

'Aye, well. Hrrm. You will come to Kinnaird, then? And on to Dundee?'

'I will send a company, to dispossess your invaders at Kinnaird. If so you wish. But I will not seek to take Dundee. Now is no time to risk being shut up in a city. I have not the men to spare, to hold it . . .'

'But it could be yours – or the King's – for the taking. I am Sheriff there . . .'

'Then *you* take it, my lord. In the King's name. His Grace would take that kindly, I am sure! And hold it, if you may. For myself, I play a game of mouse-and-cat with Baillie. Have been doing these past weeks. Dundee would be as good as a trap for me. I need space, country, wide lands to cover. My task is to destroy Baillie – if I can. Not to hold cities.'

'And the King? What of Charles?'

'I shall send him warning. Of the Leslies. Tell him better that he comes all but alone. With only Scots for company. And secretly. So long as he is back in his own Scotland, it will serve. Give me six months, with His Grace in the country – four – and he will sit his fathers' throne secure.'

'I hope so . . .'

'Now – tell me of Magdalen. And the children. Is she more herself? Less low in spirits? And are the bairns well? These soldiers – they do not harry them . . .?'

*   *   *

Southesk's visit to his son-in-law was brief, for the very next morning riders came from the Lord Gordon, at Strathbogie, thirty-five miles farther north, calling for aid and action. Both the Gordon brothers were at home, meantime. Montrose had sent Aboyne on sick-leave after Auldearn – for his damaged shoulder was not improving as it should, with all this campaigning. And Aboyne had sent urgently for George, when a new and specific command had reached Strathbogie from their absent father. Huntly straitly ordered all Gordons, all tenants and all who owed him any sort of allegiance, immediately to retire from any service with the Marquis of Montrose, on pain of his direst displeasure. The Lord Lewis would take strict note of any defaulters, and they would pay dearly when their lord returned. This fiat had been too much for Aboyne to counter on his own. He required his elder brother's authority, for once.

Now the Lord Gordon sent word of new trouble. General

Baillie, whom Montrose had been trailing back and forth across the North-East, trying to manoeuvre him into a position where his superior strength could be successfully negatived, had apparently tired of the process, and had changed tactics to harrying the Gordon lands. He was now in fact besieging the great Bog o' Gight Castle near the mouth of Spey – the same where Johnnie Graham had died. This was of little strategic importance; therefore Baillie must be doing it merely to trouble the Gordons, and possibly to coax Montrose to come to the rescue. And he was successful in this, if so, for George Gordon declared that nothing was reinforcing his father's commands like this blatant assault on the second-greatest Gordon stronghold. He could do little or nothing with his father's clansmen so long as this harrying and siege continued.

Montrose, as ever desperate for cavalry, had no option but to head north without delay. He did so, however, with his eyes wide open.

Sending his father-in-law, grumbling and more or less empty-handed, back to Kinnaird, with only a small detachment under young Napier to eject his intruders, a move was made from Corgarff.

Montrose was by no means anxious to thrust himself upon Baillie, at this stage, and well aware that Bog o' Gight might be something of a trap. Apart from the Gordons, he was suffering other detachments from his strength. Clanranald and his Moidart MacDonalds had returned to their western glens and islands – although Glengarry and his Knoydart MacDonnells remained – and Colkitto had gone with his friend to try to raise an alternative force. So the royalist army was for the moment short of both infantry and cavalry – the price which had to be paid for a purely volunteer force, unpaid save for what booty it might collect. Montrose's own fortune was by now entirely dissipated, and all his properties confiscated. Although he had total powers to requisition and tax, in theory, for policy's sake he seldom used them. This was why it had had to be cat-and-mouse with Baillie for so long – until they might fight on *his* terms.

He marched north to threaten Baillie, then – but marched warily. At Strathbogie he picked up, thankfully, the Lords Gordon and Aboyne with 250 welcome horse, and pressed on for the Spey. But not too fast. The last thing that he wanted was a pitched battle with Baillie outside Bog o' Gight. Indeed he positively dragged his feet as they neared the Speyside area. Once across Spey, he could turn Baillie's flank, get round behind him. This would have suited him very well, had he had a larger force. As it was, he must just try to coax the enemy away from the level Moray plain. And a threatened crossing of Spey, *behind* Baillie, might just do it.

His reasoning proved accurate. Baillie, well served by his scouts, came up to contest the Spey crossing. He did more, he advanced to the line of the Banffshire Isla, at Keith, which gave him a double advantage, Isla before him, Spey behind. Even a Montrose could not readily outflank him here.

And so, once again, the Graham and Baillie faced each other across a river valley, with neither able to cross it save at dire loss – especially in the case of the royalists, for Baillie had artillery drawn up on the heights. Not that Montrose had any intention of crossing. Once again he took the initiative, and went through the charade of trumpeting, parleying and challenging the other to a set battle one side of the river or the other. And with the same result. Baillie was a down-to-earth mercenary soldier, no romantic warrior. He sent word that he would fight at his own time and place; and when he did it would be the end of James Graham of Montrose and all his traitorous rebels. He reinforced this reply with a salvo from his cannon – which fell short, of course, but had its own eloquence.

Montrose waited for one inactive day. Then, in full view of the enemy, staged a dramatic interlude. He arranged an elaborate altercation between himself and the Gordons, which ended in the entire cavalry force mounting and riding away north-east-wards, pursued by the shouts of the rest. Whether Baillie interpreted this as a serious difference of opinion or not, he at least would be apt to assume that the Gordons were making for the Bog o' Gight area, to discover what had happened to their important stronghold.

Soon afterwards, minus cavalry, the royalist army packed up and headed southwards, whence it had come, in some obvious confusion.

By late evening rearward scouts brought forward the infor-mation Montrose hoped for. The ruse had worked. Baillie was following on.

The problem now was to keep the enemy cavalry at a distance, while enticing Baillie on. And this for about thirty difficult miles, two days retreating, until the Gordons could circle east-about to rejoin them unobserved. But by dint of his previous well-tried tactics of setting fire to whins and hillsides by night, and making sham ambushes, traps and obstacle-courses by day, Montrose managed it. The fact that he skirted Strathbogie again un-doubtedly helped, proximity to the Gordon heartland having an inhibiting effect on the enemy, naturally enough. On the evening of the 1st of July, Montrose crossed Don at the ford near the village of Forbes, above Alford – to find the Gordon horse drawn up under cover of woodland below the Gallows Hill, at the far side, near where the Leochal Water came in. He heaved a long sigh of relief. He was where he wanted to be, he had his cavalry back – and Baillie was only a few hours march behind.

'Now we stop trailing our wing,' he declared. 'Tomorrow, we will force Baillie to fight on ground of *our* choosing, God willing!'

* * *

James Graham, in his innumerable journeyings back and forth about the North-East, had often noted the excellence of the Ford of Forbes as a sheer copy-book battleground – at least, for *his* purposes. The long and level Howe of Alford was a flood-plain, with the Don meandering through extensive meadows for miles. This was not unusual; the same applied at the Isla, the Deveron and dozens of other rivers of the undrained land. What was un-usual was that the ford at Forbes was so wide; indeed there were really three fords, over almost a mile's extent. Moreover, there was no high ground to overlook them, until the Gallows Hill of Forbes was reached, on the south, a low, wide eminence, wooded round its base, a full mile back from the river. This meant that an opposed crossing of the Don here was almost impossible, especially with a lesser host opposing a greater. Baillie need have no fears about being able to cross here.

What was not so clear, without careful investigation, was the course and behaviour of the Leochel Burn which joined Don from the south-west just above the fords – whose deposited silt and stones, indeed, helped to form the ford's shallows. The Leochel seemed an open and placid enough stream for the first half-mile, all that might be seen from the other side of Don, broad but shallow. But thereafter it changed its character dramatically, cutting its way through rocky and steep ravines, with rapids and cauldrons, a formidable barrier. Thus it curved round the western slopes of the Gallows Hill. But half a mile farther it once again changed character, to open out in widest sprawl and spread, flooding the hollow basin at the back of the hill, and turning it into a swamp. Accordingly, though not apparent from the Don, there was only one practical way round Gallows Hill for an army, east-about – and this was much complicated by bog. The road itself steered a clear course, well to the east.

Montrose, that morning, made no attempt to hide his presence, not wishing Baillie to suspect any sort of trap. He drew up his foot on the upper and bare part of Gallows Hill, visible to all. But the rejoined cavalry he kept hidden, partly in the woodland below. Also behind the hill he kept a reinforcement he had met with on the way south, Farquharsons, Ogilvys, Hays, Baillie would see only the units he had been following all the way from Keith.

In mid-forenoon the enemy appeared, and duly made his crossing. Baillie sent his horse, some 450 of them, splashing over first, then the serried columns of foot, followed by the oxen-drawn artillery which had so held him up, with the lengthy baggage-train last. He took his time, and Montrose did not interfere. They watched each other warily.

When all were safely over, Baillie, cautious man, divided his cavalry into two, and sent half round the east base of Gallows Hill and half round the west. As would be expected of him, to avoid being outflanked and cut off on the hill-top, Montrose retired openly to a new position on the north-east face of the hill. But he did not move his hidden cavalry.

Baillie advanced his main body of infantry to the foot of the hill.

Montrose waited. Soon the east-going enemy horse would come into view of his infantry behind the hill – and vice versa. This might not upset them over-much – though they would surely send back to inform Baillie. This reserve was under the young Master of Napier, who had rejoined his uncle after expelling the Covenant guard from Kinnaird. The royalist right-wing cavalry and foot were under the command of the Lord and Nathaniel Gordon respectively, the centre infantry under Angus MacDonnell of Glengarry, the left-wing foot under O'Cahan and horse under Aboyne. All knew Montrose's plan of action.

From his point of view it was all more like an elaborate game of chess than a battle, whatever was felt by the participants in general. Every move was predicted – even though some were not exactly as timed. The Lord Gordon, for instance, left his cover too soon, and charged the enemy left-wing infantry before he should, tempting target as they made – with the result that Baillie's right-wing cavalry, riding back from the Leochel-narrows impasse, as was to be expected, were hastily switched to the other flank, and created considerable havoc – admittedly also amongst their own foot – as a cavalry battle ensued, the wretched infantry expendable amongst the lashing hooves.

Baillie, on the word that the west-about route was impossible, since he could scarcely retire across Don again with all his artillery and baggage, had either to press on east-about, or to stay where he was. But his present position was cramped and limited as to possible manoeuvre, no ground for a battle. He sought to push on.

Aboyne now charged on the left, to give this move impetus; and the Highland centre, under Glengarry, went bounding downhill in yelling fury. Bugles from Baillie recalled his left-wing cavalry in haste. This should have been Lord Gordon's task to intercept – but he was fully engaged already. Nat Gordon did his best with the right-wing foot, throwing in his men in a do-or-die effort, not to stem the new cavalry threat, since that was impossible, but, once they clashed with his young chief's hard-pressed squadron, to dash in amongst the enemy horses, dirks drawn, hamstringing the poor brutes and slitting their bellies. It was an expensive way of fighting, but effective.

O'Cahan came in then, as Baillie rallied his strung-out centre, and Aboyne was able to leave his wing altogether, on Montrose's urgent command and dash through the woodland to the aid of his brother.

It was a curious situation. On the royalist side, all went with almost clockwork precision, save for George Gordon's costly lapse. On Baillie's side, however, it was an utter confusion from start to finish, with no pattern followed or indeed possible. Even so, the enemy losses, at the start, were not great, and Baillie still had many more men in the field than had his opponent. But then young Napier came on the scene, with the reserve, afraid that his uncle had forgotten him. Loud-voiced, clamant they appeared from the back parts of the Gallows Hill, in no sort of order, a very mixed bag of raw recruits, uncertain of their target but full of fervour. They won the day, without striking a blow for as it seemed, by mutual consent, the Covenant horse broke at sight and sound of them, and turned to dash for the Ford of Forbes again, led by a group of mounted officers, notably not by Baillie himself. The infantry was unable so to escape, though much of it tried. Amidst indescribable chaos, Baillie himself was presently forced to ride off – escaping only by moments and inches, indeed, as George Gordon himself slashed his way through the press to try to grab him by the sword-belt. The Battle of Alford was over.

There was less killing thereafter than at Auldearn and Inverlochy, with Colkitto and his Irish absent, and Montrose better able to control his victorious troops. Not that he was not otherwise preoccupied. For George Gordon lay dead on the bloody field, amongst many of his clansmen. At the last moment, as he sought to capture Baillie, he had been struck down from behind by a Covenant pistol-ball.

James Graham stood over his friend, tears streaming down his cheeks unchecked. He was even more distressed than was Aboyne. The Lord Gordon was not a great soldier, or even a very notable figure on the national scene. But he was the man closest to Montrose in spirit, with whom he could talk and discuss, partner of so many evening camp-fire debates, sensitive, intelligent, conscientious, responsible. Baillie's defeat had been dear bought, as far as James Graham personally was concerned, with the heir of Gordon's fall.

The Gordon horse had, in fact, borne the brunt of the fighting, sandwiched between two assaults. Only amongst them were casualties high, or indeed more than nominal, on the royalist side. Baillie's infantry losses were large, and a great many butchered horses lay around; but basically his cavalry and officer-corps had made good their escape. The artillery and baggage, of course, remained with the visitors.

The pursuit was maintained for the rest of a long summer's day – a pursuit intensified by the extraordinary information, obtained from a captured officer, that the Marquis of Argyll himself had been with Baillie, and was now presumably fleeing northward somewhere. His presence with the army was said to be accounted for by Baillie's pleas to be allowed to resign his command, repeated more than once during the last weeks. The Campbell had not only refused this, but had come up himself in order to ensure that the reluctant general did his duty. According to Glengarry he had almost managed to dirk a richly dressed character whose description corresponded.

Hurry and Baillie both were now defeated.

The Lord Lindsay of the Byres had a small army based on Angus, local levies almost entirely – but they could be discounted. The Earl of Callender's force remained in the Border area; but it had proved itself a singularly inactive and non-aggressive body, to date. The two Leslies were still in England, although only just. Montrose might hope that the road south lay open to him, at long last.

He marched the very next day, going to Aberdeen, to inter his friend, with fullest military honours, in the great granite cathedral of St. Machar. That city did not oppose him. No city in all Scotland was likely to oppose James Graham's entry that early July of 1645.

He made but a sombre victor, nevertheless. Quite apart from the loss of George Gordon, Montrose did not forget that he had a son, and sundry good friends, to free from Edinburgh's Tolbooth. And there were reports that the plague was raging in the capital.

CHAPTER SEVEN

Some weeks before, the Earl of Southesk had urged his son-in-law to come to Kinnaird. But when he came, his reception was less than enthusiastic. Perhaps David Carnegie had some small excuse for his lukewarmness; it had never been his intention that Montrose should bring 5,000 others with him – and the vast preponderance of them Irish and Highlandmen, in the Carnegie's opinion little better than animals. Kinnaird was a handsome and civilised house, one of the first seats in all Scotland no less, and not to be defiled by such cattle.

James Graham gave him no option, however. Kinnaird was near their line of march, only three miles east of Brechin, his troops were hungry and he had spent his last penny in providing meagrely enough for them; moreover it was important at this stage that the Lowlands should not be antagonised by any whole-sale requisitioning and looting. Whereas his father-in-law was one of the richest men in the land – and, so far, his ostensible support of King Charles had cost him little. Moreover, Montrose wanted to see his wife; and it might well do Magdalen no harm to meet some of the men with whose names Scotland was ringing.

For his wife's sake mainly, then, he put on quite a show. Marching his army, unit by unit, into the great park of the castle, trumpets blaring, pipes playing, banners flying, clan slogans shouted, cavalry jingling at the trot. Never, in fact, had he had such a large force at his command since his Covenant days, for Colkitto had rejoined him at Fordoun, at the foot of the Cairn o' Mount pass the day before, and had been more successful in his recruiting in the West than hitherto. Aboyne was absent again at Strathbogie, where he had retired after his brother's funeral; but any day he was expected back, with more of the precious cavalry. Hence this breathing-space.

With his thousands marshalled in the great park, Montrose led his officers over Kinnaird's drawbridge and into the courtyard of the castle. Southesk stood there, glowering, with his youngish Countess – a second wife – his son, the Lord Carnegie, and his brother the Lord Lour. Magdalen and the two children were not present, but two small faces could be seen at an upper window of their flanking-tower, and James Graham thought that he could just distinguish the outline of a figure behind.

'Greetings, my lord,' he called out. 'You invited us to Kinnaird, a month back. We rejoice now to avail ourselves of your hospitality – in the King's good cause.'

'Man – you've brought *thousands*!' the other spluttered. 'And ... and the half o' them Hielantmen, 'fore God!'

'All His Grace's loyal subjects, sir – stout fighters for His Grace's rights.'

'But ... but ...'

'It is our hope that you will add to our numbers, at Kinnaird, my lord. With a fine troop of Carnegie horse, in especial. A captaincy for your son, my good-brother, at least.'

That closed the old man's mouth almost with a snap. He stared, appalled.

'I have the honour, my lord, to present to you some of my officers, men whose names I pronounce humbly but with pride. First, my Major-General, Alastair MacDonald of Dunaverty, Younger of Colonsay, whom men call Colkitto. The bravest of the brave!'

'Umph!' Southesk said. Highlanders and Irishmen were almost equally to be deplored, in his view. A Highlander who led Irishry was quite beyond the pale.

'We have all heard of General Colkitto,' his Countess said, admiring the blond giant's sheer rampant masculinity. 'Welcome to Kinnaird, sir.'

'*Your* welcome I would savour to the full, lady!' Alastair answered, grinning – with a distinct emphasis on that first word.

'And here is John MacDonald of Moidart, Captain of Clanranald. And Angus MacDonnell of Glengarry. Two of the most illustrious names in all Scotland.'

'Ooh, aye. No doubt.'

'Lachlan Maclean of Duart's fame must be known to you. Likewise Murdoch Maclaine of Lochbuie and Ewan Maclean of Treshnish.'

'Mm. Aye, well ...'

'Here is MacDonald of Keppoch and MacIan of Glencoe.' It was highly important to get all these Gaelic chiefs and dignitaries in their right and due order, a subject Montrose had early set himself to master. Nothing was easier than to give dire offence by a single misplacement.

'Cameron Younger of Locheil, Macpherson of Invereshie MacGregor of Glengyle . . .'

'Aye, man – aye,' Southesk interrupted testily. 'But where are the Scots ?' Like most Lowland noblemen he did not concede that Highlanders – the Erse as they named them, lumping them with the Irish – were Scots at all.

Montrose frowned. 'All are Scots, my lord. None less so than yourself.'

'Davie means your *Lowland* lords, James,' the normally silent Lord Lour intervened.

'You see here the Master of Madderty, the Master of Napier, Sir David Ogilvy son to the Earl of Airlie . . .'

'Lords he said, man – *lords*!' Southesk insisted. 'No' younglings and landless whippersnappers! Where are your solid Scots lords ?'

His son-in-law's determinedly pleasant and patient voice took on a sharp note. 'Most, I fear, are like yourself, my lord – less eager to prove their loyalty to His Grace than are their Highland brothers! A matter I shall not fail to bring to His Grace's notice.'

There was a sudden hush at that. The thing was so unlike James Graham. Even David Carnegie was struck silent at the implied threat.

It was the Countess who set things to rights. 'You are all welcome to Kinnaird, gentlemen, Highland and Lowland alike,' she declared. 'And Irish also,' she added, after just a momentary hesitation. 'But in especial, General Alastair – who is the size of man I find to my taste!'

'Lady, I improve on closer acquaintance, whatever!' Colkitto assured genially.

'As half the women in Ulster and the Highland West will vouch!' Magnus O'Cahan observed conversationally from the background.

There was a great shout of laughter, and the day was saved. In that spirit the reception broke up.

As soon as he might, James Graham went to his little family's own tower across the courtyard, only too concerned with the fact that Magdalen had not come to welcome him – and presumably had kept the children from so doing, for surely it would have been an exciting occasion in their constricted lives. But when he saw his wife, any hurt or resentment was driven from his mind. He was shocked at the sight of her, at the sheer physical deterioration. It was not so very long since since last he had seen her – three months, no more. Then she had been direly mentally depressed and heavy, lethargic in body. Now she seemed to have shrunk, her flesh dwindled on her bones. She had always been a big, well-made woman. For the first time her husband saw her looking gaunt. She gazed at him, her eyes haunted, her mouth drooping, and with no smile of greeting, no word indeed.

'Magdalen, lass – are you ill?' he cried, going to her. 'My sorrow, this is no way to find you.' He took her in his arms.

She was totally inert, passive, in his embrace. Last time she had resisted him. There was nothing of that now. Limp, unresponsive, in his arms, she might have been an inanimate thing.

Cradling her, he groaned.

He looked up, to see Robert and Jean watching them from the open doorway. He raised a hand to them, and they came forward, shyly.

'Did you see them all?' he asked. 'All the King's soldiers?'

'We saw you. And Colkitto. And Cousin Archie Napier,' Robin said. 'Colkitto is very big.'

'I saw the Hielandmen,' Jean told him. 'Why do they wear feathers in their hats?'

'That is to show that they are chiefs. Chiefs of clans. When they have three feathers. Chieftains of septs, branches, only have two. Lairds of name, but one. They are eagles' feathers . . .'

'Could *you* wear them?'

'I suppose that I could. Your grandfather Graham had a feathered bonnet, I mind – though I never saw him wear it. *An Greumach Mor*.'

'How many feathers? Three?'

'Three, yes.'

'My lord is chief of all the Grahams, silly!' her brother told her. 'And he is the King's general, too. Greater than Colkitto. Though . . . though not so big. He is the most important man in all Scotland. Perhaps he could wear *four* feathers?'

'Three would be enough. And I fear that I am not the most important man in Scotland, by any means. But . . . in this room, now!' He looked down at his wife. 'I am the important man, here. Have . . . have you no word for me, my dear?'

With an obvious effort, as though bringing her mind back from afar, she nodded. 'You are well?' she said, each word separately enunciated.

'Well, yes. I have been blessed with great good health. Would God I could say the same for you. Have you been sick, Magdalen, lass?'

'No,' she decided, after a moment or two.

'But you are so thin. And . . . and not yourself.'

'Who would wish that I should be . . . myself?' she asked, bleakly.

'Eh? I, for one, girl. Mercy on us – that's not way to talk! Your children . . .'

She said nothing.

He looked at the children, unhappily. How much of all this affected them?

'The bairns look well,' he said. 'Growing fast. A credit to their mother. They suffered no hurt when the soldiers were here?'

'No.'

'Cousin Archie Napier sent them packing!' Robin declared. 'They ran away. To Dundee. They did not even fight. I like Cousin Archie. Can I go see him, Mamma?'

'I am going to take you down, to meet my officers, my friends,' his father assured. 'Your mother too.'

'No,' she said dully.

'But yes, my heart. You will find them excellent company. You must see them. In your father's house. It will be my pleasure to present them, my good companions, to the Marchioness of Montrose. Some of the most renowned and kenspeckle names in the land.'

She shook her head.

'But, Magdalen – why? It would do you good. Take you out of yourself.'

She looked up at him, pain in those lack-lustre eyes. 'Please – no!' she whispered.

'What's wrong with you, girl? What's wrong?' he exclaimed.

'I do not know,' she answered, slowly, head drooping again, as though this brief display of decision had been too much for her. 'But . . . I must be . . . alone.'

'This is . . . this is . . .' He shook his own head, eyeing the watching, interested children. 'We shall speak of this again, Magdalen. When we are alone.' Sighing, he went and took a child's hand in each of his. 'We shall go down and see them,' he said. 'Meet Colkitto. And Clanranald. And Glengarry. And Duart. And my friend Magnus O'Cahan, the best Irishman that lives. Cousin Archie, too. And all the others. The bravest men in all this land. Shall we? And perhaps Mamma will come later, if she feels better . . .'

*   *   *

That night, quite frankly if shamefully, James Graham put off the moment when he must leave the great and cheerful company gathered round his father-in-law's hall table, and betake himself to his wife's bedchamber. He had his excuse, for his lieutenants were discussing an ambitious scheme of Nathaniel Gordon's to take a flying column to the far north of Scotland. To Strathnaver, on the very Pentland Firth, where his chief, the Marquis of Huntly was hiding himself, and to bring him south, whether he would or no, to Montrose's presence, and ultimately, the King's. Until Huntly could be persuaded to change his petty and offended attitude, the vast potential of the Clan Gordon strength could never be fully harnessed. Once they had Huntly in their hands, they could change his tune, for he was a weak and basically simple man, however proud; and honours, appointments, titles, would be apt to seduce him. Montrose's own reaction to this notion was less than enthusiastic, for severely practical reasons, in that it would demand a quite large detachment of cavalry to achieve, in any reasonable time – the very thing they could not spare. In their cups, his friends were fairly consistently and vociferously in favour, the 200-odd grievous miles conveniently shortened by wine. James Graham, sober, listened patiently. He would prick their alcoholic bubbles on the morrow.

At length, with snores – his father-in-law's the loudest – tending to overbear laughter and argument both, further delay could not be supported. Excusing himself to such of his companions as were still in a state to be concerned, the King's representative went leaden-footed towards his connubial couch.

James Graham was a wholly masculine man, however gentle of manner, and as appreciative of the other sex as any of his lusty company. His need for women was often very strong, and his denial of that need through the long campaigns no light matter. But he was a sensitive man also, and not one to find any satisfaction in forcing himself upon any woman, wife or other.

He found Magdalen's room unlit by lamp, but the northern July night was only a dove-grey. He could see his wife lying in the great four-poster, canopied bed, but whether asleep or no he could not tell. In that moment he hoped that she was.

His voice, therefore, was very low, as he spoke from the doorway. 'Are you waking, Magdalen?' he whispered.

'Yes,' she answered, after a moment.

'It is late. I am sorry. There was much discussion below.'

'Yes.'

'If you are tired, wearied, I will leave you. Sleep in the bairns' room. Tonight.'

She did not answer.

'I would not wish to disturb. When you are less than well . . .'

'No.'

He did not know what that meant. Whether she meant that he would not disturb her; or whether she agreed that she was not well, and wished him gone. 'Shall I go, then, lass?'

'I am your wife,' she said, flatly.

'Yes. But . . .' He paused. The last thing he wanted was to seem to reject her. 'If it does not . . . disturb you? Thus late?'

When she made no reply to that, he came inside and closed the door. As he took off his clothes, she did not speak, although he told her of the good impression that the children had made on his friends and colleagues, and what they had said.

When he climbed in beside her, she did not move, neither welcoming nor repulsing him. The bed was large, and he kept his distance at first, to give her time. But at length he put out an arm, to encircle her. There was no disguising the shrinking from his touch. She was naked, nevertheless. He felt her bones near the surface as never before.

He kept his arm about her, hoping for the tension to relax. But she remained stiff, silent, her breath short, shallow. Her mind apparently accepted that she should do her duty, but her body did not.

He did not press her. Instead he talked to her, gently, soothingly, speaking of many things, of their childhood and youth, when they had been good companions, of their kinsfolk and friends. Did she remember this, recollect that? Sometimes she murmured briefly, sometimes she made some monosyllabic reply; but that was as far as it went.

Slowly, almost imperceptibly, he moved his hand lower down her person. Immediately she stiffened further, drew away slightly.

Sighing, he continued to talk softly, but now with increasing intervals between remarks, for he was tired, whether she was or not. And presently he slept, although he did not intend it, still with his arm around her.

Magdalen Carnegie did not sleep – or not until just before daybreak. She lay staring up at the heraldic plaster ceiling, wide-eyed, and occasionally a great slow tear welled up and rolled unheeded down her cheek. She did not move throughout, lest she disturb the deep-breathing man at her side. She was lost, lost in a grey and endless wilderness, alone. And she would never win out. Until, until – and if – she saw her Johnnie again, beyond the grave. None understood . . .

*   *   *

In the morning Montrose received information that the plague had struck Edinburgh with great severity. And Stirling likewise. And that the Committee of the Estates had transferred itself, and the parliament it had called, for later in the month, to Perth – though it was no true parliament, since it had not the royal authority, but could be only a convention. Orders had gone out for a further 10,000 men to muster in arms, at Perth, and Baillie summoned to take command of them, his renewed resignation not accepted. Argyll was not beaten yet, it seemed.

Montrose recognised that this recrudescence should be stamped upon, if possible, before it grew into a serious threat. He ordered a move right away – to his father-in-law's uncon-cealed satisfaction. James Graham's leave-taking of his wife was harrowing for him. He knew now that she had gone far beyond his grasp, beyond any hope of return, and his heart bled for her. Previous partings had been disappointing, upsetting, resentful – but at least he had been able to ride away hurt, angry, or deter-mined to do better, emotionally roused. Now there was nothing so positive. Only the grim knowledge that she was, in spirit, little better than a corpse. And that, undoubtedly, it was in the main his neglect of her that was responsible, wherever the fault lay. Other contributory factors there were, almost certainly; but that with him lay the principle blame he could not question. It was a sorry thought to ride away with, from Kinnaird.

They made their way by the so well-known route down Strathmore, to cross the Isla near Coupar Angus and on up Tayside to their old base at Dunkeld, in the mouth of Atholl. Here, on the 24th of July, Montrose sent out his spies for detailed information – and learned that Baillie had indeed a new army, not of 10,000 but of over 5,000 foot and about 800 horse, at Perth, guarding the convention of parliament which was to open that very day. More reinforcements were said to be on their way, from Ayrshire, under the Earl of Cassillis, from Clydesdale under Hamilton's ineffable brother the Earl of Lanark, and from Fife where Balcarres was raising more cavalry. Argyll himself was at Perth, with the rest of the Covenant leadership.

When Aboyne arrived at last from Strathbogie with another 300 horse, to add to the 100 already at Dunkeld, there was no more waiting. The royalist force moved southwards, openly, by way of the Almond valley, for the Perth vicinity.

Within sight of the city walls, near their old battlefield of Tippermuir, they halted, challenging Baillie to come out and fight. But he would not.

Montrose tried a few feints and provocative gestures, circling, parading, sending forward bold forays right to the walls. But retaliatory action was not forthcoming. Any other commander but Baillie, Montrose believed he might have coaxed.

At a council of war amongst the Methven woodlands it was Colkitto, not usually a strategist, who propounded the stratagem. 'Be damned to Baillie for a fat slug!' he declared. 'Forget him. Think on his master – Argyll. The Campbell. He is the man to push, whatever.'

'Argyll got a fright at Alford, I swear, Alastair. He was never nearer capture. He will be learning Baillie's caution – or we would have had action before now.'

'Aye – but Argyll is in different case, see you, from Baillie. He has a weakness that Baillie does not have. Property! He is a great man for possessions, is Campbell. So we may move him, I think.'

'How so?'

'Castle Campbell is not far away. His house in the Ochils. Let us go spoil it. As he has spoiled *your* houses of Kincardine and Mugdock. And Keir, your kinsman's house. Burn Castle Campbell, I say. And Argyll will send Baillie out to fight!'

There was a shout of acclaim from the others round the fire. Montrose stroked his little beard thoughtfully.

'Aye – and if we get between Perth and the Forth,' Sir David Ogilvy pointed out, 'they cannot fail to see it as a threat. To cut them off from all the southlands. They must move . . .'

'Yet I would not myself wish to be trapped against the Forth,' Montrose mentioned. 'That could cut two ways, my friend. Nevertheless . . .' He drummed his fingers on his tree-trunk. 'It might serve.'

'Where would we fight, then ?' Colkitto asked.

'That I would have to consider. Not in the Ochils, certainly. We must be able to disperse back into the Highland hills should we be overborne.'

'You have never lost a battle yet, man!'

'But always I have been prepared to lose, Alastair. A way of retiral left open. That one defeat might not mean complete disaster. A general's duty is to survive defeat as well as to gain victory.'

An unexpected addition to their strength, the next morning, was the Earl of Airlie arriving with eighty more mounted Ogilvys, a most welcome accession, the old man claiming that he was now wholly recovered and fit for the wars. When he heard of the proposed descent upon Castle Campbell, he was gleeful indeed, declaring that he claimed first torch to the blaze. He had not forgotten Argyll's savage burning of his own castle of Forter, in Glen Isla, and the turning out of his pregnant countess into the wild hills.

So they marched. This was Montrose's own country, of Kincardine of Strathearn, and he knew every inch of it. They were not followed, their move apparently not perceived. By midforenoon they were at Kinross, on the shores of wide Loch Leven; and by mid-afternoon were climbing above the levels of the Forth plain, at Dollar. Castle Campbell crouched on a terrace, in a cleft of the Ochils, directly above them.

It was a strong place, in site as in building, with high square keep and towering curtain-walls rising from the naked rock of a pointed spine between two deep ravines. It might have held out for some time, for Montrose lacked artillery, as usual. But its keeper yielded at the first summons, and there was no fighting.

The spoiling of the castle went with a will, and Airlie thereafter duly applied the first flame. Great was the conflagration, for the place was most richly stocked. The smoke of its burning rose high above the green Ochil summits, for a sign that could be seen from Forth to Clyde, from the Lammermuirs to the Highland Line; its blaze a beacon which kept burning all night, while men feasted around it and in the little town below. Castle Campbell on its proud terrace blazed its message to all southern Scotland indeed. The King's Captain-General had left the North at last. Here was the token of things to come.

Wearying of the business early in the August evening, Montrose himself left it to others, and rode down to Alloa, on the shore of Forth, where the Earl of Mar, young Archie Napier's new father-in-law, had his great house.

And the following night, at dinner in Alloa Tower, James Graham received the word he awaited. Baillie was on the move. He was marching hurriedly along the north flanks of the Ochils, westwards – undoubtedly to cut off his enemy from his northern and Highland bases. Moreover, Black Pate's scouts, far ahead, reported the Earl of Lanark, with 500 horse and 1,000 foot from the Hamilton lands, had reached Glasgow and was moving up the Lower Kelvin Valley. Only thirty miles separated the two enemy forces.

It was time to be up and doing. Moreover, his Highlanders and Irish were getting out of hand in Alloa town . . .

CHAPTER EIGHT

The Campsie Fells lie south of the upper Forth valley, isolated, and could represent a strategic trap. And the hanging valley of the upper Kelvin a swamp, a waterlogged quagmire, where men must flounder and plouter and horse must sink and sprawl, is immediately to the south of the Campsies. Yet James Graham chose this to be the site of the battle which could decide the fate of Scotland. For a quagmire might be as valuable as squadrons of cavalry to him. And it was the great Flanders Moss which isolated the Campsies from the security of the Highland hill-skirts of Menteith and Strathearn – and Donald MacGregor of Glengyle knew the secret ways through that mighty morass, and could lead them safely if the worst came to the worst. Those hidden causeways, part under a foot of water, some said belonging to Roman times, had been Clan Alpine's bread and butter for generations, the route by which they brought back their stolen Lowland cattle to their Highland fastnesses.

How to bring Baillie to action where he wanted him? The enemy was following on fast enough, with Argyll and the entire Covenant leadership with him – no doubt to his grave embarrassment. Baillie had rounded the Ochils west-about, and come down Allan Water, by Dunblane, to Stirling, avoiding the plague-stricken town itself, as Montrose had done; but had delayed long enough to burn the Alexander castle of Menstrie, and re-burn Airth – no doubt Argyll's fury showing itself. Now, on the evening of the 14th of August, he was only some four or five miles away, at Hollinbush near the head of Kelvin, with 6,000 foot and 800 horse. And no more than ten miles to the west, on the other side, was Lanark and his force. They would join up on the morrow – or else seek to trap the royalists in a joint attack, front and rear. Montrose's army stood in a strong position on the ridge above the little town of Kilsyth, his back to the Campsies. It would be difficult to trap him there.

The situation was not to James Graham's taste and requirements, nevertheless. He was far *too* strongly placed. Baillie would never attack him here. Which meant that the two enemy forces would link up. And that would give Baillie at least 1,200 horse. The 7,000 foot did not worry Montrose unduly; but such number of cavalry was a serious matter.

That warm August evening, then, Montrose rode out unattended, along the Kilsyth ridge. He climbed the Campsie foothills. At last, almost two miles east of their camp he found not exactly what he was looking for, but what he believed might serve, a sizeable depression in the hills, over half a mile long and somewhat aslant as to floor. A burn came in at the head of it in a quite deep ravine, forming almost a waterfall as it came down the sudden drop. At its lower end the depression, or great hollow, opened out to a levelish apron, over which the burn spread itself wetly, before the long and gentle descent to the waterlogged Kelvin valley below, where the road from Stirling rimmed the Dullator Bog. But the central part of the hollow, because of its slight slant, was relatively dry, well-drained, the burn disciplined by gravity. The floor of it was perhaps 400 yards wide, and the slope down into it from the west, as Montrose had ridden, comparatively easy, smoothish grassland dotted with whins. The other, east, flank however, was steep and rocky, especially towards the foot, no cliff or scarp, but a difficult braeside.

For long, as the light and colour faded from the hills, the man stared, his mind busy. Then abruptly he wheeled his sure-footed Highland garron around, and trotted back to the camp.

'Sound the Rally,' he cried, to his trumpeter. 'Fires out. Assemble in companies and squadrons. We move.'

'Move?' Colkitto exclaimed, flagon in hand. 'March – now? To attack? A night attack? You will never take the cautious Baillie by surprise, man. In all those Kelvin bogs. His camp will be like a moated fortress, my God!'

'Not to attack, Alastair. To *be* attacked. If God so wills. And before Lanark and his cavalry join up.'

'You'll not force that one's hand, whatever.'

'He has the misfortune to have advisers with him! The entire Covenant leadership. They will not fail to advise him as to his duty, never fear. *I* know. I have suffered under their militant guidance. They will not let Baillie resign his command. But they will not let him command it in his own way, I swear. So – we move.'

In two hours, little more, the entire royalist army had exchanged a fine strong position for a wretched one, security for obvious hazard. Baiting traps was all very well – but the trap had to have jaws. This place was a death-trap.

James Graham smiled. '*There* are my jaws,' he said, and gestured to all the ranks of Irish and Highland infantry, settling down in their plaids for the night.

Aboyne, very much casualty-conscious since his brother's death, looked around him uneasily. 'This is no place for horse,' he said.

'Precisely, James. It is their horse that I fear. Suppose – suppose, I say, that Baillie has sent an order to my lord of Lanark that *his* horse should hasten forward, leaving the slow foot? That would give Baillie 1,200 or 1,300 cavalry. Three times our numbers. Would you accept those odds? In cavalry?'

'Holy Mother! Twelve hundred . . .! You think it possible?'

'It is what *I* would do, in his place.'

While men slept around him, James Graham settled down by a single tiny and aromatic fire of bog-pine, to read, peering, the little pocket-Bible which was his constant companion and mentor. Scouts came and went throughout the night – and none found their general asleep.

By dawn the entire camp was roused and standing to arms, eating the handfuls of raw oatmeal as they stood, washed down with burn water. If God willed, they might do better hereafter. Pate Graham informed that the enemy scouts knew where they were. Baillie, only two and a half miles east of this position, was preparing to move. As yet there was no sign of Lanark's horse, from the west.

Montrose disposed of his forces with simplicity but particular care. The Gordon cavalry he set on the right, under Nat Gordon, near the slow drop to the Kelvin valley, with the spreading water-apron and emerald-green mosses of the burn before them, and the comparatively easy western hillside behind. It was going to be a frustrating day for the Gordons, whatever happened. On the left he placed Colkitto and his veterans, 2,000 of them, crowded below the very throat of the ravine with its waterfall, allotting him Ogilvy's eighty horse as a sort of reserve. In the centre he placed the main body of the Highland infantry, 3,000 strong, under that puissant triumvirate of chiefs, Clanranald, Glengarry and Duart. All were inevitably close-packed, with little or no room to manoeuvre. Even Black Pate looked doubtful when he came hurrying in, from the eastern slopes, to announce that the enemy were on their way. It would not be long now.

Young Alexander, his lieutenant, who had shown an aptitude for scouting, still reported no hastening Clydesdale cavalry, from the west. In reserve, beside himself, Montrose kept Aboyne and a small squadron of horse, for eventualities; also a company of Gordon foot.

There was one final disposition to make, small but important. On the higher ground, up on the lip of the ravine, above the cataract, was a group of roofless, deserted cottages, the huts of a cattle-herder's shieling. Young Ewan Maclean of Treshnish was sent up there, with a token company, to hold it – and to be seen to be holding it. That done, there was nothing for it but to wait.

From his point of vantage, Maclean of Treshnish presently signalled. The enemy, in force, was in sight.

Aboyne was still unhappy, impatient. 'Suppose your stratagem does not serve?' he objected. 'Baillie is no fool. He may not fight as you would wish. What then?'

'Then there is no harm done. If we look as though we might be trapped down here, we can retire up this easy brae behind. So long as Lanark's horse does not arrive. Alexander will give us warning of that.'

'But will not Baillie seek to outflank us? Round, on this high ground to the north. Keeping high?'

'Pray you that he does, James!'

It was not long before the first ranks of the enemy began to appear over the high skyline to the east, the morning sun behind them. It was going to be another hot day, sultry, windless. Mounted outriders came first, then whole squadrons of cavalry, seemingly endless; and finally the vast cohorts of the foot, steel glinting, banners flying, regiment upon regiment.

The front ranks halted, in full view of the royalist army in the hollow, the rest pressing on. And still they came, over the swelling hill-ridge, their numbers greater than those of any previous Covenant host.

'Now we shall see!' Archie Napier said. That was almost a whisper.

Less than half a mile apart, but with 250 feet of difference in their altitudes, the two forces eyed each other.

'If he has cannon, he could smash us into bloody ruin, here,' the Master of Madderty declared.

'He cannot bring his cannon up over these rough hills. One of the reasons for my choice of battle-ground.'

A group of mounted men moved forward from the enemy front, to the very edge of the sharp drop. There they halted, peering down.

'Baillie. Argyll. Hurry. Lindsay. Balcarres. Elcho. Burleigh.' Montrose enunciated the names clearly, his fine eyes narrowed into the sun's slanting glare. 'I cannot see them, distinguish them – but they will all be there. The ministers, too. Dickson. Law. Guthrie. Traill. The men who have torn a nation apart, in the name of religion. Who have caused the deaths of thousands, in their damnable pride. So near . . .!'

The party up there reined their horses this way and that along the lip of the drop, and then gathered again in a knot. Voices, of course, could not be heard; but there could be little doubt as to what they were saying. There was no way down for cavalry, here. The brae was steep and grassy for two-thirds of the distance, then steeper and stony, at a long out-cropping escarpment. No horsed force could negotiate that descent without grievous casualties.

'What would you do if you were William Baillie, Archie?' Montrose asked his nephew.

Young Napier looked around him, nibbling his lip. 'If he sends his horse left, to the south, they must drop down into the wet ground at the tail of this valley. Or into the Kelvin bogs. He will not do that. If he sends them round to the right, they have to cross that ravine. That done, they could win on to this smooth slope behind us, and charge us down.'

'They will see young Treshnish and his lads at the cottages, on the edge of the ravine. They must assume the ravine held.'

'*I* would leave my horse out of it,' Madderty put in. 'Divide my infantry. Send the main body down this steep hill-side, straight at us. Foot could negotiate it, though horse could not. Send the rest right-about, to clear that ravine. Make a way for the cavalry to cross it. Then we are at their mercy.'

'No doubt. But Baillie well knows that we are strongest in our Highland and Irish foot, weakest in our cavalry. *He* is strong in cavalry. He will wish to use it, not merely keep it in reserve. And his foot would suffer terribly from our musketeers and bowmen as they descended. Heavy-armed infantry could not run down that hill. They would lose their footing.'

'He will do nothing, then. He is a cautious man,' Napier said. 'He will wait for *your* move.'

'He has half of the Estates advising him, up there. And the

fire-eaters of the Kirk, wanting blood! I do not see them allowing him to sit and wait.'

'What, then?'

'This smooth slope behind us must surely tempt them all. If they could but gain it, they have us. Pate – you say that they have four regiments of regular foot again? As at Auldearn. More of Leslie's army which Argyll has demanded.'

'Aye – Home's, Cassillis's, Glencairn's and Argyll's own. You can see them – their breastplates shining.'

'They will never send *them* down this brae, I swear! And Baillie knows passing well that my Highlanders and Irish like the bogs! Bogtrotters, do they not call them? He will not risk a major assault on his left, then. He will send a probe right. That is why I have put Colkitto at the foot of the ravine. If the probe is held, and cut up, he may send in more, to their aid. We may force him to fight there, around the ravine, where his horse is useless to him, where we have every advantage . . .'

It took a long time for Baillie to make up his mind. Perhaps he was arguing with his masters. The sun rose steadily in a pale sky. It was going to be unbearably hot, limp-making. Sweating already, himself, James Graham removed his shoulder-slung sword-belt, threw off his doublet and unbuttoned his shirt.

'Off with these cloying clothes!' he cried. 'Up there they roast in their iron pots! Let the sun fight for us! As well as the hills. *We* shall at least fight in comfort – if they intend to give us battle, at all! Pass the word down . . .'

Nothing could have pleased his men more, the Highlanders in especial. It was their custom, anyway, to cast aside their clothing in the heat of battle – and, oddly enough, a naked man, with naked steel, hurling himself upon one, is a deal more alarming than a man fully clad, or even armoured. So now they gladly threw aside kilts and plaids, and either tied the tails of their saffron shirts between their legs, or discarded shirts altogether. Laughter, hooting, challenge rang out, coarse jesting. Better for morale, this, than just idle, silent waiting.

As though it had been a signal, the enemy suddenly were spurred into activity. Bugle-calls resounded up there on the hill, shouts, commands. The Covenant cavalry reined round, and began to trot off, right-handed, squadron after squadron. Then the foot turned, likewise, and led by the extreme right, commenced to march in the same direction. The entire enemy army was gradually setting itself in motion.

Montrose stared, scarcely crediting what he saw. This was no probe. This was Baillie turning his entire line of battle at right angles and marching across his enemy's front. He could only be making for the ravine, or to go above it, higher still, intending to turn the royalist flank in the biggest way.

Furiously James Graham had to consider anew, scrap all his tentative plans. Never had he anticipated this, that the enemy should take so enormous a risk, so utterly unlike Baillie. However secure he believed himself to be up there, by turning into column thus, he put his army out of effective concerted action for some considerable time.

Suddenly Montrose was presented with an astonishing opportunity – if he could take it in time. He had the men to do it. But could he get his orders to them in time . . . ?

That problem solved itself. For Colkitto and Clanranald, veteran commanders and used to operating on their own, perceived the situation as swiftly as did their general. Nor were they of the sort who considered orders sacrosanct. Leaving perhaps one-third of his men, under Magnus O'Cahan, to cope with that ravine itself, Colkitto pointed his sword straight up the eastern hill-side and waved his men on, leaping forward himself, longer-strided than any. Clanranald, in the centre, was beginning to do the same even before Montrose's shouted commands were relayed to him.

And so thousands of Highland and Irish warriors launched themselves, racing and bounding, half-naked, up the steep brae-side, swords and dirks in hand, jumping, scrambling over the stones at the bottom and flinging on up the grass slope above. Only such hillmen, toughened in gruelling campaigns, could have done it, without bursting hearts and lungs.

The elongated enemy column did not at first perceive and realise its danger, for owing to the steepness of the slope and the curvature of the hill they could not see what was happening immediately below. No doubt, however, like their betters, they assumed that the ascent was unclimbable, at least for an armed force. By the time that they became aware of the true situation, it was too late to engage in any major reforming movement. They could only turn and meet the eventual charge in column, a thin end slender line indeed.

That Colkitto's and Clanranald's men had any energy and breath left to charge, after surmounting the brae, was a wonder, and a tribute to their fitness as well as enthusiasm. But charge they did, furiously if raggedly, and along a wide front, hurling themselves upon the long, extended column in waves. The first wave suffered fairly heavily from musket-fire, but thereafter it was all steel and muscle. Minutes after Baillie's trumpets had sounded the march, his army was cut, not into two but into many parts.

It was not defeat, of course, merely disruption. But since it did away, for the time being at least, of the possibility of unified command, it laid the foundations of defeat, thus early.

Perceiving that a diversion at this stage would be valuable, Treshnish opened up with musket-fire, at extreme range, from the cottages, upon the Covenant cavalry at the head of the column, thus preoccupying Balcarres. A detachment was sent to deal with him. He had only 100 men there – but the enemy could not know that. To help in this issue, Montrose sent orders to Magnus O'Cahan to advance with all speed up the eastern side of the waterfall, in the ravine itself – and to make as much noise about the business as he could. And, recognising that here was a quite extraordinary chance to strike a crippling blow, he despatched Maclean of Duart with the entire infantry reserve, up the main steep eastern slope, to join Colkitto and Clanranald on the high ground.

Aboyne, with the small cavalry reserve, was agitatedly pleading for work to do; and no doubt, on the far right, Nat Gordon and the main horsed force were equally upset. But there was no role that they could usefully fill at this stage. The same applied to Airlie's eighty Ogilvys. From the first it had been Montrose's determination that this should be no cavalry battle. He sent Aboyne up the smooth hill-side at the back, to work along to the north, towards the western lip of the ravine, as possible counter-cavalry threat – although this was really only a gesture, for the deep wooded ravine would be fatal for horse, on either side.

Baillie was not inactive in all this, of course. Cut off from most of his own foot, he still could cóntrol his cavalry. It did not take him long to perceive that much might yet be saved, and the royalist command and cavalry, at least, be defeated. He sent word to Balcarres to leave the wretched ravine area and spur on due northwards at maximum speed, up and up the long hill-side, to where the burn's channel shallowed amongst the heather and it could be crossed with ease – the best part of a mile, by the look of it. Then back down the west side and on to the smooth slope behind Montrose. A charge, in overwhelming strength, down there, and it would be the end of James Graham and the Gordon horse both.

When Montrose saw the enemy cavalry swinging away and uphill again, he swung on young Napier.

'Archie – up the ravine, after O'Cahan! Tell him to get most of his force back across the ravine. Somehow. Have them spread out as a line across the hillside. Using all the cover they can – peat-hags, burns, anything. He will know. To try to hold Balcarres's horse, when they cross higher and come down. I will get horse up to support him. Quickly, now! You understand?' He turned to Madderty. 'You, John – to my lord of Airlie, with his Ogilvys. Up this hill behind to, Aboyne. Then on up the main hillside to the north, to support O'Cahan's foot. Nat Gordon not to move meantime. You have it?'

He gazed backwards and up. Young Alexander still waited, high on a ridge to the west, giving no signal of Lanark's army. He must stay there.

Tempted as he was to leave his central stance and hurry up the steep brae in front, to see how the infantry were faring up there beyond the curve of the hill-side, James Graham sternly controlled himself. His place must remain here, where he could be seen by all, calm, assured, under the Royal Standard of Scotland, the King's Captain-General in total command of the situation. He sent one of the few aides he had left, young Alexander Ogilvy of Inverquarity, with his compliments, to Major-General Alastair, to enquire how he did? He and Black Pate were left almost alone.

'This is damnable!' that stalwart muttered. 'Standing here idle. *Watching!* Like . . . like auld wives at a marriage! Is this a battle, God's mercy?'

'If God's mercy does not forsake us, you are watching the end of the Covenant, Pate! It is a strange battle, yes. We can see little or no fighting, from here – but we see that our ally is strong! The hills – it is the hills, Pate. The hills of Scotland are fighting for us.'

'And these?' The other pointed upwards to where they could see the great mass of the Covenant cavalry streaming uphill, in no sort of order and scattered over a wide area.

'Those are Fife and Ayrshire and Lothian farm-folk, in the main. Riding low-country horses over steep heather and peat and scree. See how they flag and scatter. What state will they be in, or their beasts, when they can get across that burn-channel and come down upon our flank? The hills, I say, fight this battle for us.'

Nevertheless, the two Grahams put in a grim and trying half-hour there, in the lap of the hills, watching, waiting and unable to affect the issue for the time being. They saw the leaders of the enemy cavalry reach sufficiently high on the main spinal ridge for the burn-channel to offer little obstacle – but, even so, the emerald-green ground there was obviously very wet and progress was slow. They saw O'Cahan's line of Highlanders and Irish pouring out of the ravine, much lower, and spreading across the hill-face to form some sort of line, uneven, patchy, broken, as they utilised the natural barriers that the ground had to offer – peat-hags, hollows in the knee-high heather, outcropping rocks, burns, aprons of surface water. They saw Aboyne and Airlie spurring up to reinforce O'Cahan – but not making good time of it in the atrocious going up there. They saw Balcarres's men marshalling themselves, and then their descent upon the royalist front, a move that was so far from a charge as to be almost laughable, horsemen having to pick their way with heedful care. Soon muskets were taking their heavy toll of easy targets, men and horses both. In high old heather, which O'Cahan had deliberately chosen, horses were at a major disadvantage, as against bare-shanked Highlanders, unable to see where they were placing their hooves, turning hocks on loose stones, sinking into peat-broth, slipping on outcropping rock. Clearly it was a bloody business, up on the high hill, for both sides; but the enemy did not appear to be gaining any appreciable headway on that wicked ground.

Then young Inverquharity came leaping and slithering down the western steep to them again, scarlet faced, panting.

'Colkitto has . . . them beat!' he gasped. 'The foot. On the run. Everywhere. Dead men, dying men . . . all over the hill. Clanranald killing, killing . . .'

'Gently, lad – gently,' Montrose said. 'Take your time.'

'Yes. Yes, my lord. But . . . but, the blood! I saw a headless man . . . running . . .!'

'Aye. Your first battlefield is no bonny sight. But – your message, man. What says my Major-General?'

'To tell you, my lord, that all is near over. With the enemy. The foot. He broke them up. It was easy, he said. He was singing! Colkitto singing. He is . . . terrible! Blood all over his body. Not his own, I swear! Shouting. Laughing . . .'

'Yes, yes – I know him. But what of the four regular regiments? These I must know of. Are they still fighting?'

'They retreated. Lochbuie told me. To a line of dykes. Drystane dykes. Up the hill. As redoubt. But the Macleans leapt the dykes, Lochbuie said. And the MacDonalds. Pushed the dykes over on the enemy. Cared naught for the musket-fire. Crawled on their bellies up to the dykes, where muskets could not fire over at them. Then leapt over. They are gone, too. Home's, Cassillis's and the other regiments. Broken, fleeing, being cut down . . .'

'Glory be!' Black Pate cried. 'Then the day is ours?'

'Not quite,' his chief said. 'I thank you, Inverquharity. Now – get you back up there to the Major-General. As quickly as you came down! My congratulations to him. And request that, leaving half his men to finish off the enemy foot and make sure they do not rally, he takes the rest and gets him as quickly as he may across that ravine. To yonder battle on the great hill. You have that? Off with you, then. And you, Pate. My compliments to Nat Gordon. He has been very patient. Have them up there now, also. To Aboyne's aid, and Airlie's. The whole cavalry force. To fight it out, at last.'

But it was not to be. When Balcarres and his horsemen saw Colkitto's legions coming streaming towards them, and fresh squadrons of the Gordon horse spurring eagerly upwards, they could discern no advantage, or future, in their situation. Without any direct orders to break off battle, in fact a general disengagement began. And, in the circumstances, that soon developed into every man for himself. Uphill, downhill, over towards the ravine, northwards and westwards for the empty hills, riders broke away and fled, singly, in pairs and groups. And were pursued by bounding, hallooing Irish and Highlanders, more like wolves than men.

The Covenant leadership had not waited thus long. From an eminence well back on the eastern slopes, they had watched their hopes collapse. And well before Balcarres's horse broke, with two companies of Clanranald's half-naked MacDonalds heading purposefully in their direction, they were off, hurrying back towards Stirling, whence they had come, Argyll to the fore, Baillie amongst the last. A reinforcing body of Fife horse, come late to the battle, turned and fled with them.

The Battle of Kilsyth was over. Only the killing remained.

That killing was perhaps the most wholesale yet. Because of

the wide-scattered nature of the battle, and the subsequent flight in so many directions at once, it took longer than usual for Montrose to establish any measure of overall control. Moreover there had been a heartless and gratuitous slaughter of royalist camp-followers at Methven Wood, after the move to Castle Campbell, and revenge was much in men's minds. Much of the cavalry undoubtedly made good their escape; but the infantry in the main ran downhill, into the Dullator Bog of the Kelvin valley – overlooking the fact that their bare-shanked and lightly armed enemies were considerably more at home in bogs than were they. They died there in their hundreds, before James Graham might stop it. But not the men who gave the orders, of course; only those who obeyed them, the others being safely away in good time. That was the prime sorrow of it.

For a commander, Montrose disliked the aftermath of victory almost as much as of defeat. He felt less at one with his colleagues and subordinates then than at any other time. Disillusionment, reaction, disgust, even remorse, surged over him, instead of any sort of triumph. His lieutenants, in consequence, tended to win scant acclaim, at this stage.

When old Airlie, who had led his Ogilvy horse up that hillside like any youngling, came to him down at the Kelvin road, the congratulations tended to be one-sided.

'Magnificent, James!' he cried. 'Total victory. As great as Inverlochy.'

'Great is not the word *I* would use, I think.'

'Eh ? Och, man – great is Argyll's defeat, you'll no' deny ?'

'Perhaps. But that does not make it a great victory. Only a great slaughter. God forgive us!'

'You do not win battles without bloodshed, lad. War is not just a game of chance, of skills, with no real cost. You play it passing well, to be sure. But the reckoning is aye in men's lives.'

'I know it. But unnecessary slaughter is vile. Unworthy of our cause.'

'But not our enemies' cause, it seems! You must fight as you are fought.'

'That I cannot accept. Or we are worse than the brute creation. Besides, that way breeds hatred, continuing strife. I have a kingdom to save for His Grace. Not a desert of hatred and death. These were the King's subjects, equally with ourselves.'

'The King's rebels, in treasonable uprising, man. A difference there is. Remember our two sons in Edinburgh's Tolbooth!'

'Think you I ever forget it ? Nor the other two who lie in their graves, mine and yours both.'

'Aye. I am sorry. Forgive me, James. You have paid your price for the victory of Charles Stewart. I think that you have Scotland, now, to present to him. I hope that he is sufficient grateful.'

'You go too fast, my friend. Scotland is not ours yet, to give to the King – grateful or no.'

'I believe it may be, James. At last.'

'Wait, you,' James Graham said.

CHAPTER NINE

As the sweltering August days passed, and the reports came in, it grew to seem almost as though the Earl of Airlie had been right. Although his triumphant legions pursued the fleeing Covenant forces far past Stirling, to Fife and Lothian, and southwards and westwards towards Clydesdale and Carrick, Montrose remained at Kilsyth for a couple of days, gathering intelligence as to the national picture, to decide on his next move. He had sent a flying column, under Aboyne, to deal with Lanark and his army, to the west – only to find that hero had already fled and his people evaporated. And, that Lanark was not alone in his readings of the situation, quickly grew more apparent as the messages came in.

Baillie, it seemed, had made for Stirling town, despite the plague, and had gone to ground in the impregnable fortress-castle on its rock, along with Balcarres, Burleigh and others of the military leaders. Argyll had been much more prudent, not drawing rein until he reached South Queensferry, on the Forth, where he had actually taken ship for England no less, via Berwick-on-Tweed. The Campbell had a preference for escaping by boat. The Earls of Loudoun and Lothian were also on their way to England, on horseback – no doubt to join one or other of the Leslies, Sandy at Newcastle, David at Carlisle. The West Country earls, such as Glencairn and Cassillis, were reputed to be on their way to Ireland. The ministers, without the resources of the nobility, were dispersing to their parishes over the length and breadth of the land – possibly to their parishioners' benefit.

It seemed that no major figure remained, of the Committee of the Estates, to lead the fight against Montrose.

James Graham himself was scarcely able to credit it, however confidently jubilant were his friends. He kept enquiring of this lord or that. What of the Earl Marischal ? What of Seaforth ? What of Lindsay ? What of Balmerino ? What of the Duke, Hamilton himself ? And that fanatic Johnston of Warriston, now a Lord of Session no less ? Above all, what of James Livingstone, Earl of Callander, and his Border army ? All these could not have dissolved into the mists . . .

'Callander would not be such a fool as to assail you now,' Pate Graham of Inchbraikie averred. 'Having avoided any encounter all this while, will he hazard all now that you are master of the land?'

'It is his duty, no less. With an army in the field, unblooded. And it is folly to call me master of the land, Pate, because for the moment no host harries us.'

They were sitting alone on the hillside above Kilsyth, with the great camp outspread below them and the afternoon turning towards evening, though heat still shimmered on all the landscape and drained it of colour.

Pate eyed his friend and chief keenly. 'What has come over you, Jamie? These last days, weeks almost, you have not been yourself. Moody. You are not sick? As you were at Rothiemurchus, that time? Or is it . . . is it Magdalen? Or young James, in Edinburgh Tolbooth? That will soon be over, at least.' Almost the first thing that Montrose had done, once he heard that the Covenant forces were not reassembling against him, had been to send Archie Napier and a hard-riding squadron under Nat Gordon, to Edinburgh, to open that Tolbooth, praying the while that neither the plague nor any dread emissary from Argyll got there beforehand.

'I am well enough, Pate. Would God I could say the same for Magdalen. She is sore afflicted. I do not know what to make of her, where to turn. I have failed her grievously. But . . . I cannot blame myself for all her ill. God has laid His hand heavily on us, in this. As for Jamie, again I do blame myself. I should not have left him there, at Kinnaird, to be made hostage. Knowing the Campbell! Magdalen blames me for this, too, I know. Yet I could not take him with me on campaign. After Johnnie . . .' He shook his handsome head. 'Is there a curse on me, Pate? To bring hurt on those I love? Is it my fate to beat the air, to make great swelling gestures – and to achieve nothing save the sorrow of those close to me?'

'Achieve nothing, Man! You are losing your wits indeed, if you say that! What have you *not* achieved? One man! I mind you saying, that day at Tulliebelton, when you came to my house in guise of a groom, with William Rollo – you said, God give you one year, but one year, with the King's authority, and you would hand Charles Stewart back his Scots kingdom. That was August last. I mind not the day of it, but it was late in the month. So you have scarce had your twelve months, This is August likewise, but only the 17th. In those months you have raised armies out of nothing. Out-fought every host sent against you. Made every other general look a fool. Made the King's cause to mean something, and given Scotland hope again. And you say that you have achieved nothing, but to beat the air!'

'You are kind, Pate – but biased not a little. Winning battles without holding territory is of doubtful value – even though a necessary step. I have yet to be convinced that even this last one will solve that problem for us.'

'I say that you are too gloomy, James, by far. Their leaders are fled. What more do you ask for?'

As though in answer to that question, they perceived a small mounted party riding uphill from the camp towards them, led, they recognised, by young Alexander. There were two splendidly dressed individuals and two grooms, all in marked contrast to the campaigners' stained and tattered clothing. One of the new-comers was elderly and distinctly stout, the other of early middle years, sallow, sober.

'Visitors, my lord Marquis,' Alexander called. 'From the city of Glasgow, no less. Have I your lordship's permission to present them?'

'Glasgow, you say?' Montrose got to his feet. 'This interests me.'

'Sir Robert Douglas of Blackerston, Lord of the Manor of Gorbals and Bridgend, my lord. And Master Archibald Fleming, Commissary. Representing the Corporation of the city of Glasgow. Humbly crave audience of Your Excellency.' Gleefully, young Alexander was piling it on, rather, as they dismounted.

'I am happy to receive representatives of Glasgow,' Montrose said, 'I have happy memories of the city. I had some of my schooling there. My house of Mugdock is – or was – nearby. And my grandfather was your Provost for a while I think.'

Sir Robert Douglas, the younger of the two representatives, coughed. 'Mugdock,' he said. 'I . . . we . . . regret it. Most unhappy. That we could by no means save it.'

'Unhappy, yes.'

'Did you try?' That was a bark, from Inchbrakie.

Douglas looked uncomfortable. 'My lord Marquis of Argyll gave strictest orders . . .'

'To be sure,' Montrose nodded. 'I understand very well. Now – how can I serve you, gentlemen?'

'It is our wish to serve *you*, my lord Marquis,' the Commissary declared. 'We have the honour to seek your protection, and to offer you the hospitality of our town. In the name of the Provost, magistrates, the Dean of Guild and the Deacon-Convener of Trades.'

'Ha-a-a!' The two Grahams' glances met.

'We offer our complete support, my lord,' Douglas added.

'That I shall require, yes. In the name of the King's Grace. As I do of every other city and town. But . . . I could have done with Glasgow's sooner, see you! Before Kilsyth, rather than after! When, for instance, the Earl of Lanark marched his rebel army through your streets.'

'We are not postured for war, my lord. We are a peaceable city. Traders, merchants, craftsmen, scholars, not fighting-men . . .'

'You have city walls, strong gates, a Town Guard, train-bands, have you not ?'

The emissaries were silent.

James Graham relaxed the stern expression which he had assumed – and which indeed did not come easily to him. He was in fact greatly encouraged by this development. Perhaps it was an augury, proof that Pate and the others were right, that Scotland was at last prepared to throw over the zealots and fanatics and bigots, to acclaim the defeat of Argyll and the Covenant leaders, and to rally to the King's cause. Glasgow was a smaller city than Edinburgh or Dundee, but it was important too, the key to the South-West, its university a source of great influence, its churchmen powerful. Moreover it was very wealthy, its merchant and craft guilds the most prosperous and organised in the land.

'Belated support is better than none,' he said. 'I accept it. But for King Charles, not myself. I will inform His Grace.'

That produced no outburst of loyal enthusiasm. 'Yes, my lord,' the Commissary acceded.

'You will come to Glasgow ? Enter the city ?' Douglas asked.

'Mm. Probably. But first I shall require a token of your support. My army, after long months of campaigning, is in need of much. I shall require from your city guilds clothing, shoes, bonnets and the like. Also money.'

There was a heavy silence.

'You do not sound eager, gentlemen.'

'We must speak with our colleagues on this . . .'

'A whole army, my lord! It . . . it would be costly. Very costly.'

'Not so costly as the blood which that army has shed, sirs. Remember it, if you please. Cost is a relative matter. Moreover, I have the fullest authority – and ability – to take what I require.'

Hastily the emissaries changed their tune. The stores and supplies would be forthcoming, they were sure.

'Very well. Inform your Provost and colleagues to that effect.'

'When will you come, my lord? To Glasgow?'

'In a day or so. When you confirm this matter of supplies. That is, if you have not the plague, there? I will not put my army at risk by the pest.'

'No plague, no. It has not come to Glasgow, God be praised. The city will rejoice to honour you.'

'Will it, sir? I wonder! And why?'

'Because your lordship won a victory almost on its doorstep!' Alexander declared. 'And for no other reason. Another twenty miles, and they would have looked the other way!'

'Not so, sir. Not so. I say!' Douglas protested. 'That is not true, I swear it ...'

'You will have opportunity to prove your loyalty, never fear, gentlemen. Tell your Provost so,' Montrose said, smiling pleasantly again. 'I shall inform him of the time of my arrival. A very good day to you, friends ...'

*   *   *

So, on the 19th of August, the Captain-General and his victorious host approached the city, crossing the Molendinar Burn to the Drygait Port. Ahead, beyond the gates and walls, the Townhead area rose in a huddle of roofs and spires and towers to the vast mass of the Cathedral dominating all, with the parapets and battlements of the Archbishop's Palace and Castle near by. There was more green to be seen than in most cities, for Glasgow was a place of trees and gardens at this north-eastern end, with the cathedral-manses' orchards, and the College Garden bowered in foliage. The army metaphorically licked hungry lips at the sight – or part of the army, at any rate. For the inevitable process had already begun. The clansmen were going home, large numbers already gone. Battle won, the defeated spoiled – and there were major spoils after Kilsyth, with the entire Covenant leadership's baggage captured, to say nothing of Baillie's commissariat. Even Aboyne was anxious to be away, back to his Gordon lands, with the responsibility for the clan now his, no one knowing what Lord Lewis might be up to. Airlie himself was talking about returning to his Angus glens, where the harvest was over-ready. When the economy depended almost entirely upon cattle, as it did practically everywhere north of the Highland Line, the getting in of the oats for winter feed was a vital matter. And the hot weather had brought on the grain early.

What was left of the royalist army, then, marched to the strains of such pipers as remained to them, until the bells of Glasgow's cathedral and churches rang out a jangled welcome to compete, a new experience for them.

'It almost sounds as though they were glad to see us!' the Master of Madderty declared.

Colkitto hooted. 'They will be as glad to see us as they would the Devil!' he said. 'They'd ring the bells for *him*, whatever – if no saints were in sight to come to their aid!'

An official party was waiting to greet them just outside the Drygait Port, on the beaten dusty fairground. Here, under a silken canopy upheld on poles by halberdiers, stood Provost James Bell and his magistrates and bailies, with the Dean of Guild, the Deacon-Convener of Trades, the university dignitaries and one or two ministers, all colourful and prosperous-seeming in their robes and chains-of-office. By comparison, Montrose's army looked a shabby, ragged horde, lean, unkempt, unwashed. James Graham himself, although always he kept his person neat and as clean as might be, his bearing assured, easily commanding, was still in the stained and patched tartan doublet and trews, scuffed and battered riding-boots and shoulder-slung sword-belt he had worn while campaigning. Until his men were reclothed, he would remain thus.

The Provost was a small, ferret-like man, red-haired, with no presence but keen-eyed, shrewd, a wealthy bonnet-maker.

'My name is Bell, Lord o' Montrose – Jamie Bell. I'm the Provost,' he announced, in a sing-song West Country voice. 'And these here are the bailies.' He pronounced it bylies. 'And the Dean o' Guild. I was Dean mysel' three years back.' He sounded prouder of having been Dean than Provost. 'And this is Deacon-Convener Ninian Gilhazie – och, the trades just, ye ken. And . . . and others. You're welcome to Glasgow, you and yours.'

'I thank you, Mr. Provost, Gentlemen. I rejoice at the goodwill of this great city. I accept your submission in the King's name – whose humble servant I am.'

'Eh . . .? Submission . . .?' the Provost said. 'Whae said

anything about submission?' He glanced quickly at his companions. 'It's no' a submission lord – it's a welcome.'

'You did not offer us a welcome *before* we won Kilsyth battle, Mr. Provost. Though we were but a dozen miles off, and could have done with Glasgow's kindly aid. And you permitted my lord of Lanark and his rebel force to pass through your streets. Before that battle. Therefore I do assume that it was that battle which constrained you. To change your attitude. Correct me, pray, if I am wrong? And when battle, armed force, constrains men to change their policy, I deem it submission, sir.'

'But . . . but we never fought against you, lord . . .'

'You are a man of God. I am sure, Provost? To represent this city whose motto I well know is that it flourishes by the preaching of the Word. Then I answer you from the Word. Thus. "When saw we thee an hungered, or athirst, or a strange, or naked, or sick, or in prison, and did not minister unto thee? Then shall he answer them, saying, Verily I say unto you, inasmuch as ye did it not to one of the least of these, ye did it not to me." How say you, then? I have been fighting for King Charles's cause in Scotland for a whole year – and I have not received a man, a groat, or even a word of support, from the great and wealthy city of Glasgow. How say you, sirs, to Holy Writ?'

Provost Bell did not say anything. Nor did his companions, even the ministers. Undoubtedly they were unused to having Scripture quoted at them save from the pulpit.

'Is it submission, then? Or no?' Montrose glanced behind him, at his serried thousands. 'I would prefer not to have to *make* it so, gentlemen.'

'No! No, lord – no' that! Och, use what word you will. Submission, aye. So long . . . so long as you dinna let *them* loose in the toon! The Irishry and the Hielantmen. Anything, lord – anything but that.' The little red-lashed eyes kept looking in the direction of the gigantic Colkitto.

'Very well, Mr. Provost. Glasgow submits to the King's Captain-General, and kindly welcomes him and the King's army. Is that correct?'

'If you'll no' let them loose . . .'

'Sir – I command an army, not a rabble. If I accept your submission, then your town comes under my protection. All shall be done lawfully and in order.'

'Aye, well . . .'

'Good. Then there is the matter of the supplies, sir. Which I

123

stipulated. Shoes, clothing, bonnets and the like. And money. This is part of your welcome? A practical part – and very necessary.'

'My lord Marquis,' Commissary Fleming spoke up, from the rear. 'It is not possible to gather large quantities of these goods at short notice. You will understand, at this time of year . . . With the best will in the world, my lord. We, ah, we suggest an alternative.'

'Indeed, sir? I am not used to be offered alternatives to my legitimate requirements.'

'No, my lord. But . . . but it is difficult, see you. We suggest that you, your soldiers should be given £500 – sterling, not Scots – £500 distributed amongst them. To *buy* such things as are necessary.'

'You'll agree that's generous, lord?' the Provost added.

'Should I, sir? I shall require much more of this city than that, I assure you! But – this is for my men? In their hands? In lieu of shoes, gear and the like? Is that it?'

'Well . . . aye.' The Provost sounded doubtful, glancing around.

Hastily Sir Robert Douglas put in, from a flanking position. 'My lord Marquis – it shall all be as you say. We are in your hands, and are glad to be. We are all assured of your gracious goodwill towards our city. And your protection. We hope that you will now enter it, and test our loyalty. A banquet is prepared, feasting for all your men. Entertainment. Without stint. We must not keep you standing here, outside the walls . . .'

His points made, Montrose acceded, and moved forward in restrainedly friendly fashion to greet the bailies and guild representatives. Then he summoned the pipers once more, and after a preliminary flourish by his trumpeters, they fell in behind the musicians, one and all, and proceeded to march through the towered gateway, and into the narrow Drygait, Montrose at the front with the city deputation – and having much ado to limit his stride to their notably non-military and various gaits.

No crowds lined the narrow streets to greet them, although people were at windows and congregated in groups at close-mouths. Booths were shuttered up, stalls folded away, packmen and hucksters conspicuous by their absence. Even the poultry and pigs which normally cluttered up the wynds and alleyways had been hidden away by their prudent owners. But some attempts had been made, presumably at official level, to strike a more welcoming note, for leafy branches and bunches of fern and bracken were tied on wells, pumps, louping-on stones, braziers and the like; and now and again the head of the procession was halted for a moment or two for children dressed as angels or cherubs to present to the King's representative flowers and stammered recitals. Montrose rewarded each with a smile, a pat and one of the few coins he had managed to preserve – and was thankful for the scent of the flowers at least, for the smell of the city, in that hot airless August noonday, was appalling.

With the College in its gardens on their left, and the Archbishop's Castle on their right, unoccupied this long while and looking dejected, at the junction of the Drygait and Rotten Row, they swung northwards up the Stable Green, climbing the hill past all the cathedral manses in their orchards to the Vicar's Alley, to where the Kirk Port gave access to the mighty Cathedral of St. Mungo, Glasgow's pride – although it was now divided, in good Presbyterian fashion, into the High Kirk, the Outer Kirk, and, in the semi-subterranean crypt, the Barony Kirk. The majestic bulk of it brought back memories to Montrose, for here had been held the vital and dramatic General Assembly of 1638, the turning-point in his public life, wherein his hand was finally set to the plough. The cathedral graveyard, together with the grassy expanse of the Green outside, was the only open space large enough in the city to contain the thousands of men. On the Green oxen were already being roasted on open fires, many of them, barrels were being broached, and vast quantities of loaves laid out, using the table-stones and recumbent slabs of the graveyard as convenient dressers and benches – with the cooks and scullions furiously warding off the hordes of stray dogs which the savoury smells had brought from near and far. The swarms of flies were equally attentive. The many children, no doubt warned about the dreadful, possibly cannibalistic habits of the Irish and Highlanders, fled as the procession came up.

Here there were more speeches, by Baillie Colin Campbell – an unfortunate name, in the circumstances, which drew forth uninhibited groans from such MacDonalds and Macleans as still remained with the force – by Dean of Guild Henry Glen, and by Master Henry Gibson, the Town Clerk. All could orate better than did the Provost, but even so were listened to only by those in the immediate vicinity, and not all of those. Then the Principal of the university, the Reverend Dr. John Strang, had his say – the Chancellor, being the Duke of Hamilton, was wisely absent –

but by this time nobody wanted to listen to more talk and he got no sort of hearing, the rumbling of bellies, in consequence of the delectable aroma of cooking meats, all but drowning his precise periods. Montrose dispensed with any other reply than a series of graceful bows. He had not failed to notice that none of the city representatives had so much as mentioned the King throughout. It seemed apparent that Glasgow was paying homage to a victorious general whose power might well constrain them, rather than showing loyalty to their monarch and his cause.

Thereafter, leaving the troops to their feasting, a move was made back down the High Street, by the official party, now minus pipers, to the Tolbooth and Town House at the junction of Gallowgate and Trongate, where Montrose and his senior officers were to be entertained by the magistrates. Though not quite all of his senior officers, for he made sure that one or two were always to be on duty outside, to ensure of reasonably good behaviour on the part of the men, and to see that sentries and pickets were on the alert all round the city.

Up in the Town Hall, before ever he was sat down, Sir Robert Douglas and others were bringing individuals to present to the Captain-General. The first was none other than his old colleague and lieutenant, John Lyon, 2nd Earl of Kingborne, in ostrich-feathered hat and much beribboned.

'My lord Marquis, your servant,' Kingborne said, bowing over the hand he took – but keeping his eyes down.

'Ha – John! This is a pleasure. And a surprise. We have not seen each other in many months. You are growing fat, man, I swear. I advise more . . . activity! *Military* activity, perhaps!'

The other coughed. 'I came to offer you my congratulations, James. And to assure you of my aid and support.'

'Ah. Aid and support, John? I could have done with them this twelvemonth past – I vow I could! And wrote to you to that effect. More than once.'

'Yes. But it was . . . difficult, see you. Very difficult. Situated as I was . . .'

'No doubt. A man's duty is not always easy, my friend.'

'A man's duty is not always so clear! As it is to you . . .'

'You are one of the King's earls, are you not? Sworn to aid and defend His Grace.' He raised his glance. 'And another behind you, if I mistake not.'

'My lord Marquis – may I present the Earl of . . .'

Douglas was brushed aside. 'I need no presentation to my lord

126

of Montrose by such as yourself, sirrah,' a thin and haughty middle-aged exquisite declared, oddly dressed in sky-blue velvet and inlaid half-armour. 'We are well acquaint.'

'Yes, indeed we are,' James Graham agreed affably. 'My lord Earl of Roxburgh and I – we used both to be on the King's side! When he was His Grace's Keeper of the Privy Seal, no less.'

'I . . . my lord, I protest!' the elegant spluttered. '*Used* to be! I am the King's most loyal servant.'

'Ha – but I fear that you cannot be that, i' faith! For such position has long been filled by my esteemed goodsire, my lord of Southesk, he never fails to assure me! Would you claim to be more loyal than Southesk, my Lord Roxburgh ?'

That brought the other up short. He could scarcely insist that he was; yet Southesk's equivocal behaviour was known to all, his association with Argyll. Roxburgh compressed his lips tightly and said nothing.

'When last we forgathered, I think, it was in the Parliament Hall at Edinburgh, was it not, my lord ? I, brought from ward in the castle there, to be tried. With certain friends of mine – and of the King. You, as I mind it, had nothing to say.'

'I . . . the King. He was present. His Grace did not interfere. As one of the King's ministers, then, should I have done so ?'

'Ah. There is a question indeed. A matter for calculation. As to advantage, perhaps ?'

'As to loyalties, I say . . .'

'It may be so. And you have a sure judgment in these matters, it seems. I take it, that you now esteem the King's cause to be in the ascendancy ? Er, profitable, once more ?'

'My lord Marquis – I did not come here to be insulted!'

'I am sure that you did not. Nor do I insult you. I but remark on your judgment. Comment on your careful thought. As when I sent you a commission of lieutenancy. From Carlisle, just thirteen months ago. Seeking your aid and support when I entered Scotland, on His Grace's behalf. You judged the cause less hopeful then, I imagine – for you replied nothing. Nor have you since. Until today. You greatly encourage me, I swear! Why *did* you come, sir, may I ask ?'

'To, ah, offer my services. In the rule of this kingdom. You will require much aid and assistance. I have considerable experience in statecraft . . .'

'That you have, my lord. I shall not forget it. Now, with your permission – we hold up the good Provost . . .'

There were others queuing up to pay their respects to victory, Montrose recognising the two Johnston Earls of Annandale and Hartfell, and the Lord Linton, son of the Earl of Traquair, the Lord Erskine, and others. But, let them wait. They had kept *him*, and his master, waiting for sufficiently long. Coolly courteous, he bowed to all, and let Provost Bell lead him to his seat at the head of the great table.

It was while watching with some wry amusement the scramble thereafter, undignified but revealing, for precedency in seating, on the part of lords, knights, bailies, churchmen, university doctors and prominent citizens, that Montrose gained his clearest indication of all that the tide had turned indeed. Well down the room, a figure very familiar to him was quietly slipping into a modest place at the board, richly but restrainedly dressed. It was James, Lord Carnegie, Magdalen's brother and Southesk's heir. None could now doubt which was the cause most likely to win.

Provost Bell, presiding, seated himself on the Captain-General's left, with Colkitto on *his* left, then the Deacon-Convener. Montrose had on his right the Dean of Guild and then the Earl of Airlie. He was almost thankful that Clanranald, Glengarry, Duart and most of the other Highland chiefs had gone home so quickly; they would never have accepted this sort of placing.

'Are you fine there, lord?' the Provost asked, solicitously. 'Plentys o' room? Och, it's a right clutter, this. There's a wheen mair lords an' great folk arrived than we looked for. They must ha' smelt the guid beef roasting, eh?' He tee-heed.

'They must have smelled *something*,' James Graham agreed. 'But, yes – I am very comfortable, I thank you, Mr. Provost. Although it is many a day since I sat down at such a table.'

'Aye, well – a guid bellyfu' will set you up, man. Ayrshire beef – the best. But a bit salmon first. And hens and siclike trash after. But the beef's the thing. The claret's to your hand. And yon flagon's Bordeaux. Gie me the whisky, mysel' – there's mair body to it . . .'

Glasgow might have its own brand of ecclesiastics, and be something lacking in enthusiasm for its monarch, but there was no faulting its victuals. Quantity, quality and variety vied with each other, as course succeeded course. The heat in the great chamber grew stifling, and the noise grew with it, as the plentitude of wines and spirits began to have their effect. Montrose perceived presently that, if this occasion was to be turned to any good account, other than merely social, it would require to be done soon, while men were still in a state to apprehend it. He informed the Provost that he wished to address the gathering on matters of some importance – even though all were not yet finished eating. That worthy apprised all of the fact by merely banging on the table loud and long with his silver tankard.

James Graham rose – and from somewhere down the table Black Pate's voice rang out strongly.

'When His Grace the King's representative stands, all stand!'

There was a hasty if scarcely well-concerted effort to be up-standing, by all – save those already quite incapable of it.

Montrose gave them a moment or two. Then he raised his tankard. 'I give you the health, prosperity, long life and puissant reign of our beloved, mighty and lawful sovereign, King Charles – and damnation to his enemies!'

None refused to drink that toast – and the failure to actually acclaim it by some quite large percentage of the company was largely overwhelmed by the enthusiasm of those who did.

While they were still on their feet, Colkitto shouted, 'And another to the man who makes the King's reigning possible, whatever – Seumas Graham, *An Greumach Mor*, the Marquis!'

Few indeed allowed themselves to seem backward in drinking that toast, with so much cold steel and hot hands present. The shouting went on and on.

Montrose, noting that not a few were striving to be heard, no doubt to present other toasts, recognised that this process could well end any intelligent reception of what he had to say. He raised his hand for silence – and when that failed in effect, jerked his head towards his personal trumpeter, who sat with the ser-geant-of-the-guard and other attendants at a side-table. The subsequent bugle blast, in that confined space, all but lifted the roofing, not to mention the tops of men's heads.

In the abrupt silence that followed, James Graham bowed all around, smiling. 'I thank you. Pray resume your seats.' He paused, and went on pleasantly. 'Mr. Provost, Mr. Dean of Guild, Mr. Deacon-Convener, my lords and gentlemen. On be-half of my officers and of our good fellows who feast outside, I thank all who have provided for and contributed to our enter-tainment here. Few of us, in His Graces's forces at least, have been indulged so notably hitherto, most of us never, I am sure. Our appreciation is most obvious – in some more obvious than in others, for we have not all the same capacity . . .' And he glanced along at Colkitto, whose face was like the rising sun.

There was a shout of laughter – which was not the reaction Colkitto's presence had been creating in Glasgow earlier in the day.

'And now, my friends, I speak to you in a different voice. The voice of the King's Lieutenant for Scotland, and Captain-General of His Grace's forces.' His voice *was* different, too, and his bearing with it. Only those very far through failed to recognise it. Men sat up straighter.

'I declare to you, by the King's royal commission, that I have all the power of this ancient throne vested in me, here in Scotland, until His Grace comes here in person to reign over you. Which joyful event will, I believe, be very shortly . . .'

There was a stir and murmur at that, not all of it sounding overjoyed at the prospect, men glancing at each other questioningly.

'Before His Grace arrives, much falls to be done, in order to prepare this war-torn kingdom for him, with much of misrule, oppression and rebellion to be wiped out and set to rights. To that end I hereby decree, proclaim and call a parliament of the Estates of this realm to meet, in the King's name. Forty days of notice is required for the due calling of a parliament. Accordingly it will meet six weeks from now, on the 20th of October. And in this city of Glasgow . . .'

Again the stir and exclamation, pleased and otherwise. The Provost leaned across, behind Montrose's back, to the Dean of Guild, agitatedly.

'It is my hope that King Charles himself may be here to preside in person over this important sitting. But if not, he will appoint a High Commissioner, as proper. I need not declare to you how momentous will be this occasion, how important for all in Scotland the decisions taken thereat.' He paused, pointedly, that what lay behind his words should sink in.

Few there failed to realise the implications. It would be a day of reckoning, indeed.

'And so, Mr. Provost, you will prepare your city. As the loyal and worthy setting for this great event. I will give you and your Council all necessary powers to requisition, enforce and act accordingly. You understand, gentlemen ?'

Provost Bell darted his red head around like a weasel in a wall, uncertain whether to rejoice or wail. His colleagues looked equally unsure of themselves – but definitely more depressed than elated.

That was nothing to their expressions a moment or two later, however, as Montrose went on, 'Farther to this, I shall require forthwith for the immediate weal and governance of the kingdom, until parliament shall make proper and due provision, a loan of £50,000 Scots. From this city. This loan, which must be paid to me by tomorrow's evening, will no doubt be repaid by that parliament hereafter.'

There was no doubt about the wailing now. Like a chorus of the damned the Glasgow representatives raised their voices in agonised protest, loud and continuous.

'Do not tell me that a wealthy city such as this could find it difficult to raise such paltry sum for their lord the King?'

'It's no' possible, lord – Goad, it's no'!' the Provost croaked. 'Fifty thousand! We . . . we couldna get you money the likes o' that.'

'You got Argyll more, five years past! And the next year sent him a further £10,000, I was told.'

'Nine thousand, lord – only £9,000!' Bell quavered. 'And the first was the toon's siller. The whole plate and treasure . . .'

'Save perhaps these silver tankards and dishes we sup from, sir?'

'*Twenty* thousand we might find, my lord Marquis . . .' Commissary Fleming put in.

'I am not here to bargain and chaffer like any huckster!' they were told sternly. 'Fifty thousand I require. By tomorrow night. Or I requisition what is necessary. And that will be no *loan*!'

A halberdier of the Town Guard came, to hurry apologetically to the Provost's side, pluck at his robe, and whisper.

Bell started up. 'Hech, hech – lord there's a riot! In the streets. Booths afire. Your Hielantmen. Robbery! Looting . . .!'

Montrose looked down. 'I am not finished, Mr. Provost. I will not be interrupted. If what you declare is true, it is against my strictest orders. Any such disobedience is punishable with the utmost severity. In the matter of conduct in the streets – or of failure to obey my other commands. Such as producing this money for loan.' He looked up. 'Colonel Graham, Younger of Inchbrakie – you will go investigate. If you find looting, take the leaders and hang them. Where all may see. And put the officers who should have stopped it in close ward. I will deal with such later. I will not have looting or riot – or disobedience – by any soever.'

'Yes, my lord Marquis.' Black Pate strode from the room.

131

There was a throbbing silence as men contemplated this abrupt display of harsh realism, in all the talking, and the sheer authority which could command it. The lesson was not lost on those present, nor the threat implied to other than rioters.

James Graham remained on his feet. 'I further have to announce that all men assembled in arms, save those under my authority or otherwise in the King's service, must disperse forthwith or be treated as rebels and traitors; and all who command them to be guilty of high treason. All lords, lairds, chiefs of clans and of names, all landed men, must apply to me, in default of parliament, for licence to muster any tail of armed men, in excess of a dozen, sufficient to guard their persons and homes. All comforting, sheltering and abetting former rebel leaders will also be deemed to be in treason to the Crown. But such rebels, who give themselves up and acknowledge their error, and yield due allegiance to the King, will be treated with the utmost clemency. My word upon it. These decrees will be promulgated throughout the land.'

None raised voice in comment.

'Now, as regards requisitioning for my army. I shall require . . .'

Montrose was interrupted again, this time by the sound of upraised voices, and the door being flung open. Two men pushed past the protesting Town Guards – the Master of Napier and Nat Gordon. James Graham's brows had risen – but it was the sight of the faces which now appeared behind his two lieutenants which caught his breath. And caught the breaths of more than he.

It was as though a party of spectres was filing into Glasgow's Town Hall, pale, gaunt, shrunken, stooping, shuffling, sunken-eyed. Absolute silence fell on the crowded chamber.

It was Montrose himself who broke it. 'Dear God – Archie!' he cried, in a strangled voice; and thrusting aside his chair, hurried forward to greet the newcomers. 'And George! I . . . I . . .' Helplessly he shook his head, unable to continue.

'Jamie!' the Lord Napier of Merchiston, his brother-in-law and one-time guardian, whispered. 'God be praised for this day! To set eyes on you again. Oh, Jamie, Jamie . . .'

Montrose clasped the other to him – and almost choked at the slight and brittle insubstantiality of what he held, the mere skeleton of a man. Young Archie had been supporting his father; clearly he was too weak to stand upright, had become an old, white-headed broken totterer. James Graham took over the duty.

Holding the other, he turned to Sir George Stirling of Keir, holding out his hand, silent. For Stirling, although a youngish man, was only in slightly better shape than his uncle, Napier, hunched, parchment-skinned, luminous-eyed, the reddened galling of manacles on his wrists the only colour to his person.

'Victory, James!' Keir got out, stammering. 'At last, victory.'

'Victory, George – at a price!' Montrose dashed a tear from his eye. 'God forgive me – this was my doing. Because you are linked with me, it is, that they did this to you.'

'What matters it, James? Now. We have the victory you fought for, won – although we only rotted in prison . . .'

His words were lost, indeed he was all but knocked over, as old Airlie rushed past them to reach and embrace his son. The Lord Ogilvy had just hobbled in, no longer the fresh-faced enthusiast of the English campaigns but a haggard scarecrow looking aged enough to be his own father.

Montrose, shocked, appalled, reached out to him also. 'James – you too!' he groaned. 'The brave one, the stalwart of the Angus glens!' He glanced behind still, biting his lip, as more walking ghosts shuffled in, some with as illustrious names as any in the land. Anxiously he scanned them. Then, feeling Napier reeling within his arm, he half carried him to his own chair.

'Cherish these!' he cried. 'The most honoured men in all Scotland. These paid Argyll in different coin to yours! Make way for them, I say . . .!'

There was no lack of aid, now, sympathy and welcome, for the pathetic band. All were eager to help and comfort. Montrose went from one to another greeting, commiserating, exclaiming – even though always his eyes searched behind all, to the still open door.

'Thirty-two in all, my lord Marquis,' Nat Gordon came up to report. 'Including the ladies. These we brought to Keir, on our way here. Where they might have attention. They . . . they were in ill case. These, the men, insisted on coming on, to pay respects to your lordship. We had not the heart to refuse them. My Lord Napier and Sir George we lifted out of Linlithgow town's jail, in the by-going. The rest were in the Tolbooth of Edinburgh. Held in stinking vaults. No light, no room to stand upright, filth covering the floor. Some were too sick and weak even to ride . . .'

'Aye, man. It is beyond belief. But – my son?' Montrose could stand it no longer. 'My *son*! Jamie? What of him? Where is he?'

'He is well, my lord. But they have him secure in Edinburgh Castle. The town itself yielded to us – but not the castle. They moved him there over a month back. We offered them any they might name, as hostage, in exchange for the Lord James. But they would not. Nor would he, indeed. We spoke with him, he standing on the gatehouse parapet, shouting. He said to tell his father not to waste exchange of a good man for one too young to fight. He said it would ill become his father's son to deprive the King of a single fighter.'

'He said that? Jamie truly said that, Nat?'

'Aye.' The Gordon grinned. 'He said more. He said that a man in the castle was teaching him to build boats.'

A faint flicker of a smile crossed Montrose's face. 'Aye – that is Jamie! But – what of the plague? Does it not rage sorely? Is he in danger?'

'The castle is high above the mists and stews of the city. The plague has not touched it. Indeed, Edinburgh is not so sore hit as is Stirling town.'

'You say so? Ah, well – so his mother will not see Jamie yet awhile.' He sighed. 'Edinburgh yielded, then? You had no trouble?'

'None. We sent messengers ahead, as you instructed us, demanding that the city submitted, in the King's name. They sent out a deputation of magistrates and the like, to plead with us to spare the town – as though we were a great army. A mere squadron of horse! They said that they were ever loyal to the King – only that their city had been used by wicked and unscrupulous men, who had now fled and left them defenceless. They offered us money, what we would – but besought us to have mercy. For the hand of God was sore upon them, with this plague. We said that we had come only for the prisoners and hostages – and that your lordship would decide Edinburgh's fate in due course! And suggested that you had little cause to love the place . . .!'

'Yes – this is the pattern, then. I am told that Dundee is likewise clamouring to be admitted to the King's peace. No doubt Aberdeen the same. But – they could turn against us again tomorrow, should our fortunes seem to change. Poor devils – I scarce blame them. They are at the mercy of whosoever wields the heaviest stick! We must gain from them what we can *while* we can.' He paused. 'But, Nat, there is one man I have looked for here. Doctor Wishart, the divine. I have not seen him ...'

'I am here, my lord,' a voice spoke, from behind them.

Montrose turned, and stared – and realised that his eyes had slid over this man, more than once, unrecognising. The lesson had not fully sunk in. George Wishart, one of the ministers of St. Andrews, and a notably learned man, had been ousted for being a King's man, and had fled to Newcastle. There Montrose had met him, when with Leslie's army, and they had discovered that they saw eye to eye on many matters. No doubt because of this friendship he had been taken into custody at the later surrender of Newcastle by the royalists, and confined to Edinburgh's Tolbooth, He was only three years older than Montrose – but now looked thirty.

'George! George Wishart ...! Oh, my friend – forgive me! That I did not know you. Save us – you, you ...!' He swallowed, shaking his head.

'That is no matter, my lord. What matters is yourself. I have never seen you look better – for which God be thanked. It is worth all the weary days and nights in that place. To see you well, triumphant, the noblest face in this land ...!' The voice, which seemed to have deepened, broke.

James Graham gripped his arm. 'What am I to say to you? When you have suffered so much. My friend. And not to know you...'

'Say, my lord, that I may stay with you, now. Be your secretary, perhaps, your chaplain. If you will have me. I ask no greater favour, privilege. Take me with you hereafter. I shall serve you, with all my heart.'

Much moved, Montrose nodded, finding words difficult. 'Aye – it shall be so. To be sure, George. To my joy. I will no doubt require a secretary, now. But ... what did they do to you? Those marks. On your face. Did they – did they misuse you so ...?'

'Rats,' the other informed, briefly. 'There were more than prisoners in that Tolbooth!'

The banquet broke up quickly thereafter, Montrose having lost all taste for junketing, as for speech-making and social civilities. He wanted to be alone with Archie Napier, George Sterling, James Ogilvy and George Wishart – and was not in a mood for disguising his preferences. Glasgow's representatives were despatched to collect their £50,000 Scots, and sundry other requirements, and the King's Lieutenant took over their Town

House and Tolbooth for the use of his forces, his first act thereafter to order the cells to be opened below it, and their inmates freed, fed and pardoned, whatever the reason for their incarceration.

CHAPTER TEN

The great castle of Bothwell, although ruinous, made a magnificent backcloth for the event, towering above the level haughlands of the Clyde. There was space on those flats, dry at this time of the year, for all the complicated manoeuvres and displays that Montrose had planned. At the same time, the site held tactical possibilities, in the unlikely event of trouble. And there was sufficient accommodation in the courtyard and outbuildings of the castle, still roofed, to provide for what might be called his Court – and those lofty personages attending who found such conditions too spartan could roost in the little town nearby, if so they elected.

It was the 3rd of September, and the royalist army had been at Bothwell for over a week. Montrose had cut short this stay at Glasgow, remaining there for only two days in fact. It had been discovered that plague had reached the city; moreover, it was increasingly difficult to control many of the soldiery, who, with insufficient to do and too much liquor to drink, found the temptations towards plunder beyond them. Bothwell was only eight miles south-east of Glasgow, and convenient for a variety of reasons.

To all outwards appearances today's programme was a triumph, a successful flourish by an all-conquering general, the fitting climax to a brilliant campaign. The conqueror reviewed his troops and displayed his might and authority for all to see – and to note. A normal, indeed almost obligatory gesture of total victory. None realised – except perhaps Black Pate Graham, from whom his chief had few secrets – that it was, in fact, something of a last desperate throw, the resort of a worried and distracted man.

This review was perhaps unique in that it was organised and laid on not mainly for public edification and impression but for the sake of the army itself. Or what was left of it. For, of the near 6,000 with which he had fought Kilsyth, Montrose had now less than half. Worse than that, not only was Aboyne threatening to leave any day for the North with his Gordon horse, but

Colkitto himself was insisting on a campaign in Argyll, to pay back old MacDonald scores against the Campbells. In vain James Graham had pointed out that this was no valid activity for the King's army, that it was the way to lose Scotland again. Colkitto, urged on by his clansmen, remained obdurate.

This review, then, was an effort to hold together an army, to re-arouse a spirit of military pride, glory and unity – and to display to the rest of Scotland a show of armed might and confident power while yet he had it to display.

Montrose had planned it all almost as carefully as he would a battle. In a way it *was* a battle, a struggle for the adherence of a highly important part of his strength. A great march past, cavalry manoeuvres, Highland charges, a mock battle and the like, were to be followed by less military events and games, archery contests, races, wrestling, piping and dancing, football. All Clydesdale, Cunningham, Kyle and Carrick was invited to attend – though not plague-struck Glasgow – and it was hoped that not a little recruiting would be a by-product of the day.

Anxious to make under 3,000 men seem more than in fact they were, he had split up his forces into a great many lesser units, and improvised a host of flags and banners. There had been much reclothing, mainly at Glasgow's expense. Extra pipers had actually been hired.

Punctually at noon, the King's Lieutenant and his Court emerged from the castle. And it was a Court now, for half the nobility and gentry of Southern Scotland flooded to join him. For the past six days they had been coming in, in ever-growing numbers. As an indication of public opinion they were welcome – but otherwise more of an embarrassment and problem.

The issuing of the official party was the awaited signal. Cannon boomed out from four different batteries – there was no lack of artillery now that it was not needed, with half a dozen Lowland fortresses to draw upon. The sound of the bagpipes swelled and throbbed on the warm September air. The vice-regal procession moved down towards the saluting base just above the spreading haughland.

It was then, just as the first of the remaining clan regiments was marching in, that there was an unscheduled interlude. A small mounted party came trotting across the Clyde meadows from a south-easterly direction, all colour, nodding plumes, jingling spurs and gallantry. Many such had ridden in this last week, but this group seemed to exude a peculiarly pronounced air of confidence and self-assurance, careless authority in every line of them. Montrose had not seen the like. Here were no humble suppliants for his favours, at any rate.

At the head of the strolling, chattering, magpie throng, James Graham halted, and waited for the new arrivals. He was a little concerned that delay might upset the carefully timed arrangements – but showed no sign of this. He did send Black Pate to slow up the first marchers.

A hush fell on all that far-from-hushed company as the identity of the newcomers' leader was recognised – although it took Montrose himself a few moments to place the extravagantly clad florid individual as William Douglas, Marquis thereof. Willie Douglas had put on a deal of weight, since James Graham had left him, at Padua, to go search fruitlessly for his missing sister Katherine amongst the stews of Europe. Then Willie had been Earl of Angus, and they had been doing the Grand Tour in company. Always something of a playboy, the Marquis, succeeding to the title, had since then managed skilfully to avoid entanglement in matters political, religious or national, an odd condition of the head of the mighty house of Douglas, living largely abroad and ignoring all appeals from either side. That he should have appeared, unsummoned, at Bothwell this day was something of a triumph for Montrose – and all there perceived it. He was the *owner* of the castle, of course. However non-military and superficial, William Douglas was the richest man in Scotland, and could, if he so wished, muster more man-power, and horsed man-power at that, than any save Huntly himself, from the wide Douglas lands of Douglasdale, Clydesdale and Dumfriesshire.

'Jamie! Jamie Graham – well met!' this plumply mature dandy exclaimed, flourishing his wide-brimmed, ostrich-plumed bearer in an elaborate but half-mocking bow from the saddle. 'Dammit, man – you are lean as a fox! And as brown, I swear! How d'ye do it, I say?' They were almost of an age, these two, though the Douglas looked ten years the senior despite his pink, chubby cheeks.

'By going to and fro in the land – on the King's business, Willie,' Montrose answered, moving forward to shake the other's hand. 'I recommend it, my friend! You should try it! But – it is good to see you, after all these years. Old Bloody Heart!' This was always the reigning Douglas's nick-name, from the blood-red symbol they bore on their coat-of-arms, representing the great Bruce's heart taken on crusade by their ancestor, the Good Sir James Douglas, on his dying master's command.

'You ever were a restless devil, James. Full of conscience!
Thank God, an ill that never afflicted me! So – now you are as
good as king in Scotland, eh?'

'No. Sir – I am not! I am but the King's servant. As are you,
and all here. I but wait to hand over all to His Grace – and thankfully retire to mind my own affairs again. Which, unlike yours
Willie, I fear are in sorry state!'

'Mm. Aye. To be sure. A costly matter, conscience!' The
Douglas smoothed a hand over his double chins. He did not have
to be reminded that amongst his hereditary privileges was that of
leading the van of the royal army of Scotland in battle, as well as
the first vote in Parliament or Council and carrying the crown at
coronations – none of them activities Willie Douglas would have
chosen. Moreover, he had married as second wife Huntly's sister,
and his brother-in-law's views were not unknown to him. He
cleared his throat, and looked round. 'You'll be acquaint with my
lord of Home?'

'We know each other, yes,' Montrose tried to force some
cordiality into his voice. This James, 10th lord and 3rd Earl of
Home was something of a trimmer, ostensibly a King's man but
as liable to support the other side. He had signed the Cumber-
nauld Bond in 1641, but had done nothing to support that signature so far. But he was kin to Douglas, and moreover could
produce a large fighting tail of Border moss-troopers and Merse-
men. The King's Captain-General was in no position to offend
such as James Home. 'My lord of Home is very welcome,' he
said.

'Aye. Here, too, is Sir John Dalziel, brother to the Earl of
Carnwath – whose fame you will know!'

'Ah, yes – to be sure.' Carnwath had fought for Charles in
England, after his fashion, but had refused to accept Montrose's
commission from the King and serve under him. He was still in
England, an extraordinary character who kept a hard-riding
mistress with him on campaign, wearing man's dress, using the
name of Captain Francis Dalziel, and leading a troop of horse in
fiery style – an unusual arrangement by any standards. The
Covenant had outlawed him. His brother might be a useful
adherent, for they had large lands in the Upper Ward of
Lanarkshire.

Douglas introduced others of his gay entourage, but Montrose
intervened to point out that his fighting-men would be getting

impatient, unused to being held up, however illustrious the cause. A move was made to the saluting base. Like a pride of posturing peacocks, this particular cross-section of the Lowland nobility and gentry followed on.

As the pipes resumed, and the clansmen came marching into the great arena from one side, the Gordon horsed squadrons rode in from the other. James Graham stood out in front of the rest, under the Royal Standard which stirred only faintly in the warm breeze, aware that his heart had lifted again. Although sanguine of temperament, he had been much concerned over his inability to hold together his victorious army, now that the fighting was over, however little he dared allow his anxiety to show. The sudden adherence of all these nobles was encouraging, but not really important – for they would all be gone as quickly as they had come, at the first hint of reverse. But William Douglas was in a different category. Having taken all this time to make up his mind, being as devoid of ambition as of political interest, with no need to add to his riches or position, it was conceivable that he might stay the course and be able to provide that source of armed strength and influence which the King's cause so greatly needed. Clydesdale and Douglasdale was one of the greatest horse-rearing areas of the land. Montrose was calculating just how many squadrons of cavalry Douglas might be able to raise, when his dreams were rudely broken into. Despite the fact that his Gordon horse were at that moment trotting in gallant ordered ranks across their front, the Viscount Aboyne came spurring to Montrose's side.

'My Lord James,' he cried, careless of who heard him. 'I do protest! The Lord Crawford has taken command of my men. There he rides at their head. Gordons! It is insufferable! I will not have it. You must remove him . . .'

'*Must*, James? That is scarcely the word, I think?' the other said quietly. 'And might I ask you to lower your voice?'

'But . . . but I will not be treated so. I, Aboyne. And heir to Gordon. By this, this arrogant fool! Even if he is senior earl of Scotland! I ask you to remove him from my squadrons, and forthwith. Or . . . or I withdraw them from this play-acting folly!'

Montrose took his patience in both hands. 'James – the Earl of Crawford is one of His Grace's Major-Generals. He should not have superseded you, taken over your command. But I cannot call him off like some underling. Not before all these. I will speak with him hereafter . . .'

'I fear that I must ask you to do so, my lord Marquis,' the younger man said stiffly. 'I have been insulted. In front of my own clansmen. They are not His Grace's troops, I would remind you. But *mine*. Or my father's. Crawford has no right to ride at their head . . .'

'No right, I agree. But some small excuse, perhaps. He is Major-General of Horse. Yours, and a few Ogilvys, are the only cavalry in the King's Scottish army. At present Crawford has no command. And he has been rotting in Edinburgh Tolbooth. Can you not allow him a little flourish, James ?'

'In front of all these . . . ?'

'All here know well the true position. That you are heir of Gordon and Colonel of Aboyne's Horse. Go back, James, and ride at Crawford's side.'

'I will not!' the other declared stubbornly, flushing. 'I will not go back. To eat dirt before that . . . that interloper! Nor will I allow my Gordons to be commanded by any Lindsay, Major-General or none! That will be his next move, for a wager! I shall withdraw my men, as I wished to do before, and return to Strathbogie.'

Montrose raised his head a little higher. 'You will do what you must, James. But so long as you bear the King's commission under my hand, you will obey my commands. Go back to your place, Colonel. And after this ceremonial ride is over, require Major-General the Lord Crawford to report to me.'

Dark-browed, Aboyne rode off, leaving his leader a deal more perturbed than he seemed.

There were no more hitches, and the review proceeded satisfactorily enough, the skilful dispositions, groupings and rearrangement of formations giving the impression of much greater man-power than was actually involved. To avoid the true numbers becoming evident, the final march past in the formal part of the proceedings, was restricted to colour-parties only, bearing banners. Practically the entire remaining man-power was indeed on parade as alleged colour-parties, and a goodly show they made. If any of the spectators realised that it was all bluff, play-acting as Aboyne had called it, they did not publicise their discovery.

This over, and his officers assembling before the games, races, mock-battles and contests commenced, Montrose had devised a little ceremony. At a sign from him, a middle-aged gentleman of great dignity stepped forward from the over-dressed throng, Sir

Robert Spottiswoode, the King's Secretary of State for Scotland. He had arrived at Bothwell two days earlier, from England, bearing letters and appointments from King Charles. He now read out a letter sent from Hereford on the 25th of June, before the Battles of Alford and Kilsyth, expressing Charles's joy and gratitude for the great victory at Auldearn, and all other suc-successes, declaring that he would come to Scotland at the earliest moment possible, and saying that, thanks to his beloved Marquis of Montrose, his sacred cause was now assured of success. All loyal men in England had taken renewed heart from the Scottish triumphs, and so a great surge forward there was imminent. His Grace, therefore, could not come north imme-diately; but he had commanded the Lord Digby and Sir Marmaduke Langdale to ride to Scotland with a major cavalry force, for the Marquis of Montrose's support.

The fact that this cavalry support had not yet materialised, by the end of August, and that the war had gone from bad to worse in England, was not commented upon.

When the polite applause subsided, James Graham thanked Sir Robert, and called upon Sir Archibald Primrose, Clerk to the Privy Council, to read a royal proclamation which Sir Robert had also brought with him. Primrose cannot have enjoyed the occasion, for he was of the opposition party, but he put a good lawyer's face upon it. The proclamation appointed the King's well-beloved James, Marquis of Montrose, to be Lieutenant-Governor and Viceroy of the realm of Scotland, in addition to being Captain-General of its forces, with all the King's powers during his royal absence, the right to call parliament, preside at Privy Councils, create knights, appoint judges and sheriffs, and otherwise rule and govern the King's Scottish subjects. All men soever were ordered and commanded to give the said Marquis of Montrose fullest aid, duty and support. On pain of high treason. Etcetra.

There was rather louder applause for this, led noticeably by Montrose's own officers, for which James Graham bowed acknowledgment.

'I have to announce, my lords and gentlemen, that by this authority I shall tomorrow hold a Council of State, to deal with sundry urgent matters of government and to prepare for the Parliament called for October. This will not be a Privy Council, since that Council is at present in no state to meet.' He did not add that a goodly proportion of its members were indeed fled the country. 'To this meeting most here will be called to attend, and I shall greatly value your advice and guidance.' He paused. 'And now, by the same authority, rather than as commander of the King's forces, I ask Major-General Alastair MacDonald of Dunaverty, Younger of Colonsay, to stand forward.'

Wondering, obviously, but assuming a typically swaggering air to cover his uncertainty, the giant Highlander pushed his way through the throng. He was very fine today, in a strange mixture of Highland and cavalier garb, hung about with Celtic jewellery, ceremonial dirks and the like. Men drew back from his passage heedfully, for this man's name was more feared in Scotland than any other save that of Argyll himself.

'My friends,' Montrose went on, 'before you, you see one to whom the King's cause owes more than to any other in the land. Most of you know him as Colkitto. Without him and his Ulstermen and Highlanders and Islesmen, we could by no means be here today. We have won victories, yes – but without this man we might well have won none. Auldearn, of which you have just heard the King's praise, was almost wholly *his* victory. To unnumbered others we owe much – but to this man most. So I ask you to kneel, Alastair.'

'Kneel?' that stalwart exclaimed, '*Me* kneel? God's eyes – Colkitto kneels to no man. Not even you, Seumas Graham! Not even the King's Grace!'

'Then kneel before your God, man – for this is done in His name. You'll not grudge your Maker a knee?'

Doubtfully the other sank – but only on one knee, stiffly.

James Graham drew his sword, and tapped the gigantic Islesman on each massive shoulder. 'I dub thee knight, Alastair MacDonald,' he said. 'In the sight of God and of all men. Walk humbly before that God, serve the King as you have well done, assist the poor and needy, set thine hand against tyranny and evil, and remain a good and true knight until thy life's end. Arise, Sir Alastair MacDonald.' He paused, and glanced around. 'This in the King's authority. For myself, I name you Captain-General of the Clans, in the King's army.'

Speechless, his face scarlet, Colkitto got up, looked about him shaking his head like a dog, and then stumbled back to his place, forgetting entirely even to bow, much less to swagger. The buzz of exclamation and comment arose.

Montrose had thought to knight Aboyne also; policy dictated no less. But there was no sign of the Gordon; and if he was indeed hiding himself somewhere, sulking, to call out for him would but publish his absence.

He raised his hand. 'It is enough, gentlemen. Now for the contests of strength, the games. There will be victuals, refreshments, for all. Now – a word with you, if you please, my lord Earl of Crawford . . .'

*　　*　　*

Next morning, as Montrose was dressing himself with unusual care for the Council of State – for today he was acting the King's part, and concerned to do so worthily – his chaplain and secretary came to inform him that the Lord Aboyne was seeking interview.

'So early, George ? He would see me *now* ?'

'Yes, my lord.' Wishart was looking a different man already from the scarecrow which had entered Glasgow's Town Hall. 'He says that it is urgent. And . . . he is dressed for the road, I think!'

'Eh . . . ? You say so.' James Graham frowned. 'Then I must see him.' He sighed.

Aboyne came in, booted and spurred. 'I have come to take my leave, my lord Marquis,' he blurted out, even as he crossed the threshold. 'I ride north forthwith.'

Montrose eyed him levelly. 'I could say, James, that you come to *seek* leave of absence,' he observed. 'But never heed. I am sorry that you feel that you must go. Is there anything that I may do to change your mind ?'

'No. Nothing.'

'That is unfortunate. But – I hope that you will return. And soon.'

'I think not.'

'James – it is not all this foolish matter of Crawford ? I spoke with him last night. I do not think that he will so offend again. Indeed, I may be able to send him on an errand to His Grace, in England – for I love him little more than do you.'

'It is not only Crawford. There will be others like him. And you have made Ogilvy a Colonel of Horse likewise, equal with me. He has a mere eighty troopers – or his father does . . .'

'Ogilvy, James, is a good officer, as you well know. You were companions-in-arms for long, my two good lieutenants, when in England. Do you grudge him this, after a year in a prison cell ? I need experienced officers still, to lead the new squadrons I intend to raise here in the Lowlands. The King's cause is not won yet, I'd remind you.'

'Who is there to fight you now?' the younger man demanded. 'You have all these, these time-servers coming to laud you, to seek positions, commands. No doubt some of *them* you will make colonels, major-generals! Who have done nothing, hazarded nothing . . .'

'You wish to be a major-general, James?'

'I . . . I care not. I am Gordon. And you owe much to Gordon.'

'I do. I have always declared it. You are an excellent commander of light horse, James – one of the best. But are you a general officer? Capable of commanding a general army in the field? In strategy and tactics? You may well be – even though you are very young for it. We do not know. You have never tried, had occasion to do so . . .'

'I am as capable of it as the Earl of Crawford, God knows!'

'No doubt. But *I* did not make Crawford general. I never would have done so. That was the King's doing. I do not see a general's position as a kind of honour. When the lives of thousands, the decision of battles, are in his hands. Knighthood – now that is something different . . .'

'Gordon needs no knighthoods! No, my lord – we ride forthwith. My father – he commands it. I have given the orders to my men. They await me.'

'Your men? So – it is not only yourself, James? You remove your Gordon horse from my army? My main cavalry!'

'Yes. We are to return to Strathbogie.'

'You realise what this means? For the royal cause? Five hundred trained and experienced horse. Leaving me with a mere 100 or so others . . .'

'The fighting is by with. And you will get more. Now that you have the Lowlands. This Douglas, and the rest. Time that they played *their* part. My father demands that we return. I have disobeyed him for long enough. And my brother Lewis is taking my place, at Strathbogie. Making himself master, in my father's absence. *I* am heir to Gordon now, and must take my place. I am sorry . . .'

'I will not beg of you, James. But . . . this is a sore blow. My information is that David Leslie is at Carlisle. Not so very far away. He is the best soldier the enemy have. Better by far than old Sandy, Lord Leven, his kinsman. And he has an army of 10,000, half of them cavalry. *Half* – 5,000 horse! He plans to get between the King and myself. And His Grace delays. All is seeming triumph here – but *is* not! I am weak, man – weak. And your going will make me direly weaker.'

'If it comes to fighting again, I can return, my lord. Time enough for that when Leslie crosses the border.'

Montrose bowed to the inevitable. He held out his hand. 'So be it. God go with you, then, James. I am sorry that we part thus. After so long a companionship. So many dangers shared. I thank you, from my heart, for all that you have done, you and yours. The King, all Scotland, myself – we are all greatly in your debt. More than words can ever say. I hope that you find affairs none so ill at Strathbogie.'

The other gripped his hand, muttered something incoherent, and hurried from the room.

Grave-faced, James Graham continued with his dressing.

Later, on his way to the Council, Montrose saw a tall, dark, sardonic-looking figure idling near the Great Hall doorway. 'Nat!' he exclaimed. 'You, still here? You have not gone, with the others?'

'I have not, my lord,' Colonel Nathaniel Gordon said. 'My place is at *your* side. Huntly may whistle for me, as he will!'

The other stepped over to grip the Gordon's arm, silently, before he moved on into the crowded hall.

If some of his officers found their General somewhat constrained, aloof, stern, at the great Council of State that followed, they could account for it by the exceptional nature of the occasion.

In a brief introductory he outlined the programme. The forthcoming parliament would establish and settle much. But meantime the country was in a lawless and leaderless state. Temporary measures had to be taken, and quickly. The previous rulers had largely abdicated their responsibilities, and fled the country. Half the sheriffdoms of the land were vacant. The Court of Session itself had not sat for months. Taxes and duties went ungathered – and many of them were iniquitous and harsh anyway. Broken soldiery terrorised the land. The plague raged unchecked in cities, and refugees roamed the countryside destitute. Certain nobles had not yet disbanded their private forces, and were using them to ravage their neighbours' property. Moreover certain castles and fortresses still held out against the King's authority, Edinburgh the most prominent. He did not stress that his own son was held therein, but all knew it. Famine would take hold if this present harvest was not ingathered quickly. So much to be done . . .

Nothing was said about raising men for the army. Instinctively Montrose felt that this was a matter for private negotiation – and Napier agreed. When James Alexander sought to raise the subject, on his own initiative, he was courteously but firmly headed off on another tack. It was far too delicate and vital a matter to be tossed around in public discussion.

The afternoon session was devoted to the drawing up of a manifesto or declaration of policy and faith, declaring continued support for the terms of the original National Covenant – though by no means the Solemn League and Covenant – freedom of religious observance and from the domination and tyranny of either prelates or Kirk, the maintenance of government by King and Parliament. They were most of the way through this, without overmuch acrimony – for men were growing sleepy in the sunshine – when Pate Graham came whispering at his chief's ear.

'A messenger. Urgent. From the South.' And when the other looked enquiringly at him. 'Ill news, I fear.'

'Bring him to me. But . . . bid him be discreet. And speak low!'

A dusty, weary-looking man in jack and leather was led in, distinctly abashed by the stare of all the great company. 'My lord Marquis – a message from my Lord Digby,' the man muttered, in a North Country English voice. 'He, and Sir Marmaduke Langdale . . . ambushed! By a force of Ironsides. Psalm-singing devils of the man Cromwell. Routed. With their whole force. Crossing Yorkshire. A great slaughter. On their way to you, in Scotland. All gone, destroyed . . .'

'A-a-ah!' James Graham sought to school his features before that closely watching assembly, but his fingers drummed a tattoo on the table.

'My lord and Sir Marmaduke made good their escape. They head across Lancashire. For Carlisle. They hope to raise another force, see you, in Cumberland. To bring to your side. I was to tell you this, my lord. But . . . ' The messenger left the rest unsaid.

'Thank you.' Chokingly Montrose got it out. 'I . . . ah, understand. It is the fortunes of war. And you, friend? You will be tired. Hungry. Colonel Graham will see to your refreshment. And reward.' He paused. 'The King? What of the King? Have you news of His Grace?'

'The King is still on the Welsh marches, my lord.'

'Aye.' That was a sigh. 'My thanks.' Turning back to the

battery of eyes, Montrose drew a long breath. 'Forgive me, gentlemen. A despatch from my Lord Digby, one of His Grace's generals. Who nears the borders. He raises cavalry in Cumberland. As I did once. Intends to bring them north to Scotland in due course. It is my hope, however, that we shall not require them. But we are grateful for His Grace's thought for us. Now – let us proceed. This matter of ensuring the Kirk's support . . .'

James Graham when he decently could, brought the proceedings to a close.

That evening there was much noise and stir in the Irish and Islesmen's camp, to the west of the haugh. Montrose, seeking to convince the Marquis of Douglas to muster a cavalry force and start its training as soon as possible – while not alarming him with the situation as regards the King and Digby – ignored the to-do, for Colkitto's people were often noisy. But when a cannon-shot crashed out from quite close at hand, to be followed by another, shaking the castle walls, he excused himself from the high-born company and went with Pate and young Napier to investigate.

They found the Gaelic host in high spirits, with much drink taken, dancing, singing, squabbling, the cannon-fire seemingly just *joie-de-vivre*, using up the unaccustomed plenty of gunpowder.

'A saint's day, it must be,' Montrose observed. 'Our Irish friends have saints innumerable. They celebrate.'

'Late in the day for it,' Pate demurred. 'But they celebrate *something*.' He called to a young major of gallow-glasses. 'O'Gorman – wherefore the jollity?'

'*Dia* – do you not know? We march . . .' He hiccupped. 'We march tomorrow, by the Mass! Against the Campbells. At last! Mother o' God – we'll teach them who's m-master in Scotland now . . .!'

Pate and Napier glanced at their chief, and then at each other, quickly.

'Where is Colkitto?' Montrose asked, expressionlessly.

They found the Major-General sitting on an upturned powder-barrel, drinking from a tankard.

'Ha – Seumas! My lord Seumas himself!' the big man cried. 'A drink? A drink for the Captain-General! Have you left all your fine gentlemen, to visit us poor bare-shanked barbarians, heh? Come – sit you. A barrel for Seumas Graham. And a drink, whatever . . .'

'Thank you, no, Sir Alastair,' Montrose declared formally. 'I am not drinking, meantime. I am seeking information. I hear word that there is an expedition against the Campbells, planned. To Argyll?'

'And no lie. We march at tomorrow's dawn. With Your Honour's permission, of course! I was just after coming to inform you.'

James Graham smoothed his tiny beard. 'You know that I need your men *here*. That I can by no means spare them. I have told you. Moreover you know that I am against punitory raiding, Campbells or other.'

'Tut, man – you will not need us for a week or so. My lads grow rusty here, idle in these fat Lowlands. And we have scores to pay in Argyll – by God we have!'

'Nevertheless, Alastair – I ask you not to go.'

'But, save us – what's the difference? You are not fighting, nor like to be. We could be back in four days, whatever – three. We serve you nothing here. Send me word when Leslie crosses the Border, and I will be back with you before he is.'

'That is scarce the point. The point is that it will leave me with a bare 1,000 men. Weak, for all to see. Our enemies will not fail to note. And our nervous friends, likewise. Many will hold back. That you may be sure. Roxburgh, Home, Dalziel and the others. Possibly even Douglas. They will contribute nothing to weakness. Only to obvious strength.'

'You are strong enough, never fear, man. Whether the Marquis of Montrose has 1,000 men more or less matters nothing. Your name will serve you sufficiently well. And the Campbells may well be mustering against you. As they have done before, see you. It is not in that devil Argyll not to do so . . .'

'I will not seek to command you, Alastair. But I *ask* you. Do not go.'

'I must, man. I have given them my word. My gallow-glasses. My MacDonalds. I cannot go back on it now, mercy to God! We march at dawn. But – we will be back, never fear.'

James Graham turned away, to walk slowly back whence he had come.

'You fool, Colkitto!' Black Pate said quietly. 'You great, stiff-necked, Hielant fool! You are failing the finest man in this land, God forgive you!'

Next morning early, as they watched the Gaelic host march off, pipes playing, gallant, devil-may-care, Pate repeated his allegation.

'There goes a fool, a great Hielant stot!' he declared. 'Look at him – the knighted ox!'

'There goes the finest infantry leader in all Christendom,' Montrose corrected, a catch in his voice. 'Aye, and the finest fighting-men, too. All gone. Shall we ever see them back? Or their like, again?'

'Not *all* gone, my lord,' a quiet voice said, from behind.

They turned, to find Colonel Magnus O'Cahan standing there.

'Magnus! You . . . you are not going?'

'I am not, my lord James. There are some of us sane. And loyal. Though, God knows, Alastair is that, whatever else. Only headstrong. I, and 500 from Ulster, who think as I do, remain. At your service.'

Montrose looked away quickly. 'Thank you, my friend,' he got out. 'My very good friend . . .'

CHAPTER ELEVEN

With the Marquis of Douglas agreeing to raise a cavalry force in his wide Dumfriesshire properties – and the Lord Ogilvy sent with him to guide and advise, and to ensure that he kept his less than enthusiasitcally given word – Montrose marched eastwards from Bothwell on the 4th of September, with about 1,200 men, his assemblage of the illustrious and the high-born dispersing, to meet again at the parliament on the 20th of October. He left Bothwell more to prevent any further defection of his forces than for any particular need to move, with the parliament to be held in Glasgow; but he felt instinctively that he would be more able to hold his remaining numbers together on the march, in at least a posture of campaigning, then idling in camp. Moreover, the only three nobles who had promised any substantial numbers of the now so necessary reinforcements were the Earls of Home, Roxburgh and Traquair. And these all had their lands in the East and Middle Marches of the border. James Graham was of the opinion that he would never see these reinforcements unless he actually went there for them. The situation being as it was, therefore, he was as well making a military progress east and south, while Ogilvy and Douglas went south and west. They would rendezvous centrally as soon as possible, and march in strength towards Glasgow, in plenty of time for the parliament – unless an emergency dictated earlier action.

So then 1,200 marched across country, out of Lanarkshire, by West Lothian, skirting the southern flanks of the Pentland Hills, to pick up some extra horsemen from the Dalziel lands around Carnwath and the Fleming lands of Biggar. In two days unhurried marching they were at Cranstoun eight miles south-east of Edinburgh, carefully avoiding that still plague-stricken city, however much Montrose tended to cast his glance towards its distant fortress towering high on its rock, wherein young Jamie was held. A siege of that all but impregnable citadel was utterly out of the question, in the circumstances; it would fall like a ripe plum in due course. Nevertheless, now that he could command what artillery he wanted, the temptation was there.

On Saturday the 6th September, Montrose ordered a great open-air service of prayer and praise for the morrow, at this Cranstoun on the ridge above Dalkeith. He always made a point of marking the Lord's Day especially, if at all practicable; but since most of his army had been Catholic, in the past, he had not gone in for any mammoth church parades. Now, with the Catholic element so direly reduced, and the advisability of displaying to the Presbyterian Lowlands that he was no Papist monster, as was so often alleged, he took the opportunity. The local parish minister was invited to take the service – but for prudence's sake, George Wishart was to preach.

But it was not to be. The Lord Erskine, heir to the Earl of Mar, rode into camp in the early evening, in a great state of excitement. He had left Bothwell earlier, with Home and Roxburgh, for the Merse. They had barely arrived at Home Castle, when the dread news reached them. General David Leslie was on the East March, indeed was crossing Tweed at Berwick that very day. And with 5,000 seasoned cavalry, the pick of Scotland's regular army in England, however many foot he might have.

To say that Montrose was appalled was not strictly accurate. He had all along been all too well aware of this possibility; indeed, despite all the seeming triumph, the thing had haunted him for many a night. Hence his distress over the defection of Aboyne and Colkitto. But he had understood Leslie to be tied up in the West, at Carlisle, where he might have been expected to be preoccupied with Digby's and Langdale's efforts to raise an army amongst the Cumberland loyalists, and where Callander was said to have moved south to join him with his carefully keeping-out-of-the-way force. This switch to the east, therefore, and actual crossing into Scotland at this stage, was a surprise. As was the figure of 5,000 cavalry – a devastating prospect, when Montrose had a bare 100 Ogilvys and perhaps fifty others. The Tweed at Berwick was not forty miles away.

But this was by no means all Erskine's news. At Berwick-on-Tweed Leslie had been joined by a group of the Covenant leaders who had been hiding in Northern England since Kilsyth – including Argyll himself, the Earl of Lanark and the Lord Lindsay. This no doubt was what had brought Leslie across country so unexpectedly – orders from Argyll.

Given this daunting information, Montrose did not waste valuable time on fruitless lamentation or discussion. He ordered immediate striking of camp and readiness to move. He sent Black Pate off southwards, at his old task in charge of scouts. And he despatched urgent couriers to ride day and night northwards to Strathbogie and north-westwards to Colkitto in Argyll; also south-west to Douglas and Ogilvy, and southwards to Traquair in the Ettrick Forest. Then he gave orders to march.

Erskine's information was that Leslie was making northwards along the coast road, by Coldingham and the Lammermuir passes of Pease and Cockburnspath, no doubt hoping to reach the waist of Scotland between Forth and Clyde, and so cut off the royalists from their northern and Highland bases. He could do it, too, in the present circumstances, with all that cavalry. Montrose decided to deny him the opportunity. He would march southwards, as Leslie marched north, but well to the west, inland. Once more he would strive to make the land fight for him. He must remain in the hills, where cavalry were least effective, where ambush offered opportunity, where he and his would be at home. They would go south by Gala Water, for the Ettrick Forest, refuge of so many a desperate band from Wallace and Bruce onwards.

By Soutra and Fala Muir they crossed the hills to the long, hidden valley of the Gala Water, that September night, fairly certain that Leslie's scouts would not have observed them, nor would even look for them here.

Next day, half-way to the Tweed and the Forest, Montrose sent fast messengers ahead, into the Merse, south-eastwards, to the Earls of Home and Roxburgh, with instructions to meet him, in the King's name, with all available strength, at Kelso, at the junction of Tweed and Teviot, by midday following.

Black Pate, now behind them with his scouts, sent word that Leslie and his army, with Argyll and the others, were at Dunbar and still proceeding northwards. They had eluded them, this time, gained a breathing-space, at least.

But at Kelso, down Tweed, the next day there was no sign of the Lords Home or Roxburgh, with their levies. Montrose waited an entire dangerous day for them – and dared risk nothing longer. Kelso was too far from the hills, on the edge of the wide open Merse, cavalry country. He turned back for the Forest of Ettrick and the lonely heights.

They went by Teviot. Jedburgh they passed by, for if Roxburgh – who was Kerr of Cessford – had failed them, his kinsman, the earl of Lothian, Kerr of Ferniehirst here, was actually a general of horse in Leslie's army. But at Jedburgh, at least they learned interesting tidings. Home and Roxburgh were now with Leslie, allegedly as prisoners – but since neither of their strong castles of Home and Cessford had been besieged, or even assailed, it seemed obvious that they had elected to give themselves up rather than risk any further association with Montrose. Apparently the tide has turned once more, in Scotland.

There was still Douglas and Ogilvy, and the rendezvous in the Forest. And on the way to it, they might see what John Stewart, Earl of Traquair, could do to help, former Lord High Commissioner from the King, and Treasurer of Scotland. After all, he had sent his son to Bothwell with assurances of loyal support, in men and money; and Linton, a cheerful youngster, was still with them.

They reached the handsome white and venerable house of Traquair, on the Tweed near Innerleithen, on the evening of the 11th. It was a peaceful spot, a rich oasis in the great Forest of Ettrick. Too peaceful by far, for though the Earl was at home, and had received Montrose's message days before, there was no sign of any mustering of men.

If Traquair did not actually slam his door in the face of the King's Captain-General, he did everything but. Cold to the point of rudeness, he declared that he had no men to spare – and indeed ordered his son to withdraw from the royalist force forthwith. He said that he had no reason to believe that the King was coming north, and he had heard that Digby had been utterly defeated on the way. In consequence it was folly to oppose the Committee of the Estates at this juncture, and he for one would have none of it. He urged the Marquis of Montrose to retire with all speed possible to his Highland fastnesses, and the redisperse his force.

James Graham recognised that he ought to have learned his lesson by now: never to put any trust in the Scots nobility – or nine-tenths of it. He was sorry to lose young Lord Linton. He had to restrain some of his men from violently showing Traquair what they thought of him.

They moved down Tweed again, to camp near Elibank. They did not see the messenger whom Traquair despatched northwards in haste.

That evening, at least some of James Graham's trust in his fellow-aristocrats was restored. For into the Elibank camp came marching the Marquis of Douglas and the Lord Ogilvy, with some 400 mounted Douglas levies from Dumfriesshire, a sight to quicken the hearts of all present – even though these were wholly untrained, raw dalesmen from Annandale and Nithsdale. They were cavalry, of a sort, and welcome indeed. And as welcome, indeed, was the fact that some men kept their word. And this was not all. More Douglas and Johnston levies would be coming, when they had been horsed and equipped in two or three days. They were to make for the original rendezvous in the heart of the Forest, at St. Mary's Loch, up Yarrow, on the only practical road over the hills from Moffat and the head of far-away Annandale – how Douglas and Ogilvy had just come. Montrose decided to continue on to this area now, to wait for them. There was levelish ground, around the loch, and there they could lie safe while he licked his new cavalry into shape.

Next day, then, they made their way in that direction, following Tweed down to its junction with Ettrick, at Sunderland, just south of Galashiels and then turning up Ettrick for some three miles, to where Yarrow joined it below the ancient burgh of Selkirk. Here, on the riverside meadows of Philiphaugh, they camped again. One day's more marching up Yarrow would bring them to the St. Mary's Loch rendezvous. There was no hurry, however.

As ever, Montrose chose his night's position with care. It was a fairly strong tactical site, flanked by the river on east and south, with the Yarrow's confluence protecting their rear and steep hillsides to the west. Assault could come only from the Tweed area to the north-east, or down Ettrick from the south-south-west – which latter seemed unlikely, from the Forest fastnesses. Montrose felt reasonably secure here – but he did send Charteris of Amisfield, who had come with Douglas and who claimed to know the district well and was eager to act the soldier, with a picket to watch the junction of Ettrick and Tweed and give warning should there be any approach from the north.

They could sleep secure – or most of them. Montrose himself had a lengthy despatch and memorandum to send to the King, which would take him most of the night. With Douglas, Airlie and others he forded the Ettrick – which was running fairly low after all the good weather – and rode uphill to the little burgh of Selkirk. He got no welcome from the townsfolk.

It was very late before James Graham extinguished the lamp in his lodging in the West Port, his companions asleep hours before. He had ended his letter to Charles urgently requesting a personal appearance in Scotland, alone if he need be, at the earliest possible moment, campaigning season or none.

He was at breakfast not very many hours later, when one of Pate Graham's scout officers, Blackadder by name, burst in on the company unceremoniously, with the dire news.

'We are attacked, my lord!' he exclaimed. 'On two fronts. Both sides of the river. Cavalry attack. In this damned mist . . . !'

Montrose's chair fell with a crash as he jumped to his feet, reaching for his sword. 'Attacks, man? Who attacks? What cavalry? How many?'

'Many. Colonel Graham says regular cavalry. Dragoons . . .'

'Dear God – Leslie!' James Graham was already flinging through the doorway. 'Why was he not seen? Reported? Ere this . . . ?' But he did not wait for an answer.

Neither did he wait for his horse to be saddled, but galloped off bare-back down the hill to the Ettrick haughlands. A white mist rolled thickly over all the lower ground, as so often of a night and early morning blankets the border valleys. He could see neither his own forces nor the enemy under the billowing shroud – but he could hear musketry, shooting.

In the seething jumble of his thoughts the musketry registered – and set him thinking clearly, himself again. That mist was far too thick for musket-fire. Therefore it could only be shooting blind. But it was being kept up. Therefore it was a device. To keep a flank occupied. The only point in that would be from across the river – *this* side. Pinning down forces there. To prevent a crossing. Presumably while the main action developed on the other side. Reasonable tactics in a surprise attack, in mist. The chances were, then, that there would be no assault across the river while the mist remained. Time – time he desperately needed.

Keeping well to the left, upstream, of the shooting, he splashed across Ettrick, his companions not far behind. He cursed its autumnal shallowness now. If it had been running high, as so often, no attack across it would have been possible – and he could not have crossed to Selkirk last night. No point in recriminations and regrets now against himself or others. Somebody had blundered. He had relied too much on others – and so failed in his duty. Now he needed time . . .

He needed more than time, however. When he reached the camp, a scene of dire confusion, it was to find Nathaniel Gordon temporarily in command, the Ogilvy cavalry waiting uncertainly for orders. Colonel O'Cahan was forward somewhere, Gordon reported, beating off an attack from the north. And Colonel

Graham was out in the mist, with his scouts, seeking information. This hellish mist . . . !

'We must make it fight for us, now!' Montrose snapped. 'O'Cahan has all his Ulstermen forward? Then, the rest of the foot? Where?'

'Lining the river-side. Under Lords Erskine and Fleming. To prevent a crossing in flank, my lord.'

'There will be no crossing while the mist lasts. That is a feint, meantime. The cavalry? The Ogilvys are here. What of the Douglas horse? And the rest?'

Gordon coughed. The Marquis of Douglas and the Earl of Crawford had just come up, with Airlie and the others. 'I fear they have . . . dispersed, my lord,' he said. 'At the first charge of Leslie's dragoons. I could not hold them. God knows where they are! This accursed mist . . .'

'Aye. My Lords Crawford and Douglas – search for and find, if you may, these missing squadrons. They will be confused, at a loss. Their first action – and leaderless. Gather them, and hold them ready in reserve. Nat – where is Lord Ogilvy?'

'He has gone seeking to rally the Douglas horse.'

'Yes. My Lord Crawford – when you find him, send my Lord Ogilvy back to me. At once. Nat – marshal the remaining cavalry into two squadrons. The hundred Ogilvys, and a mixed lot of fifty. Now – my trumpeters . . .'

Pate Graham came running up, panting. 'Thank God you are here, James!' For almost the first time, he forgot to address his friend and chief honorifically in public. 'Here's a brawl! There's been treachery – our position betrayed. Traquair, for a wager! No sign of Charteris or his picket. Leslie's entire cavalry army is here, I reckon. I've been forward with O'Cahan. There's a hero! He is holding four regiments of horse, at least, with his 500 Ulster foot. At a burn-channel. But with heavy losses. My scouts say there are two regiments of dragoons across the river – 1,500 at least . . .'

'Any encircling move to the left? On the high ground?'

'Not that I know of. That way the Douglas horse fled. At the first charge.'

'They are untrained, raw. Their first engagement.' He turned. 'Where is Airlie?'

'Here, James,' the old Earl said, quietly, from behind.

'May I take your Ogilvys, my friend? To O'Cahan's aid? Myself?'

'To be sure. I come with you.'

'Nat – command here at the centre, meantime. I cannot order a battle, blind. I go forward with the Ogilvy squadron. To discover the position, and aid O'Cahan. Send the Lord Ogilvy after me. Hold all others in reserve until you receive my orders, foot and horse. The camp here a strong-point.' He mounted a saddled horse. 'All trumpeters sound the Advance!' he called. He raised drawn sword to the Ogilvy ranks. 'Come!'

Mist or none there was no doubt as to which direction to take, at least. Down-river, due northwards, the noise of battle was evident enough, though muffled. The trumpets ringing out eerily, they advanced at as fast a trot as was practicable, in the obscurity. Soon their mounts were shying and tripping over dead bodies, some dead and dying horses also. These seemed to be mainly Douglases. A charge had got thus far – although O'Cahan was still forward of it.

They came upon the Irish line suddenly, almost rode it down indeed, where O'Cahan was skilfully using a tree-lined burn-channel as extended trench. Men and horses, moaning, screaming many of them, lay thick here, in the swirling eddies, a scene out of hell. They found O'Cahan himself, in the centre, his shirt-sleeve ripped off to act as bandage and to keep the blood from a sabre cut out of his eyes. He was calm and cool as ever, however.

'Ha, my lord – here's warm work! We were taken by surprise, this once.'

'Aye, Magnus – I blame myself. But – that can wait. You have a good line here, old friend. You I could trust, at least! Pate says you have lost heavily? In saving us all.'

The other shrugged. 'We have casualties, yes. Half of our 500 perhaps. But – I have the other half, yet.!'

'Dear God – so many lost! Already? My brave Irish! And your head, man?'

'A nothing. Think you this mist is lifting, my lord? Or thinning?'

'A little, yes. I know not whether to be glad or sorry. To see – and to be seen! Our scant numbers.' He nodded forward. 'They come in waves? They can scarce charge in this . . . ?'

'They come at a trot. A regiment at a time. We have had Middleton's first. Dalhousie's. Eglinton's. Leven's own. No foot. Pate Graham says that Kirkcudbright's and Fraser's are across the river . . .'

'The entire Covenant cavalry army! God knows how they got

here. David Leslie is something new in their generals! Not many would have dared an attack in this. With cavalry. This burn-channel – it makes a fair barrier. How far does it extend? Upwards?'

'As far as I have men to hold it! Farther. For we are thin on the ground, thin.'

'I have the Ogilvys, here. One hundred. Are they better dismounted, and aiding you? Or horsed? To counter the next attack?'

'So long as the mist remains thick, dismounted I'd say.'

'I agree. I will keep them close, not scattered. In case . . .'

Montrose gave orders for his troopers to dismount, but to remain centrally grouped around himself and O'Cahan. The Irish to spread out farther. Horses to be taken a little way back.

Even as this manoeuvre was being carried out, they were all but taken by surprise. For Leslie too had recognised that foot were the more effective in these circumstances, and had sent forward a dismounted attack – and kept it as quiet as might be. Only the hollow clumping of heavy thigh-boots and the occasional jingle of spurs, with the muffled curse of a stumbling cavalryman out of his element, gave them a little warning. Then the mass of grey figures loomed out of the billowing vapours, to fling themselves on the defended line of the burn.

Montrose was almost glad to lose himself in hard hand-to-hand fighting. But he well knew that this was not his role, however tempting as an alternative to hard and responsible thinking. Deliberately he disentangled himself, and drew back. As well that he did. For, on a soft area of wet ground where the burn had been apt to overflow, he distinctly felt the earth trembling slightly beneath his feet. That could only be horses' hooves. He could not tell from which side it came; but it was highly unlikely that the Douglas yeomen could have been rounded up and brought back into battle so quickly. The chances were that Leslie was putting in a mounted attack on the heels of the dismounted one – a sound tactic.

James Graham yelled for his Ogilvys to break off, to remount. Airlie and his son Sir David took up the cry. Somehow they got back to their horses, and up, however raggedly. Montrose by no means waited for the last of them. Leading his people forward in no sort of formation, he drove his mount through the press of struggling men in the burn-channel, pushing through the scrub trees and stumbling through the shallow water, slashing at dismounted dragoons. Across, waiting agitatedly for the others, hearing the oncoming cavalry now, he found himself joined by the Lord Ogilvy.

'Thank Heaven you are here, James!' he gasped. 'Help me get them into an arrowhead. A wedge-formation. Quickly – we have only moments.'

Desperately they herded their troopers into some sort of tight wedge-shaped grouping, with Airlie, his two sons, and Montrose himself, at the tip. Then, not waiting for any refinement, he shouted for his trumpeter whose duty it was always to be at his master's heels, to sound the stirring cavalry Charge. Breathless but recognisable the well-known and dread strains blared out. Ignoring the fact that he could not see where he was going, James Graham dug in his spurs, yelling 'A Graham! A Graham!'

The shout was taken up at his back, interspersed with 'An Ogilvy! An Ogilvy!' and knee-to-knee they plunged onwards blindly, straight into a canter.

It was seconds only before they saw the trotting line of advancing dragoons – or at least that part of it immediately in front of them; how far it stretched on either hand, none could tell. It was a daunting sight, at a mere thirty yards or so – but safe to say not nearly so daunting as the charging compact mass that bore down upon the enemy, yelling. The dragoons' line was only four deep, and inevitably only three or four files were at the actual point of impact. Small wonder then that they tended to rein back, aside, anywhere, to be out of the path of that hurtling, menacing band. The wedge slammed through almost without a blow struck, cutting the enemy line in seconds.

Montrose was thankful that it was the veteran Ogilvy horse which were involved, with Airlie and his sons in command. For such a breakthrough could be of little advantage, indeed could be a positive death-trap, if not skilfully exploited and followed up, if the enemy ranks closed again and massed, cutting off the attackers from their own base. Now, he shouted to the Lord Ogilvy to take the left flank, himself taking the right. The wedge split into two behind him, and without appreciable loss of momentum began to roll up the two lines of dragoons – which now had to draw up, turn about in the mist, and try to counter this assault of unknown dimension at their rear.

It was a chaotic business on both sides. But at least Montrose's people knew what they were seeking to do and held the initiative.

Probably they inflicted no large number of casualties; but they broke up that assault completely and sent the enemy fleeing blindly in all directions. Montrose had his trumpeter sound the Recall, and led his section trotting back to the burn-channel. The quite distinct upward trend of the ground from east to west at least allowed them to recognise which way to go. They came up against many of the dismounted first wave retiring, and were able to punish these severely. Ogilvy was back with O'Cahan before them.

'Merry work, my lord,' the Irishman acclaimed.' That will set Leslie thinking.'

'Aye – he will learn that mist can be a two-sided blade. But . . . it lifts, I think ?'

'To be sure. Where will the advantage lie, then ?'

'Not with us, I think. They must then see how pitifully few we are. Our dire lack of cavalry. Save that it allowed them to creep up on us, the mist was to *our* advantage.'

'Yes. And in this position we cannot retire, I think ? Can we ?'

'I would give much to know. I would break off and retire, yes – if I might. To fight on better terms another day. But I much fear we may be trapped, Magnus. David Leslie is an able general – and bold. Bolder than any we have had to face, as yet – or he would not be here this morning, attacking in the mist. He knows our position. He has sent regiments along the *east* side of Ettrick. They wait there now. Think you he will have neglected to stop the gap behind us ? Up Yarrow ? *I* would not, in his place – with all the regiments of horse he has. And if Yarrow is blocked, we are held. I have sent Blackadder to discover it. But I am not hopeful.'

'We must cut our way through then,' Ogilvy said.

'*We* might. But the foot could not.'

'They could disperse. Up into the hills.'

'It may come to that. But not yet . . .'

They watched the mist lighten, the morning brighten, with ever larger clear patches. No new attack developed. Leslie had learned his lesson and was waiting for clear vision.

A rider from the Marquis of Douglas came to announce that he and Crawford had collected over 100 of the Douglas horse, and more were coming in. His men had not been craven, merely leaderless and confused. Montrose sent the messenger back with orders to use all men to guard the river-bank meantime.

Gradually visibility improved, with an ominous quiet over

the battlefield. Even the rattle of musketry from across Ettrick died away. The quiet was only relative, of course, since it included the cries and moans of wounded men and the whinnying and screaming of hamstrung and broken-legged horses.

Captain Blackadder cantered up to report that the narrows of the vale of Yarrow behind them were blocked by cavalry. They must have found their way across the hills during the early morning. That way there was no escape.

Montrose nodded grimly.

'What happened to Charteris of Amisfield – tell me that!' the Lord Ogilvy demanded. 'He was sent forward to guard the northern approach. All this descends upon us, and he sends us no word.'

'He may have been overwhelmed. Cut off. I blame myself for sending a man insufficiently experienced. But – I had no reason to believe that Leslie was within fifty miles of us!' Montrose spread his hands. 'That does not absolve me from blame. I have failed in this. Taken too much for granted.'

'Do not assail yourself, James,' old Airlie exclaimed. 'There has been treachery, that is certain. I say Traquair is at the back of it. *He* knew where we were heading for, our state, our numbers – the King's Lord Treasurer! I swear he sent word hot-foot to Leslie. A rider sent forthwith and fast could have reached Leslie, in Lothian, by dawn yesterday. And his cavalry, riding south all yesterday and part of last night, could have reached Tweed in time for this.'

'That is true . . .'

All the time he had been peering ahead of him, northwards. Now, at last, they were beginning to see the enemy. Actually they saw those across the Ettrick first, less than the two regiments reported, probably only one, mounted, waiting. They were unlikely to wait much longer.

The main mass of Leslie's force however was massed half a mile to the north, on the haughland west of the river, a cavalry host under a forest of banners, a gallant and colourful sight such as James Graham, for one, had always most dreaded to see. Amidst all his campaigning he had dreamed of this, and awakened sweating in the night – to see a huge and overwhelming host of well-trained and veteran horse, hopelessly outnumbering his own, and with no avenue of escape open to him. Even counting the Douglas contingent as effective, Leslie outnumbered him in cavalry twenty to one. The nightmare had come true. Lacking his experienced Gordons, to say nothing of Colkitto's warriors, he was as a man naked in the face of his foes.

He dared not show the least hint of his despair, of course. Nor did he let himself dwell on the hopelessness of the situation. He was faced with a grievous choice – to fight the best battle possible, and go down bravely and with honour; or to seek to save as much as he could from the wreckage, at all costs, for the King's cause.

He had no doubts in his mind as to his own preference. He had fought a good enough fight hitherto, and he would choose to end it in the same fashion. His own life was not so full of joy and felicity that he must cling to it, award it over-high a value – so long as his honour survived. But nor was he in any doubt but that this was a selfish attitude, well enough for a private soldier. He was not that. He was a general, and must take a general's view. He was the King's representative, and responsible mean-time for the entire future of the royal cause in Scotland. There could be no question as to his over-riding duty, however repugnant to himself. He was not the first commander faced with the same grim choice.

Fortunately he did not have to spell it out to his companions. Magnus O'Cahan did it for him.

'My lord Marquis – neither tactics nor strategy will serve to win this day for us – even yours. The thing is plain to see. But you can still save much that is of value to the King's Grace. The foot can by no means escape this trap – but much of the horse can. You must cut your way out, my lord. As you cut through those, just now. It is the only way, now. All Leslie's cavalry are here. When they attack, on three fronts, you are lost.'

'And leave you, and your Ulstermen? And the rest of my brave infantry? To your fate, Magnus?'

'We are in God's hands,' the other said simply. 'And we have no choice. Nor have you. You must save what you can, my lord.'

There was a murmur of agreement from the other officers clustered around.

Montrose moistened dry lips. 'It may come to that,' he acceded, low-voiced. 'But not yet. Leslie has us cornered, yes – but he has yet to spring the trap. He may yet make a wrong move.'

Bugles blowing to the northwards were the signal for the enemy assault. The attack across the river, being nearest at hand, developed first; but the entire main body began to move forward at the trot. Perhaps a thrust would come from the rear likewise; but the mist had not yet lifted from the narrow mouth of the Yarrow valley, and the commander there might hold back, preferring to act only as stop-gap.

Looking to the right, then front, then right again, Montrose made his decision. 'Try to hold your position, Magnus, for a little,' he jerked, pointing forward. 'Enormous odds. But I will be back, I promise you.' Turning to the waiting Ogilvys, he pointed right-handed, eastwards. 'To the river!' he shouted.

The Covenant regiment there was in process of fording Ettrick, on a fairly wide front, a difficult proceeding when opposed. But with perhaps 1,000 of them, against an opposition of no more than 300, they could hardly fail to succeed.

Montrose neither went to reinforce the defenders nor led directly against the enemy. Instead he spurred down to the river, a fair way below the fording regiment, and plunged straight across, the Ogilvys after him, splashing water high.

Unopposed, and less careful of their horses' footing than the heavier dragoons, they made the crossing a deal more quickly than their foes – who indeed were now faltering doubtfully, some even beginning to turn back. Clambering up the far bank, Montrose swung right-handed, upstream. And now his 100 were behind the enemy. They bore down upon those struggling to get back to dry land, swords slashing.

Caught in a direly exposed and unsteady position in the river, the dragoons' commander was in a quandary, entrenched opposition in front, cavalry behind. That there was only a comparatively small number of the latter was obvious – but so also was the Royal Standard of Scotland which Montrose's trumpeter bore aloft behind his master, worth another squadron in itself, so renowned was the Captain-General's reputation. The dragoons chose to press forward.

Or some of them did. Others decided that survival was more important than victory, and turned off up and down the river, seeking escape. Far from desiring to discourage this, Montrose drew his horse-pistol and pointed at the central splashing group.

'The main body!' he cried. 'Shoot at the main body. Leave these others.'

It was short range, and even pistols were fairly effective. The musketeers on the far bank redoubled their efforts. The dragoons fell like ninepins, amidst considerable panic and confusion. When their colonel splashed heavily into the Ettrick, chaos took over.

But already the sounds of clash were evident from the north, where Leslie's main force had come up against O'Cahan's thin line defending the vital burn-channel. Clearly this could not last long.

Reining his mount round, James Graham waved to his Ogilvys to break off and follow him. He spurred into a full gallop, still down the east bank.

Leslie could not fail to see it, nor the small numbers involved. Still, it might effect some slight easement of the pressure on O'Cahan.

They rode on down Ettrick, the Lion Rampant fluttering above them bravely, well past the level of the enemy ranks. Inevitably Leslie had to detach one of his regiments, to turn back to deal with them. Whenever Montrose saw this, he swung down to ford the river again, at once – before they in turn were faced with an opposed crossing. It was not the best stretch for fording; but nowhere was it so deep, at this season, that horses could not cross. They splashed and floundered over, just in time.

Now they were faced with an entire regiment advancing upon them. But once again this was in extended formation, not in column. Shouting to form wedge behind him again, Montrose wasted not a moment to give the enemy time to reform, but lashed his horse into the charge, there and then.

The spearhead had only just formed at his back, and less tightly than desirable, when Montrose crashed into a section of the enemy line, smiting, Airlie at one knee, Ogilvy at the other, the trumpeter with the banner immediately behind. The shock was fierce and he was all but unseated, but sheer pressure from the others kept him up. He was vaguely aware of a sword grazing his shoulder and clanging against his breastplate, also of a man screaming, open-mouthed but unheard, before him and falling away, with another behind him reining desperately aside. Then they were through, pushed on by the thundering mass at their backs.

This time he did not, dared not, signal for any swing right and left behind the broken line. The dragoons were far too many for anything of the sort. Instead he pressed right on, slantwise, across the haughland, making for the high ground.

Leslie could not ignore this, of course, at his immediate rear. Bugles blowing, he turned most of his remaining force to face the north again.

There was no question of any attack on this major formation

which had turned to face them. And the regiment behind would be re-forming, since it had been only broken, not shattered Montrose swung away, climbing.

The land steepened quickly, and no enemy barred the way. There was a real temptation just to ride on, and away, over the hills – as Magnus had advised. Save at least this Ogilvy horse intact. None could stop them now. It was never seriously considered as a programme, however. Part-way up the hill-side, they reined up.

'Well, my friends,' James Graham panted, 'you see it all. We are trapped. Or our foot is, and Douglas. Here is a battle we can by no means win. Your advice, gentlemen?'

'What *is* there to say, James?' Airlie demanded. 'We go down fighting. What else?'

'Or *some* of us do,' his heir amended. 'My Lord James, and yourself, sir, should go. Now leave the field. While you may. Save at least the high command. Ride off, over this hill. And fight, to win, another day.'

'So say I,' his brother, Sir David, agreed.

'That is all your advice, my friends? To fall, or to flee?'

'What else can we do, James? We are no more than a gadfly against this host. We can dart and sting and harass it. But we cannot beat it. Or even greatly harm it.' That was Airlie.

'A gad-fly may yet sting a man into anger which can breed folly! And folly as we know, can lose battles. I intend to sting further. Before I flee! Or fall.' Montrose raised his hand, to point southwards. 'The enemy force sent to stop the mouth of Yarrow have not moved. Have not shown themselves. That could mean that they are the weakest link in this chain that binds us. If we could break that . . . ?'

The mist had all gone now, and a golden, mellow September sun illumined the Borderland. It glinted on steel, there where the wooded hillsides guarded the entrance to Yarrow's valley; but it was impossible to say how many men might be there.

'It may be strongly held . . .'

'It may. But, if you were Leslie, would you send a strong force there? Merely to block our retreat? Not to attack us. With the position itself strong.'

'No-o-o.'

'Nor would I. It is a chance, a mere chance. But lacking any other chances I am inclined to take it.'

'How so?'

'A charge down to the river again. They will try to stop us – but will not, I think. Across, at speed. Then upstream, as before we came down. But farther. Up to the junction of Ettrick and Yarrow rivers. Cross Ettrick again, higher. Into those woods between the two rivers. Then ford Yarrow *behind* that force. They would not see us. Not until we were upon them.'

'Phe-e-ew!'

'That would take time, James.'

'Less time than if we ran away! Or fell! It will not take so long – as I intend to ride! Two miles in all – less. Six minutes?'

'My lord – the regiment we broke up, at the first fording, has re-formed. Beyond the river. It is drawn up there . . .'

'I see it, David. But we have smashed through them once, and can do so again. They will be the more ready to break. And the fact that they have formed up there, across the river again, shows that they have little belly for fight. My lord Viscount Kirk-cudbright's dragoons!'

'We could go more quickly behind. Up this hill. And down upon Yarrow from above,' Lord Ogilvy suggested. 'And save a clash on the way.'

'To be sure. But part of our duty is to aid O'Cahan. This may help him a little. The other would not. Would seem as though we fled. Come, then – enough of talk. The wedge again – and forward!'

Straight into the charge they plunged downhill. Leslie's main force was stretched in a long line to their right, just out of musket-range of O'Cahan; and the regiment which they had already cut through was re-formed and now tightly grouped between them and the river. The sudden headlong advance probably took Leslie by surprise, for there was no visible reaction for a little – and time was of the essence, with only half a mile for the galloping horses to cover to the Ettrick. They were, in fact, half-way there before the long line of the main body began to move forward. The single regiment stayed where it was.

Montrose, concerned at the difficulty in keeping his tight formation at this speed on broken ground, abruptly perceived their dire danger. Leslie's massive line was not hastening forward – as it required to do if it was to try to intercept their rush to the river. It moved only at a trot. This could mean only one thing – musket-fire. Because he had never had dragoons to command, he had forgotten; these were heavy cavalry, equipped not with horse-pistols but with short-barrelled muskets, carbines. These had four times the range of pistols, as well as much greater accuracy. If they rode within range of these, massed close as his people were, it would be massacre, a target none could miss. Cursing his lack of previous perception, Montrose raised his sword high, to gesture with it half-left, to swing away north-wards. And at the same time he yelled to disperse, break up the formation, open out.

It was not so easy. Speed, impetus, the downhill slope, even lack of understanding amongst the men, ensured that. The mass was still far too tight-knit, even though veering well to the left, when the first shots cracked out.

Now, at least, there was no need to explain, to persuade. Only fools would fail to see the danger. Lashing their beasts, horse-men sought to draw away from their fellows, as men and horses began to fall.

Now along the entire, long, enemy front there was firing. The range was in most cases extreme. But lead was flying thickly – and finding marks all too frequently. The Ogilvy horse was running the gauntlet.

The ordeal did not last for long, with the targets pulling away even more to the left, and the distance to the river closing fast. But it was grim indeed for a few moments, and losses heavy.

And now there was the second menace. For the isolated regiment, Middleton's Montrose now recognised, had seen its opportunity, the foe no longer a hard-hitting wedge but a scatter of individuals. It strung out to intercept carbines firing here also.

That any sizeable proportion of the royalist cavalry got through the barrier was due to impetus, the advantage of the fast-moving over the static. Montrose, suffering no more than a graze on the thigh from a musket-ball, slashed his way through, with his standard-bearer and old Airlie still close at his back. But neither of the Ogilvy sons were there now. Down to the river they plunged, and across. Barely three minutes had passed since the order to advance.

Across the water, they drew up and looked back, Airlie's features as set as those of James Graham. Men were splashing over, wide scattered – but it was clear that they would be fortu-nate to muster much more than half of their original strength.

They could not wait for stragglers, for Middleton's regiment, its confidence restored, was coming after them, and shooting as it came. Sir David Ogilvy turned up at the last moment, slightly wounded; but there was no sign of his elder brother.

'I am sorry,' Montrose jerked, to the father. 'He may be well enough. Dismounted only. Did you see him fall?'

Airlie shook his grey head, and rode on.

Less than sixty of them now, they galloped upstream. They could see Kirkcudbright's regiment – or what remained of it – assembled in front of them, back a little from the river-side, out of range of Nat Gordon's muskets. Without surprise, or any other advantage now, any straightforward attack on them would be madness, with the odds still possibly five-to-one. They would never get through. Montrose's plan had to be scrapped. Anyway, it was doubtful whether he now had enough men to mount a surprise assault on the rear of the Yarrow stop-gap.

He pointed across the river, to their own camp area. Much of Middleton's regiment was in hot pursuit not far behind.

They were barely over Ettrick, water dripping off the horses, when Montrose was shouting.

'Nat – a runner to O'Cahan. To retire. If he can. To a shorter line. Yonder shallow ravine. We are too extended. My Lord Douglas – how many have you gathered?'

'Near 200, Jamie. We have held these others off...'

'Aye. Pate – how many in that Yarrow gap. Have you a notion?'

'A complete regiment, my lord. Fraser's, I think.'

'One regiment? Then we must try to fight our way through it. Our only hope. The woodlands. We will hold this river-line till O'Cahan can get back. Then a leap-frogging retiral. Up Yarrow. My Lord Crawford – take two troops of Douglas horse. Up-river. To that bend, there. Wait there, where these enemy may see you. You will pose a threat. Of an upper crossing. The Ogilvys will take your place here, meantime. If Middleton is with his regiment over there, we are like to have another attack. He is no shrinking lily! He will spur on Kirkcudbright's reluctant warriors...'

With or without Colonel John Middleton – who had once served under Montrose – when his dragoons did join up with the waiting ranks across the river, there was a prompt and positive reaction. The combined force was swiftly split up into troops of about seventy strong, some ten of these, to be sent off, up and down stream, to line the banks about 100 yards apart. At a bugle's blast they all began the fording process simultaneously.

Montrose bit his lip. He could not hope to cope with this successfully, with his small numbers. Some must get over almost unopposed. He spread his available men as best he could – but all realised that it was hopeless.

They made the enemy pay dearly for that crossing. But before they were outflanked Montrose issued orders to retire to higher ground, calling back Crawford.

As they moved back, Pate Graham raced up to announce that O'Cahan, with barely 100 men remaining of his 500, had fallen back, as ordered, but could not hold the second line with so few. He proposed to stand, form a square, a hedgehog, and go down to the last man.

James Graham groaned aloud. 'My stout Magnus! Not that – not that! Back to him, Pate. Tell him . . .'

He was interrupted by a horseman clattering up, wounded, hatless, one of Blackadder's scout officers. 'My lord,' he gasped, 'Fraser's regiment advances. To attack your rear. Out of Yarrow. See there . . .' And in the act of turning in his saddle to point, he swayed and crashed to the ground.

Montrose raised his head in a strange gesture that was almost relief, and stared around him. It would all be over in ten minutes now. Complete and utter defeat.

A clamour of voices were urging, demanding, a dash for it immediately – Douglas's, Fleming's, Erskine's, young Archie Napier's, Nat Gordon's – though not Airlie's, whose heir was somewhere on that stricken field. Montrose could do no more, they declared. He was the King's Viceroy. The royal cause must go on. Fight another day. Flee, now . . .

Slowly, gravely, James Graham nodded his head. 'As you will,' he said. 'I accept the full responsibility for this decision. Pate – my salute to Colonel O'Cahan. Tell him that he is *not* to fight on. My command. His men to disperse. Into the hills and woods. As best they can. Some will escape. And, Pate – tell Magnus of my love for him. The truest and bravest! Tell him that when next we meet, God willing, he will be Sir Magnus! Off with you. Then follow me southwards. Up Yarrow. Rendezvous, the Loch of St. Mary. God-speed, Pate . . .!'

As his friend hurried off, Crawford rode up. 'The river-line breaks, Montrose. We cannot hold them longer . . .'

'I know it, my lord. It is enough. My command to all. Horse to me here, quickly. All foot to disperse. Save themselves as best they can. Run. Not to yield – run! Our enemies' slogan is "Jesus and No Quarter!" Remind all. To my sorrow and shame. But my grateful thanks . . .' He turned. 'And now, gentlemen – another wedge! For the last time. All remaining horse. Fraser's regiment has not tasted our steel yet. Form up. We shall give these others a moment to come up.' He reached out to grip Airlie's forearm. 'I am sorry, old friend . . .'

'I leave . . . my son . . . in God's hands,' the other muttered. 'Again!'

In the event, that final dash was less taxing than most feared. The cavalry wedge, about eighty strong, got away before the regiment from the river reached the camp area, and before Leslie's main body had got past O'Cahan. And spurring uphill, they found Fraser's regiment in troop formation, spread over the widest front – ideal to catch stragglers of a defeated army, but hopeless to counter a determined arrowhead charge. In fact, actual contact was with only one troop, and this made a gesture rather than any real attempt to halt them. Then they were past, and driving on hard. Yarrow's wooded hill-sides swallowed them up.

It was all too easy, swift, anti-climax. If pursuit there was, none was evident. It still lacked an hour till noon.

James Graham would have wept if he could, as he rode. But he was beyond tears.

CHAPTER TWELVE

St. Mary's Loch was far too close to Philiphaugh to be a safe rendezvous at which to linger long. Picking up a few stragglers there, including Pate Graham, the fugitives pressed on, due northwards now, deciding that to hang about in the Ettrick Forest area waiting for possible Douglas recruits would be un-realistic in the circumstances. They went by Mountbenger and the heights of Minchmoor, and so down to the Quair Water. They hammered on Traquair's door in the by-going, but gained no response. That particular bird appeared to have flown.

The Lord Fleming pointed out that his house at Biggar was within riding distance. They could eat and rest there; none would seek them in the Upper Ward of Lanarkshire, that night. So, in the dusk, they climbed out of Tweeddale and westwards over lower green hills, weary, hungry, jaded. But by no means in despair. Fiercely James Graham had put anything such from him. He had suffered his first major defeat, and sacrificed some of his good friends; but he still had much – or the cause had. He had chosen to keep alight the King's cause, and he would do so.

That determination was reinforced when a single horseman, pursuing them was allowed to catch up, in the Skirling area. To their surprise, it was an infantryman, one of O'Cahan's Irish officers, MacDermott by name. Flinging aside the Highland plaid he wore, he revealed himself to be still more colourfully clad. Wrapped around him were the silken folds of the Ulster Brigade's standard. He handed it to Montrose, with a flourish.

'You will find another company to serve under it, sir – but you will never find a better!' he panted.

'That I well know, friend,' Montrose agreed, touched. 'I thank you. But – how come you here, thus?'

'There was a great slaughter at the end, lord. We left it too late. I feigned dead. Amongst the dead. This flag was nearby. Under Captain O'Donnell. I dragged it beneath myself. And so lay. Until they left us. And I found me a riderless horse. Och, there were many of them . . .'

'A great slaughter, you say? And you left it too late? Do you mean that your people did not disperse? That O'Cahan was taken?'

'Aye, sir. *He* was taken. But the rest slain. Cut down there and then.'

'You mean that they took them prisoner? And then slew them, defenceless?'

'I do so. Every one, yes, by God! Barring Colonel O'Cahan himself. And Major Lachlan. And my own self, whom they thought dead. God's curse on them! They cut them down, standing there. Their priests, it was – the black crows! The ministers . . .'

'Jesus and No Quarter!' Fleming snarled.

'You tell me that Leslie killed all prisoners save the officers?' Montrose's voice quivered. 'At the demand of the ministers?'

'Not all officers, sir. Only the highest were spared. Spared to be hanged they said!'

'Dear God! Magnus . . .!'

'I told him, Jamie,' Pate Graham put in. 'I said you commanded him to disperse. To run for it. I said the Covenant zealots were merciless. He still had time, opportunity . . .'

'He aimed to keep the enemy busy, lord,' MacDermott explained. 'Until *yourself* had got clear away. That was the size of him!'

James Graham bowed his head.

Into the hush, the Earl of Airlie spoke uncertainly. 'My son . . .? The Lord Ogilvy? Did you see aught of him?'

'Aye, lord. He is prisoner. I saw him. Wounded. Colonel Gordon, also. And the lame one, Rollo. And the other Ogilvy, the young captain . . .'

'Inverquharity.' Airlie sighed, with a mixture of relief and apprehension. 'Thank God he is alive, at the least. So far!'

None commented on the Earl's last words.

'Did you see the Marquis of Argyll, Captain? Was he there?' Montrose asked.

'I know him not, lord. But many great folk rode up. When the fighting was over. With the ministers – flocks of the ministers.'

With much to think upon, they rode on to Biggar.

After only a few hours for rest and refreshment they were off again next morning, before dawn, still heading northwards, Montrose determined to get back into the Highlands where he could summon renewed support, get Colkitto back, and Aboyne.

He must regroup, and re-attack. He was in a hurry now. Hangings had to be prevented, at all costs. This would best be done by posing a threat. And that required men, many men. The Athollmen who had so gallantly aided him in the past, and were quickly mustered, would have won in their harvest by now. Atholl had been the first to give him large-scale support. He would go to Atholl.

The crossings of Forth would almost certainly be held against him. It must be the secret, devious causeways of the Flanders Moss again, then. Avoiding Stirling, they would make for the Campsie Fells.

They were not challenged, that hard-riding company, as they raced up the centre of Lowland Scotland. The word of the Philiphaugh disaster had not yet reached the country at large, and until it did the Marquis of Montrose was still master of the kingdom – even though Leslie would never have neglected to send swift orders ahead to guard the Forth, the ferries east of Stirling, and the bridges there and to the west.

They passed close to Kilsyth that evening, the site of triumph only a few brief weeks before – a wryly humbling experience. Threading the lonely Carron valley of the Campsies thereafter, they camped therein again, only eight miles from the edge of the great Flanders Moss. They dared not seek to cross that watery waste, in darkness, without MacGregor guides.

At daybreak, amongst the mists, they did so, unimpeded, leading their horses over the under-water causeways and twisting deer-tracks, arousing clouds of protesting wildfowl. Wet and muddy, but relieved, they climbed out beyond, into the Menteith uplands. They were safe now. These were the foothills of the Highland Line. Therein no Lowlander would lay hands on James Graham and his friends.

They spent two days at the hospitable MacGregor house of Glengyle, near Loch Katrine – despite the fact that the mistress of the house was a Campbell – resting themselves and their beasts, and treating wounds. Montrose's own superficial thigh-wound had stiffened up, so that he could barely walk, with even riding painful. Donald MacGregor of Glengyle had left the army after Kilsyth, like so many another, to attend to his harvest. Now it was gathered in, and he was a free man again. He would come with them, and seventy of his clansmen. It was an encouraging start.

The two days were by no means wasted, for Montrose used

them to send out messengers far and near, summoning men to Atholl at the earliest possible moment. He wrote in the King's name, and peremptorily.

On the second evening at Glengyle another refugee from Philiphaugh turned up, son of MacGregor of Comar, who had been with Nat Gordon at the Ettrick. That he had got so far and so quickly, on foot, was a tribute to his stamina as it was to his ability. He had escaped the final massacre by throwing himself into the river, and lying for hours under an overhanging bank. He had not seen the terrible things that were done, therefore – but he had heard them. And had later seen the heaps of slain. The ministers had behaved like madmen, he said, screaming about the Sword of the Lord and of Gideon, and slaying the Ishmaelites, and treading down the Winepress of God. They were drunk with blood. And not only on the battlefield of Philiphaugh. All over the Lowlands all who could be linked with the name of Montrose were being rounded up and slaughtered, camp-followers, villagers who had given food and shelter to the royalist army, the folk of districts where they had camped. There were hangings, shootings, drownings. As far north as Linlithgow Bridge, scores were flung over the bridge-parapet into the Avon – and those who tried to swim ashore driven back by musket-butts to drown, men, women and children. Everywhere terror reigned, with the zealots, not the military, in command. Argyll was master of Scotland again.

Montrose did not sleep that night.

Next morning they rode on northwards, though Breadalbane, to Atholl.

Not to involve too grievously the young Earl of Atholl, who had already suffered much from Argyll's reprisals, Montrose did not make his headquarters at Blair-in-Atholl but in the quiet side-glen of Fincastle, off Tummel, whose Stewart laird was sympathetic. From here he wrote a stiff and formal letter to Argyll. He told him that he was unbelievedly shocked at what was being done to their fellow-subjects of King Charles, the more so as apparently it was done in the name of religion, the final blasphemy. He warned the Campbell, and his colleagues, that all such slaughters and savageries must stop immediately, or the consequences would be visited drastically upon his Campbell lands of Lorne and Argyll, which were now within his, Montrose's, grasp. His Major-General Sir Alastair MacDonald was there now, and could be instructed to take the most vehement reprisals. Also he, Montrose, held a number of Covenant hostages and prisoners and could collect many more. If any hurt came to the prisoners, taken after Philiphaugh, these would be the first to suffer – but only the first.

James Graham did not know how much of this threat he could bring himself to carry out. But the writing of the letter did him good – and might have some effect.

Soon the hanging valley of Glen Fincastle was an armed camp, with contingents coming in from all over Atholl, and from the Graham lands of Strathearn and Mentieth and the Drummond and Hay territories of Almond and Gowrie. There was still no sign of Colkitto from the West, or of the Gordons from the North. But Airlie had gone off, with Douglas, to recruit in Angus – where the latter had large lands, being in fact also Earl of Angus. Individuals arrived, singly and in groups, finding their way to these remote fastnesses by devious routes – and all telling grim tales of the reign of terror prevailing in the South. Amongst them came the old Lord Napier, actually carried in a litter by stalwart MacGregor clansmen, a frail, sick man, but determined – and with probably the shrewdest political brain in Scotland, now that Sir Thomas Hope was laid low. By the end of September, Montrose had 600 men assembled, with twice as many promised.

Soon after, he had a letter from the King. It expressed Charles's condolences in the set-back, his continued confidence in his Captain-General, and his promise of armed assistance. He also expressed renewed optimism over the successful outcome of his affairs in England. All would yet be well.

Montrose did not find cause for major rejoicing over this royal epistle although he made the most of it. Next day, news was brought from Edinburgh. Magnus O'Cahan had been hanged, without trial, on the Castle-hill there, as an Irish interloper and brigand, without rights. And the parliament called for the 20th of October was changed to be a meeting of the Committee of Estates, to sit in judgment on the other prisoners and malignants, on charges of treason against the realm, Sir Archibald Johnston of Warriston prosecuting for the Crown.

James Graham shut himself up in a room of the house of Fincastle, a man desolate. He mourned Magnus O'Cahan as he would his own brother. And the bitterness swelled within him.

It was not in the man, however, to mope inactive. To do what he intended, to save those others who faced a similar fate, he required an army, not of 600 but of 6,000. And above all, cavalry. With still nothing from Aboyne and the Gordons, he decided on a lightning dash across the Mounth, in person, to Strathbogie. Pride could find no place in this; the lives of fine men were at stake.

So he and Pate Graham hurried across the Grampians, by Moulin and Strathardle and Glen Shee, to the Dee. And still northwards, over the Mounth passes, in wild free-riding, to come down to the low ground again just south of Strathbogie.

James Graham had a strange encounter with Aboyne, that young man torn between guilt and defiance, sympathy and uncertainty. While not conceding that his Gordons would have made all the difference at Philiphaugh, he pressed for details of the battle and indicated where mistakes had been made. He was loud in his condemnation of Colkitto, and stigmatised the Douglas horse as south-country sheep. He bewailed the capture of his old colleague Ogilvy, but pointed out that he had ever been rash. Nat Gordon, he declared, deserved all that came to him, little better than a bandit. It was all a grievous business – but the fortunes of war.

Montrose listened to all this, drawing on his reserves of forbearance – for he needed what only this young man could supply. What of the future, he asked? What of Gordon power? Had Aboyne received his messages?

The other admitted that he had – but that it was difficult, difficult. After some beating about the bush he informed that he had in fact some 1,500 men mustered, ready – but his father's hand was heavy. Huntly was, indeed, uncomfortably close at hand, having left his refuge in far-away Strathnaver and come south to the castle of Gight, no less. He was insisting that no move could be made without his authority. And so close as Gight, none could deny that he was still Cock o' the North, master of all the Gordons.

Montrose made up his mind there and then. He must see Huntly in person.

Not to allow that strangely wary and atypical magnate to slip away and avoid him, James Graham did not inform Aboyne of his project until ready to set out – for the sly and hostile Lord Lewis was at Strathbogie and might well warn his father. Then they rode as hard as they might for Gight. But it was not to be, not possible in Gordon country apparently, to approach the Gordon chief unawares. Huntly was gone by the time they reached Gight, having left word with his major-domo that he was gone for some days, destination unspecified.

Disappointed but determined, Montrose set to work again on Aboyne. He had gone counter to his father's unreasonable commands before – why not now ? When so much hung upon it – the King's entire cause in Scotland ? His father claimed to be the King's friend, was his hereditary Lieutenant of the North. If a blow was not struck now against the King's enemies, the campaign would possibly collapse. To say nothing of the lives of many illustrious captives.

Aboyne capitulated. He would give orders to march the next day. Almost he seemed in a hurry, now, the decision taken.

Unfortunately, next day, the Lord Lewis insisted on accompanying them. Montrose could scarcely forbid it, especially as many Gordons looked on the younger brother as their leader, in Huntly's absence, rather than Aboyne who had been so long in England. He was only just nineteen but had been out of control and acting the brigand-leader since he was thirteen. They marched southwards at the head of no fewer than 1,800 Gordons.

It did not take long for Montrose's misgivings to be justified. The second day out, in the Dee valley, the Lord Lewis announced that a messenger had arrived from his father. Middleton, now promoted Major-General for his part at Philiphaugh, with 1,000 horse, had come north to Aberdeenshire, specifically to threaten Gordon – or so said Huntly – and was now at Turriff, enrolling local levies from Forbes, Fraser and other enemies of Gordon. The host was to return at once. Huntly however, according to his younger son, sent the Marquis of Montrose his good wishes, and assured him of his continuing support of the King's cause.

Montrose, trusting neither Lewis nor his sire, was prepared to believe that it was all a trick – but could scarcely say so. Aboyne wanted him to turn back with them, to deal with Middleton. But even if the threat at Turriff was genuine, this was the last thing that James Graham was prepared to do at this juncture. His eyes were firmly fixed on the main danger, in the South, and on the saving of the lives of his captured lieutenants. He insisted that they march on. Huntly could raise 5,000 Gordons if so he wished. He did not need this 1,800. And if he required sons to officer his force, he had four others. And Lord Lewis might like to return to lead them ?

Lewis would return, assuredly – but he would take the Gordons with him. It came to another unseemly clash, the two brothers at loggerheads – and ended with Lewis marching back northwards again, with all who would follow him, slightly more than half the total.

And next day, in Glen Shee, with another and more peremptory command coming from Huntly, Aboyne also turned back, with the remainder of the force.

Montrose humiliated, frustrated, returned to the Dee, and sent urgent messages to Huntly, pointing out that he was Viceroy and Captain-General. He had complete royal authority, in Scotland, to dispose the King's forces as he thought best. Middleton could never seriously threaten Gordon with a force of 1,000 dragoons, two regiments. Let him, Montrose, have the Gordon strength to spearhead a swift assault on Glasgow, before the Committee of Estates' meeting and trials, and to deal with Leslie; then he promised that he would hurry back to the North to dispose of Middleton – if Huntly had not already done so.

While he impatiently waited for a reply, he busied himself with recruiting in Mar and Deeside, raising Farquharsons, Irvines and some northern Douglases. No reply came from Huntly, and when inexorable time allowed him to wait no longer, sore at heart he left Braemar for Atholl, with a bare 300 men, only half of them horsed.

At Fincastle he found Airlie and Douglas already returned, with some 600 recruits. There were also other miscellaneous adherents arrived – but no sign of Colkitto. They now had a force of some 1,600, about one third cavalry – but totally untrained cavalry. And Montrose had no time to train it. It was the 22nd of October, and the ominous meetings of the Committee would have started. He had to do what he could with what he had. He ordered a march on Glasgow.

They were at Loch Earn the day following when a relay of messengers caught up with them. One was from the Reverend Zachary Boyd in Glasgow, announcing that the Committee, concerned at Montrose's near presence, had postponed its meetings, as such, but had started forthwith on hasty trials. Sir William Rollo, Montrose's lame friend who had doggedly taken part in most of the campaigns, had been tried, condemned and executed at the Mercat Cross the same day. Sir Philip Nisbet, who had fought with Montrose in England, had followed him to the scaffold. Then young Ogilvy of Inverquharity, although still only in his teens – and despite many pleas for clemency. There was a long list to follow. This messenger also announced that Leslie was in Glasgow for the moment, to receive the thanks of the Committee, and a gift of 50,000 merks – Middleton also, 30,000 – out of the confiscated estate of the Marquis of Douglas; but that Leslie's army was in the main still in Central Scotland, with rumours of royalist assault from England.

The second courier was, in fact, from the King, He announced that Digby and Langdale were once again on their way north, with 1,500 trained horse. They should reach the border by the end of the month, and Charles requested his Captain-General to move south to meet them there.

The third message was from Aboyne, who declared that he had now convinced his father that Middleton was no major threat meantime, and that 1,000 Gordons might be spared. He hoped therefore to join Montrose in a few days time.

James Graham, it is to be feared, did not nowadays accord his illustrious sovereign's pronouncements the respect that would be seemly in a viceroy. He would believe in Digby's 1,500 when he saw them, and not before. Aboyne's 1,000 likewise. He certainly would not go rushing south to the border. But the execution of Rollo, young Inverquharity and Nisbet appalled him, and the threat of more of it forced his hand. He could not wait for further reinforcements. He had to continue his march on Glasgow forthwith.

Keeping within the skirts of the Highlands, he hastened west by south, burning now, deliberately, as he went. For all the Lennox foothill area formed Glasgow's skyline to the north, and the sight of smoke-clouds drawing ever nearer – even if they were only caused by burning stubbles and heather – could have a salutory effect. If terror was to stalk Scotland, he must try to induce some of it. The MacGregors, to whom this sort of thing was second nature, co-operated enthusiastically.

Montrose's own Graham lands of Fintry, Endrick and Mugdock had been harried and ravaged unmercifully times without number, and were little better than a desert. He halted therefore at Buchanan, at the foot of Loch Lomond, a mere dozen miles north of the city – where he could make a quick retreat into the mountains if necessary – and summoned Glasgow to surrender to the King's forces, on pain of sack. And to deliver up to himself all members of the Committee of Estates therein, and all other rebels and murderers.

He prayed God that the threat would be enough.

To some extent it was. The trials were hastily abandoned, and the inquisitors fled – unfortunately taking their prisoners with them. Provost Bell sent Sir Robert Douglas again, to Montrose, assuring him of the city's goodwill and loyalty, complete lack of sympathy with the Committee of Estates, but lack of power to halt their escape. He sent urgent pleas that no armed descent upon the town should be countenanced. Any reasonable demands for money, provision and gear would be met . . .

Douglas, privately, informed that Leslie, allegedly sickened with atrocities, had hurried off to Stirling where a large part of his force was presently stationed.

Satisfied meantime, James Graham sent in his requisitions, and sat down to wait, at Buchanan – with a weather-eye to the eastwards, for Leslie. With a mere 1,600 men he was very vulnerable; but he would not be caught unawares again, and had a way of retreat kept open.

On the last day of October the news reached him that Digby had been defeated once again, at Skipton in Yorkshire. He and Langdale were allegedly fleeing north to join him – but only as hunted refugees, history repeating itself. There was no sign, nor word, of Aboyne. Nor yet of Colkitto – whom rumour declared to have crossed over to Ulster on affairs of his own.

Restive, well recognising that his present position was dangerous as well as unlikely to be profitable, yet anxious not to seem to withdraw the threat which could keep his captive friends alive, Montrose, early in November, decided that he must do better than this. He left a token force of MacGregors and other local clans at Buchanan, under Glengyle, to maintain the illusion of pressure against Glasgow. He moved his main force back into the mountains of Menteith and Balquhidder, from which they could make frequent forays and keep the South-West in a stir, flourishing the Royal Standard, but safe from Leslie. Then, with a small party of close associates, he set out again, fast and secretly, for the North. He was going to have it out, one way or another, with Huntly.

Not unexpectedly, he had great difficulty in running that elusive Cock o' the North to earth, when he did not want to be found. They criss-crossed Aberdeenshire and Banffshire in the early winter weather, with the first snow already on the hill-tops and hard frosts at night. At last they cornered him at Bog o' Gight Castle, at the mouth of Spey, in a snowstorm. Huntly's horse had slipped on the ice and thrown its master, damaging an ankle.

It was years since Montrose had actually seen George Gordon, 2nd Marquis of Huntly, now in his late fifties but looking older – and was surprised at the change in his appearance. He had always been fairly good-looking, in a well-built, red-haired, foxy-faced way; now he was puffy, flabby, his features coarsened, his beard straggling and flecked with white. The sharp foxy look was almost gone; in its place a frowning concentration which could not disguise a general vagueness, alternating with sudden darting, blinking glances and a constant lip-licking. James Graham wondered if there might not be just the beginnings of madness there. The Gordon was dressed in clothes which had once been rich, highly decorative, but were now tarnished, stained, soiled, as was the broad diagonal ribbon of the Garter which he wore on all occasions, frayed as it was. Even before a roaring log fire in his hall, he had a plaid wrapped round his shoulders like a shawl.

'Well, my lord – I have sought you long,' Montrose greeted. 'I regretted to hear of your fall – but rejoice that it has enabled me to come up with you. You know my friends, I think – the Marquis of Douglas, the Lords Reay, Erskine, Fleming, the Master of Napier, Sir John Dalziel and Colonel Graham of Inchbrakie? Some have already visited you on my behalf!'

'Aye,' the other said, pursing his lips. 'No doubt. You are welcome to my house. In this ill weather. I can offer you shelter, refreshment. If nothing more.'

'We hope for more than that, my lord – from the most powerful man in the North of Scotland. Since we come in the King's name and authority. But we shall be glad of your hospitality, sir.'

'The King's authority, you say? Charles Stewart is far away, man. And free with his authority, his commissions! *I* am his Lieutenant of the North, see you.'

'That I acknowledge,' Montrose agreed diplomatically. 'It is to the King's Lieutenant of the North that I appeal, as his Captain-General, for troops, cavalry, to fight the King's battle.'

'The King's battle? Or *yours*, Graham?' the other jerked, with one of his darting glances.

'*Mine*, my lord? How could it be mine?' Astonished, Montrose gazed at the man. 'What have I ever gained, by fighting for the King's cause? It has all been loss to me – save that I did my duty.'

'Many a man will forfeit much for power, James Graham. The power that you seek. To rule a kingdom. If you win this battle – for which you need my Gordons – who will rule Scotland? Not King Charles, I swear – for he will never live in this land. He's ower fond of London. Like his father. James Graham will rule in Scotland. And why should good Gordons die for that, tell me?'

Montrose frowned, looking over at his friends, as honestly distressed as he was taken aback. 'My lord – you do me wrong, I assure you. I have no desire to rule Scotland. I do not see myself as ruler. I have become a soldier, reluctantly, because the King's Grace needed such, grievously. But as to ruling afterwards, this is for the King and Parliament to decide. When the fighting is over. I shall not be a candidate for government – for I wish to live my own life hereafter. As I have not done for nine years. Believe me, that is the truth of it.'

Huntly peered, blinking, and tugged at his beard.

'You, sir,' Montrose went on, 'could save the King's cause.' He paused, glancing round. 'My lord Marquis of Douglas, here, can do much – has already done much. Supplying men and horses and moneys. But – he has not the cavalry which Gordon has. The large numbers trained to arms. His Borderers, of Eskdale and Annandale and Nithsdale, are excellent material – but they are hard to muster, unused to serving together, to obeying a single voice. They are not of one clan, but many, unlike Gordon. With no chief whose word is their law.' James Graham was picking his words with care. He was concerned not to offend Douglas – yet anxious to play him off against his fellow-marquis. There were in fact only four marquesses in Scotland, now that Hamilton was made duke, and three of them were in this draughty hall, Argyll the fourth. If he could make Huntly jealous of Douglas, without setting them at each others' throats, make him desire to outdo the other, show his superior power and inffuence ...

'My lord of Douglas has taken long to hear Charles Stewart calling!' the Gordon jerked. 'He has some way to make up, I swear!'

'I know it, my lord,' Douglas acceded, mildly enough. 'But better perhaps to come to His Grace's aid late than to desert him in his need?'

'I have never deserted the King. Always I have been his friend. I fought for him when James Graham fought *against* him! What happened at Turriff? Ask *him*! Who has won most of his battles for him, since? My Gordon horse. And when they are no longer there? As at this Philiphaugh. Defeat! Do not speak to me of my duty to the King!'

'For all of which His Grace will show his royal gratitude, I am sure,' Montrose put in smoothly. 'As his viceroy, I myself might offer some small and inadequate recognition, even now. A commission as Major-General, perhaps? The sheriffship of Moray? Certain lands of the rebel Lord Forbes, contiguous to Gordon territory – at the King's victory? Even, it might be, the recommendation to His Grace for the bestowal of a dukedom . . . !'

Huntly moistened his lips. 'A . . . a dukedom!' He almost rose from his chair, but thought better of it. 'Duke – of Gordon!'

'Perhaps. You understand, my lord, that I cannot commit His Grace in any way. But I can strongly recommend.'

The other swivelled those strange eyes sideways, in the direction of Douglas. 'And this – would he be Duke of Douglas?'

'I have no such ambition or desire,' that nobleman said quickly. 'I am not of the stuff of dukes!'

Huntly drummed his fingers on his chair-arm. 'How many men would you want, Graham? I could by no means spare many, mind you.'

Montrose sought to keep his voice steady. 'A minimum of, say, 2,000, my lord. At first. Although, the more you provide, the more quickly will this sorry business be over, and . . . results achieved!'

'Aye – maybe so. But, see you – I will allow you my men under one condition only. That they do not leave the North. I will not have them taken south. They must remain where they may guard my Gordon lands from any attack. That is understood?'

'But – I cannot field an army under these conditions, sir. If it is Middleton who disturbs you, we will deal with him, yes. But then I must return to the South. The King's cause will not be won here in the North.'

'Middleton has moved to Inverness. He is raiding into my lands of upper Spey and Badenoch. And he chaffers with that snake Seaforth! The Mackenzie will turn his coat once again, and bring the northern clans down upon us. If Inverness is held against us, all the North is lost to the King.'

'Seaforth sent me assurances of his fullest support.' But that was before Philiphaugh. Montrose looked at the Gordon thoughtfully. Was this a private feud of his own, against Seaforth?

The Lord Reay, who was chief of the Mackays, the most northerly clan of all, spoke up. 'If Seaforth takes to arms against you, James, then you will never get the northern MacDonalds to rejoin your banner – Clanranald, Glengarry, Sleat and the rest.

And leave their lands open to the threat of the Mackenzies. In this, Inverness is key to all the North and West.'

'True, Donald.' Was this what had been holding up Colkitto? 'But – Leslie and Argyll are in the South. And the prisoners – such as are still alive. I have to balance it all out . . .'

'My Gordons do not move south of Tay,' Huntly insisted, finally.

'Very well, sir. I will ride south forthwith. Make some gesture there, to keep the hostages from being murdered, if I may. Then bring my main force north again as quickly as possible. Meanwhile you muster your Gordons. Then we will make a joint attack on Middleton. Thereafter deal with Leslie and Argyll.' He did not say that once he had the Gordon host fighting under his command again, he believed that it might go where *he* wanted.

And so, before they so much as tasted of Huntly's proffered refreshment, the thing was settled – after a fashion.

Making it work, with the Cock o' the North for partner, was, all recognised, another matter.

*   *   *

The next months were amongst the most galling and frustrating of James Graham's military career – as well as the saddest. For return to Fincastle revealed that Lord Napier, his brother-in-law, friend and one-time guardian, had just died there while his son, the Master, was away with Montrose. And two days later, news came that Nat Gordon had been hanged, at St. Andrews. And the next day, even Sir Robert Spottiswoode, the King's Secretary of State and former Lord President of the Court of Session – who had sent a dying message to Montrose urging him, in the mercy of Christ, not to indulge in reprisals. There was one bright gleam, however, as other judicial murders were reported; the Lord Ogilvy, condemned to death, feigned sickness, and when his sister obtained leave to visit him for the last time, contrived to escape in women's clothes she brought him. His arrival at Fincastle was a joyous occasion, for once.

But it was Huntly who made that first half of 1646 a misery for James Graham. His interpretation of their agreement and relationship was extraordinary. He produced his Gordon host, yes – but not only did he keep it entirely under his own command, preferring always to use the Lord Lewis rather than Aboyne as lieutenant, but made little or no attempt to co-operate militarily with Montrose or his part of the army. Indeed frequently he acted in exactly contrary fashion, deliberately, blatantly – and Lewis insolently. He declared openly that, since *he* was the King's Lieutenant of the North, and this campaign was taking place in the North, his position was superior to that of Montrose. Moreover, since he had more men under arms – for his force, though ever fluctuating in numbers, often amounted to as many as 3,000 men – *his* decisions on tactics and strategy should prevail.

In theory they were besieging Middleton in Inverness; in practice Huntly was pursuing vendettas of his own all over the North, sometimes two or three at a time, and Middleton was left to Montrose. Aboyne elected usually to stay with Montrose, despite his father, but was unable to detach more than one squadron of horse. As a result, the royalist force was normally greatly inferior in cavalry to that which it was allegedly besieging, however many in theory it might claim in the background. And they were again without artillery, so that they could not hope to take a walled town by storm, when it was alerted and well-defended. Frequently Montrose had to retire precipitately before Middleton's cavalry thrusts from the town. Yet if the Gordon cavalry had been there in force they could have rolled up the enemy time and again. It was a maddening situation. Its only virtue was that it made the cautious Seaforth think again, and retire once more to his northern fastnesses. In consequence, Montrose could still hope for MacDonald participation thereafter. Colkitto was now known to be in Ulster, negotiating with the MacDonnell Earl of Antrim for a joint expedition to Scotland in the late spring – a piece of independent initiative his Captain-General found singularly inept.

It was a hard winter, and campaigning unpleasant anyway. Argyll and Leslie appeared to have accepted the fact that it was not practical, militarily, and operations in the South were in abeyance. Indeed Leslie returned to Leven's army in England temporarily – no doubt glad to get away from the religious zealots who now ruled in Scotland's southern half. Montrose, however, kept up his activities, for he was concerned that the population at large should recognise that Philiphaugh was only a temporary set-back, and that he was still very much a force to be reckoned with. He intended to be in a good position to take the initiative, on a national scale, when the new campaigning season started.

In pursuance of this intention, and in view of the ineffectiveness of the present follies around Inverness and Strathspey, he sent two sections of his force southwards again, under Lord Ogilvy and the new Lord Napier, to keep the Lowlands preoccupied and to reinforce Donald MacGregor of Glengyle's efforts in the Lennox. He would have gone himself, in disgust – but he feared that without his influence in the North, Huntly might run completely mad. Moreover the man was no longer young, and might weary of his brigandage; in which case Montrose wished to be on hand to ensure that the vital cavalry came into Aboyne's command rather than Lewis Gordon's. So he sat it out, at least largely immobilising Middleton – who was the only Covenant leader who appeared to be prepared to fight in winter conditions – seeking meanwhile to stomach Huntly's arrogance and Lewis's sheer impertinence. It made a grim interlude.

But with the lengthening days, and the melting snows, the position began to improve. Both Ogilvy and Napier reported successes. Antrim and Colkitto actually landed on the Hebridean seaboard, concerned mainly with harrying Argyll and Lorne apparently, but who must be coaxed into more productive warfare – Antrim, curiously enough, announcing himself to be the King's General of the Isles and Highlands. Clanranald sent word that, despite Antrim, he would be at Montrose's disposal, with 2,000 MacDonalds, whenever the first hay was in. And the weathercock Seaforth sent a new set of assurances as to his loyalty to the Throne and his good wishes for Montrose. He was ever the first to reflect a change of wind.

At this stage, for some undisclosed reason, Huntly changed direction altogether and led his force southwards to assault, take and sack Aberdeen – all in the name of King Charles. Horrified, Montrose hurried thither in an attempt to undo as much of the harm as he might. But the Gordon, as ever, got word of his coming, and disappeared into deepest Aberdeenshire, leaving only the Lord Lewis to face the Captain-General – which he did with his usual swaggering audacity, announcing that he took his orders from his father, the Lieutenant of the North and from no other, etcetera. And he had thousands of Gordon horse to back his youthful contumely.

Wearily, at long last, James Graham recognised that he had come to the end of the road as far as the Gordons were concerned. There was a limit even to *his* patience. Moreover the harm now being done to the King's cause all over the North was so great that unless he disassociated himself from Huntly, clearly enough for all to see, he must lose all support and credence. Reluctantly he issued a proclamation declaring that, as the King's Viceroy and Captain-General, he could no longer accept the Marquis of Huntly as a true servant of His Grace and colleague of his own, all men to take note. By the same token he ordered Huntly to disband his forces and return to his own territories.

It was in this extraordinary situation, at the end of May 1646, in Strathspey, that the final blow fell. A messenger arrived with a letter from Charles Stewart – but not from Oxford or any other royalist stronghold. It came, by the hand of Colonel Robin Kerr, from the Earl of Leven's Scottish army headquarters in England. And it announced that the King had decided to do as his good and faithful friend the Marquis of Montrose had long advised, abandon his failing cause in England and throw himself upon the loyal affections of his Scottish subjects. To that end he had secretly left Oxford, in the guise of a servant, and committed himself to the care and keeping of the Earl of Leven, the Earl of Lothian, General David Leslie and others commanding the Scottish army, assured of their leal goodwill. As a result of discussions with them he had agreed to certain terms. He would sign the Covenant and order the royalist forces in England to lay down their arms. Accordingly, he commanded his trusted friend the Marquis of Montrose likewise to disarm and disband the royal forces in Scotland, and enter into discussions with the Covenant leadership there, forthwith.

This official letter was privately amplified by Colonel Kerr. His Grace's treatment by the Leslies and Lothian, on Argyll's instructions, was harsh and unbending, and hardly indicative of clemency in Scotland. The King privately advised Montrose to make the best terms he could over the disbandment of his forces, and then to flee to France – where he would send him further instructions in due course.

Utterly bewildered and appalled, James Graham saw all that he had fought and striven for dissolving, crumbling, thrown away. Like a man mortally wounded his head sank on his chest. This, then was what he had given his all for, and what so many fine men had died for. This was the end of it all – abject folly triumphant.

PART TWO

CHAPTER THIRTEEN

James Graham steadied himself against the thrumming cordage as the vessel rolled and pitched, and stared back at the receding land. Already the features and details of the coastline, dramatic as it was, were fading, levelling out, and the great mass of the inland mountains seemed to grow, to come closer to the shore, to dominate all, in their blue, shadow-slashed infinity – those mountains which for so long had been both his sure ally and his continuing challenge, his refuge and yet his constant problem. Would he ever look on them again, he wondered?

He could no longer distinguish the mouths of the two Esks, North and South, or even the towers and spires of the town of Montrose between the rivers and the rising backcloth of the land. He could not pinpoint exactly where lay Old Montrose and Kinnaird, at the head of the great landlocked bay, where last night he had secretly said goodbye to his wife and children, in as unsatisfactory a parting as might be imagined. Magdalen, he well recognised, he might never see again in this life, the mere husk of a woman, mentally and physically, already next to death in all but name. Surely he need not feel responsibility for all of that? But the children – that was different. What sort of a father had he proved to them, sacrificed on the altar of his crumbled faith, an altar to a false god, a noble image with feet of clay? At least he had got Jamie safely out of Edinburgh Castle – though not out of Covenant tutelage and back to his mother – part of the terms he had won from Middleton over the disbandment of the army. He would have liked to have brought the boy away with him; but even if it had been allowed, it would not have been fair to Magdalen. Nor to Jamie himself, probably, for God alone knew into what sort of exile he was sailing. The lad was better left behind, for Southesk had promised to keep an eye on him – and Southesk at least knew the art of self-preservation. Perhaps he had reason to be thankful for David Carnegie's trimming propensities now, for his family's sake.

A little way to the side, in the shelter of the sloop's deckhouse, a small group of men watched him – all that remained of the galaxy that had attended on the Viceroy and Captain-General of Scotland, and none his closest friends. Respecting Montrose's mood and his need for a measure of privacy, these kept their distance – even the brashest of them, Sir John Hurry, of all men. That extraordinary soldier of misfortune was indeed with them. After his defeats, in such bad odour was he with Argyll and the Estates leadership that, a mercenary at heart anyway, he had decided to sell his sword to the other side. It had proved a bad time to make the change; but there was no going back, in the Scotland that now was. But he had soldiered in the Continental wars before – with more success than at home – and could do so again. That he was on this ship, getting safe out of a country too hot to hold him, was the measure of his former enemy's generosity of spirit, and the respect of one soldier for another.

George Wishart, secretary and chaplain, had organised this escape into exile. He knew, as did Montrose himself, that the moment that the strange conferences with Middleton were over and the army actually disbanded, whatever the terms might say, James Graham himself would be arrested, his protection gone – Archibald Campbell would see to that. Aberdeen harbour had been well watched, as had Montrose itself; but Wishart had discovered a small Norwegian vessel at Stonehaven, unloading, and had paid its master well, too well for their slender resources, to forgo a cargo and slip off in the darkness down the coast, to stand out to sea during that day, and then to move in at evening and pick up, off the mouth of the South Esk, a fishing-coble that had rowed out of Montrose Basin, with a minister of the Kirk aboard, the Reverend James Wood, and his servant. That servant had been James Graham, who was now on his way to Bergen.

Montrose, however bitter and grievous his thoughts as he watched the shoreline of his native land recede, was not at heart despairing or hopeless, of course – for that was not in the nature of the man. His private affairs were in ruin, and his faith in his monarch's judgment and word gone; but the cause to which he had sacrificed all could yet be saved, *must* yet be saved. He now identified himself almost wholly with that cause – since his personal life had been so sacrificed as to be all but non-existent. But Charles Stewart and his throne might yet be saved; it was unthinkable to believe otherwise, whatever the folly of the King. He, James Graham, could and would save it, given a modicum of co-operation, understanding, trust. Before ever he came to terms with Middleton, as commanded, he had in fact received a secret letter from Charles, smuggled out from his semi-captivity with Leven's army, in which he had urged Montrose to bear with him, not to desert him, good cause as he had to do so. He appointed him special ambassador to the Courts of Europe, to solicit money, aid, men and arms, from his fellow-monarchs of Christendom, to build up an army which would return to sweep their enemies from England and Scotland both, of which army Montrose was to be supreme commander. Meantime to make his way, if he could, to the Court of Queen Henrietta Maria, who would welcome him, and who had managed to have most of the royal treasure conveyed into her keeping at St. Germain, in France. Shaking his head not a little over this typical Charlesian outpouring, Montrose had nevertheless managed to send the Earl of Crawford secretly out of the country, for France, to prepare the way, to promise the Queen the restoration of her husband to freedom and at least the Scottish throne, given the men and money and authority. Since Charles's hands were tied meantime, his wife was to be his deputy, acting for him and the young Prince of Wales. With her help, James Graham intended to wipe out this present shame and folly, God willing. So this was not really goodbye to Scotland, he prayed. He would be back.

When he could no longer see even the loom of the land, he turned, sought to speak cheerfully to his friends and went below.

With strong but consistent south-west winds the sloop made a fairly fast passage across the North Sea, to arrive at Bergen in six days, on the 10th of September. Under the shadow of different and more jagged mountains, snow-streaked, harsh, they anchored. But though the surly ship-master, Jens Gunnarsen, wanted to be rid of his passengers and off north to his home port of Trondhjem, Montrose refused to disembark until he was apprised of conditions here. His first main objective was to reach King Christian IV of Denmark, who was King Charles's uncle, brother of his late mother Anne of Denmark. From him he might expect aid for his nephew's cause. But the northern kingdom, Norway, was in only doubtful allegiance and security at this time, the Peace of Broemsebro being only two years old. Montrose's foreign travels could well be cut short before they had rightly begun. So he sent Sir John Hurry, who had campaigned here, with George Wishart, ashore to prospect the situation.

They came back in good cheer, Hurry positively gleeful.

Bergen, it seemed, was sound for King Christian, and the Bergenhus, its castle, whose cannon commanded the harbour and had yawned menacingly at them, was in fact under the command of a former lieutenant of Hurry's own in the Thirty Years War, a Scot named Thomas Gray, now Lieutenant-colonel of the Trondhjem Infantry Regiment. He would be honoured to welcome the Marquis of Montrose.

Just how welcome he was Montrose learned with real astonishment. He had barely set his foot on dry land before a salvo of cannon-fire saluted him, the gates of the castle were flung open and the entire garrison marched forth with flags and banners, a band playing. At their head, on a white horse, resplendent in feathered hat and half-armour, rode Colonel Gray.

Reining up before them, he leapt down, flourished off his hat, and actually sank on one knee, almost as though to royalty.

'My lord Marquis of Montrose – hail!' he cried dramatically. 'I welcome the greatest soldier in Christendom to my master's domains. In the name of His Majesty of Denmark, Norway, Schleswig, Holstein and Oldenburg – hail!'

Distinctly embarrassed, Montrose raised him up. 'You do me overmuch honour, sir,' he protested. 'For a defeated general! But I thank you for your warm welcome and kind words. I am . . . somewhat unused to the like, I confess!'

'No man can do you too much honour, my lord. The world rings with your deeds. My house is yours, and all at my command. Mount this horse, if you will, and come taste of honest meats. You will be deeved with shipboard fare . . .'

It was a strange experience to be fêted. During his all too brief months of rule in Scotland, men had bowed to him as victor, governor, fearing his enmity or desiring favours. But disinterested acclaim and admiration was something different. And it was not only Colonel Gray and his officers, but all the notables of Bergen who thronged to pay their respects. It had never occurred to James Graham that he had been building up a reputation outside Scotland. In Norway, at least, he found himself to be a hero.

Pleasing as it was to savour such esteem and boundless hospitality, Montrose did not long delay at Bergen. Christiania, where he hoped to find King Christian, was his immediate objective. But he quickly discovered that Norway was not a land to ride over readily, even for toughened travellers. Savage mountains of rock and ice, rising steep and trackless from the deep dark fiords which probed vast distances inland, barred the way. Christiania was less than 200 miles away, as the crow flew – but as man must travel more than twice that. The quickest way would have been to go by ship. But their previous vessel had left for Trondhjem, to the north, just as soon as it got rid of its passengers, and no other sea-going craft was immediately available. Moreover, Montrose was practically penniless. Skipper Gunnarsen had required almost all their scant funds to compensate for abandoning his return cargo at Stonehaven. And hero or none, the last thing James Graham would consider was to start borrowing money from his new friends. They would travel by land, as best they could.

In fact, they did sail for almost 100 miles, but in a small fishing-craft, between the mosaic of the clustered offshore islands and then up the long, long gut of Sogne Fiord, between scowling fierce mountains, a spectacular and latterly grim waterway which probed deep into the desolate heart of Norway. At its head, at Laerdalsoyri, they disembarked, cramped and cold, and managed to hire there a guide and a dozen shaggy ponies, not unlike their own Highland garrons, to take them on over the high mountain tracks, eastwards.

The days that followed taxed some of the little party to the utmost, George Wishart, not yet fully recovered from his long incarceration in Edinburgh's Tolbooth, in especial. But not Montrose himself. The physical effort, the constant struggle against a harsh and challenging land, were as meat and drink to him, after the frustrations, disappointments and enforced inactivities of the past. He indeed drugged himself with sheer exertion, embracing the weariness which overwhelmed all regrets, repinings, self-questioning. Despite his comparatively slight and slender build, he was superbly fit, his body the tried servant of his will. Moreover the scenery was magnificent, defiant, a dare in itself, and he was a man to whom such meant much, a poet. If he had had little opportunity, or heart, for poetry these last years, perhaps he might do better hereafter.

Climbing over the lofty, ice-bound watershed above Laerdal and so down into the Valdres valley and along the fifty mile long lake of Randsfiord it took them a week to reach Christiania at the head of the Oslo Fiord – there to find that King Christian had gone to Copenhagen, in his other kindgom of Denmark, for the winter – which seemed to set in earlier here than in Scotland. Christian's Norwegian ministers treated the travellers well, making much of Montrose, before despatching them onwards, down the eastern coast of the Oslo Fiord, on the Gothenburg road. They crossed the Swedish border near Kornsjo – which would not have been possible two years before, when Christian made the Peace of Broemsebro with Queen Christina, Gustavus Adolphus's daughter. Even so, although the Scandinavian nations were now nominally at harmony, it was considered unwise for travellers from Christiania to proceed right to Gothenburg, the great new city Gustavus had founded; so they made the crossing to Denmark from Marstrand, a small port a little to the north, over the stormy Kattegat, to Copenhagen.

Here they were disconcerted to learn that the King had departed for Hamburg, for a conference concerned with trying to bring order out of the end of the Thirty Years War which had for so long so decimated Northern Europe. No speedy return was anticipated. So it was onwards again, southwards. At least this time their almost non-existent funds did not have to stretch to the cost, for despatches and papers of State were being sent to the King by the hands of junior ministers, and Montrose and his party were welcome to travel in the royal sloop.

So, in fair comfort, they crossed the south-west corner of the Baltic – although suffering the usual jangle of seas where the cold current from the Gulf of Bothnia met the constricted waters of the Kattegat off the island of Mon. Disembarking at Lubeck, they crossed the level, cattle-dotted lands of Holstein to Altona, and so into the free Hanse city of Hamburg in the Holy Roman Empire, one of the richest towns in the world. The Danish envoys installed the travellers in a canal-side inn, and declared that they would announce Montrose's presence to His Majesty at the Rathaus.

James Graham knew Hamburg of old, having visited it on his Grand Tour of Europe. That was only twelve years before; but it might have been in another life, so different a man had he become from the idealistic, impulsive youth of those days. Somehow the place seemed smaller, less impressive and exciting, despite all its obvious riches, more drab for all the palaces of its merchant-princes, its magnificent churches all overtopped by St. Catherine's with its 400-foot spire, the tall bulging warehouses that overhung the narrow twisting streets, the houses of pleasure with their painted and half naked whores, the picturesque medley of traders, seamen and Jews which thronged every thoroughfare, market-place and canal-side. All seemed somehow lessened, tarnished, from a mere dozen years before. Or was that merely age talking? At thirty-four, no less. James Graham suspected that it might be.

In anticipation of a summons to the Danish King's presence, he was concerned to be as fittingly attired as was possible. Always neat, almost simple in his dress, eschewing the florid extravagance of most of the cavaliers, he nevertheless liked to dress well, indeed with a sort of sober richness that came natural to him. But his present garb was travel-stained where it was not battle-worn, and he had not the means to purchase better. His friends offered him the best of their own – but such were apt to be as hard-worn as his, besides tending to be the wrong size and shape. He could only spruce all up as best he might.

He was so engaged when his room door was thrown open, and one of the Danish envoys, Jorgensen, stood there. 'Excellence,' he declared, 'His Majesty the King will speak with you.'

'Ha – I thank you, sir. A moment, and I will come with you.'

'But no! He is here. King Christian himself is here.' And Jorgensen stood aside, bowing low.

A tall and heavy elderly man with a black eye-patch, who stooped, clad in dark, nondescript clothes, came into the room, peering about him, with but one eye from under grey bushy eyebrows. Astonished, Montrose and his companions made hurried genuflexions.

'Your Majesty – this, this is a scarcely believable honour!' James Graham, still in his shirt-sleeves, got out. 'To – to come here . . .!' For once that assured and eloquent man stammered.

'Honour, my lord? Of God's truth, the honour is mine!' Christian barked, in a hoarse voice, his English excellent though thickly accented. He came forward, hand outstretched. '*You* honour this Hamburg, and every man in it, by your presence here. Permit that I shake the hand of the greatest soldier in Europe!'

Quite overcome, Montrose grasped the proffered hand, and bowing deeply, sought to bring it to his lips. But the other would have none of it, insisting on a hearty handshake.

'Stand up, man. Christian of Denmark has more need to bow to the great Marquis of Montrose. As a soldier, I am not worthy to hold your stirrup!'

'Your Majesty – I pray you not to cozen me! You – one of the most experienced campaigners in all Christendom. You, who even mastered Gustavus Adolphus . . .!'

'Only once – and that by his ill-luck,' the King gave back, in his jerky, harsh voice. '*You*, now, would have fought Gustavus into the earth! With you as my general, *I* would have been Lion of the North, not Adolphus. God's Death – and you young enough to be my grandson!'

'Scarce that, Sire. I am thirty-four – and feel older! But – for Your Majesty to come to me, to this lowly tavern! It is too much . . .'

'Tush – where Montrose is must be the most illustrious place in this, or any city, I say! Not that I will not have you out of here, this kennel, forthwith. That Montrose should be stalled thus, in a city of palaces! We shall see to it.'

'You are too good, Sire. But – may I present my friends? Sir John Hurry, Major-General, whom you may know. The Reverend Dr. George Wishart, my secretary, chaplain and guide. Drummond of Balloch, John Spottiswoode, nephew to Sir Robert, King Charles's late Secretary of State. All good servants of your royal nephew.' Which was being generous to Hurry, at least.

Nodding impatiently, Christian sat himself down, unbidden, on one of the rough benches. 'My royal nephew is a fool!' he said bluntly. 'Only a fool could have lost his throne with you as general! My good-son James, his father, was little better than a mountebank, God knows – but he would not have thrown away two kingdoms for a quibble of religion. Charles is an ass. Not worth your support, my lord.'

James Graham bit his lip. 'I cannot believe that Your Majesty is fair to His Grace,' he said. 'King Charles has made mistakes amany. His judgment, I fear, is often at fault. And he has been unfortunate in his choice of advisers. But he is a noble man . . .'

'A noble blockhead, sir! A saintly numbskull! If he must be a saint, he should have abdicated his throne. Kings cannot afford to be saints. I vow his sister Elizabeth, my niece, would have made a better monarch! She is more of a man than Charles will ever be. To allow himself to be bought and sold like, like a slave!'

'Bought and sold, Sire? What jest is this . . . ?'

'No jest, sirrah! I'd have you know I do not jest about the fate of kings! Have you not heard, man? Charles has been sold by the Scots, by your Argyll and Leven and Lothian. To Cromwell and the English. For £200,000. Sold and delivered.'

'No!' Montrose stared, forgetting that one did not contradict reigning monarchs. 'I'll not believe it! Here is some error, some mistaken story . . .'

'No mistake. I have it, in writing, from my ambassador in London. Charles was handed over at Newcastle. He is taken by the English parliamentmen to Hampton Court. A prisoner . . .'

'They gave him up? For money? £200,000 you said? From the English? For the King of Scots?'

'They did – and joyfully. They declared that it was for the proper payment of Leven's army. The first payment of £100,000 is already made – and divided up. Not to the army, by God! £30,000 for the Duke of Hamilton. £30,000 for the Marquis of Argyll. £15,000 to be divided up amongst those named by Argyll. And, see you, the Scots army will not leave English soil until they get the other £100,000!'

'No-o-o! Merciful God – no!' James Graham groaned. 'This is beyond all conception. Even for Argyll . . .!'

'It is the truth. I believed Hamburg to be the city of merchants. Your Scots lords, it seems, can teach them their business! But – enough of that. I came to speak of more savoury matters. Of things military. At Oldurn now – that is how you say it? Ah, Auldearn – yes. You scarcely used your cavalry there, I heard? They stood by, while your foot did all. And at Alward – Alford, yes – your horse, they say, all but lost you the battle. How could this be? Foot against cavalry hosts? I do not understand.'

When, presently, Jorgensen ventured to remind his master that emissaries at the Rathaus were still awaiting him, the old monarch reluctantly got to his feet.

'We will talk more of this, my lord,' he declared. 'My sorrow that I must go now and talk and chaffer over lands and boundaries and appointments, with hucksters, not soldiers. Meanwhile, Jorgensen will find you a house more suitable to your requirements.'

'You are kind, Sire – but I think that I had best remain here, if Your Majesty pleases.'

'In this hovel? Why, man?'

'Because, Sire, I fear that my resources are not such as to pay for better. Scarce even this.'

'Resources? Money? God's death – are *you*, Montrose, to concern yourself with gold pieces?'

'I must – since I have none! All the little we could bring away has been spent in our journeying. Until Queen Henrietta sends me some from St. Germain, we must harbour our groats!'

'Nonsense, man! The greatest soldier in Europe live like a pauper? Not while Christian of Denmark draws breath. See to it, Jorgensen. A good house – one of these merchant's palaces – for the Marquis of Montrose. And an allowance suitable for his dignity.'

'Sire – I thank you, from my heart. But – I cannot accept your charity. Even from Your Majesty. A small loan, perhaps, until the Queen sends me money? I have expended my all on King Charles's service, and I am to draw on the royal revenues she has, while I build up an army to go to his aid. Draw modestly . . .'

'Charity, sir? Who talks of charity? You will receive the payment of a General-Marshal of the Danish Army – which position I request the honour to bestow upon you. You will not say me nay, my lord?'

His breath all but taken away by this announcement, Montrose could only stammer, and shake his head. Without waiting for thanks or even acceptance, the tall old crane of a monarch turned and stalked from the room – before even his audience had so much as time to bow.

*   *   *

Less than willingly Montrose settled down for the winter in Hamburg. His intention had been to press on to France, to St. Germain, where the Queen held her exiled Court – although, as a French princess she was more at home there than ever she had been in England. But Henrietta Maria did not answer his letters, did not send him any money, and did not issue the official authority which he required – and which King Charles wrote that he had instructed her to do – appointing Montrose ambassador-extraordinary to the monarchs of Europe, to raise funds and man-power for the liberation attempt. Without this, his required credentials, James Graham had nothing to show as authority save a mere paragraph in a private letter from Charles, unsealed, unauthenticated. Requiring more, he perforce must wait, while sending more urgent messages to St. Germain.

They were all very comfortable, however, in the palatial merchant's house in the Alsterstrasse which Jorgensen had rented for them; and Montrose would have been more than human if he had not found some satisfaction in the high esteem in which he was held in Hamburg, and with the compliments and honours showered upon him, the constant stream of distinguished visitors who came from far and near to be presented to the most consistently victorious general in Christendom. After the treatment he had received at home, for long, it was a heady experience. His salary as a Danish general, duly and meticulously paid by King Christian, monthly, was a great help – although not sufficient to support his friends and entourage, penniless as himself, in any great style, and certainly not enough to tour Europe in the character of King Charles's ambassador.

Christian was consistently friendly, and they spent much time in each other's company. But despite all the generosity, Montrose could not pin the King down to promising any substantial number of soldiers for the liberation attempt. Christian conceded that he would supply a number of officers, and would encourage Scots mercenaries in his employ to volunteer for service back in Scotland, at his expense. Also he would provide funds to an unspecified amount, and shipping perhaps. Further than that he would not go – and Montrose was in no position to press him unduly. The fact was, Christian of Oldenburg scarcely judged his nephew Charles Stewart worth the trouble – a difficult situation for the suppliants to get round.

So, in a winter of snow and ice much more severe than they were used to in Scotland, they passed the time pleasantly enough, even though Montrose fretted to be up and doing. At least it was a change, to have leisure and to live in comfort, and in civilised conditions.

The high spot of the winter was the Yuletide festival, carried out on a scale the visitors had never experienced, three solid weeks of celebration, feasting and winter carnival in which the religious aspect of Christmas was very largely swallowed up in only thinly disguised pagan revelry. Hamburg was a cosmopolitan free city, with multi-religious background, but with German and Scandinavian Lutheran sympathies dominant. For all that, licence and gaiety at this season was worthy of the Old Church at its most unreformed and worldly, and enough to set Presbyterian Scotland by the ears. The two divines, Wishart and Wood, were distinctly upset.

It was in the midst of this festive interlude that Montrose one day received a command to attend at King Christian's official quarters in a wing of the Rathaus, where he was passing the winter as the guest of the city-state, and conducting protracted negotiations regarding the Baltic lands. James Graham had been there many times – although it was more usual for the King to come to him, privately, as it were incognito. But this was in the nature of a peremptory royal summons. Conditioned ever to receive bad news – and having felt for some time that this pleasant interlude could not last – he dressed with care, and walked through the icebound streets to the Rathaus.

Known to all in Hamburg now, he was conducted without delay to the royal apartments, through successive floridly gorgeous reception-rooms. A major-domo with a gold-tipped staff of office tapped three times on great double-doors, and after the requisite pause, threw them open and announced:

'His Excellency the General-Marshal Montrose craves audience of His Serene and Gracious Majesty, King of Denmark and Norway, Duke of Holstein and Schleswig, Count of Oldenburg and Lord of Bornholm.'

James Graham perceived firstly that the King was dressed very differently from his normal careless and undistinguished garb, very fine in a quiet way, being in full royal fig. The second perception was that there were three other persons in the great chamber with its four roaring log fires, and all women.

'Come, my lord,' Christian greeted him warmly. 'It is my privilege to present you to a renowned and beautiful lady, who has expressed a hearty desire to meet you. Indeed I believe that she is come to Hamburg for that principal purpose – for she does not often honour her old uncle with her presence! You are well acquainted with her two sons, I understand. Her daughters, here, dazzle my old eyes. But not more than their mother, my niece.' That was quite a courtier's speech for the old warrior. 'Her Majesty Elizabeth of Bohemia.'

Montrose swallowed, as well he might. Christian was by no means exaggerating about the beauty and renown. The woman who held out her hand to James Graham was in fact the most lovely of feature that man had ever set eyes upon, accepted as the most beautiful in Europe, as well as the most talented. Elizabeth Stewart, Queen of Bohemia and Princess-Royal of Great Britain, was an extraordinary daughter for Shaughlin' Jamie, the Wisest Fool in Christendom, James VI and I – though not quite so extraordinary to be the grand-daughter of Mary Queen of Scots. Almost as strange that she should be the sister of King Charles, nobly handsome as he was – for they were clearly poles apart in their natures. This was the celebrated Winter Queen, the Queen of Hearts to all Europe, to whom fate had been so unkind, yet who was acknowledged to be the most lively royal lady in generations.

'Majesty!' the Graham exclaimed, having a little difficulty with his breathing – and for once could think of nothing more to say.

'My lord of Montrose – Jamie, as my son Rupert calls you. I have longed to see you, speak with you. Up, my lord – do not bow to me. One day, it is my hope, you will allow me also to name you Jamie!' Her voice was light but strong, musical and with a lilt, a joy in itself. Tall, she had a magnificent figure, though scarcely slender, for she had had no less than thirteen children, but her carriage was as lively as the rest of her, though proud. She was dressed all in black and silver, but gave no impression of darkness, only of lightsome vigour, vehement loveliness allied to laughter, the epitome of spirited womanhood, ageless, her hair thick and still fair – although she was exactly fifty. Reaching out, she took both his hands.

'Madam . . . you are good. Kind. Gracious. It is my great joy to see you. I have heard so much of Your Majesty. From Prince Rupert. And Prince Maurice. And others. All of it in your praise . . .'

'La – enough! I would not have believed the Marquis Jamie a flatterer! A courtier! My sons will not always speak well of me, I swear! When I chide them – as they need chiding, now and again! As indeed do these two.' Elizabeth turned. 'My daughters, Louise and Sophia. Come, my dears, and pay your respects to the Hero of Scotland!'

The two young women, watching, reacted differently. One curtsied deep, the other bobbed an almost boyish nod, and grinned. They were indeed very different in almost every way. Sophia was fair, plumpish, conventionally pretty, with large blue eyes of seeming innocence, her yellow hair in ringlets, dressed with a sort of artful simplicity, not extravagantly – for her widowed mother, dispossessed and exiled, was not wealthy – but in the latest style and fashion. Whereas her sister was dark, taller, more slender with finely sculptured features, a wide mouth and strong chin, with a strange sort of watchful self-sufficiency about her – wholly womanly but with this boyish streak, and recognisably Prince Rupert's sister.

'Highnesses,' Montrose said, bowing. 'It has not been my good fortune to see at one time so much beauty as graces this room. I am privileged as I am overwhelmed.'

The Princess Sophia giggled, but the Princess Louise eyed him, frankly assessing, saying nothing.

'My daughters are not usually lacking in words!' the Queen observed, drily. 'Your presence, and reputation, must be too much for them, my Lord Jamie.'

'Not so, Mamma,' Sophia protested. 'But none told us the Marquis was so handsome as well as, as . . .' She flushed, prettily. 'Forgive me, my lord.'

'It seems that these minxes take after me in something, at least,' Elizabeth added, with a trill of laughter. 'For I have a sad weakness for good-looking men! So be it they *are* men!'

'Oh, Mamma . . . !'

King Christian chuckled raspingly. 'A captain of men and women both, on my soul!' he said. 'Captain-General, indeed!'

James Graham coughed, not a little embarrassed. 'Not so,' he objected, again forgetting that one did not contradict reigning monarchs. 'You mistake, Sire. I am no lady's man. Or, or . . . Your pardon, Majesty, Highnesses! Say that I lack success with your sex, I think. I am a plain man, in truth. Simple. And no great soldier, either – and that is a fact. I have been fortunate. In war, in some measure. In things military. Though, not altogether.' It was not often that Montrose made such a botch of any pronouncement.

'Then all the world is wrong about the Great Marquis!' Elizabeth cried. 'Or can it be that his judgment lacks something? As to war and women both? I think it must.'

'I would like to draw Your Lordship,' Princess Louise had not spoken until now. Her quite deep and slightly husky voice surprised the man, as much as her strange abrupt statement.

'Draw . . . ?' he echoed.

'Ha – that is the supreme accolade, sir! When Louise would draw a man,' her mother informed. 'She has a certain skill with crayon and brush. Now you *know* that you are a success!'

'Except that Louie is concerned to draw the ugly as much as the handsome!' her sister put in demurely. 'Indeed, her favourite sitter is a pet monkey.'

'Pert, miss!' the Queen said, though not sharply.

'It is character that I am concerned with, not beauty,' Louise declared, but with a shrug, as though the matter was of no importance. She seemed to have a casual way with her, highly unusual in a young woman of no more than twenty.

Montrose eyed her keenly, nevertheless. 'You are a painter, Highness?'

'I am not – although I would wish to be,' she answered, frankly.

'She has done some very fair work,' her mother told him. 'And will do better when she has lived longer, more fully. Gerard van Honthorst, who honours us at the Hague, gives her lessons and has hopes for her. When you come to the Hague – as come you must – you will see something of it.'

'Daubs of paint on canvas,' Sophia decried, in mock criticism. 'In the main, monkeys and ugly old men . . .'

'At least *I* paint canvas – you only your face!' her sister gave back, smilingly, without rancour.

'Ah – I think that the awe of the mighty Marquis of Montrose begins to wear off,' the Queen commented. 'Perhaps we should banish these two to another chamber, Uncle, and so be able to talk in adult fashion.'

'No, Madam – if you please,' Montrose pleaded. 'I would hear more. This of character – it is all, is it not ? All important. What distinguishes men from clods, and masters from men. Character is the essence of a man. Or a woman. But of the *full* man. For it is not something born, I think, but achieved. The painter – the Princess Louise – looks for character to draw. On canvas. I also have ever been concerned with character, in my small way. Not in paint, but in words. And in the assessment of men . . .'

'Ah, yes – you are a poet, of course,' Elizabeth nodded. 'Rupert said so – I had forgot. Forgive me.'

'God's Eyes – a poet !' King Christian looked shocked.

'Scarce that, Your Majesties. A mere versifier, a rhymster, now and again. A makar, as we say in Scotland. I scribble, lacking only talent, not will nor feeling . . .'

'As I draw and paint,' Louise added.

'Much better, I should think !' Sophia averred. 'Now I come to think of it, my lord has the looks of a poet.'

'God forbid !' Christian jerked. 'I would not wish to enrol a poet as General-Marshal of Denmark !'

'You need have no fear, Sire,' Montrose smiled. 'My weakness I keep well in hand. But – Your Majesty may decry poetry but not, surely, the search for character in men, which poetry, *my* poetry, seeks to express ? And the Princess's brush. For is not kingcraft, successful kingcraft, dependent upon the true judgment of character ? If a monarch cannot distinguish character in others, cannot choose the right men to serve him, how can his kingdom stand ?'

'You are right in that, at least,' the King agreed. 'Would God my nephew Charles had learned it.'

'Amen!' Elizabeth said, simply.

At the sudden pause, the change in atmosphere in that great room was very noticeable. It was as though a shadow had fallen over them, a noble but somewhat pathetic shadow of nephew, brother, uncle and sovereign, now captive in cruel and mocking hands, bought and sold like merchandise, failed, betrayed, rejected, yet still a King. Montrose, who had not made his references lightly, spoke carefully.

'King Charles and his kingdom can yet be saved – in especial his Scots kingdom. Of England, I do not know. But the Scots I do know. They will not do without their King, the successor of the Kenneths and Malcolms and Alexanders, of the Bruce and the Stewarts, the line that has endured for a thousand years. The monarch, *Ard Righ*, the High King of the Celtic peoples, is something that is part of the Scots, something which completes their polity, which they will not, cannot, do without, and remain themselves. It is otherwise in England, I think, where the monarch was ever the master, rather than the father. Wicked self-seeking men, in Scotland today, have pushed their King aside meantime – one man, in particular, who sees himself as master of the land. But the people are not with him and his supporters – despite the Kirk which he uses and which would use him . . .'

'Yes – the Kirk ?' Elizabeth interposed. 'What of Scotland's Church ? If it is against him . . . ?'

'The Kirk has gained all that it sought from the King. Freedom of worship, the revenues of the dioceses, even the suppression of the bishops. Only the fanatic few, the zealots who rave and rant, are against the King. And the nobles hate Argyll. Scotland would fall to any competent general – had he the cavalry I always lacked. To that end I am here, in Europe – to gather together the core of that invasion army, its arms and munitions of war. And the moneys to gain it that cavalry. With it, I will put King Charles on his Scottish throne again, if not his English.'

Elizabeth of Bohemia shook her beautiful head. 'Would I could aid you in your noble project, for my brother, my lord,' she said. 'God knows I would if I might. But I am poor, with barely sufficient to maintain my own house and family. I live an exile's life. But . . . I will do what I can to influence others. I have my friends . . .'

That was the reason for Montrose's rather lengthy statement.

He knew well that the Queen herself could not supply him with what he needed. But she was beloved of many, and might sway powerful men. Not least King Christian himself. She might well bring him to the stage of committing men, money and supplies for the venture.

'How will you win Charles out of the man Cromwell's hands, my friend?' the King asked, then. 'The English Parliament will be loth to let go a prize they have paid so highly for!'

'Once I sit in strength in Edinburgh, Sire, I believe they will quickly yield up King Charles – if they have not already done so. I would tell them that I was coming for him! I conceive it to be the last thing that Cromwell and his friends would wish would be another Scottish invasion, this time openly *against* them. There are over-many royalists in England, still. They would trade the King, for peace. Of this I am sure.'

'And then? With Charles back on the Scots throne? What then?'

'Then, Sire, it would be *my* advice to let England be. Meantime. It will not run away! In due course it will, I think, return to its allegiance. To its lawful monarch! Although – do I not know. I think, perhaps, it might be better for His Majesty to be content with being King of Scots, as were his forefathers. The English throne has brought little but sorrow and trouble . . .'

'And wealth! Forget not the wealth, man. Do not tell me that Charles Stewart will be content with ruling Scotland only, when he has ruled England also. He will not be in Scotland a month before he is seeking to get back to London. This is what I fear, why I, and others, hesitate. To see our men and aid squandered in a long campaign with England with Charles in foolish, unsure command. He and his friends have shown that they have no notion of soldiering, dabblers all. Madam's Rupert was the best of them – and him Charles threw out after Bristol siege. To *you*, sir I would trust my men. To my nephew Charles, never!'

Montrose bit his lip. 'Lend *me* the men then, Majesty – and you have my word that, whenever Scotland is won, you will have them back. At once.'

'*You* say so. But what my royal nephew say? He would over-rule you I swear. How think you, Elizabeth?'

'I would trust the Lord Jamie, Uncle. He has failed none, as yet – only been failed by others. Especially my foolish brother, God forgive him. I agree that it were wise to consider the Scots throne only, meantime. In this pass. Tie your aid to the sole command of my lord, here. That clear from the outset. Charles cannot demur. He has no choice.'

'Mm. I cannot provide sufficient of men and arms for the task. I will do what I can. Ships I can find . . .'

'But there are others,' Elizabeth declared. 'The Emperor. The Archduke Leopold. The Prince of Orange. The Electors – Hanover, Brandenburg. The King of France, indeed : . .'

'If I, and other Protestants, take this up, the Catholics will not touch it.'

'All Christian monarchs must deplore the unseating of a fellow-king, by his own subjects,' Montrose put in. 'Religion should not enter into this. Here is a cause to unite Protestant and Catholic both. Although, I admit it, Scotland would take more kindly to Protestant aid.'

'I have friends in both camps,' the Queen said. 'I shall appeal to all – but the Protestants first. I shall be your scribe and adjutant, my Lord Jamie. And enrol my sons Rupert and Maurice first of all!'

The Princess Sophia clapped her hands. 'We will all recruit for the Marquis. I swear I can persuade not a few young officers to go campaigning . . .!'

'Hush, girl – this is serious talk,' her mother told her. 'Not some knightly adventure. Though if any man can make war knightly, it will be this one, I think! But we must plan it with great care. *Our* campaign . . .'

Montrose cleared his throat. 'Madam, you are kind, kindness itself. I shall greatly esteem your royal and gracious help. But I must remind Your Majesty that I, we, require first the Queen's authority. The other Queen – Henrietta. King Charles has sent me to her. She is his deputy, while he is a prisoner. Any request for men and arms to invade his kingdom must go out with her authority . . .'

'That woman! That, that . . .!' Elizabeth swallowed, her fine eyes flashing. 'You must excuse me, my lord. I forget myself. But Henrietta Maria is . . . difficult. No wife for a man in Charles's situation. She is courageous, yes. She has spirit. But she is shallow as she is obstinate. Oh, you will say that all women are that! But Henrietta is like a weathercock. And selfish. She has little care for aught but her own comfort, I think.'

'Mamma would think more kindly of Aunt Henrietta if she were a man!' the innocently pert Sophia observed.

Elizabeth laughed frankly. 'Perhaps there is some truth in

that. Though it ill becomes my daughter to say it! But I do fear that if you depend on Henrietta, my lord, you are like to suffer much, in delay, procrastination, perhaps betrayal. And you have been betrayed overmuch already. I have known her for over twenty years, and never loved her. She is so *French* – and hàlf a Medici, at that!'

Both daughters laughed at that, and Louise made one of her few contributions. 'Rupert at least agrees with Mamma. He once called her Aunt Hetty – and she boxed his ears!'

'But she also likes good-looking men!' her sister pointed out. 'My lord may be more fortunate than you, Mamma!'

'Our tastes in men scarce coincide!' the Queen commented, drily.

Montrose inclined his head. 'Her Majesty admires my lord Duke of Hamilton,' he said, and left it at that.

'You have not heard from her yet ?' King Christian enquired.

'No, Sire. I still await a reply to my letters.'

'And you have no authority, true authority, without her ? To raise forces in Charles's name ?'

'No written authority. Only a private letter, in the King's own hand, but the page unsigned, unsealed. Instructing me to obtain authority, as ambassador extraordinary, from the Queen.'

'A fool in this, as in all!' Christian grunted. 'The woman is not to be trusted – like the rest of her house. She surrounds herself with time-servers and toadys. Rupert and Maurice soon had enough of her Court, and fled it.'

'All I need from the Queen, Sire, is a paper. Sealed. And some money, if I may . . .'

'Then, when you have got your paper, come back to the Hague, my Lord Jamie, and we will plan our campaign,' Elizabeth told him. 'But do not mention my name to Henrietta Maria, if you are wise!'

'It may not be necessary to go to St. Germain, Madam. If the Queen will but send me the letters of accreditation. As I have requested . . .'

They moved through to an antechamber, to eat, a fairly plain meal considering the illustriousness of the little company, for Christian had no patience with things fancy, in food as in other spheres. Montrose greatly enjoyed the company of the ladies, smiling and laughing and blossoming out more than he had done for long years. He found the Queen a truly kindred spirit, and was wholly captivated by her beauty, her verve, her warm outgoing manner – and by her wits, for he perceived her ability and acute mind, recognising what Christian had meant when he had said that Elizabeth Stewart was more of a man than Charles would ever be. Obviously she had inherited much of her extraordinary father's shrewdness, if apparently little else of his. As for the daughters, the man found the lively and so deceptively demure Sophia a constant challenge – though his eyes tended to stray more often to her quieter sister. Though quiet was hardly the word to apply to Louise; watchful, latent, smouldering, perhaps. She gave the impression of intense vitality, something of her mother's spirits, held as it were on leash, her finely moulded features, high arched brows and slightly hooded dark eyes eloquent of hidden fires. Apparently there were other daughters in this lively family.

It was with a real reluctance that James Graham eventually forced himself to make his adieus, seeking royal permission to retire, determined not to linger over-long in company so lofty, to outstay what was suitable in a first encounter – however much the ladies united in urging him to remain. He promised to visit them at the Queen's place of exile at the Hague, as soon as he might.

When Queen Elizabeth gave him one hand to kiss, she held his other with her own, squeezing it frankly. 'Be not too long in coming, Lord Jamie,' she told him. 'I am old enough to grudge the passage of time!' She was exactly fifty, and looked fifteen years younger.

The princesses bade farewell in typical fashion, Sophia breathless, prominent bosom heaving flatteringly, glance dipping but provocative, fluttering diffident but calculated compliments; Louise brief, almost casual, but her glowing eyes looking deep into the Graham's for a moment before she turned away.

That look stayed longer with the man than her sister's dimpling, as he made his way through the snow-decked streets of Hamburg to his own lodging. But it was their mother's image and presence and voice which presently pushed them both to the back of his mind. Something told him that he had been looking for Elizabeth Stewart all his days.

CHAPTER FOURTEEN

The early months of 1647 were of mixed satisfaction for James Graham. He had seldom been more comfortably quartered. He was still being most flatteringly treated, a constant stream of distinguished visitors coming to greet him and express appreciation and admiration. Invitations came from various Courts, to attend. He had leisure, as seldom before, and a remarkable lack of immediate responsibilities. Moreover, he had a warm feeling somewhere at the back of his mind, which he did not examine too closely but of which he was seldom unaware – and which was the inspiration of more poetry than he had written since his Grand Tour days, even if this tended to be torn up and burned before any other eyes could rest on it. A peculiar sense of well-being permeated the man – even though guilt for it was as consistent. For the thought of his wife and family, and all his friends, back in Scotland, seldom was far from him. That he could do nothing about them was at once both the hurt and the relief of it.

Frustration of a more immediate sort was as constant, however. For the waited-for reply from Queen Henrietta did not come, no royal summons to Paris. He fretted, being the man he was, his work, his duty, held up. His affairs had been awry, now, for so long that he almost forgot what it was like to be otherwise. But in the past action had been the anodyne for his problems and troubles – even with Magdalen and the children, with his estates and tenantry, with his involvement in national affairs, vigorous action had been the saving of his peace of mind. Now, action was denied him; but relaxation did not follow, with all that he stood for trembling on the brink, and he safe, comfortable, but unable to affect the issue. The image of that woman who was not his wife and was not, could not be, for him, while it warmed him like a steady fire, scarcely soothed the frustration.

Elizabeth of Bohemia wrote him a friendly, cheerful and encouraging letter – and uncertain how to answer her, he sent her a careful verse – after tearing up five.

He waited.

Then, in a bitter cold February, he had a letter from King Charles, much delayed in transit. It was warm, almost fulsome, assuring his well-beloved cousin and friend of his continuing reliance, affection and trust, commending him to the Queen, hoping for great things – but giving Montrose nothing that he needed. Charles continued to run true to form. No proper credentials, no constructive commands or instructions, no recognition of the Graham's helplessness in foreign lands, lacking funds or authority, however resounding his fame. There were even royal commendations, to him, of sundry utterly useless courtiers and captains, now on the Continent, proven incompetents and worse, who would co-operate with the King's Captain-General.

James Graham all but wept.

Then, at last, at the end of February, the long-awaited letter from Queen Henrietta arrived at Hamburg. But it contained no credentials, no authority of any sort, not even a promise thereof, or of funds. Merely platitudes, ineffectual felicitations, and assurances of welcome at her Court at the Louvre should he choose to call there in his sojournings on the Continent of Europe. She promised to write him further despatches hereafter, and signed herself his very good and affectionate cousin and friend.

Sorrowfully, Montrose decided that he had waited sufficiently long. Anyway, King Christian was not well, and was going back to Copenhagen, where he might be in his own palace. James Graham had wrung as much, in promises, out of the old warrior as he was likely to get. He wrote briefly to Henrietta that he was on his way to Paris, with the intention of collecting his credentials, as King Charles had instructed, closed up the house in Hamburg, took a rather troubled leave of King Christian, who had suddenly begun to age noticeably, thanked the Free City's council for its hospitality, and set off westwards, by sea, at the beginning of March.

It was convenient to sail to the Hague, and then to travel overland, by Brabant and Flanders. Elizabeth, in her second letter, had said that Rupert was proposing to be with her that month.

With contrary westerly winds, and fogs off the Friesian islands, it was late in the afternoon, three days later, when their vessel put in at Schevenigen, the port of the Hague, and midevening before Montrose could present himself at the couple of large and rambling houses, the Hof te Wassenaer and the

Naaldwijk Hof, which William II, Prince of Orange, had generously made available to his aunt-by-marriage – he was wed to King Charles's daughter Mary – on the Kneuterdijk, at the western end óf the tree-lined Lange Voorhout and near the city's central Vijver pond. The two adjacent houses scarcely made up a palace, but they served to house quite the gayest and most lively royal establishment in Europe, a mecca for talent, wit and beauty, where laughter, music, good talking and artistic expression flourished, despite the comparative poverty of the exiled Queen.

Impoverished or not, lights were everywhere as James Graham was conducted up a short avenue and into a courtyard surrounded on three sides by a many gabled and dormered red-brick house with notably steep roofs and ornamented chimneys. He heard the music before ever a servant informed him that an orchestral concert was in full swing. But a very gallant young man quickly materialised, to usher him into an ante-room, explaining the situation and announcing that Her Majesty sent assurances to the Lord Marquis that she would not long keep him waiting. Protesting that he had no intention of disturbing the evening's performance, and declaring that he would seek audience the next day, he was for prompt retiral. But any such thing was prevented by the arrival of an imperious young woman, not beautiful but dark with fine eyes, to whom the gallant bowed low, and introduced as the Princess Elizabeth. She looked Montrose up and down, assessingly, evidently decided that she approved of what she saw, and smiled faintly – and her smile transformed features just a little heavy.

'Mamma was right, and Sophia was wrong,' she observed, cryptically, and held out her hand to be kissed.

'I rejoice to meet one more of a family splendid as it is renowned, Highness,' he said. 'But – do I congratulate myself, or otherwise, on this judgment of right and wrong ?'

'That is for yourself to decide, my lord. My mother said that she wished that you were ten years older, my sister that you were ten years younger!'

'Ha!' Giving himself time to ponder that intriguing disclosure, the man cleared his throat. 'And . . . what did the Princess Louise say, Highness ?'

'Louie keeps her own counsel, sir. But she told Sophie not to be a fool!'

'So – I must make the best I can out of that ?' He considered this, at twenty-eight, the eldest daughter of this spirited family, known as Eliza to distinguish her from her mother. 'You also would prefer me ten years older, Highness?'

'Twenty, sir. Then you might be less dangerous to us women-folk!'

He sighed, ruefully. 'The danger, I swear, is all the other way. I am a poor soldier, lacking defences against beautiful women.' He bowed. 'I confess to having had little practice in such . . . campaigning. Circumstances have been less than propitious, I fear.'

'Are your Scotswomen so backward, then? Or blind? You cozen us, I think. You agree, Comte Henri? The Marquis is a cozener, a dangerous man?'

The younger man spread his hands. 'All the world knows of his victories, Highness. And a man who wins victories in one sphere, usually knows how to do so in others.'

'Exactly. Was Her Majesty wise in inviting this, this victor to the Hague, I wonder.'

'The said victor retires, stricken, forthwith,' James Graham assured her. 'I will return again tomorrow, if I may? Girded for battle . . .!'

'Indeed, my lord, and you will do no such thing! My royal mamma would not forgive me if I let the Marquis of Montrose go now – nothing more sure. If your lordship wearies of me, shall I send out Sophie . . . ?'

'God forbid, Highness! But – I did not come to intrude. Upon a concert. An entertainment. I will come back . . .'

'Concerts we have, like poverty, always with us – but Montrose is a rare bird! Come, sir – I was to take you to my mother's boudoir. No buts, my lord – a royal command! This way. Henri – I have come to the conclusion that you may safely leave me with my Lord of Montrose . . .!'

So the visitor was conducted, by rather shabby corridors and passages, to a small private apartment, opening on to a bed-chamber, where a wood-fire burned brightly and an elderly serving-woman sat knitting beside it, a homely and domestic scene. The woman was hobbling out, after bobbing a sort of curtsy, when the Princess restrained her.

'Wait, Martha. My lord – this is Martha. Martha Duncan, from Scotland. Who was Mamma's nurse, once. And my own likewise. Martha – here is the great Marquis of Montrose. Of whom we have so often spoken.'

'Mistress Duncan – your servant.' Montrose bowed as low as he had done to Eliza. 'Whoever nursed these ladies deserves the praise of all!'

'Och, mercy – himsel', is it?' the woman exclaimed, in the strong, slightly harsh voice of central Scotland. 'James Graham! God be thankit I have lived to see the face o' King Charles's truest friend! Gin there had been but yin mair like yoursel', sir, the pair gentlemen wouldna be where he is the day.' And coming forward again, she took Montrose's hand and kissed it, then almost flung it away, in a strange gesture, part fervid, part defiant.

Moved, the man shook his head. 'King Charles has been ill-served, yes. But I fear you all have been misled as to my poor efforts. What have I achieved, after all? That has lasted? I have been but ploughing the sands. And so many have paid for that ploughing, so much more dearly than have I.' He changed his sigh to a smile. 'But, I thank you. I see that Her Majesty of Bohemia has been under an excellent Scots influence, this while!'

'Och, I'm frae Falkland, in the Kingdom o' Fife, just. When Her Majesty's mither, the Queen Anne came, nae mair'n a lassie frae Denmark, I was a bit maid in the palace there, dochter to Pate Duncan, the falconer. That was fifty year ago and mair, mind ...'

A great flurry of activity interrupted her. The door was flung open and two large dogs bounded in, a greyhound and a beagle, all tail-wagging joy. And behind them came Elizabeth of Bohemia, hurrying, breathless. Obviously she had run up the stairs. Yet somehow she remained queenly, assured, mistress of herself and all else. And vivid – so vivid that her daughter and the old Scotswoman might not have been there. Her presence was an extraordinary one, magnetic, positive, compulsive – yet less imperious than that of his eldest daughter. She was like a bright light which makes all lesser luminaries seem dimmer than they really are, by comparison. Yet her brilliance had a gaiety and warmth which countered any hurt and grudging which it might have aroused amongst her own sex.

'My Lord Jamie – forgive me! The good musicians would have been hurt had I left them in mid-flood! Here is delight, to see you in my house. I rejoice that you have come.' She stopped short of an actual embrace of her visitor, but only just, gripping his arm, his shoulder, smiling into his eyes. 'Am I pardoned?'

Quite overwhelmed, James Graham wagged his head. 'Majesty – what can I say ? You shame me, I declare! Mine is all the privilege. That you should receive me in your house, at all. I have interrupted your music, spoiled your concert . . .'

'It is an interruption we relish, my friend. Oh, the music was well enough. But your coming changes all. The word of it went round that salon like a flash, I swear – the great Marquis of Montrose is here! None listened any more.' She laughed. 'Save only I, who most desired to come away. I must make a show of heeding. The Queen must ever set example! Ah, me!'

Her daughter looked heavenwards. 'Mamma – how *can* you!'

'I can, must and do, girl. And gain scant help from my unruly offspring. How has she been entertaining you, my lord ? With the sharp edge of her tongue, this one, I vow! And Martha, here ? Did I hear her declaring my sorry fifty years ? Shame on you, Martha! When my Lord Jamie might have conceived me less. Such treachery!'

'Och wheesht, Mam – it was *my* age, no' yours, I was at. The day *you* look your right age, there'll no' be a weel-favoured man left walking this good earth!'

'Mercy – I do not think I like the sound of that!' the Queen exclaimed, grimacing. 'As you can see, sir, I am accorded scant respect in my own house. My daughters have a conspiracy to keep me down. And this old witch shamefully abets them. But – at least it gives me just cause to banish them now, from my royal presence. So that I may have you to myself, my lord! Begone – both of you! You are dismissed.' With a lofty flourish, Elizabeth waved them out.

'I do not know how to thank Your Majesty for your gracious reception and favour,' Montrose said, when they were alone. 'And for your kind letters, advice and offer of aid. It is for your royal brother's sake, I well know. But it is none the less an enormous satisfaction, encouragement to me. The more so in that others prove less helpful.'

'Ah – you mean Henrietta Maria, I expect ? Has she not sent you your authority yet ? Or moneys ?'

'Neither, Madam. As yet. Only a vague letter. But she has now sent invitation, of a sort, to attend her Court – should I choose to travel in France! So that I may now go to the Louvre. Am on my way there, now, I took the opportunity to call upon Your Majesty, en route. To seek your further guidance. And in hope of seeing Prince Rupert . . .'

'Alas, Rupert is not come. Nor likely to come, for some time, I fear. He is seeking to build up a fleet of ships. For his uncle's aid. And, no doubt, to transport *your* army in due course. But there is trouble – there is always trouble. He is in South Zeeland, I think. A mutiny, no less. He lacks money also, to be sure. To pay the men, as well as to hire the vessels.'

'Aye, money is ever the stumbling-block. And yet, what is money, mere gold, compared with the lives of men? Shame it is that blood is cheap, but gold, silver, are dear indeed.'

'True – how very true. My sorrow that *I* cannot give you the money that you require. Any more than I can give it to Rupert. I live here in comfort yes – but only on the bounty of others, now that nothing comes to me from England. I am still the Princess-Royal of England – aye, even the First Daughter of Scotland! I have lands, properties, moneys owed me from both kingdoms. But not a groat have I seen from either, for years. Bohemia avails me nothing. And such Palatinate revenues as survive are insufficient even for my son Charles-Louis, the Elector. Were it not for my kinsman, William of Orange, here. And Uncle Christian...'

'Majesty – you must not distress yourself so. Myself also,' James Graham cried. 'I did not come to you, seeking money – God forbid! I pray you say no more on that score. I am sorry that I shall not see Prince Rupert. But it was for other help, guidance, introductions, that I sought Your Majesty's good offices...'

'Ah, me – and myself foolishly hoping that it might be something of my poor self that brought you. But never heed – at least accept my guidance in this, that we cease, when we are alone, this nonsense of majesty and lordship, and be ourselves. My name is Elizabeth – and I shall call you Jamie. As does Rupert. As, indeed, I intended, from the start! It was my father's name, and so my mother called him – although that may not commend itself to you? For not all men found my strange sire to their taste! But at least he knew how to manage men – which my brother does not.' She pointed to a chair. 'Come – sit with me by the fire, here. And tell me how Elizabeth Stewart may serve Jamie Graham.'

A little bemused, overwhelmed still, by all this, he waited for the Queen to sit, and then took his chair, at a discreet distance. That would not do.

'Draw close,' she commanded. 'For this Holland and its

creeping mist is plaguey cold of a winter, as it is hot and dusty of a summer. Dear God – how often I long and long for my own pleasant land.' She sighed, who was not a woman for sighing. 'I have been an exile for over thirty years. Almost all your lifetime, Jamie.'

'You would go back? If you might? To England? To Scotland?'

'Scotland I left at the age of six. Forty-four years ago. You see, I insist upon my full fifty years! If *I* do not, my daughters will! And you are but thirty-five. I have made it my business to find that out! So you are quite safe from Elizabeth Stewart, the woman, and may sit close to the fire with her, secure, James Graham. Not back there, as though the flames might scorch you!' She laughed, a shade ruefully. 'Forgive an elderly woman's havers, Jamie. And remember that I am Mary Stewart's grand-daughter. Also god-daughter of Elizabeth Tudor! A fatal heritage for any female, you will agree?'

He bit his lip, but did draw his chair closer. 'It's not the fire that might scorch me, I think,' he said carefully. 'In some matters, many I fear, I am but a weakly man, Madam . . .'

'Elizabeth.'

'Elizabeth.' He nodded. 'I believe that you underestimate your . . . potency. Which has nothing to do with age or years. Or rank, indeed.'

'I underestimate nothing, my friend. Myself – nor you! Nor sad facts. Facts I have been living with, all my days. I am not likely to blink them now.' She sat back a little. 'Your wife, Jamie? Your children? Tell me of them.'

He drew a long breath. 'I do not know. How they do. Now. I left the children well, Magdalen less so. I hope, I believe, that they will not suffer further. On my account. Magdalen's father, the Earl of Southesk, is a careful man. He seldom finds himself at odds with the winning side! He remains friendly with those who rule Scotland today. And she, Magdalen, has long lived with him. In his house. Under his protection. With the younger children. They should be safe, I think.'

Elizabeth considered that. 'Your wife prefers her father's course to yours?'

'She has had reason to, I have brought her little but sorrow and hurt. Our first son died. On campaign with me. Although but fourteen years. Our second is a prisoner, a hostage. Magdalen has suffered for my actions, always.'

'It is a wife's lot and duty, is it not? And yours has the greatest soldier in Europe to husband.'

'I cannot think that she would esteem that – even if it were true. Besides, she is unwell. Much troubled. Has been, for long...'

'In her mind? Or her body?'

'In both, I think. And, God forgive me, I have been no help to her, in this, either.'

'You have had much else to consider.'

'So I tell myself. But is it sufficient excuse? For a husband?'

She eyed him shrewdly. 'So James Graham blames himself? You have spent more than your treasure, and the risk of your life, in my brother's cause, it seems.'

'A man must be prepared to give all for what he believes in. But... it is grievous when the price must be paid by others, who had no choice in the matter.'

'Your wife did not choose? To support you in this your fight?'

'No-o-o. She believed always that I made the wrong choice. Perhaps I did. But, having made it, set my hand to it, taken the lead indeed, I must needs see it through. Cost what it may. Or... so *I* saw it.'

'Yes – that is how Montrose would see it. So – you lack support in your own house, as well as in my brother's? More than Charles Stewart is not worthy of James Graham, I think.'

'No – you misjudge, Madam. Elizabeth. You misjudge it. I have thought much on this. Magdalen was married to me as a child, a mere child. Myself I was not seventeen. She had no choice – nor indeed did I. But we were happy enough. For three years. But in her father's house. I blame much on that. It was part of the marriage contract that my guardians drew up – and David Carnegie himself was one of them – that for at least three years after the wedding, until I was of age, his daughter should continue to live in *his* house. So she never escaped from his influence. And he is a dominant man, and thinks other than do I. And I grew to rebel against it. Then, when my good-brother Colquhoun ran off with my younger sister Katherine, to the Continent, I took matters into my own hands and went after her, at the age of twenty. To try to save her, bring her back from shame. It meant putting forward my projected tour of Europe. But I did not take Magdalen with me. I had a wife and two bairns – and I left them behind, in her father's house. For three years. I did not find Katherine, and I lost Magdalen, in those years. She became her father's daughter, rather than my wife, and has remained so. For when I came home at last, it was almost at once to become concerned in Scotland's troubles. I have been no husband to Magdalen Carnegie. And her's not the blame.'

For a while there was silence in that chamber, apart from the snuffling of the two dogs, men's dogs but seemingly the Queen's own, and the whuff and crackle of the wood fire.

Gently Elizabeth spoke, at length. 'Tell me of your children, Jamie. Three survive, I think . . . ?'

He spoke to her of Jamie, and his defiant gesture, imprisoned in Edinburgh Castle; of David who died young; of little Robert and young Jean. Nor did he hide his painful pride in Johnnie, who had played the man before his time, and died in his father's arms. So they talked by the flickering fire, and the man found a comfort in the talking such as he had not known in long years – even though comfort was not usually one of the emotions inspired by this woman. Elizabeth, the Queen of Hearts. She proved herself an excellent listener, understanding, responsive, sympathetic – but never merely that, stimulating, leading on. And she, presently, in return, told him much of her own affairs; of her beloved Frederick's death, by plague, fifteen years previously; of the trials of an exiled widow with no fewer than ten children still to rear; of the problems of maintaining royal state without a kingdom or its revenues; of her pride in her valiant son Rupert, her satisfaction over the more solid Maurice and her disillusion with the eldest, the Elector Palatine Charles-Louis; and so on. She even, ruefully, related something of the semi-scandalous affair of the Sieur de Vaux, Colonel Jacques de l'Epinay, who had come to the Hague a year before and paid court in shameless and flagrant fashion both to herself and to her daughter Louie – and had had his hat knocked off by her nineteen year old son Philip in consequence, this resulting first in a duel between the two, which was interrupted, and then in a more deadly encounter ending in the death of de Vaux and the flight of Prince Philip. The Queen did not seem unduly upset over the gallant Colonel's demise, and her head-shaking over the spirits of her sons gave the impression of being formal rather than distressed. Montrose's grave observation that he was duly warned as to the dangers of association with the Bohemian royal family, brought forth a quick hand to his arm, a chuckle, and the reminder that none of her sons happened to be at the Hague in the meantime.

So it was late when James Graham finally forced himself to depart, still without anything to the point said on the subject of his visit, advice over his approaches to Henrietta Maria and introductions to various crowned heads of Europe. That must await their next interview. The Queen herself saw him down back-stairs and passages to a side-door – a delightfully personal, almost conspiratorial proceeding, that sent the man off through the misty, night-bound streets in a warm glow of sheer pleasure such as had not been his lot to experience heretofore. He was to come back the next day, and with all his little party, to take up residence in the Wassenaer Hoff, before he moved on towards Paris – that was another royal command.

* * *

Montrose spent a full week at the Hague, entirely pleasantly, indeed enjoyably. Moreover, his ever-active conscience did not greatly trouble him over the delay, for at his next audience with Elizabeth he discovered that, although peace had theoretically descended at last upon war-torn Europe, much of it was still an armed camp and travel across it still impossible without permits and letters of passage. Flanders had to be crossed to reach France, and the Governor of the Spanish Netherlands, the Archduke Leopold, brother of the Emperor Ferdinand III, still scarcely welcomed travellers from Protestant Holland. But he was well-disposed to the Queen of Bohemia it seemed, and she would send to him for a safe-conduct for the Marquis of Montrose. Meantime he had no option, she pointed out, but to put up with her company and that of her daughters.

This was no hardship. Four daughters, though no sons, were presently at the Hague with their mother – Eliza, Louise, Sophia and Henrietta, the last a gentle and pretty girl of twenty-one. They all showed considerable interest in their visitor, each in a different fashion, and the man underwent the highly unusual experience of passing his days amidst a whirl of attractive, high-spirited and demanding womanhood. He did not again have opportunity for any lengthy and purely private association with the Queen; but there was a rapport and sympathy between them, amongst all the flurry and activity of that lively and somewhat overcrowded little Court which did not have to be emphasised by confidential encounters. A glance, a tossed word, an understanding or cryptic allusion, as well as an open and undisguised mutual admiration, served eloquently to link them in a form of delightful intimacy such as James Graham, at least, had never envisaged as linking a man and a woman. It was a strange and totally unlooked for development – but he was scarcely given time to brood on its implications or problems.

Through it all he was aware, too, of other eyes that were apt to dwell on him, in thoughtful, assessing fashion, Sophia flirted with him outrageously, Eliza fenced with him in a kind of intellectual in-fighting, and Henrietta plainly hero-worshipped. But Louise considered him, he was aware, with deeper, more searching scrutiny, from those lustrous eyes. There was no rude staring; but Montrose was a little uncomfortably sensible of being carefully weighed in some sort of balance. Whether this was all in the interests of art and feature delineation, he tended to doubt. Nevertheless, without deliberately debating the matter with himself, he came to accept that the Princess Louise was his favourite amongst the royal daughters.

A most agreeable surprise for James Graham was the fortuitous arrival at the Hague, that week, of the young Lord Napier, direct from Scotland. Archie was, in fact, on his way to Paris, seeking Montrose, and unable to bear Scotland without him any longer; but the only vessel he had been able to find passage in had been bound for Haarlem and Schevenigen. Uncle and nephew made a joyful reunion. They had parted, in sad farewell at Rattray, on the northern rim of Strathmore, the previous July, when Montrose had disbanded what remained of his army, on the King's command and according to the terms he had had to agree with Middleton.

Napier had much and varied news from home. He had not seen Magdalen and the children, but the Lord Carnegie had told him that his sister might as well be dead, for all her interest in living. She was still with her father at Kinnaird. The children were well, and the Lord James still a hostage but not being maltreated.

With this Montrose had to be satisfied.

For the rest of his news, the younger man confirmed the sale of the King for £200,000 – but said that only half had been paid by the English Parliament. Argyll was master in Scotland but, strangely, the Estates were proving more difficult towards him than heretofore. The selling of the King had shocked the Scottish people, of all ranks, and the men responsible were highly unpopular. Hamilton and Argyll had fallen out, whether over their respective shares in the money, or otherwise, was not clear;

but the Duke was now seeking to form a monarchical party – presumably in the interests of King Hamilton instead of King Campbell. The Kirk was split, and the fanatic zealots had lost ground – although the moderates had suffered a blow in the death of Alexander Henderson . . .

Montrose grieved to hear this last. He and Henderson had scarcely agreed these last years; but he had always esteemed the minister honest, and recognised his notable qualities. Scotland in her present sorry state could ill spare Henderson.

As for the rest, the 'pardon' and reversal of all forfeitures, which James Graham had managed to gain for his supporters, by his treaty with Middleton and the disbandment of his army, though grumbled at by the Estates had been respected in the main, and there seemed to have been no major reprisals. Nevertheless, life was made sufficiently difficult for all who had been King's men, with pinpricks innumerable, threats and continued ostracism. But greetings and assurances of renewed support came from all Montrose's former lieutenants and friends – Airlie and his sons, Madderty, Douglas, Atholl, Kinnoull, Wigton, even the Laird of Grant – and, of course, all the Grahams, Inchbrakie in particular, who was like a shackled lion, denied action and his master's presence. They all asked, when would he come back to free Scotland from its purgatory?

Montrose was touched, moved – but frustrated, in his turn. God knew, he was as anxious as they for his return. But he was under the King's command to raise an army, munitions and money, for that purpose, yet was still denied all the necessary authority to do so. He was, in fact, little farther on than when he had left Scotland, save in the good offices and sponsorship of the Queen of Bohemia, and in certain promises of Christian of Denmark. At this rate he could hold out no hope of any speedy return, grieve him as it did to say so.

Then let him go back to Scotland alone, on his own, his nephew urged, with all the enthusiasm of his twenty-three years. Forget the foreign aid and rely on Scotland itself, Many would rise again, rejoicing at their leader's return, and they would sweep Argyll and Hamilton, with all the sour prophets of doom and hell-fire, from the face of a fair land. As they had done before. Montrose could be master of Scotland again in six months, would he but return and raise his standard.

Patiently his uncle demurred. Was something not being forgotten? King Charles, and his commands. He, Montrose, had no right, or desire, to be master of Scotland. His only authority to raise any standard was the King's. He was Charles's Captain-General, yes – but it was on the King's command that he had disbanded his army and left Scotland. He could not just return on his *own* authority – not as Captain-General.

While Napier deflatedly considered this, Montrose went on to ask about the Gordons. What of Huntly? Of Aboyne? Aye, and what of Colkitto? And the Clan Donald? Despite the older man's realism as to the priorities of the situation, there was no hiding the eagerness behind the enquiries.

The Gordons were just the Gordons, his nephew asserted. Huntly was lying low, safe behind his ramparts of man-power and vast territories. Aboyne was no one knew where, and the Lord Lewis, a curse on him, to all intents leader of the clan and approved of by Argyll. As for Colkitto, it was said that he had gone back to Ulster in the meantime. Clan Donald was back to internecine feuding, and baiting Seaforth and the Mackenzies. All was folly and a beating of the air. But if Montrose returned . . .

James Graham digested his nephew's news with mixed feelings, glad as he was to see the young man. It made him, at least, the more urgent to get to Henrietta Maria in France, whatever the present delights of the Hague. Indeed when, two days later, the awaited safe-conduct arrived from the Archduke Leopold, plus a pressing invitation to call at the vice-regal seat of Ghent in the by-going, it was Archie Napier who would have held back and dallied amongst the feminine attractions of the Wassenaer Hof.

The young women would have held their visitors back, but the Queen rebuked them. 'Let them go, stupids!' she said. 'No man worth the name thinks the more of women who seek to detain him when he has business on his mind. And the Lord Jamie has much on his – whatever the Lord Archie may have! Let him go while still he loves us – and he will come back the sooner!'

'Her Majesty is as wise as she is beautiful,' Montrose acknowledged. 'Would that we might linger. But with work to do, pressing work – for men's lives are in this – we would make ill company biding in this felicity against our consciences.' And if that sounded too sententious, he added, smiling, 'We are Scots Presbyterians, recollect – uncomfortable folk, wary of all the world's pleasures!'

'You will scarce feel at home where you are going, then!'

Elizabeth declared. 'We shall not quarrel with that, never fear – and welcome you back thereafter to our soberer company!'

So they left the Hague on the 10th of March for Ghent, on horseback now, over the canal-seamed levels of the Flanders plain.

*   *   *

The Archduke Leopold, son of the late Emperor Ferdinand II and brother of the present Ferdinand, was Governor of the Spanish Netherlands. He greeted them effusively, loud in his praise of Montrose's achievements, vehement in his vocal support, hinting at translating it into arms and men in due course. This was encouraging, but at the same time somewhat embarrassing. For, of course, this was Catholic support; and if it was over-enthusiastic, or made too much of, Protestant princes might refuse to co-operate. Moreover, any Catholic preponderance in the proposed invasion force would be highly unpopular in Scotland, where Montrose's Catholic supporters had already been too prominent. Money, now – that was different. Catholic money smelled the same as any other. But Leopold, a sallow and rather sinister-looking Hapsburg in his late thirties, with a slight squint in one eye which chillingly reminded James Graham of Argyll, however much he smiled, had nothing to say about money. So his visitor found himself in the strange position of seeking to play down enthusiasm for his cause, meantime. Perhaps he would come back to the Archduke.

On the second day at the great fortress-city of Ghent, another English-speaking visitor arrived – and seeking Montrose, not Leopold. This was a Mr. John Ashburnham, one of Queen Henrietta Maria's Gentlemen-in-Waiting. He had been sent to intercept the Marquis on his way to Paris.

When they could be alone, in the long vaulted gallery of the twelfth-century castle on the Scheldt, the stylishly languid Mr. Ashburnham, slightly older than Montrose and apparently somewhat weary of living, after expressing the Queen's great regard for his lordship and his own humble satisfaction at greeting so eminent a soldier, went on to declare that it therefore gave him no little pleasure to be the means of shortening his lordship's inevitably tedious journey through these benighted lands, and save him much time and trouble. All on Her Majesty's gracious behalf, of course. Even a sympathetic yawn was achieved here.

'You mean, sir, that you have brought me my letters of

credence and appointment? As His Majesty's ambassador-extraordinary? You have them with you?' Montrose was indeed prepared to look more kindly on this saturnine and sighful elegant, with his scented gloves, powder and ringlets if he carried the long-sought authority.

'Hm. Not precisely that, my lord. But, shall we say, new and improved instructions? Her Majesty desires you, instead of further delay here on the Continent, to return to Scotland forthwith, there to gather an army and lead it south into England against the man Cromwell, this Fairfax, and the other rebels. In conjunction with a thrust from Ireland, to be led by my lord of Ormonde.'

James Graham stared, bereft of any speech.

'Her Majesty believes that this will be much more profitable to the King's cause than your making of a tour of Europe. Here is a letter, from the Queen, making plain her instructions. So there will be no need for your lordship to continue on this journey to the Louvre.'

Montrose drew a long breath. 'Do I hear aright? Or am I losing my senses?' he demanded. 'You are telling me that Queen Henrietta proposes that I turn back? Do not see her. But instead return to Scotland. Just as I am. Alone! Without men, or money. Or, indeed, credit. And there, in Argyll's Covenant-dominated land, raise an army and invade England! That is what you are saying, sir? And conceiving as possible?'

'You have done it before, my lord, have you not? And can do it again.'

Long seconds passed as the other strove to master his emotions and speak with a controlled voice. 'No, sir,' he said, at length. 'I have not done so before. When last I entered Scotland, to raise it for the King, I was a rich man. With a clan to raise; friends, also rich, and hopeful. The King's cause, in England, was still sound, battles still being won. Now, I am a man utterly impoverished – as are my friends. At the King's command I disbanded my army, submitted myself to his enemies, disappointed all who were loyal to His Grace in Scotland. And now you would have me go back, empty-handed, discredited, alone, and start all over again. One man . . .'

'Scarce discredited, my lord. As a soldier, you still have credit. Your name alone will be sufficient, I vow, to rally thousands to you . . .'

'God save us – do you know anything of soldiering, of armies, warfare, man? Anything at all, to speak of?' It was not often that James Graham was provoked into such discourteous speech.

Offended, Ashburnham turned away, to move to one of the small windows. 'I have served His Majesty in the field, my lord, I assure you,' he threw back over his padded shoulder. 'And not without success. But – I am here to express the Queen's desires and instructions, not my own.'

'Queen Henrietta can know nothing of war. Therefore she takes the advice of others, in this. If not yours, sir – whose?'

'That is not my place to say. I am here conveying the royal commands.'

'Commands? I take my commands, sir, from my master – and yours – King Charles.'

'Her Majesty acts for the King. Since he is imprisoned and cannot act for himself. Read Her Majesty's letter if you doubt my competence, my lord.'

Montrose did break the seals and scanned the neat clerk's penwork with Henrietta's floriate signature at the foot. Ashburnham had not gone beyond his remit. The Queen had indeed requested her well-beloved cousin and friend to return to Scotland forthwith, there to raise an army and invade England.

Helplessly he shook his head. 'Whoever advised Her Grace to this course was a fool!' he declared. 'I cannot accept it.'

'But . . . my lord! It is the Queen's expressed wish that you should. Clear and beyond question. You cannot reject Her Majesty's written authority.'

'I am the *King*'s Captain-General and ambassador-designate. With the King's personal instructions to visit the Courts of Europe on his behalf. To gain men and materials and shipping from them, to lead a properly equipped and officered invasion of Scotland,' he said. '*That* command I cannot reject, on the whim of his wife, advised by incompetents.'

'You refuse to obey Her Majesty, my lord?'

'No. But I will not carry out foolish proposals without first seeing her, and advising her otherwise. As the King's principal officer and adviser on Scottish affairs. I shall continue on my journey to Paris, sir.'

'Hm.' John Ashburnham turned, and spoke in a rather different tone of voice. 'That will not be necessary, I am sure, my lord Marquis. I have, er, other matters to put to you, which may make you see this policy in a different light.'

'Ah. I wondered why one of the Queen's Gentlemen should

have brought this letter to me, rather than a mere courier. There is more than meets the eye, here?'

'There is policy, my lord – to meet the new situation. The King's captivity and harsh treatment by Fairfax and Cromwell. In the circumstances, we must think anew. How best to serve His Majesty's interests. My Lord Jermyn is convinced that the time has come to make a new and statesmanlike move. In conformity with His Majesty's own wishes.'

'So – it is Jermyn! Harry Jermyn is a lord now! He was ever close to the Queen's ear. So much so that King Charles sentenced him to eternal banishment! So this is where Her Majesty gleans her advice!'

'Lord Jermyn is amongst the ablest of the Queen's advisers, sir.' That was stiffly said.

'And knows little more of warfare and soldiering than does the lady herself!'

'This is policy, statecraft, rather than soldiering, my lord. The Scots, the Covenant Scots, have fallen out with their English allies, with Cromwell and Fairfax and the Independents. They have been paid only half the price they bargained for the King – £200,000. The rest is withheld – not going to be paid, it is clear. Moreover, the Independents have rejected Presbyterianism – Cromwell will have none of it. That was to be the cornerstone of Argyll's Commonwealth of the two kingdoms – Presbyterian worship and government for both. So there is ill-will. We must turn it to the King's advantage. Do you not agree?'

'I await Lord Jermyn's superior understanding of statecraft, sir, to enlighten me as to how this unsavoury squabble between traitors and hucksters may serve the King?'

'Why, it is simple, I'd have thought. The true enemy is Parliament, Cromwell and the Independents, the rebels who hold the King prisoner. The Scots business is a mere nothing, by comparison. So – make friends with the Scots, and use them against the English rebels.'

'Make friends with the Scots?' Montrose searched the man's face. 'The Scots people are the King's friends *now*. His loyal subjects. Can it be . . . can you possibly mean to make friends with the Covenant leadership? Argyll? And the zealot ministers? Not that – you cannot mean that!'

'But yes. Why not? To make use of them against the King's enemies.'

'Dear God! Do you know what you say? *Use* Archibald

Campbell! You and your like? Mercy of heaven – have you, and Jermyn, taken leave of your wits?'

'I think you forget yourself, my lord!' Ashburnham said, haughtily. 'I am not accustomed to be spoken to so. Especially when on the Queen's business. This is not some camp of mercenary soldiers, in the Scottish wilds!'

'Then I beg your pardon, sir, if my disbelief offends you. I would offend no man, without cause. But – still I cannot conceive you to be in earnest in this.'

'And why not? The Marquis of Argyll is an able and astute nobleman – if prejudiced. He will perceive advantage to himself and his Presbyterians in uniting with the King's forces against the English Parliament, which witholds his money. And, once the King is safely back on his throne, he can deal with the Presbyterian fanatics. As he has done before. And if Argyll and his faction will not co-operate, then be sure that the Duke of Hamilton and his *will*. Already he has set up a King's party in Scotland . . .'

'Hamilton, now!' James Graham had difficulty in breathing. Abruptly he turned and paced the length of the gallery and back before committing himself to speech.

'Mr. Ashburnham,' he said, tightly, 'Hamilton is only second to Argyll as the King's enemy and betrayer. He is a fool, where the Campbell is clever – but a dangerous fool. None, of any integrity, or plain sense, would trust him a yard!'

'You must not allow your personal humours and dislikes to sway you in matters of State, my lord Marquis,' the other reproved, raising his brows. 'We cannot all delight in those we work with.'

Somehow Montrose kept his Graham temper. 'Sir – would you work with one who had just *sold* your King, and his? For money. And pocketed £30,000 therefor? Dividing the forty pieces of silver with Argyll! And now weeps because another £30,000 is not forthcoming? You would work with such?'

'I would *use* such. On the King's service and behalf. Use them to fight the King's greater enemies. They will fight as well as the next, will they not? Especially when led by a general so able as the Marquis of Montrose.'

'Which they will not be, I assure you, sir!' That was forceful, grim. 'I would no more consider working with these forsworn traitors than would they agree to be led by me. We are anathema to each other.'

231

'And if your monarch's interests demand it? And your Queen's commands?'

'See you, sir – how can I make you understand? Argyll is a shrewd man, utterly unscrupulous. Compared with him, you and Jermyn – aye, and my own self – are babes at breast! He has played a long, difficult and hazardous game to win to where he is now – ruler of Scotland. He has betrayed, tortured, slaughtered, as few men have ever done, to reach that goal. Think you he will allow *any* to use him now? Will not see through any manoeuvre that you, or I, might envisage? He would no more allow an invasion of England, on the King's behalf, than he would yield the style of *MacCailean Mor* to one of his clansmen. Argyll must be *defeated* before any such move may be attempted. Defeated in the field, and then before the Estates. And defeated soundly. Driven from Scotland.'

'Hamilton, then? The Duke.'

'Fails in all he touches. Save only in imposing on the King. And the Queen! Fails and betrays. Death to any cause. I would not work with him under any circumstances. That is final.'

'You are a harsh judge, my lord.'

'On the contrary. Others claim that I am too trusting. But these two are beyond all association.'

'There are others in the Covenant ranks. Even you, sir, will not call Lauderdale, Lothian. Lanark . . .'

'They have sold their monarch once. They would do so again.'

'*You* would be there to ensure that they did not.'

'No, sir. I will not be there. Save with an army at my back. Now – enough. You know my mind. I shall not change it.'

'The Queen's Majesty will be much displeased.'

'Better that than betrayed, her husband's cause further violated. But – I will speak with Her Majesty on this. I ride on to the Louvre, Mr. Ashburnham . . .'

CHAPTER FIFTEEN

There was need for haste now, Montrose recognised – for Ashburnham would not linger in getting back to Paris with his news and steps might well be taken to injure, or at least retard, his interests there. But an invited guest of a ruling prince could not just pack up and depart unceremoniously, and James Graham had to take his leave of the Archduke Leopold in due and proper fashion. This could not be done before noon next day – and meanwhile Ashburnham had a major start on the 200-mile road to Paris.

So, once they did win clear of Ghent, Montrose, Napier and Wishart – for Hurry had departed to sell his sword to the highest bidder, and the other exiles gone their own ways – settled down to sheer and sustained hard riding. It was almost like old days, exhilarating indeed, after too much hanging about and soft living, to stretch themselves, to test horse-flesh and their own endurance to the full. Over the flat, poplar-dotted plains and straight hedgeless roads of Flanders, Hainault and Picardy they raced, on and on through a fertile country-side still shamefully devastated by the long years of war, with ruin, neglect and havoc everywhere. Compared with Scotland, however, it was easy riding, the endless canals, ditches, and rivers with often damaged bridges the greatest obstacles. Darkness did not halt them, and they rode on through the night, only the weariness of their horses the limiting factor. By late afternoon of the second day they were riding down the forested reaches of the wide valley of the Oise.

At St. Denis, only four miles from Paris, Montrose sent Archie Napier on ahead, to the Louvre – but he himself slowed his pace only a little. A stratagem was necessary, he believed. If Ashburnham was still ahead, and hurried to inform his mistress that her commands and desires were being contested, Henrietta Maria, a proud and headstrong woman, might possibly refuse to receive her visitor – or her advisers might so sway her. Apart from his personal feelings in the matter, it would do his embassage no good if it was whispered round the Continent that the Marquis of Montrose had either been refused audience of his

Queen, or kept kicking his heels for any lengthy time before she would deign to see him. He must ensure, if at all possible, that this did not happen.

The magnificent royal palace of the Louvre, on the north bank of Seine, had not been occupied by the French royal family since the death of Louis XIII in 1643. His widow, Anne of Austria, mother of the child Louis XIV, had generously handed it over to her exiled sister-in-law with a monthly pension of no less than 30,000 livres, and here the so-called Court of England was set up in surroundings of almost unbelievable splendour, in vast premises and amongst a treasure-house of art, sculpture, tapestries and the like. Nevertheless, despite the pension, the innumerable occupants of this huge establishment were, by this 1647, not a little threadbare, if not tarnished. Henrietta conceived it her duty to maintain a large Court. Support for King Charles's cause amongst his fellow-monarchs of Christendom, she pointed out, would nowise be advanced by the presence of any seedy and second-rate household for his Queen and representative. She was the wife of the reigning monarch of one of the major States of Europe – not the widow of the ex-King of a small country, like her sister-in-law of Bohemia; and it was only suitable and consonant with her husband's dignity that she should maintain a worthy style and entourage. Moreover, she was a Daughter of France, sister of the late King Louis, and in France its princesses were expected to live in a fashion commensurate with the household of His Most Christian Majesty. Hence the princely pension. Unfortunately, Henrietta had always been extravagant however, and though she had in the past engaged in much money-raising for King Charles's cause – the object of her return to France – more and more her Court establishment ate up not only her revenues but also the hoard of jewellery she had brought her from England at an early stage of the Civil War – including the Crown Jewels. The value of that royal treasure had been enormous – King James had remarked at his daughter Elizabeth's wedding to the Elector Palatine in 1612 that he and his wife, Anne of Denmark, between them wore jewellery to the value of over £900,000. But all this was long since gone, and Henrietta was hard put to it to keep her establishment in the style she conceived necessary, much less to find funds for adventures in England and Scotland.

Nevertheless, superficially at least, impoverishment was by no means obvious – compared, for instance with Queen Elizabeth's little establishment at the Hague. In numbers of adherents, for one thing; scores, almost hundreds, of high-born but at present mainly impecunious courtiers decorated the Louvre's already over-decorative halls and salons, English and French, with their families and servants. Gaiety, colour and amusement by no means suffered, and were indeed even more in evidence than when the Court had flourished, at peace, in England. Henrietta Maria was a woman of spirit, although of a very different order from Elizabeth, and was not to be unduly depressed by circumstances. Her Court glittered, and if the glitter was apt to be more tinsel than solid specie, it corruscated but the more brittly brilliant.

Montrose knew enough of this to be prepared, and cautious. The last thing he desired was to antagonise this Queen. Elizabeth's entourage at the Hague was nothing to by go; its friendly, hospitable informality was unlikely to be paralleled by any other in Europe. Courts-in-exile were often the fiercest sticklers for form of any; and Henrietta's, on past performance, was more than likely to be of that order. In theory, he should not approach the royal presence without being summoned. She had, of course, invited him to visit her; but her later request for him to return to Scotland at once might be claimed to have countermanded that invitation. Nevertheless, he was Viceroy of Scotland, in name at least, and ambassador-designate, and as such surely had the *right* to approach the King's consort as one of her advisers. While sending Napier ahead to inform the Master of the Queen's Household of his arrival, therefore, he followed closely enough in the other's wake not to be halted by any hastily decided ban.

He had taken dress into consideration, likewise, and halted for a brief time at an inn on the outskirts of Paris, to change, not into Court dress deliberately, but into clothing sufficiently neat not to stand out offensively in evening company.

Nevertheless, when he entered the ornate portico of the magnificent quarter-mile-long façade of the Louvre Palace, ablaze with lights, and strode authoritatively past the uncertain guards into the first of the great reception-rooms, discarding his travelling-cloak, in the peacock brilliance of the seething, chattering throng his sober black-and-silver garb stood out like a daw's. He moved quietly but purposefully through the staring, painted, posturing groupings.

His purpose, of course, required that he should not now be

kept waiting for any lengthy period, at the royal displeasure, before all – although such of these people as spared him more than a disapproving glance probably assumed him to be a secretary or messenger somehow strayed into the wrong part of the palace, or possibly one of the musicians for the dancing which was in progress in the huge main gallery.

Where the thickest throng was, there he anticipated he would find the Queen. He was fortunate to arrive just as a cotillon was approaching its final measures, in the 300-foot-long pilastered and arcaded gallery under the coved, gilt and painted ceilings and the flashing crystal chandeliers, its blaze and colour reflected to infinity in vast ornate mirrors. Henrietta herself was treading it, at the far top end of the apartment, partnered by a florid, thick-set and fair-headed youngish man with a somewhat petulant mouth, who would have looked better dressed other than in yellow satin – an old acquaintance though scarcely a friend of Montrose's, the Lord Digby, heir to the Earl of Bristol and the former junior commander of royalist forces who had twice failed to come to Scotland. The high throne-like chair raised on the dais-platform at the head of the gallery was obviously where the Queen would make for at the end of the dance. James Graham worked his way thitherwards unobtrusively, as the final flourishes of the orchestra led up to a climax. It all could not have been much more convenient.

But, standing beside the throne, waiting with some evident impatience, was a very large and bulky gentleman, red faced, powdered-haired, dressed in maroon velvet with orange bows and garters and gold lace. Montrose knew this man also – Harry, first Lord Jermyn of St. Edmundsbury, Chamberlain and Master of the Household to Henrietta – and declared by many to be the Queen's lover, likewise. Their eyes met.

'Christ God – Montrose!' Jermyn gasped. 'Here! Already!'

'Greetings, my lord. Accept my belated congratulations on your, hm, elevation. Not unearned, I warrant!' That was smoothly said.

'But . . . damme, sir – my lord . . .' The other's rather prominent blue eyes goggled unhappily. He was superficially an amiable man, and lazy, an unlikely intriguer and meddler in State affairs; but since the Queen had so largely influenced the King, and Jermyn had long found himself in a position to influence the Queen, he had gradually achieved a power which seemed to sit but unsuitably on his massive but rather ungainly person. Now, although he was obviously much upset by the Graham's appearance upon the scene, he found it difficult to be authoritatively angry in the face of this proud interloper. He was the son only of a simple country knight, and was not at his best with such as Montrose.

'Yes, my lord?' the other encouraged, smiling gently – and thereby causing the greater unease.

'Did you not . . .? I sent Napier . . . I told him to tell your lordship that, that . . .'

'That Her Majesty would be happy to greet her principal adviser on Scottish affairs? I have, as you see, hastened to present myself to Her Majesty, as is right and proper, immediately on my arrival in Paris, straight from the saddle. I could do no less.'

'No, my lord Marquis.' Jermyn had partly recovered himself. 'That was not my intention. I sent the Lord Napier back to you, to inform you that it was not possible for Her Majesty to grant you audience. Not at present. Not yet. Until she has considered well. Considered your, your contumely.' The big man puffed. 'Your refusal to obey Her Majesty's specific commands. Reported to me only a short time ago. Scarcely believable, sir – but proved as accurate by your presence here. When you should be on your way to Scotland. I must request you to leave, my lord. To leave the palace at once. Until Her Majesty has had time to consider your situation.'

'You jest, sir! How can Her Majesty consider my, and the Scottish situation, when she is uninformed upon it? Is decision to be taken on Scotland, with Scotland's Lieutenant outside the door?'

'You are no longer Scotland's Lieutenant, my lord. And when the Queen requires your advice, she will send for it. You may not thrust it upon her. She has her advisers on Scottish affairs, never fear.' Those lack-lustre eyes which could look so sleepy darted their glance now towards the dance-floor. The music had ceased and the dancers were bowing. Henrietta Maria was making for the dais, on Digby's arm. 'Now – go, sir. And quickly. Her Majesty approaches.'

'I shall do no such thing. You cannot be serious, sir?'

'God's death, I am! Would you provoke a scene, in front of the Queen's Majesty, man?'

'My lord – I am here on the King's behalf, not the Queen's. In that cause I have made more than dance-floor scenes! I wish nothing such – but am prepared for it, and worse, if thereby His Majesty may be served. I bide.'

Jermyn bit fleshy lips, calculated how close was Henrietta and recognised that there was no time for further argument. He could scarcely summon minions to eject the Marquis of Montrose. All he could do was to step forward to warn the Queen, and put himself between her and the unwanted visitor.

Montrose anticipated just such move. He accordingly stepped out at the same time as the other, smiling, and side by side they paced together to meet the Queen and Digby, Jermyn's red, round face a study.

Henrietta Maria was a tiny and still vivacious creature of thirty-eight years, not beautiful although she had been pretty as a young woman, having too large a nose, heavy eyelids and features becoming a little gaunt; but she was undeniably attractive, despite much ill-health, and all the sorrows of her marriage and motherhood. She was now painfully thin compared with the last time Montrose had seen her, at Oxford four years earlier, having been grievously ill on her flight to France, with the birth of the Princess Henrietta-Anne and childbed-fever en route. But she could summon vigour and energy when she would, and her darkly imperious eyes could sparkle strangely under those misleadingly heavy lids. The dance's exertions had brought colour to cheeks already painted. Her visitor realised that she was *more* formidable, rather than less so, than on their previous encounters.

As she caught sight of him, she hesitated in her step – but only for an instant. She was a great lady, daughter of the renowned Henry of Navarre himself, and both by breeding and her training able to cope with the unexpected in better fashion than did such as Jermyn. She inclined her head very slightly, and spoke – but to Digby at her side, not to James Graham.

'My lord of Montrose, I see, has honoured our Court with his unexpected presence,' she said, her accent still pronounced but her words sufficiently clear, as clear as the intimation to all that he had come lacking her royal summons.

'Majesty – I come straight from the saddle to your presence,' Montrose said quickly, before Jermyn could speak. 'Forgive this attire. But, after so long, it was incumbent upon me to come and pay my respects and duty, at the first possible moment. As representing your royal husband's ancient kingdom of Scotland.'

'Madam – I tried . . .' Jermyn protested, but got no further.

The Graham had stepped the extra two paces forward, and dropping on one knee reached for and took the Queen's beringed hand, to raise it to his lips. Almost she seemed as though she would resist him, but did not actually do so – although she took the hand back quickly, all but snatched it indeed.

'We had anticipated that you would be on your way to Scotland, my lord,' she said shortly.

He rose, as quickly. 'The sooner that the King your husband's cause takes me back to Scotland, the happier I shall be, Your Majesty. But meantime you would not deny me a brief glimpse of the sun? In my master's service it has been mainly cloud and storm which has been my lot. The opportunity to bask, even for a brief moment, in the presence of his renowned and fair consort was not to be missed. None will blame me for this, I think?'

It was fulsome, courtier's stuff – but it had its effect. Unexpected from Montrose, it gave the Queen pause. And she was woman enough, and Frenchwoman, to be affected by the sheer beauty of this man and his winsome personality – wholly manly as these were. Allied to his dazzling reputation as a soldier and leader of men, plus the aura of tragedy which went with him, they added up to a total not readily cast aside by any woman.

Henrietta nodded, and moving over to her throne, sat down.

Montrose had been accepted at Court, after a fashion.

He was under no illusions, however, that he was welcome. He was not exactly shunned, thereafter, and was indeed the target for all eyes; but most people kept their distance, and such as greeted him did so briefly, formally, warily. The Queen was stiffly gracious, Digby civil but restrained, Jermyn pointedly ignored him now. The only Scot apparently present, at least in this great gallery, was none other than the Earl of Crawford, Major-General, whom Montrose himself had sent here from Scotland, as forerunner and envoy eight months before, at the King's suggestion – and who, judging by results, seemed to have been as unsuccessful diplomatically as he usually was militarily. He at least greeted his Captain-General affably, but with the sort of patronising effusiveness of the old hand for the new boy – which the other found very little to his taste. The Graham and the Lindsay, heads of two of the oldest lines in Scotland, had never found each other congenial company.

Montrose, having established his position and right, formed a base for future assault, recognised that this was no time to press his case. A strategic retiral was indicated, meantime, and a return at a more suitable moment for discussion of affairs. But Court procedure did not permit that he just up and left. Those with whom the Queen had spoken, or in any way close to her person, might not leave before her, save by her pleasure.

He sought to move close to the throne therefore – but Henrietta was now surrounded by a tight throng of her courtiers, male and female, chattering, laughing, posturing. Undoubtedly the Queen saw that he tried to win close enough to speak – but she gave no sign. He perforce had to wait.

James Graham was not an unduly impatient man – or, at least, he kept his tendency to impatience under close rein; and though proud, he was not prideful. But it taxed his self-control to the full to stand there humbly awaiting for a pause in the inanities and simperings and giggling, in order to take his leave. He told himself that this was a different world from his own, and since he had elected to enter it for the time being, he must adjust himself to it. But he found it hard.

The Court of Great Britain – or England, as it ignorantly called itself – in Paris, certainly was a different world from anything James Graham had known. When he had visited Court at Whitehall and at Oxford, he had been sufficiently disenchanted; but there, at least, the King's personally noble presence had had some restraining effect. Here, there seemed to be none. He recognised, of course, that this was un-Reformed France, not Presbyterian Scotland or even Cavalier England, where different standards applied; and that exiles, in the uncertainty of their future, often tended to a feverish gaiety and search for pleasure. But even making allowances, what he saw about him in this Louvre Palace shocked and dismayed him. License was the prevailing theme here, obviously, extreme depravity in dress, talk, manner and behaviour. Men were painted, powdered and prinked out much as were the women, perfumed, hair-styled, high-heeled, beribboned. Women's bosoms had been prominent enough at Whitehall, with peeping, rouged nipples the smart thing, but here breasts thrust or hung openly out of gowns which scarcely existed above the waist – and men handled and fondled them as they would. Skirts, though as voluminous as the men's breeches, were frequently split, dividing frankly; while others were almost wholly diaphanous, worn without shift or petticoats, revealing gartered silken stockings and bare flesh. Kissing, embracing and intimate caresses went on shamelessly in every alcove and bay amongst the erotic statuary, men with women, men with men, women with women. Wine flowed, drunken casualties of both sexes were dragged into corners, but the music and dancing went on, growing ever the wilder. Henrietta Maria, daughter of the depraved Medicis as well as of the gallant Navarre, had always been known as a fast and sensual woman who had shocked Charles's England – though oddly religious also, with her Jesuit confessor, Father Walter Montagu, ever nearby. It was a strange commentary on her doting husband's complex and at least superficially saintly character, that she had never seemed to shock him.

At length, James Graham could stand neither the scene nor the waiting any longer. It occurred to him, who was not rank-conscious, that in fact he was almost certainly the highest-ranking individual in that palace, next to the Queen herself; he had seen no one loftier than an earl – Crawford. Courteously but authoritatively, he stepped in, to move people firmly aside, right and left, ignoring the gasps and stifled protests, until he found himself once more at Lord Jermyn's bulky side and looking down on the Queen in her chair. Jermyn was speaking, and undoubtedly would go on doing so.

'Majesty,' Montrose said, not loudly but very clearly. 'The Lord Jermyn will forgive me, as I hope you will also, if I make so bold as to intervene. For only a moment. I will not claim seniority, in this – only his indulgence. To seek Your Majesty's permission to retire.'

Henrietta looked from one to the other of them, and said nothing. Jermyn cleared his throat, frowning, but doubtfully. That word seniority, from a marquis to a baron, was not lost on him.

'I have been in the saddle two days and a night, from Ghent, Majesty, coming here. And only came thus immediately, to present myself before you, my liege lord's lady, as in duty bound, and then to seek my couch. I am scarcely in a state to associate with the company I find around me. If I may retire – and seek Your Majesty's presence hereafter – I shall esteem myself fortunate.'

The Queen considered that curious assertion for a moment, and then shrugged her thin, bare shoulders. 'Very well, my lord. You may go. I bid you a good-night. I shall bring myself to overlook your desertion. Like your . . . *recalcitrance*!'

Their eyes met, dark brown and blue-grey, and each realised that the other was no mean opponent – but an opponent, certainly. Smiling faintly, slowly, James Graham bowed twice, once low, a second time two paces back, and briefly – and their eyes held. Then he turned and strode off through the rainbow throng.

In the outer vestibule, itself a palatial salon, he found Archie Napier asleep on a gilded bench and George Wishart pacing the marble floor anxiously.

'Come, my friends,' he said, 'Let us out of this shameful bordello and breathe some clean air! The cheapest inn in Paris will savour sweeter than this Louvre!'

'You were rejected . . . ?'

'No-o-o. Not rejected. But not accepted, either. Challenged, it may be. Aye, challenged. And sickened! That this should be the scene and centre of our liege lord's hopes! God save the King indeed!'

*   *   *

Montrose was right about the challenge. He had won the first round, by speed and strategy, with Henrietta and her friends; but that it was only the first round was soon made apparent. It was one thing to be accepted at Court; another to gain the Queen's private ear, or to attend on her as a counsellor. It quickly became obvious that Henrietta intended to play with him as a cat with a mouse; and was therefore equally obvious that she had little intention of giving him what he wanted, letters of accreditation for his ambassadorial tour. He applied, and reapplied, for a private audience – and was sent formally gracious acknowledgments and assurances that this would be arranged so soon as it was possible; but it was never arranged. Montrose discovered, if he had not realised it before, that nothing was more difficult than to obtain a personal interview with a queen who does not so desire. And his own nature and character militated against him in this – for he would not crawl and toady to her close associates, to try to arrange it; nor would he hang about in the corridors or gardens of the Louvre, indefinitely, like some wistful and consistently rejected suitor.

He did see, even spoke with, Henrietta Maria on not a few occasions, of course – but never when she was not surrounded by a protective circle of her courtiers. He even, in these circumstances, attempted some initiation of discussion as to his purpose in Paris – but made no progress at all in what was quite obviously a private and State matter unsuitable for public airing. Without being curt or rude, the Queen, on her own ground, was able easily to counter all his efforts.

If grievously and infuriatingly held up in his purpose, however, the man was not left neglected or forlorn elsewhere. His fame and renown seemed to be as greatly acclaimed in France as in other lands; and once it became known that he was in Paris, callers, invitations, honours, descended upon him in a flood. Only at the Louvre, it seemed, was he to be held at arm's length. Princes and great nobles sought him out and gave receptions in honour of the First Soldier of Christendom. Ambassadors of other States and Powers brought him glowing invitations to visit their countries and rulers. Deputations of the municipality, the Sorbonne, the Scots College, the officer-corps, learned societies and the like waited upon him, urging attendance at banquets and gatherings, asking him to address their members. He acceded to many, partly on policy, to make friends for the King's cause; partly because he had little else to do – and moreover was far from antisocial and normally enjoyed the company of his fellow-men, and partly in the hope that word of it all might in some way affect Henrietta in her enclosed, hothouse world at the Louvre.

If the last was in fact achieved, in any degree, no sign of it reached James Graham that spring of 1647.

He was much heartened and warmed, however, to receive a letter at the end of April from that other and so different queen, Elizabeth. She wrote in the most natural and affectionate terms, wondering how he fared, warning him now to escape the Paris ague, and playfully urging him to be on his guard against Frenchwomen, indeed all designing females – save only those at the Hague, whose designs were wholly either artistic or altruistic. Which led her to tell him that Louie's portrait of him was nearly finished and requiring only the sitter's return to give it the final touches – for which return the artist was as impatient as was her mother. She would forbear to comment on the work of art, since she was perhaps prejudiced in having her own picture of Jamie Graham which she conceived to be rather different from her daughter's perhaps. But it might be that she should warn him, in the by-going, that she had a notion that Louie might just possibly have fallen in love with her sitter – a dire matter for an artist, however unexceptionable in less rarefied and mature mortals.

She went on to inform him that she had had a letter from the

Emperor Ferdinand, in answer to her own, to the effect that he would eagerly welcome the Marquis of Montrose to his Imperial Court at Prague, and would pay as sympathetic attention to the Marquis's representations as was in his power. Also the warlike and valiant Elector Frederic William of Brandenburg had sent her word that he was prepared to consider allotting men and money for her brother's cause if the Marquis of Montrose would give him detailed information and surety as to its satisfactory employment – and that was *Protestant* aid. She added that her long-standing benefactor and 'landlord' Frederick Henry, Prince of Orange, had fallen seriously ill at the nearby Binnenhoff Palace, where his fifteen and a half year old daughter-in-law, Charles's and Henrietta's elder daughter Mary, was declared to be with child. The girl's brother, the young Charles, Prince of Wales, had arrived – allegedly not so much to comfort his sister during her trial as to try to get some money out of her father-in-law before he died, for the illness was said to be grave. Elizabeth confided that she found her seventeen year old nephew excellent company and a laughing cynic – but she would not trust him an inch! It was hardly his fault, of course, but there was too much of his grandmother's Medici blood in him for her taste. She ended by declaring that she was afraid that she was getting stout, and would certainly turn into a fat old woman very soon now – but was attempting to rumble away the noxious flesh with hard daily horse-riding – no hardship – tennis and archery – of little use – and sawing firewood for faggots – the best of all since it warmed one twice. She looked forward to instructing Jamie Graham in the saw just as soon as he could find his way back to the Hague.

James Graham cherished that letter more than he would admit, even to himself, reading and re-reading it. It helped to make up for so much. The bit about the Princess Louise caused him just a little unease; but, with all the rest, should probably not be taken too seriously, he assured himself. Almost at once he sat down to write a lengthy reply, pouring out his troubles, difficulties and frustrations to one whom he knew could perceive, understand and sympathise – perhaps the only one.

Though that might be unfair to George Wishart, Montrose was not the only writer busy in the modest Trois Plumes *auberge* where they had taken up residence. Wishart was nowadays almost consistently so employed, compiling something which he had begun some time before in a small way and was now tackling seriously – a book on the life and activities of his friend, hero and employer. When he first heard of this, James Graham was far from enthusiastic; but with Wishart pointing out that his enemies would most certainly seek to misrepresent him in every way, his motives, aims and behaviour, to the detriment of his cause as well as his personal honour and reputation, he began to see that there might be some point in it. Accordingly he submitted to much questioning, searching of memory and some embarrassment; and gradually the stack of paper had grown. Now, the first part, ending with his hero's departure from Scotland, was almost completed, and Montrose quite intrigued.

In May, as Montrose was becoming almost desperate about his affairs, there was a development which although at first it seemed just one more empty honour, might well hold the seeds of better things. A clerical messenger, a Vicar-General no less, called upon him at his inn, one morning, to request that the Marquis of Montrose, of his goodness, might honour the Archbishop-Coadjutor of Paris with his company at private dinner the following day. Surprised – for he had heard much of Monseigneur l'Abbé Jean François Paul de Gondi de Retz – James Graham accepted without hesitation. All knew that de Retz, whatever his reputation, held the key to the door of the corridors of power, in France.

So next evening, Montrose presented himself at the huge Archiepiscopal Palace, and was conducted to a small but richly furnished Moroccan-leather panelled chamber in a side-wing, where he found a tall, good-looking, flashing-eyed youngish man of approximately his own age, dressed in the height of fashion and with no hint of the ecclesiastic about him, indeed a dress sword at his side. The Vicar-General, however, introduced him as the Illustrious and Exalted Archbishop-Coadjutor of Paris.

'Greetings to today's reincarnation of the true Roman hero – born into a sadly degenerate world!' this extraordinary character cried, in highly exaggerated fashion, as though taking part in a theatrical masque. 'I am enchanted to meet the victor of a hundred battles, fought against the enemies of Christ!'

Montrose cleared his throat. 'Half a dozen, Excellency,' he amended flatly. 'And my opponents would debate with much vigour, aye and scriptural texts, as to which of us was Christ's enemy! I, the excommunicate, or they the Elect! But . . . I thank you for your courtesy.'

'It is my privilege, Marquis. But – you are young! So much younger than I had realised.'

The other almost said that the same thought had occurred to himself – but perhaps it was less than tactful to comment on an archbishop's youth whatever was the case with a soldier. Especially when one realised that the archbishopric had been obtained by other than normal promotion within the episcopate.

But de Retz went on, in flowery flood. 'Younger – but no less gallant, Monsieur – than I had anticipated. More so, I vow to God! Alas – I had feared the day of the hero dead!'

'The same God knows that I am no hero, Excellency,' James Graham contested, almost roughly for him – the effect of the other's dramatics on his Scots restraint. 'Merely a general, a reluctant general, who was fortunate in his fighting-men. And an unsuccessful one – or I would scarce be here, begging through Europe!' He bowed slightly, and he hoped, less ironically than he felt. 'For success, I had better look to you, Your Eminence.'

'Ha – say it not, Marquis! Eminence is only for cardinals – and I am not that. Not yet!' De Retz laughed gaily. 'Give me another year or two. Perhaps a grey hair, to go with a red hat! It looks the better. It looks the better, yes – especially to the ladies. And it is important to please the ladies, is it not? Especially in France! And, perhaps, in the Netherlands also?'

Montrose looked at this strange Archbishop quickly, at that, and recognised that there was shrewdness in those brilliant dark eyes, as well as dramatics and laughter and quick-silver changes of expression. There would be, of course, must be. For this slightly swarthy man-about-town of a cleric was not the second most powerful figure in France by accident. Of fairly humble and Italian stock – like Mazarin himself – he had risen by his own efforts, even though some criticised his methods, like all else about him. But it had not been the usual and easy way, by toadying to the Throne and Court intrigue. Unlikely as it might seem, de Retz was actually a reformer, a liberal, almost a radical, a leader of the liberal-reform party – which was to be called the Fronde, but not quiet yet – and which had campaigned against the undue assumption of power by the Throne, as represented by the late Cardinal Richelieu, to the hurt of Church, nobility and to some extent, people. He had been prepared to make himself unpopular with the highest power in the land, and won in that struggle. He had the great advantage, of course, of having as uncle the Archbishop of Paris; and with the old man's descent towards senility, had got himself appointed, first secretary, then Archbishop-Coadjutor, and gradually taken the archiepiscopal power wholly into his own capable hands – as David Beaton had done, in Scotland, a century before. This despite the fact that he had never wished to enter the Church, indeed had sought a military career more suitable in the son of a general of galleys. Not that he had let episcopal office, or political reforming fervour either, interfere unduly with his private life, as his many amours, affairs of honour settled by the sword, and uninhibited conversation testified. But all that only enhanced his popularity with the people of Paris, and so had the effect of strengthening his position in the Estates – whatever it did with his fellow-clerics. Cardinal Mazarin and he were known to hate each other. But it had come to this that it was only through co-operation with de Retz that Mazarin ruled France, in the name of the infant King Louis XIV.

'Success, Marquis, is relative, qualified and impermanent. Heroism is not,' the Archbishop-Coadjutor went on – and there seemed no doubt that he was speaking seriously. 'In a century – or half as much, perhaps – none will know *my* name. But yours will live for all time. No – not because you won battles. Others have done that, by the score – Wallenstein, Arnim, Tilly, Wrangel. But because you won by gallantry, against overwhelming odds, never counting the cost, leading all in person, sustaining all, doing the impossible. And, I heard, giving God the credit! For that the name of Montrose will never die.'

James Graham looked down, suddenly much moved. He had not thought that it was possible, with this seeming mountebank. But there was obviously much more to Jean François de Retz than appeared at first or second sight.

'I fear that you have mis-heard, Archbishop. Been wrongly informed.' he said. 'Or misinterpreted. Others, you see, think a deal less highly!'

'That I take leave to doubt, Monsieur. Others recognise your greatness – but may hate it. Men like yourself are often a menace to lesser men. And women! Never forget it. But, come – a glass of wine, before we eat. My shame, to have kept you standing thus . . .'

De Retz was not all praise and flattery. He proved to be keenly interested in strategy and military affairs, and knowledgeable too, asking pointed questions, and making accurate deductions from the answers. Also he was particularly concerned with the character, motives and activities of the Marquis of Argyll, whom he declared, he had been at a loss to understand. But, in due course, during an excellent repast, he came to the point of the invitation to this private dinner.

'I have been requested to approach you, Marquis, on your further intentions and employment,' he remarked, apropos of nothing. 'So eminent and talented a commander should not be having to kick his heels, dancing attendance on the whims of royal ladies, however charming! Here, or at the Hague.'

A hot retort almost sprang to James Graham's lips, especially at that last word. But he bit it back. He recognised that this man was probably as well informed as anyone in Europe; nor was he one for a penniless exile to offend.

'My further intentions have never been in doubt, Archbishop,' he said, instead, as calmly as he might. 'If attendance at Courts, Queen Henrietta's or others, is a necessary preliminary, then I must needs accept it. Meantime.'

'You mean, my friend, that you still think to try to build up an army, here on the Continent of Europe? To go to the aid of King Charles?'

'I do. Or, if not a full army, at least the equipment, munitions and officer-corps for a Scots army. And the money to pay for it. These were my master the King's commands.'

'No doubt. But – do you see them ever likely to be fulfilled, Marquis?'

James Graham turned to look at him. 'If I did not, I would not be here.'

'But you are finding little success in your quest, I think? And, I fear, will continue so to find. King Charles's cause is, shall we say, scarcely the most hopeful. Unfortunately. Not all would wish to risk supporting it.'

'It is my business, then, to convince them otherwise. I know better than most the possibilities of success, Excellency. Not in England, perhaps, at first. But in Scotland. Given some support, I can win back Scotland for King Charles – this I am sure. His ancient kingdom.'

'Perhaps. But, I think, not all to whom you appeal are interested in Scotland. England is the prize. Am I not right?'

'That is the short-sighted view, if I may say so, Archbishop. Scotland is the first priority. Where the Stewart line belongs.'

'I think that *you* are not greatly concerned with the English

248

throne, my friend? Others are. It is a score of times richer, is it not?'

'Richer? Richer in what, sir? Money? Gold? Numbers? Are these what matter? Or should it be the *kind* of throne, the quality and worth of it, the most ancient throne in Europe? In Scotland Charles is *Ard Righ*, High King. That is, in fact, King of Kings. Is there another in Christendom? Once there was, in Ireland, another land of our ancient Celtic race. But not now for long. Only in Scotland. England's throne is a later, less worthy, thing – a conqueror's. Scotland's a father's.'

The other was keenly interested, obviously. 'So you claim small Scotland's crown superior? To all others?'

'I do. Because it represents something superior. The King of Scots is just that – not the King of Scotland. It is important. He can never be a tyrant, as can, almost *must*, be other kings. For he is not only a king of kings; he must reign through, with and on behalf of his lesser kings. It is the patriarchal system, the father of the family, the chief of the clan – our Celtic heritage. It has been Charles Stewart's great loss and failing that he did not understand it. His father did, however little he loved Scotland. And all his forefathers. He, Charles, must learn it again.'

'Fascinating, Marquis. I knew nothing of this. Tell me – who are these lesser kings? In Scotland. Where does one find them?'

'You need not look far, Archbishop. One sits at your side! The lesser kings are the earls of Scotland. Not perhaps the new earls, of whom Charles has made over-many, after the English pattern. A mistake. Proof that he does not understand. As, indeed, he made me marquis. And Hamilton duke. Alien, all but meaningless titles, in Scotland. The ancient Earls of Scotland, and certain great chiefs such as the Lords of the Isle, descended from the former mormaors – these are the lesser kings to *Ard Righ Albann*. Whose duty was, and is, to guide, advise, support and rule with the High King of Scots, for the good of the whole people and community of the realm. Not for the power of the throne. Do you understand?'

'I think that I do, yes. And a noble concept. I do not wish to dispirit you, Marquis. Nor to cause you offence. But it is my belief, from what I know and hear, that you will not be successful in your project. Even amongst those from whom you would most look for help. They do not seek adventures, change. And such as might move have their eyes set on England. Moreover you are unfortunately beset by the jealousy of smaller men.

Forgive my plain speaking. But it would be wise to look facts in the face. As a commander ever must.'

The Graham waited.

'Matters may improve – who knows? Much will depend on Charles himself. How he comports himself with this Cromwell and the English Parliament. But – an invasion of England is out of the question. And of Scotland, I fear, few see the advantage. Meantime, the greatest soldier in Europe is . . . *désœuvré*. Unemployed! Save as an unsuccessful importuner. Almost a beggar – shame as this is. Do I speak too plain, Marquis?'

'I prefer plain speech, sir. But – I am prepared to go on begging. That I may fight the better hereafter.'

'Spoken like Montrose! But why be a beggar? Why be humiliated when you should be raised to the heights you deserve?' De Retz paused. 'I have been authorised to sound you as to certain suggestions, my friend. I am but an intermediary, in this. But the offers are authoritative – that I assure you.'

'Offers, Archbishop? Suggestions? For my cause?'

'For your person, Marquis. Meantime. In the service of France. High service.'

'But . . . I am grateful. But how should that help my master?'

'It is *you* whom we would honour, Marquis, rather than your monarch. But I think it would do his cause no harm to be represented by one highly placed in the service of France.'

'You are kind. But . . .'

'Wait, Monsieur. Hear what is proposed. Firstly, that you should be made Lieutenant-General of the Army of France – a command, my friend, not just an honour. Command over all the Mareschals-of-the-field. Secondly, that you should be, not only commander of the *Garde Ecossais* but general of all the Scots soldiers in France – and, as you know, there are many. Your *private* command. Thirdly, that you be appointed Captain of the Corps of Gentlemen-at-Arms, so placing you ever close to the French throne. And this, my friend, carries a statutory annual payment of 12,000 crowns, with a pension over and above! Lastly, in a year's time – since it could not, by regulation, be done before – you to be appointed Mareschal of France, and Captain of the King's Guard.'

Speechless, Montrose stared at him.

'Is it a fair offer – for one of the lesser kings of the Scots?'

'You . . . you cannot be serious?' his hearer got out. 'Not . . . all this!'

'But, yes. The suggestion comes from, shall we say, the highest source. As indeed it would have to.'

'Mazarin? This is scarcely to be believed. So much. So great a position. For a foreigner. And outsider . . .'

'Scarcely that. The Auld Alliance is not yet forgotten, Marquis. The Scots have always held an especial position here in France. And the privilege would be France's. To possess the greatest soldier in Christendom.'

That word possess brought James Graham up with a jerk. It was not intended in any derogatory way, nothing is more certain – but it was significant. It put all into perspective, brought Montrose abruptly out of his euphoria.

'I thank you,' he said. 'And he who instructed you. From the bottom of my heart. For a most signal honour, undeserved. But – no, sir. My sincere regrets – but it cannot be. I am sorry, but I must refuse. Refuse all.'

The other leaned over to search his guest's face closely. 'You say so? Take longer to think of it, my friend. This is no matter for instant decision. Think well.'

'There is no need, Archbishop. No choice, indeed. I am King Charles's servant, only. I cannot transfer my allegiance to the King of France. Or any other. My service must be to my own High King, and he in need. You must perceive it. I am honoured far beyond my deserts – but I have no choice.'

The Archbishop-Coadjutor let out his breath in a long sigh, almost a whistle. 'So-o-o! I was right. I told the Cardinal – the Marquis of Montrose is incorruptible! I said that I feared that you would not have it. That is why he would have *me* put it to you. Not himself. He, the Minister of the Crown, could not have a refusal, you understand. So – I was right. But I am sorry, nevertheless. I know no other who would have refused so great an offer. That is why it *was* so great. The Cardinal believed none could refuse so much. Why – the Captaincy of the King's Guard alone is a position the highest in the land will pay 150,000 crowns to fill!' He smiled. 'All the more reason for Montrose to refuse it, eh?'

The other shook his head. 'I would not have you think me prudishly pretentious, sir. Puritanical. But when so much hangs in the balance, for King Charles and for Scotland, I cannot involve myself in other matters, however flattered I feel. You understand?'

'I understand – and admire the more. I only wish

that I could aid you in your great and unpromising task.'

'Perhaps you can, Archbishop – if you will?'

'Try me, Monsieur – so be it that it is in my power.'

'I wish to have private speech with the Queen. Yes, my *own* Queen! For though I should be her adviser, she will not see me alone, or even in council. As I think you know well?' As de Retz nodded, he went on. 'It occurs to me that you, or the Cardinal, might arrange it. Of your kindness. *Outside* the Louvre. I need my letters of credence, and time passes. If I am to achieve anything for the King. His wife is badly advised, God knows. If I could but gain private speech with her. Some function to which we were both invited, perhaps? She depends much on the goodwill of France . . .'

The Archbishop-Coadjutor nodded. 'Leave it with me, Monsieur. I will see what may be done. I think the Cardinal will be sympathetic – although disappointed. Though whether such speech will serve you anything to the point, I doubt. But we can try . . .'

CHAPTER SIXTEEN

James Graham was on his travels again, and thankfully, his accreditation, signed and sealed by Henrietta Maria, in his pouch. But it had taken a long time. The Archbishop-Coadjutor de Retz had been as good as his word, and with Cardinal Mazarin's help had engineered an interview between Montrose and his Queen – not indeed in private, but at a great banquet in the Archiepiscopal Palace. Each summer, the Queen Regent, Anne of Austria, removed with her small son and Court to the Palace of Fontainebleau, and Queen Henrietta, with her entourage, to St. Germain-en-Laye, to avoid the heat and smells of Paris. To as it were celebrate this annual departure for the country, the Cardinal had invited the two queens to this farewell entertainment – with Montrose as extra guest-of-honour, but this only divulged at the last moment. He had been ushered in, with trumpets, to a great ovation, only when all the other guests, including the two royal ladies, were already seated, eulogised in a welcoming speech – to his supreme embarrassment – by the swarthy Italianate Mazarin, and then led forward to take his seat beside his Queen. It had all looked natural and uncontrived – and Henrietta could by no means object. Especially with the Queen Regent present and applauding, and Mazarin, her host, in a position to stop her French pension and use of the royal palaces – for he guided Anne in all things. Actually, after an initial stiffness, they had got on fairly well together. Henrietta, true Frenchwoman, was a realist, and no doubt recognised that with such powerful friends any further overt offence to the Graham would be injudicious. Perhaps she allowed herself to savour, just a little, her fellow-guests, undoubted attractiveness to her sex. At any rate, they had conversed amicably enough throughout an interminable repast of no fewer than fifteen courses, interspersed with entertainments; and though it was hardly the occasion for discussion of policies or strategy, the man had managed to say most of what he wanted. She had listened, sounded even gracious, if non-committal towards his needs and requests, and he believed that he had made some impression.

She was not a woman that he could understand, or even like; but he was prepared to accept that she had her qualities, even though her ideas and loyalties were very different from his own. He had at least gained from her an undertaking to let him have the long-awaited and necessary credentials.

Fulfilment had taken a long time, even so. The removal to St. Germain and consequent upheaval and holiday spirit, plus the subsequent round of distracting country pursuits and visits, riding, hunting, hawking, picnics, pageants and the like, all served to delay. Montrose would have been wholly out of patience again, had it not been that a letter from Queen Elizabeth informed that Prince Rupert was intending to visit his aunt and seek her aid, plus official French aid, in his building up of a fleet to help King Charles's cause. A joint assault on Henrietta Maria, with so potent an ally as Rupert, was worth waiting for. But unfortunately Rupert had not come. At length, James Graham had got his papers – though no promise of money for his army, or indeed any firm commitment of active support. He had requested permission to leave Court there and then – and was granted it a deal more promptly than any other requests of his.

So now, at last, he was doing what Charles had sent him to do, after all the wasted months, making a tour of the States and Courts of Europe, a selective tour.

It was a strange progress, by any standards, an absurd mixture of welcome and rejection, of personal success and causal failure. He left George Wishart behind in Paris to finish his book and superintend the printing and publication thereof – which, he had come to recognise, might well prove a useful weapon of propaganda – and with Archie Napier for company made first for Protestant Geneva. But the democratic Swiss, though greatly admiring of Montrose the Victor, would have admired him more were his pockets full of gold. Moreover, they had little interest in saving monarchs, their history being concerned almost wholly with keeping all such at bay. Though notable purveyors of mercenary fighters, rivalling Scotland herself in the commodity, the Swiss demanded cash down for such aid, and certainly were not prepared to subsidise applicants, however illustrious. If the Marquis of Montrose came back with a full purse, they would not fail him. Meanwhile they commended him to Calvin's God.

On through the other cantons of the Swiss Confederation he travelled, experiencing similar receptions, flanking the Bernese

Oberland by the upper Rhone valley, climbing the St. Gotthard Pass and down the Vorder Rhein into the Tyrol. This was Austria, Catholic and in the domains of the Emperor. Montrose had heard that Ferdinand was here, but this proved to be false, and Vienna his goal. But he took the opportunity of approaching the princely and ducal rulers of this part of the Empire in the by-going – and was everywhere received with enormous respect and consistent acclaim, a triumphant succession calculated to turn the head of anyone less used to disappointment than was James Graham. But nowhere could he arouse the least enthusiasm for King Charles's cause. Sympathy with his plight, yes; outrage at upstarts and traitorous subjects, who could thus treat a crowned monarch; acknowledgment that here was a highly dangerous precedent and warning for other rulers. But possible involvement, commitment, no.

It was the same at Munich and Ratisbon, in Bavaria, whither he went on his way to Vienna. The elderly Duke Maximilian of Wittelsbach, with whom Elizabeth of Bohemia had been in touch – although he, as leader of the Catholic League had been mainly responsible for driving her and her husband out of Bohemia in 1619 – greeted Montrose like a long-lost brother, and conferred on him the Order of St. Hubert, to add to the others he had collected, but remained dumb as regards aid and offered not one penny to the campaign-chest.

Jean François de Retz had been right.

At Vienna also he drew a blank – although he was given a civic welcome. The Emperor Ferdinand seemed to rattle about his vast domains like a weaver's shuttle, and had now gone to his winter palace at Prague. Since the Emperor's help and influence with all the lesser rulers could be enormous, possibly decisive, and Montrose was getting desperate, he set out forthwith to travel the further 150 miles northwards. He was already 650 miles from Paris, and the harsh winter of Central Europe upon him.

On the fourth day after leaving Vienna, with a messenger gone on before, and the beautiful and famous walled city of Prague, in its vast amphitheatre ahead, James Graham was brought the extraordinary news that the Emperor himself had come out to meet and receive him. And in due course, at the end of the magnificent sixteen-arched and towered bridge over the Moldau, with the tiered city rising behind, Ferdinand and much of his Court stamped about in the snow beside huge bonfires lit to warm them, waiting to greet the Hero of Scotland, an honour to put all others in the shade.

Ferdinand was much more Germanic in appearance than his brother Leopold, a big, bull-necked, solidly built man of forty, inclining to fatness, beside whom Montrose looked slight and slender. He threw his arms around his guest, embracing him before all, and then took him on his own sled over the bridge with its serried statues and through the narrow crowded streets lined with cheering citizens, to climb to the vast palace-castle of Hrads on its ridge, almost a city in itself, where all 440 of its rooms appeared to be ablaze with light. Debating with himself the reason for this so flattering reception, Montrose sought to keep his hopes from rising too high. No doubt there would be a price to pay. And, of course this was again *Catholic* support, next to the Pope the most Catholic of all, the Holy Roman Empire. He acknowledged to himself, however, that he was reaching the stage where he would clutch at *any* support, so long as it was in more than words.

He was not kept long in doubt as to the Emperor's reasons for all this enthusiasm. The very next day, at a great banquet which followed a review of troops, at which Montrose had stood by Ferdinand's side to take the salute, the Emperor, now just a little drunk, after toasting his honoured guest and brother-in-arms as the most successful general since their own much-lamented Wallenstein, announced his immediate appointment to the Order of the Golden Fleece, the most sought-after decoration in the world. He also declared that he intended to make the Marquis of Montrose an honorary citizen by creating him a Count of the Holy Roman Empire. And this – Ferdinand turned, staggering just a little, and jerking a stiff bob – would in turn make him eligible to receive the highest honour that it was in the Emperor's power to bestow. He would receive the baton of a Marshal of the Empire. The Emperor repeated that, beaming – a Marshal of the Empire. And then added, very slightly slurring his consonants, that he would then have the greatest strategist in Christendom in his ranks – and where would those French condottieri, Turenne and Condé, be then ? Chasing their tails back to Paris! Long live the Empire's new Marshal!

As the roar of applause burst out, and continued, and Ferdinand sat down beaming, James Graham stared set-faced before him. So that was it! Those last two sentences, added no doubt only because wine had loosened the imperial tongue, revealed all. And not only this present 'honour'. As in a flash he saw what had really been behind Mazarin's equally flattering offers in Paris – and which, in his own simplicity of mind, had never occurred to him. These great powers, the Empire and France, were not really concerned to honour him, the man, at all. They were at each other's throats, in this unending state of war, and each had seen in the unemployed soldier James Graham, with his reputation for strategy and successful tactics, a means of stealing a march on the other. He was but a pawn in this power-game, this struggle for the hegemony of Europe – for the Thirty Years War had developed into that, between the Empire and France, rather than the religious struggle between Catholicism and Protestantism with which it had started. He was not being given ovations for what he had done for King Charles, but bargained for as a useful weapon. And, by the same token, the last thing either side would wish would be to see him disappear back to Scotland with an army. What an innocent he had been!

Nevertheless, it was necessary that the honoured Marquis of Montrose should get to his feet, there and then, and express his thanks, his sense of deep and humble gratitude, for these signal, indeed unheard-of marks of favour being shown to him – for this was not an offer, like Mazarin's, but a bestowal, an edict not a suggestion, and public refusal was unthinkable. In fairish German – for he had always been good at languages – he expressed his appreciation, although without saying anything about actual military service. And all the time he was sick at heart.

He retired to bed, long afterwards, in the magnificent quarters allotted to him in the Castle of Hrads that night, Golden Fleece, Count and Marshal of the Empire notwithstanding, a saddened and a wiser man. Would he ever, indeed, return with an army to save Scotland from Argyll and for his King?

*   *   *

When the weather eased somewhat, one influence more than any other detained James Graham in Prague. This was the Emperor Ferdinand himself, the man's character, and the stirrings of hope it offered Montrose. For he proved to be a fairly simple man, and friendly, almost childlike in some things, something of a hero-worshipper. He had been a soldier himself before he succeeded his father in 1637, indeed had nominally won a great victory over the Swedes at Nordlingen in 1634, having succeeded the murdered Wallenstein as imperial generalissimo – although

257

Count Matthias of Gallas was the true victor. Since he ascended the throne he had not lead troops in person. But his admiration of Montrose, as a general, was at least informed and sincere, knowing in fact no bounds. A friendly tussle developed between these two, on one side to manoeuvre the new Marshal into actual command in the field, and so to challenge the French; on the other, to avoid anything of the sort, and at the same time gain concessions which would aid the Scots' cause. It was inevitably a prolonged process – but since Montrose clearly had the stronger character and the nimbler brain, he grew steadily the more hopeful. Nor did he see that he could be more usefully employed elsewhere, in the prevailing circumstances.

So he accompanied the Emperor that spring of 1648, when the snows would let them, in the eastern part of the imperial domains, visiting armies, garrisons and strategically placed rulers – all with hunting, sport and varied junketing as ostensible primary purpose. The war situation had been quiescent for some time, although this last year or two the Empire had done but poorly militarily – in part the reason for Montrose's enthusiastic welcome undoubtedly. But as spring wore on, signs of renewing hostilities were not lacking. By May Turenne and the Swedish General Wrangel were advancing from southern France into Bavaria, and presently achieved a major victory over the imperial forces under Count Melander of Holzappel, at Zusmarhausen. The Elector Maximilian of Bavaria came in flight to Prague. Suddenly it was no longer hypothetical but actual war – and Montrose found himself liable to be caught up in it, willy-nilly.

It went against the grain to seem to desert the Emperor just as danger threatened, and moreover he needed a skilful strategist as never before. But to become actively involved in this massive struggle, which meant nothing to him, would not only have been contrary to his principles but fatal for King Charles's cause – as well as anathema to all Protestants. Moreover, the fighting would in fact be mainly against the French, which was out of the question for Montrose. The Emperor, with Maximilian, marched south to Linz on the Danube, there to threaten the invaders' flank in Bavaria. And there, at last, James Graham went to him and finally told him that, with his gracious permission, he must leave. He could on no account allow himself to appear to be in arms against his master's wife, a French princess, with the royal Court of Great Britain on French soil. He was sorry, but the time had come to part.

In the end, Ferdinand took it in good part, Montrose having established a considerable ascendancy over him. Probably he had seen it coming. Recognising realities, he agreed, made a fine ceremony of presenting the crimson baton of the Empire to his departing Marshal at the castle of Linz, on the 12th of June; and followed it up, at last with what the other had been angling for for so long – the imperial written authority to raise troops under his own command, and to appoint his own colonels and other officers therefor. Clearly neither Austria, Bohemia nor Bavaria was the place to attempt this – but Ferdinand gave him a letter to his brother the Archduke Leopold, in the Netherlands, where there was a large army, with many mercenaries, remote from the present theatre of war and convenient for shipping to Scotland. Leopold would help.

Grateful, and feeling almost absurdly guilty, James Graham took his leave, at last – leaving behind, as his considered advice to his imperial friend that he would be wise to conclude a truce, if not a full peace, with the forces invading Bavaria, just as soon as possible. Before matters got worse. He believed, in fact, that the Emperor could not win.

Feeling like deserters, he and Archie Napier set off actually eastwards from Linz, through Moravia to Cracow on the Polish Marches, to make northwards thereafter, for Danzig. A Swedish army was known to be now threatening the northern German States, and was liable to make travel exceedingly difficult. Montrose would seek to avoid it, and other complications, by skirting eastwards, to make for Denmark. There he would try to keep Christian to his promise regarding shipping. Then by sea to the Spanish Netherlands and the Archduke Leopold.

At last, it almost looked as though he might be getting somewhere. It was his belief that Ferdinand would be forced to make peace, and fairly quickly, to prevent further losses to his Empire. By the time that he himself reached Leopold, the war might well be over – with consequently many soldiers suddenly available for new employment. If only he had the moneys he ought to have, to hire them . . .

CHAPTER SEVENTEEN

The familiar hammer-blows of fate recommenced for James Graham. At Danzig, he learned that Christian of Denmark's illness had proved fatal. The old King had died at Copenhagen on the last day of February. Montrose grieved for the harsh old warrior whom he had come to look upon as a friend; and he was anxious for his cause. The new monarch was Christian's middle-aged son Frederic III, an unknown quantity of no pronounced character, of whom his father had spoken little. He had spoken much, however of his son-in-law Korsitz Ulfeldt, the Lord High Steward, a strong and ambitious man who dominated the Rigsraad, or Parliament. All said that there would be troubles in Denmark. If even Christian had been lukewarm about aid for his nephew Charles, was the new regime likely even to go so far?

Nevertheless they sailed, as planned, from Danzig port, arriving at Copenhagen in high August. They found Frederic amiable, but a weak man compared with his sire – and already moreover shorn of much of his authority, Ulfeldt having played upon the nobles and Rigsraad to unite and to compel the new monarch to accept much reduced powers. Montrose was well received; but it was clear from the first that hopes of substantial aid must be scaled down, and any idea of a sizeable fleet of ships could be abandoned – unless money was forthcoming to hire them commercially. Frederic had difficulties enough of his own, without rushing to his cousin's rescue. Montrose felt compelled to offer, in the circumstances, the termination of the very useful salary which Christian had conferred upon him – which offer was accepted.

James Graham's reaction was controlled. Control was, indeed, becoming almost the dominant factor in this man's life – an unnatural state in which he himself recognised the dangers of rigidity, of atrophy. Moreover, only half of his mind was engaged, concerned. For other letters either awaited him, or caught up with him, at Copenhagen. One of them informed him that Magdalen was dead.

The effect of this news upon him was greater than might have been anticipated. For long his wife had been detached from him, emotionally as well as physically, and indeed more or less withdrawn from the whole business of living. The final break could scarcely come as a great surprise. The letter bringing the tidings was from his father-in-law Southesk, who wrote curtly, giving no details other than using the phrase that she had 'lost all will to live', and had died in the spring. There should have been nothing of shock in this. And yet, James Graham was shocked. Those words bit deeper probably than the writer knew. The reader did not fail to ask himself – if Magdalen had lost the wish to live, whose fault was it? Only his own, surely. They had been joined together, man and wife, one entity before God. And one of them had chosen to die. The other could not escape the indictment. However ill-matched, however little she had seemed to try to conform herself to him and his way of life, his career, his fate, he had almost certainly failed her. And so, basically, was responsible for her death at the age of thirty-two. That he had also, to some extent, been responsible for their son Johnnie's death, after Inverlochy, was a recognition which he had never sought to blink. Added to this, it was a thought which wakened him of a night, sweating. Also, he had been, in a fashion, responsible for the deaths of so many others, foes, soldiers, friends – this was grievous burden enough, though one any leader or commander in the field had to carry. But this of his wife was different. Even Johnnie had not *blamed* him – however entitled he might have been to do so. But undoubtedly Magdalen had done so. She had said as much.

If, at the back of his mind, there was the recognition of a new freedom, some kind of relief that that chapter was for the time being closed, it was overlaid not only by the feeling of guilt but by sheer sorrow, sadness, for the withered and spoiled life of the comely girl he had married.

News of his master, as well as of his wife, awaited Montrose in Copenhagen. In November, Charles had effected his escape from detention at Hampton Court, unwisely as it now seemed, and fled to the Isle of Wight, en route for France. There, for some reason, he had committed himself to one Colonel Hammond, governor of the royal castle of Carisbrooke. But Hammond was a kinsman of Oliver Cromwell himself, and had detained the King. So now he was a closer prisoner than ever, at Carisbrooke, and in worse case; for while there he had entered into negotiations with Scots emissaries, and the terms he was alleged to have agreed with these, anent the imposition of the Covenant and Presbyterianism to both kingdoms, had infuriated the English Parliamentarians. There was even wild talk of bringing the King to trial for treason against his English realm, as though that were possible.

Montrose groaned for his sovereign lord. Had he no one with any wits or wisdom to advise him?

James Graham had been in Copenhagen only a few days when another Scots visitor arrived in Denmark – William Hay, 3rd Earl of Kinnoull, once Viscount Dupplin, who had joined Montrose after Tippermuir and thought better of it after Fyvie and before Inverlochy. Now, apparently he could stand Covenant-ruled Scotland no longer. Having heard that Montrose was about to invade England with a great army and fleet, from Denmark, he had come to participate.

'Invade England, Will? Are you out of your wits!' The Graham stared at his visitor. 'What nonsense is this?'

'Why, James – is it nonsense, then?' Kinnoull was a stocky, stolid man of early middle years, rather like one of his own Perthshire bulls. He shook his head now, as though to clear it. 'All Scotland resounds with it. And England too, they say. All have heard how great has been your reception by these foreigners. All the crowned heads of Europe showering titles on you, making you marshal, general, offering you men, guns, ships, whatever you seek. Cromwell himself, a curse on the man, has moved his troops, they do say, to East Anglia, to repel your descent upon London. Myself, I'd liefer you came to Scotland, but...'

'Save us – Cromwell is no such fool, I'll swear! Dear God, I'm in no state to invade the Isle of May! You see there my sole following – Archie Napier! I have no army, no ships. Titles, honours, yes, but nothing that I can grasp. Not yet. Heaven knows, it is not for want of trying. But this Europe has its own troubles...'

'My God – it is all nothing, then? Wind! Fables! Your success...?'

'Scarce that, sir!' Napier put in, warmly. 'My lord Marquis has everywhere been received as in a Roman triumph. Hailed saluted, garlanded. He has the Emperor's authority to recruit, as Marshal...'

'But no recruits, as yet, Archie! Nothing to show but a marshal's baton – and an empty purse! Not what my lord came to Denmark to find. I am sorry, Will, that you – and so many others, it seems – have been misinformed...'

'Sink me – all Scotland has, James. Even the Estates. Argyll himself. I do not believe that he would ever have allowed the Engagers to have their way, had he not believed it was better so than your invasion. He would never have let them go to Carisbrooke – no, nor to the Queen, either – without the threat of your sword constraining him. And it is all ... nothing!'

'Argyll, you say, believes this? And this of engagers? Who engages? And what?'

Kinnoull stared. 'Do you not know, James? The Engagement. Hamilton, Lauderdale and the rest?'

'I heard Hamilton was seeking to form some new party in Scotland, supposedly favouring the King – but we know Hamilton's favours! Is that what you mean?'

'No, no. It grew out of it, yes. They called themselves the Moderate Covenanters. When the King escaped to this Carisbrooke, they realised that he would never agree with the English Parliament. So they sent emissaries to Charles there – Loudoun, the Chancellor. Lanark, Hamilton's brother. And Lauderdale...'

'Loudoun! But he is a Campbell. In Argyll's pocket!'

'Aye – Argyll ever keeps a road of escape open! As you know well. So, although against these others, he set Loudoun with them. And they came to an agreement with the King. This was at last Yule. It was agreed that Charles should impose the Covenant on England. Impose Presbyterianism as the religion there, for at least three years. And ban all sectaries, the Independents. In return, the Scots would urge on the English Parliament the King's release and restoration to the throne – and if they would not have it, invade England from Scotland, on the King's behalf. That was the Engagement. Covenanted Uniformity, they call it – that is the goal.'

'Sweet March! You are not telling me ... you do not say that any man could believe in any of this! Back to the old folly. The Solemn League and Covenant again. Impose Presbyterianism on the English, against their wishes! Charles – and the Scots! Ban the Independents – and Cromwell an Independent! God save us – invade against Cromwell's New Model Army!'

'It is true. Those were the agreed terms. Secret, of course. But they leaked out...'

'I swear they did! I swear Argyll sent a galloper with them, hot-foot to his friend Cromwell! Loudoun agreed to this madness, you say? Then it would be only to betray it.'

'Perhaps. It split the Estates, anyway. In a larger parliament than there has been for years. Over fifty lords alone.' Kinnoull coughed, but did not declare that, obviously, he himself had attended and voted. 'In March, it was. They won a great majority. All thinking to aid the King. Then they sent envoys to the Queen and the Prince of Wales, in Paris . . .'

'Ha! So that was it. When was this?'

'April, it would be.'

Montrose exchanged glances with his nephew. 'April! And we were there, in Paris. We did not leave until June. Were not told of their presence at Court. Kept out!' He took a deep breath. 'This was Hamilton, eh? Ever the Queen favoured him. But – what came of it?'

'Why, the invasion. Invasion of England. In July. Hamilton's invasion. The Kirk and Argyll were against it, but the Estates gave him permission . . .'

'If Argyll was against it, he could have stopped it. But did not? Then he saw a way of getting rid of Hamilton!' James Graham groaned aloud. 'So – they actually did it? Marched into England. Under Hamilton? That under-witted clothes-horse! With whom, as general?'

'Himself as general. Callander second-in-command. Baillie as chief-of-staff. Middleton as master-of-horse. Ten thousand men . . .'

'Middleton? He, at least, should have known better. How far did they get?'

'To Preston, only. In Lancashire. The English royalists did not rise, as hoped for . . .'

'Can you wonder at it? To have Presbyterianism imposed upon them!'

'Langdale, from Cumberland, only. With a small force. Hamilton split his army – why, I know not. Callander and Middleton, with the horse, rode on to the south, to Wigan. Cromwell came up, over the hills from the east, and fell on Hamilton. It was a complete rout. Thousands died. Hamilton surrendered. He is still a prisoner. It was disaster.'

'So-o-o!' Montrose shook his head, helplessly. 'Every move of it could have been foreseen. The sorry folly of it! And the King in worse case than ever, in consequence. What happened to Callander and Middleton? The rest of the Scots?'

'They won back to Scotland, in due course. Without battle. Just ahead of the man Cromwell himself.'

'Cromwell ? You mean – he invaded Scotland, then ?'

'No, no. Not that. He came alone. A private visit. To see Argyll. They got on very well, it is said.'

'I vow they did! They are hand-in-glove, those two – the King's greatest enemies. I doubt not but that it was all planned between them. Argyll got rid of Hamilton, and Cromwell got rid of the Scots threat. And has a further charge against the King. And Queen Henrietta, if she supported Hamilton, has no doubt thrown away on him what moneys she could raise. It is hardly to be believed that there could be so much of foolish incompetence and error.'

'If only they had listened to *you*,' Napier burst out. 'The King's Captain-General and Viceroy! And the only soldier who could have out-fought Cromwell. Yet they turned their backs on you. Why ? When the rest of the world unites to do you homage ?'

None attempted to answer that rhetorical question.

'So now all wait for you to invade England,' Kinnoull ended. 'It is believed that you have a great mercenary army. All Scotland believes it. And – you have not!'

There was silence in that room of the Rosenborg Castle, as three peers of Scotland contemplated the unhappy state of their native land.

*   *   *

Montrose was going to Gothenburg, across the Kattegat, in Sweden, to seek out, not official aid – which could hardly be looked for with Christina now at active war with the Empire – but the private help of a Scottish merchant-prince there, one John Maclear, immensely rich and said to be prepared to assist King Charles's cause. It might be less than consonant with the dignity of the King's Lieutenant to go cap-in-hand in search of a mere merchant, but James Graham was never one to consider anything of the sort. And he had time to spare, anyway, for the Archduke Leopold himself was now involved in the hostilities, and had left Ghent at the head of his troops – scarcely the best moment to approach him for military aid. The Thirty Years War, which had seemed to be over at last, save for a few local adjustments, apparently and unhappily was warming up again – to the sorrow of more than Montrose.

But on the eve of his setting sail for Gothenburg, news

reached Copenhagen that changed all. The Archduke had been met and soundly defeated by a French army under Marshal the Prince Louis of Condé, at Lens near Liege, on the 20th of August, losing 7,000 men. He had retreated to Tournai. With his brother still unable to avenge the May defeat in Bavaria, and the Swedes now actually besieging Prague, the Empire was making overtures for peace – and apparently prepared to pay the price for it. Mazarin and Christina were sending negotiators to meet the Emperor at Munster. If a final peace was concluded, as seemed likely, it behoved Montrose to be on hand when the Archduke began the inevitable disbandment of his army. It was westwards, therefore, that he must sail, meantime, not eastwards.

With Kinnoull and Napier he was embarking on a Dutch coaster for Groningen, in Holland, when King Frederic sent after them two packages which had just come from thereabouts, addressed to Montrose. One was a letter from George Wishart, enclosing a copy of the first edition of his book, published at the Hague under the imprint of one Samuel Browne and pleasingly bound in calf, the text in Latin, recording the *Annus Mirabilis* of the campaigns of the illustrious Marquis of Montrose. The second was sealed with the royal arms of Bohemia – and this the recipient refrained from opening until he was alone in his tiny cabin and they were tossing their way up the Kattegat. It read:

Jamie Graham,

I have heard that you make for Copenhagen, where my good uncle has died. If he rests in peace now, I swear it will be more than he ever did in life. I send this letter to my cousin Frederic's hand, in hope that it will come to yours in as little time as may be.

This is to greet you, with all my heart. And to wish you well. We have heard here, with much joy, of your triumphs wherever you go and your deserved honours. Will you be too grand, Marshal of the Empire, when you return to the Netherlands, to keep company with an elderly lady of respectable birth but reduced fortune, and her peculiar daughters? I pray not.

You have been too long away, Marshal Jamie, and I urge you to return so soon as you may. Not only for my own selfish sake, who find your company to my taste. But for your own good, and for the cause we both do cherish. You may have heard of Leopold's defeat at Lens. It was not expected. I have heard that the Emperor has been making moves towards peace for some time. This defeat will, I am sure, expedite the matter. Indeed peace may be signed ere you receive this. In which case you should be here, in the Netherlands, I do believe. Although it was beat – by bad generalship, it is said – the Archduke's army is in being and as good for your purposes as any you will find in Europe. The Spanishers you will not want, but there are in the army many mercenary corps, men not a few of them Scots, with much experience of war. These will be disbanded, if there is true peace, you may be sure. You might gain whole regiments of veteran soldiers. If so be it that you can hire them. Of this I know not, but hope that you have found the moneys, or some, such as you need – and which alas this impoverished friend cannot find you.

There is more reason than this for your return to the Hague. My nephew Prince Charles is now here, lodging with his sister, Mary, now Princess of Orange. At the age of eighteen he is advanced for his years, but needs better company than he keeps. He is a youth of parts – but not all of the parts such as a king should display – and one day, God willing, he will be King in his father's room. Who am I to speak who, according to my daughters but seldom decently act the queen ? But then, *my* kingdom can be only in the hearts of my friends, Jamie – whereas young Charles will have the rule over many. He does admire you, and speaks of the Great Marquis often. But others about him, I fear, are less admiring – Willoughby, Hopton, Colepeper. That gross fellow-countryman of yours, Earl of Lauderdale, in especial is now ever at his ear. You know him ? A depraved ruffian, but cunning. He came as ambassador of the so-called Engagers, of whom you will certainly have heard, and when their foolhardy cause went down, he bided here. Safer, I doubt not, than back in Scotland at this moment. But he drinks and whores too much with young Charles, gaining over-great an influence. And would persuade him to other courses than yours, I swear. For my brother's sake, as well as for the country's sake, his son requires a better guide and adviser than any he has here. Despite Lauderdale, I reckon that he still conceives James Graham as hero. The more so, I do believe, since he heard the story of your scandal with his mother. It may be that you have not yourself heard of this, my handsome James – but the story being put out from Henrietta's Court is that you left it in haste after making unsuitable advances upon that poor lady's virtue, and boasting indecently of her favours towards you afterwards. Young Charles, who knows his mother – although not quite so well as I do – is highly intrigued. But for myself, I prefer to await the tale from your own lips rather than from such as surround my sister-in-law.

My sons Rupert and Maurice have now built up a fair fleet at Helvoetsluys, but continue to have much trouble in manning it, lacking money also. With Prince Charles they made a sally, by sea across Channel to the mouth of Thames, in August, on Henrietta's instructions, as part of this mismanaged Engagement of Hamilton's. But nothing came of it, and Rupert is angry and sore with waiting. He is determined to sail his ships to Ireland, to join Ormonde, where he conceives there is now more hope for his uncle's cause than in England or Scotland. If you were here it might be that you could convince him otherwise. You will require ships to sail your army to Scotland. Uncle Christian might have given you them, but I think not my cousin Frederic.

Come back to the Hague then, Jamie Graham, to the much comfort and satisfaction of

> your affectionate and entirely loving friend,
>   ELIZABETH.

At the end there was scrawled a postscript, in larger, hasty almost defiant writing:

Louie would send a letter with this, if she but dared. She has written two, to my knowledge. She does not usually lack, daring.

James Graham read and re-read that characteristic epistle, his emotions in a turmoil. He did not know whether to be more disturbed by the postscript or by the canard about himself and Henrietta Maria. The former, probably – since no one who really knew him would believe the latter, surely. Not that these two items bulked overlarge in his mind, or spoiled the rest for him. That letter generated a warmth within him which, deliberately, he did not seek to analyse, which indeed he dared not analyse.

CHAPTER EIGHTEEN

Landing in the Ems estuary for Groningen, in North-East Holland, Montrose and his companions rode due south through an October countryside alive with talk of peace, heady but confused, through Drente and Gelderland and Brabant to Flanders. Some said that the Emperor had already signed the peace treaty at Münster, yielding much that men had died for but bringing hope to the lives of countless more. Just what had been at stake was by now less than clear to most; certainly not any clear-cut religious decision, for Protestants and Catholics had been fighting on both sides. But the power of the Empire and the Pope had suffered a major blow obviously, and that of France an enhancement.

When the travellers arrived at length at Tournai, only a few miles from the French border, it was to discover that the Archduke Leopold had already left for Brussels to meet the States-General. But peace was indeed concluded, and the Spanish-Netherlands' imperial army was kicking its heels in idleness, still at Tournai, disgruntled over its shameful and unnecessary defeat, concerned with future unemployment, discipline relaxed, a trouble to itself and everybody else. Montrose could have recruited thousands there and then – had he the money to pay them. As it was, he interviewed many senior officers, especially Scots ones – of whom there were large numbers – seeking to persuade, promising, all but pleading. He had the fullest authority to enrol them, the Emperor's signed commission to do so; and they wanted to be enrolled. But though some few might be prepared to take a chance on it, not unnaturally most required financial inducement. And the King's Captain-General had now insufficient money even to pay his own daily expenses, and was reduced to spending Kinnoull's. One of the Scots officers here was none other than Sir John Hurry, acting colonel of one of the mercenary regiments. Poor Hurry was not very fortunate in his employment, these days. But he remained the cheerful soldier of fortune, prepared to take the rough with the smooth. Perceiving no better prospects on the present rather gloomy military horizon, he once more attached himself to Montrose's party – and promptly resumed the rank and status of major-general.

Having obtained tentative agreements to join his expeditionary force for Scotland, when the necessary funds were available – unless better alternative employment turned up in the meantime – from a large number of experienced officers, some colonels promising their entire regiments also, James Graham repaired to Brussels in search of the Archduke. His Marshal's baton, commission and letter of recommendation from the Emperor meant less than they had done when they were granted, admittedly, but they must still have value within the imperial domains.

Brussels was the seat of the States-General of the Spanish Netherlands, and the new political situation in Europe consequent on what was now being called the Peace of Westphalia, signed at Münster by the Emperor, meant great changes in the position and influence of this Catholic and Walloon southern section of the Low Countries. Very much on the wrong side in this settlement, it had to swallow much that was unpalatable, and its ruling body, the States-General, was in constant session, the Governor-General, Leopold, no longer the military dictator he had been during a state of war, and in almost as constant attendance. In these circumstances, Montrose was under no illusions as to the difficulties of his task.

Leopold, a harassed man, and never a towering figure personally, received his visitor civilly enough – but did not fail to indicate that he could have done with this new Marshal of the Empire's renowned military services somewhat earlier in the day. He accepted, however, his brother the Emperor's expressed wishes in this matter – even though he all but implied that he could scarcely understand why Ferdinand should have taken so much trouble at this difficult time. The affairs of King Charles, Scotland and England, could hardly be of less importance to the troubled Empire, he inferred. Nevertheless, his brother's word was his command, and all that had been promised the Marquis of Montrose would be fulfilled as far as it was in his – the Archduke's – power to ensure. He could recruit, enlist, appoint his own colonels and officers, marshal and train his force in the imperial domains, and embark it at imperial ports.

All of which was, of course, satisfactory so far as it went. But since Montrose had not funds left to hire himself a body-servant, much less an army, it did not in fact go very far. And when the subject of money was raised, a subvention-in-aid, either loan, credit or outright grant, Leopold Hapsburg referred him to the States-General. Anything such was entirely and solely within the province of that body, which now controlled the exchequer. He himself had no funds at his disposal other than his private purse and what the States-General voted him for expenses, he declared. He could not offer a penny. What he could and would do, however, was to commend an application for financial aid from Montrose to the States-General – and meantime house him in Brussels in a fashion suitable for a Marshal of the Empire. Perhaps, if approached, the Emperor might even grant a small pension...?

With that James Graham had to be satisfied – and seem grateful. He pointed out that the aid required was for King Charles and his kingdom of Great Britain, not in any way for himself; and that, as such, could and would undoubtedly be repaid if and when Charles was restored to his rightful throne. The Archduke advised that he inserted a clause to that effect in a written application to the States-General, and he would undertake to present it, sympathetically. But he warned that it must inevitably take time – for the business before the assembly was lengthy, far-reaching and urgent. Meanwhile, his lordship was to consider himself the guest of the Governor-General.

And so Montrose settled himself down, in a wing of the royal palace in huddled, steep-climbing Brussels, to the familiar and soul-destroying business of waiting, through that winter of 1648/49.

He kept in touch with the residue of the professional army, therefore, with Hurry as his link – and would dearly have liked to move into it in person, to try to save it from demoralisation and indisciplined rampage. But even as a Marshal he had no claim or authority to do anything of the sort, until there was at least some indication that he would be in a position to employ it, or any portion of it. Born to wealth and inherited power, James Graham seemed to himself to have been a beggar for too long.

He was by no means idle that winter, apart from constant lobbying and interviewing soldiers. He wrote long letters. Those he wrote to Elizabeth of Bohemia were indeed in the nature of safety-valves, some release for his pent-up anxieties and impatience. But he also sent messages to her son Rupert and her nephew Prince Charles. Rupert he urged to think again over the projected expedition to Ireland, and instead to help him with the

Scottish project, which he believed to be infinitely more likely to succeed, as well as much more effective for the King's restoration. Especially to hold his fleet available to transport the troops. To young Charles he appealed for help in his plea to the States-General, as indication that the Scottish invasion was indeed royal policy and not just some wild theory of his own. This was important, for Henrietta Maria's influence could be guaranteed to be working against him, and these cautious Flemings had to be convinced that they had at least the chance of getting their money back. He wrote with much tact, for he was in effect asking the son to work against his mother; but it was *for* his father in dire need. Also he urged Charles to approach his sister on his, Montrose's behalf – this on Elizabeth's suggestion. The Princess Mary's husband was now ruling Prince of of Orange, Stadtholder of the Protestant Netherlands, on the winning side, and as such in a position to influence his neighbours. Moreover he was wealthy – and Mary herself had been given a considerable fortune in jewels by her father on her marriage. She was only seventeen, and apparently not concerned with much other than her own domestic affairs; but some of those jewels, sold, could solve the financial problem of this expedition's start.

Rupert replied in friendly fashion, declaring his great admiration for Montrose, and his desire to help, but pointing out that he was hardly his own master, and more or less committed to the Irish venture, with Ormonde, and could not just postpone it indefinitely. The longer he remained in port, with his ships, the more difficulties he had to contend with. If Jamie Graham would give him an approximate date, in the not-distant future, when the Scots expedition would be ready to embark, he would put it to his colleagues that here was a practical proposition. If not, he feared that plans to sail for Ireland, already far advanced, must inevitably go ahead.

Jamie Graham, unable of course to give any possible date, wrote back begging patience, and suggesting a meeting to discuss the whole situation, including overall strategy.

Charles, Prince of Wales, did not reply.

Rupert did continue with the correspondence, to the effect that they were now preparing to embark troops – but that there had been another mutiny amongst the ships' crews, engineered with the aid of English parliamentary gold. He could not leave Helvoetsluys in these circumstances, for a meeting, but would be delighted to see his old friend there on the Dutch coast.

Montrose, expecting any day to be summoned before the States-General to elaborate on his appeal, wrote that he would come just so soon as he might. Meantime, for the King's and old friendship's sake, not to sail away on an Irish expedition which, in truth, even if successful, could not win Charles Stewart his freedom or regain him his throne, as could the Scottish one.

By this time Yule-tide had passed, Montrose's third on the Continent. In a letter of seasonable greetings and good wishes to Elizabeth and her family, he urged her, if she would, to use her influence with her nephew Charles to reply to his overture and proposals, as time was of the essence. With this he enclosed, as Christmas gift, an inscribed copy of the new edition of his book by Wishart – in English now. The first edition was already sold out, and a second printing.

Before the end of January he did, in consequence, receive a reply from Prince Charles, at last – not written but by the lips of a messenger. Unfortunately, the day before he had had a final letter from Rupert, sending his greetings and regrets, but that he was sailing with the morrow's tide. A sudden financial godsend, in the shape of the proceeds of the sale of his cousin the Princess of Orange's jewellery, had enabled him to buy the so necessary provisions and munitions, and at last to pay his mutinous and absentee crews. He had to thank the Prince of Wales for this, he understood. It would be folly to delay longer and risk further trouble. He wished his old comrade-in-arms very well, and hoped that they might indeed meet together before long – preferably somewhere in England, in a joint Irish and Scottish thrust on London. Meantime, God aid them both and King Charles likewise.

It was, in consequence, in a distinctly doubtful not to say incensed frame of mind, that James Graham learned that Sir Edward Nicholas, secretary to the Prince of Wales, waited in an ante-room of the Palais Royale in Brussels, craving an interview.

The very thin, almost emaciated man of late middle years who awaited him in the ante-room, soberly dressed, with deep-set dark eyes and careful speech, seemed an unlikely representative, on the face of it, for the allegedly gay and imprudent Prince of Wales. Montrose had heard of Edward Nicholas, of course – one of the King's former Secretaries of State, no less, appointed by an anxious father, when things were in dissolution around him, to be the guide and secretary to a youthful son and heir lacking parental control. Rumour had it that he was wise, but insufficiently strong of character to exert influence over his high-spirited charge. That he himself had made the journey to Brussels, on Charles's behalf, was at least encouraging.

After mutually courteous greetings, Nicholas did not beat about the bush. 'Your lordship – His Highness has sent me to you in person, rather than commit words to writing,' he declared in a softly lilting Welsh voice. 'That I may explain his situation to you. We conceived it too dangerous to write. His Highness hopes, therefore, that you will forgive the delay in answering your lordship's letter.'

'A delay, sir, which has had dire results! All these weeks I have waited. And now Prince Rupert has sailed, with his fleet, for Ireland. Enabled to do so by the moneys which might have set up a Scottish expedition of infinitely more value. I cannot think that His Highness was well advised in this. Nor in failing to send support for my appeal for credit to the States-General here. The King's cause, I believe, is the sufferer.'

'My lord Marquis – your disappointment and concern are well understood. Personally I agree with you,' the other said earnestly. 'But you must understand the Prince's most difficult position. He has the greatest admiration for you, as a commander, and recognises that you have done more for his royal father than any man living. He conceives you also to be better informed and have a wiser head, than most others who would advise him. Or than Prince Rupert, his cousin, indeed. But his situation is most delicate. And you, my lord, have . . . enemies. In high places.'

'Of that I am well aware, sir. To my sorrow. But need that have prevented a reply to my letter? All this delay? And no message to the States-General?'

'I fear that it needs must. His Highness is heir to the throne, yes – but only eighteen years, and with no true authority of his own. As yet. Whereas his mother, the Queen, has the authority. *She* is His Majesty's personal representative and mouthpiece, in this unhappy situation – by the King's express command. Not his son. Indeed, His Majesty has instructed His Highness to obey his mother in everything. The Queen's authority you have had occasion to know, I think, my lord! Not unnaturally, therefore, she brings strong influence to bear on Prince Charles. She provides most of the members of his household. To be frank with you, his household at the Hague is little more than a nest of spies! The Queen is informed, in the course of two or three days, of everything His Highness says and does. And he is, of course, kept grievously short of money – for the pension which the French Treasury allows him is paid through Her Majesty, who withholds what she sees fit. I am his secretary, and know, to my cost! The Queen undoubtedly *means* well, my lord – but she still has the power gravely to influence and control His Highness. Save in, h'm, private and personal matters.'

'Ah, yes. I have heard of these. The present young woman – Walters, is it? Mistress Walters has had her child. What says Her Majesty to that?'

'Little or nothing, my lord. Indeed, I think that so long as the Prince does her wishes in matters of State, she cares little how he behaves in private.'

'So – you say that His Highness could not write to me for fear of the Queen's spies knowing of it?'

'Partly that, my lord. We know that his couriers are frequently tampered with. As his other servants. That is why *I* am come here today – in secret. And that is not all, see you. There are the damned Scots also . . .!' Nicholas drew a quick breath, blinking those deep eyes. 'Your pardon, my lord Marquis – a slip of the tongue. No offence meant, I do assure. But – we have at the Hague the Earl of Lauderdale and his party. If you know him . . . ? Then you will understand! *They* have plenty of money, I swear! Where it comes from, who knows?'

'But I understood Lauderdale, whom I much dislike, was something of an exile himself? A refugee, now that the Engagement folly is done with?'

'But it is not done with, my lord. *Hamilton*'s bolt is shot, yes. But the Engagers seem to be very much a power in Scotland still, and Lauderdale their representative here. Indeed, it is whispered that the Marquis of Argyll himself now encourages them, *sub rosa*. If it is so, this could be where their money comes from.'

'If that is true, then it is all for his own evil ends.'

'No doubt. Which is why we have to be so careful, so wary. Secret. And Lauderdale never ceases to speak against your lordship and your enterprises. He holds out to His Highness much hope of support in Scotland – but claims that *you* must be put aside, that you are the stumbling-block of his Scottish support. You will understand, therefore, how His Highness is pulled in many ways. He would have you to meet and confer with Sir Edward Hyde, my lord. If you will. In secret also. On the whole matter of your policy and plans. Hyde is the King's Chancellor.

But not in the Queen's pocket. He has a good head and is to be trusted.'

'I know Ned Hyde. A lawyer, though sourish. Able – but no soldier.'

'No. But a good judge of the practical. He is the King's most senior minister, and the Prince trusts him.'

'Where do I meet him, then? The sooner the better. Can he come here – for I cannot risk to be away from Brussels while the States-General may call upon me.'

'I will take back a message to Hyde from you, my lord. Name a place and date, and I will seek to arrange it . . .'

So it was agreed. Nicholas took back to the Hague with him, that 20th day of January, Montrose's letters to Prince Charles himself and to Sir Edward Hyde, the King's minister.

It was exactly two weeks later, to the hour, that one of the Archduke's men handed a letter to George Wishart, for his master, from Hyde, written from the Hague. He brought it to Montrose as he sat at his desk by a bright log fire, writing – for it was a cold and snowy day of February. James Graham did not open it at once, finishing the paragraph which he was penning, to Elizabeth. Then, breaking the seal, spreading the paper and raising it to gain added light from the fire, he began to read.

Suddenly Wishart, at his own writings, heard a strange choking sound. Glancing up he saw the other to be tugging convulsively at the deep white linen collar at his neck, and swaying noticeably in his chair. The letter had fluttered to the floor. Alarmed, he rose and hurried over.

'My lord – are you unwell? What's to do?' he demanded. 'Of a mercy – what's this?'

Only a strangled gasping came from James Graham, who appeared to be taking some sort of seizure.

Desperately Wishart sought to support his master's and friend's slumping person, to loosen the collar. He shouted for help. The Lord Napier was somewhere about.

Montrose was evidently struggling, fighting some staggering attack upon body or mind, eyes staring but unfocussed, lips trembling but seeking to form words. With one hand he clutched at his friend's arm, with the other he seemed to be pointing downwards, to the floor. Obviously it was the letter that he indicated.

Wishart held him upright, gabbling assurances, comforts, appeals to the Deity.

Archie Napier came in, eyes widening at what he saw. He sprang forward to his uncle's side, with a flood of questions.

'He is ill! Quick – wine!' Wishart panted. 'There – on the board. No – hold him. I will get it . . .'

But when they tried to force wine between Montrose's slack lips, he managed to shake his head, with some kind of decision, mumbling.

'What does he say? In God's name – what is it?' Napier cried.

'It sounds like, like the King,' Wishart muttered.

The deep groan from the chair confirmed that. Again there was the palsied pointing towards the floor.

'The letter . . .' Wishart stooped to pick it up.

'What letter? Who from? Christ God – what does it say?'

'Hyde. From Sir Edward Hyde, the Chancellor . . .' The other was swiftly scanning the writing, as he spoke. Then he gagged, gulping for air in his turn. 'They . . . they . . . have slain . . . the King! Dear God – dead! Executed – dead! They have, have cut off King Charles's head! Oh, merciful Jesu . . . !'

Napier snatched the paper from the other's hand, to read. And James Graham, unsupported, collapsed forward over his desk, a tight-coiled spring snapped, broken.

CHAPTER NINETEEN

It was two whole days before Montrose dared emerge from his bedchamber and face the world again, two days in which his friends had tiptoed about their palace suite, continually coming to listen and whisper at the locked door, lost, frightened, as though the death was here, not in far-away London. When he did emerge, however, James Graham was calm, quiet, set-faced, but himself – even though it was a rather different self, steely, eyes hooded, remote. In level tones he apologised for any inconvenience and anxiety he had caused, and declared that he was now fully recovered – but that, of course, His Majesty's death changed all. None there, even the somewhat insensitive Kinnoull, who had hurriedly returned, nor the brash Hurry, thought to discuss or elaborate with him on the King's trial and execution by Cromwell and the Parliamentarians.

And indeed it did change all, for Montrose as for so many others. Any authority Montrose had had stemmed from his monarch. He was no longer, therefore, Viceroy of Scotland, or Captain-General either. He had no further right to appeal to Leopold or the States-General or to seek enlist an army. He was suddenly no more than a private individual, who had staked all – and lost. His desperate grief for Charles Stewart, and his surging hurt and anger at those who had dared to slay the Lord's Anointed, did not blind him to the fact that here was a wholly, radically, new situation, for himself and all his hopes and plans. He might still be a commander of some renown, a Marshal of the Empire; but the *raison d'etre* for it all – indeed for his whole existence, as it seemed – was no longer there. In consequence, he could no longer trespass on the Archduke Leopold's hospitality, nor further impose his claims on the States-General. He sat down at once to write formal statements of withdrawal and expressions of gratitude.

But another aspect of the utterly changed situation did not fail to impress itself ever more clearly upon his recognition. There was no King Charles I to serve, any more; but there was now a King Charles II. Eighteen year old Charles was no longer Prince

278

of Wales but King, in undoubted right and succession – King of Scots, in particular, however much the English Parliamentarians might talk about a Republic or Commonwealth. There was no such possibility for Scotland. Even the most fanatic ministers and Covenanting zealots had never conceived Scotland without a king. Young Charles, whatever else he was, was *Ard Righ*, the High King of Scots. And to be accepted as King of Great Britain also, meantime.

All of which had highly important implications, in its turn. Authority now rested with Charles himself, however immature. At eighteen, and of sound mind, he was beyond the age for regency control. Henrietta Maria was no longer the King's representative in Europe. In theory at least, all the Crown revenues, prerogatives, privileges and powers were his. Honours, appointments, dispensations, charters, were within his gift; treaties, official negotiations, State decisions, were his to make or break. Cromwell, Fairfax, Milton and their friends had, by their wicked sacrilege, exchanged a captive and helpless monarch whom they could dominate and press, whose aim latterly had been to escape to the Continent, for a free monarch who was already there. Apart from the ethics of it all, they had scarcely been well-advised.

It behoved James Graham, therefore, as a loyal subject and moreover one of the Earls of Scotland, to present himself and his allegiance to his new High King forthwith, as well as to be available to advise on Scottish matters. Nothing altered that hereditary privilege and duty. He must repair to the Hague.

*　　*　　*

'Her Majesty requests that you will come this way, Marquis,' the young Count Henri informed. 'If you will follow me – and forgive, h'm, the *desarroi*, *desordre*? A reception is in progress in the principal salons. For the ministers of the Elector Palatine, Her Majesty's son, who have come to pay their respects to the new King Charles.'

'Then, sir, let me come again. On another, more suitable occasion.'

'No, Marquis. The Queen commands your attendance. But – this way!'

If Count Henri felt that he must apologise for leading the visitor by the distinctly seedy and humbly domestic back-passages and corridors of the Wassenaer Hof, he did not know, of course, that Montrose had traversed them before, and in good company. The newcomer's heart lifted, indeed, to their shabby intimacy as he followed the younger man.

Climbing the remembered private stairway at the end of one passage, to the better proportioned and decorated but still far from palatial bedroom floor, his escort handed Montrose over to the old Scotswoman, Martha Duncan, who stood waiting there, and discreetly withdrew.

She took him through the dressing room, littered with women's clothing, shaking her grey head and tut-tutting at the untidy sight, and opened the door beyond. But she opened it only a little, to insert her head and peer within. Then she nodded again, opened it wider, and gestured through.

'Aye, well,' she observed, with her own significance, gave him the slightest push in, and shut the door behind him.

Elizabeth stood in the firelight, with no lamps or candles further lighting her boudoir – for it was a grey day of late February sleet. Regally clad – for the reception, of course – the flickering half-light played about her magnificent figure and lovely features. She stood watching him, in a strangely alert, almost wary, questioning stance, as she searched his face. She did not speak.

He bowed low. 'Your Majesty,' he murmured. 'Your . . . very proud . . . servant.'

She drew a long, quite audible breath, and also drew herself up from the slightly tense and peering posture. And she raised her arms, forwards towards him, still unspeaking.

He moved into the room, with a trace of hesitance. 'I intrude, as ever,' he said. 'Interrupt Your Majesty's affairs. I . . .'

He it was who was interrupted. She did not wait for his careful advance, 'Jamie! Jamie!' she cried, and moved swiftly forward, to throw herself directly into his arms.

'Elizabeth!' The name came out almost as a groan, as he enfolded her in his embrace. 'Elizabeth, my dear.' And he buried his lips in her hair.

For long moments they clung thus, saying no more. The man was trembling, and knew it, and the Queen's splendid bosom heaved frankly, strongly against him. She was a big, well-made woman, challenging to any masculine arms and person.

At length she straightened up, and drew a little away – but still held him by both forearms, so that he did not feel compelled to drop his own arms from her sides.

'Jamie – forgive this . . . display!' she breathed, panting just a little her face close to his own. 'A weak woman's foolishness. I should keep myself . . . better in hand. Should I not?'

Gravely he considered that, and her. 'Should you?' he asked.

As seriously, she nodded. 'Unseemly. That is what it is. Inappropriate. Everyone would say so. Do you not think so?' But she did not release his arms.

'As a queen? As a royal lady, to an impoverished Scots lord?'

'As an old woman! To a man fifteen years younger. There is surely no folly to equal an elderly woman's presumptuous folly! See – I lit no lights lest you should notice the lines on my face!'

'Is this folly, then? I suppose that it is. For James Graham. But – it is the dearest folly that I have ever known.' He comprehensively scanned the lightly upturned features so near his own. 'Lines? I see no lines. Only the fairest face that it has ever been my joy to behold. And the kindest, truest, most noble. As for age, there is none so full of years in all this world, I sometimes think, as am I. If this be folly, Elizabeth – let us be fools a little longer!'

'With all my heart!' she said, and her parted lips rose to his.

When at length they moved, it was still hand-in-hand, going slowly over to stare down into the red glow of the fire, silent, too full for words. But presently Elizabeth shook her head, blinking a little.

'Jamie, dear Jamie – bless you! And Elizabeth Stewart, too. God bless us both! This, of all things most wonderful! So very good. See – I am weeping. Weeping for joy. I never thought to do that again. Our folly is . . . blessed. I think that we have paid for it, in advance, you and I! And may pay further, indeed. But we have something, here, now, which no one can ever take from us. Jamie and Elizabeth. Sweet God – Jamie . . . and Elizabeth!'

'Yes,' he said.

'What does the future hold for us, Jamie? Placed as are you and I?'

'I am no seer, Elizabeth – save to see that you will ever reign in my heart, here and in eternity.'

'That, then, is perhaps sufficient, my lord! If we have eternity, present uncertainties, problems, obstacles, become the less sore to contemplate. Or should do. As even now, my dear, at this precious moment. Which should be ours, and ours alone. Alas, I have to return to my stupid, honest Germans! Already they will be asking what has become of the Queen? And Charles Louis, the Elector Palatine, the eldest of my brood – and the least lovable, a pompous ass, indeed! – will be huffing and puffing, at my seeming discourtesy to the ministers he has brought. Aye, and the girls will be doing their best for me – and raising eyebrows to each other over their scandalous mamma! Not that I care, for them – or for Charles Louis. But these German burghers – that is different. I have my duty.' She sighed. 'Charles Louis has arranged – and will pay for, since I cannot – a banquet for them. Seemingly of my giving. Young Charles will be there. He it is they have come to greet – the new British King. If you care to honour it, you will be the most welcome guest. But . . .'

'No – I thank you. Since I cannot be with you this night, I would wish to be by myself. Alone. Where I may hug this joy to me, clutch it to myself, lose myself in it. Is that selfish ? To sit through a banquet, with you there, but be unable to talk with you, touch you . . .!' His hand slid from hers, and his arm encircled her, to tighten and draw her close again fiercely, possessively.

'I know, I know . . .'

When she could, breathlessly, she went on. 'I must go, Jamie. But – we have said nothing of, of my brother.'

'No.' He drew a deep breath. 'I dared not. I do not think that I can dare it, even now, Elizabeth. And, and for you . . .!'

'I was less close to Charles than, perhaps, I should have been. I served him not one-tenth so well as did you. But I grieve for him sorely. For all he was – and for all he failed to be. He had great virtues, of a sort. Not as a king. That was the sorrow of it – he was unfitted to be King. If only my brother Henry had lived! But – Charles did not deserve to pay so hideously for his failure.' She stopped, as she perceived the man's face working. 'Oh, forgive me, my dear. I forget myself. Your Lord Napier told me of your, your great hurt. I am sorry . . .'

He shook his head.

She turned, within his arm.' Jamie – we have both had a dire bereavement since last we were together. Myself a brother, you, a wife! You said that you dared not speak of Charles. I, likewise, can scarce dare to speak . . . of her.'

'Then do not,' he said, thickly, almost harshly. 'Magdalen is with God. And better there than she was with me for husband. We were . . . ill-matched. I failed her. But life failed her also. She had no joy in it, for years. Who knows why it should be so ? The fault was not her's. But she wished to be gone. It would be as wrong to grudge her the going as it would be to pretend that I did not know a certain . . . relief.'

'Yes. You were ever honest. As, I hope, am I. For I do not pretend that I am sorry. Save for her. For you, I think that I am glad. For myself, more so. Is that cruel? Heartless? I would not have permitted myself this, this happiness, indulgence, had not, had not this happened. Had she still lived.'

He nodded, slowly. 'Nor I. Nor, strangely, Elizabeth, had the *King* lived, I think. You see, I was *his* servant, before all, his instrument, a weapon for his hand. I was not my own man, while he remained constrained in need of my services. I left all for his cause – and must have continued to do so. But . . . I am, God help me, free of that servitude now. After ten years of it. *Both* deaths brought us to this, Elizabeth – for better or worse. Both of them.'

She raised a hand to touch his cheek, wordless.

He turned to her, with something almost like desperation. 'I was lost – a lost man. Suddenly. Do you understand? I came to you. What I have found, in this room, I cannot yet gauge, cannot foresee the end of. But . . . I am not lost, any more.'

'I thank God for that!' she breathed. And then, 'But you come to see young Charles, do you not? Oh, I know that you came to me, as a woman. But – *he* is now your King, is he not? Do you serve him, then, as you served his father?'

'I must serve him, yes – as my liege lord. But . . . it is not quite the same. As you will understand. My full duty I do not yet see. It may be that *you* will show me it.'

'No! Do not put that responsibility upon me, James Graham. I have sufficient, without that! But – I will speak to Charles. Tonight. Arrange that you see him. Privately. And quickly. This I can do. But as to your decision thereafter – that you must take yourself, my dear. For I, I would but work and intrigue to keep you by *my* side! I think that I shall do that, anyway, I warn you!'

He smiled, at last. 'I shall be on my guard! But not tonight. Now I have been overlong at your side, kept you from your guests and duty. Go, my dear – before your delightful daughters come searching for their mother, and find her thus! Which would not do.'

'Would not do . . . ? You think . . . it will not . . . do?' Her voice faltered unqueenlike.

'Net yet, at any rate, I judge. We must be discreet. Very. You are a queen . . .'

'I have never been discreet, all my life! Must I start now – for Jamie Graham?'

'Yes,' he said. 'And for Elizabeth Stewart, too.'

She searched his eyes, in the firelight, and clung to him.

They embraced again, passionately. Then she broke away, and hurried to the door.

She turned there. 'Tomorrow you will come again. For all to see. Meet all again, my family. Then you will stay here, in this my house. I will not have you staying in an inn. And we shall contrive to be together, frequently.' She was all the Queen again. 'However discreetly . . .!'

'Do you think that wise?'

'Wise? Wise! There is more than wisdom and discretion to living!' Then, in a different voice. 'But, Jamie – be kind to Louie, will you? For a little. I . . . I would not wish her hurt. She cares for you, I know. As I do not think she has done for others. It may pass – you are a hero, and shamefully good-looking – and she is young. You will think of it?'

'Yes, my dear. I will be kind with Louise. And find it no hardship.'

'But not too kind, sir! I will not see my daughter's affections trifled with!' She held out two hands towards him, and then, as he came forward again, shook her head, turned, and opening the door, hurried out.

CHAPTER TWENTY

The plump and slightly pompous little man in the rich but sober clothing, eyed Montrose warily and scarcely warmly from prominent but shrewd if watery eyes. 'His Majesty is informed, my lord, and will grant you audience presently,' he said. 'Private audience. Save for my humble self, as adviser. As is necessary.' He did not sound humble. But then, why should he? Sir Edward Hyde, although humbly enough born, the son of a country squire, was senior minister of the Crown – whatever the English and Scottish Parliaments might proclaim – Chancellor of the Exchequer, however empty its coffers, and principal adviser to the new King Charles II.

Montrose had never liked the self-important little man, who seemed so much older than his forty years, but he recognised him as able, gifted and moreover honest, attributes not so common at the Courts of monarchs as not to be appreciated when discovered.

The door opened quite suddenly and a young man slipped into this small and obscure chamber of the Naaldwijk Hof, a house adjacent to the Wassenaer Hof and linked thereto for use as overflow by the Bohemian Court. It was no regal entrance – just as this was no regal apartment – merely the unannounced arrival of a tall and angular youth who, by his breathing, had apparently run up the stairs to get here. Coming in, and his glance going straight to Montrose, he halted, began to bow, recollected his station, and raised a hand in a kind of involuntary salute – which itself was cut short as probably unsuitable.

'My lord Marquis,' he said – and smiled ruefully.

James Graham, taken by surprise at such entry, after a first keen gaze, bowed deeply. 'Your Grace!' he said. Then, straightening up, he stepped forward, to take the young man's hand between both of his own, palms vertical, and holding them thus to go down on one knee. 'I take, and hold you for liege lord and High King,' he declared.

Wonderingly Charles Stewart looked down at him, and as the other rose again, shook his dark head. 'My lord – it is rather for me to greet the great Montrose in such lowly fashion, than you me, I swear . . .' he began, and then stopped, biting his lip.

'Lowly, Sire? That is the proudest fashion in which I may greet any man living! *An Greumach Mor* to his *Ard Righ*, in first acceptance. The ancient usage of an Earl of Scotland to his liege, cousin and High King.'

'Ha – I had not heard of this, my lord. I have not been greeted so before. Forgive me. And forgive me also for keeping you waiting. I . . . I was detained. My cousin Sophie . . .'

'Ah, yes.' Gravely James Graham inclined his head. 'The Princess Sophia is most detaining, I agree, Sir. Like all the rest of her family!' And he smiled a little.

The young King grinned at that – and a rather ugly face was quite transformed. Montrose had not been prepared for his appearance, any more than for his abrupt entry. Charles was totally unlike his father, in looks as evidently in all else. He was surprisingly tall, for a Stewart – although his great-grandmother Mary had been tall – and he had little of the traditional Stewart good looks, being sallow, irregularly featured, with too large a mouth. But his eyes were good, large, dark and lustrous – Stewart eyes; but more lively than had been his father's, with something vivid in them, quick-silver. A Medici inheritance, perhaps. It was a strangely contradictory face, young-old, casual-calculating, debonair but wary too.

'Yes. Yes, my aunt and her daughters are not to be denied!' he agreed. 'I wish . . .' He stopped, shrugging eloquently, in true Gallic fashion, his quick glance darting towards Hyde, for the first time. 'But I forget myself, my lord. May I welcome you to the Hague, and my, er, presence, if not my Court! Even in these modest quarters. And say how greatly I am honoured to see you, the greatest soldier in Europe. I, I have longed to meet you, sir – but it has never been possible. But now that I am my own master – or almost . . .' He looked again at Hyde, with that quick-silver smile.

'You are too kind, Sire. I am sure that you have met much greater soldiers than am I, trained soldiers – Condé, Turenne, Wrangel? But, whatever my qualities, successes or failings, I am now at Your Grace's service. As I was . . . at your father's.'

'And you served my father better than did any other, my lord Marquis. He would have me say it, I think.'

Wordless, James Graham shook his head.

Charles looked at him quickly, and changed the subject. Perhaps his aunt had warned him. 'My royal mother, however, has not always fully appreciated your worth, I fear. I am sorry. She has been ill-advised, I think. In this as in other matters. But – that is past, my lord.'

Montrose bowed again, unspeaking.

'I wish to avail myself of your services to the full,' the young man went on. 'I rejoice that they are . . . available. However secret they must be, at this stage.'

'Secret, Sire . . . ?'

'Perhaps secret is not the word? Kept undeclared, untrumpeted . . . ?' Charles looked for help to Hyde.

'Secret, my lord, is, I would say, fair, accurate. In the circumstances prevailing,' the little man said judicially. 'Secrecy was necessary when we sent Sir Edward Nicholas to you at Brussels. It is still more necessary now.'

'I am afraid that I do not understand, Sir Edward. Conditions have wholly changed, since then. Your master, here, is now King. King of Scots, in fact; King of Great Britain to be. His Grace now commands all. And must be seen to do so. You must explain to me this need for secrecy. Between the King of Scots and one of his earls.'

'But that's it, my lord! It is the confounded Scots that are at the back of it! H'r'm.' The little lawyer had risen on tiptoe, flushing, blinking, puffing. He recovered himself, however. 'I beg Your Majesty's pardon. And yours, my lord Marquis. But – it is all most difficult, most unfortunate. The secrecy is not of *my* choosing, I assure you. Or of His Majesty's.'

'Perhaps if you explained, Ned?' Charles suggested. 'His lordship clearly does not fully comprehend the fix we are in.'

'As Your Majesty wishes. You know, my lord, that the Earl of Lauderdale is here at the Hague. Has been for some time. Representing the Engagers' party in Scotland. He, ah, mislikes yourself. As do his friends, unfortunately. For reasons we need not go into. But now, since his late Majesty's shameful murder, the position is changed somewhat. In this, as in other issues. Lauderdale now represents more than the Engagers. Letters of authority have come from Scotland. Now he represents the whole Estates of that realm. Other representatives are on their way to the Hague, to join him. To explain new proposals to His Majesty. It seems that Scotland is as shocked by his late Majesty's death as, as are we.'

'I rejoice to hear it, sir. I knew it, of course – that it would be so. Scotland's position is wholly different from England's. That is why I said that in *fact* His Grace is already King of Scots and only to *be* King of Great Britain.'

'I noticed that, my lord – and did not quite take your meaning?' Charles said.

'It is because the Scots monarchy is different, Sire. In quality and essence. More patriarchal. The King of Scots cannot be unseated. It seems that the King of England can! If he is a bad king, he may be forced to govern through a regency. As Robert III was. But there *must* be a King of Scots, always. Without interval. At your royal father's last breath, Your Grace became the High King. Your coronation will follow, one day – but you are King now. You need not await any recognition, from the Estates or others. Even from the lesser kings of Scotland, the Earls. Although on *their* acceptance the fullest authority of your reigning depends. That is the Scots monarchial position.'

'I see. This is something I had not known, fully. None ever explained it so.' Charles raised an eyebrow towards his official adviser, even a little annoyed.

'That may be so, my lord. In theory,' the Chancellor declared, frowning. 'But we are, I fear, more concerned with practice. The facts of the situation.'

'And these demand secrecy, sir?

'So far as your lordship is concerned, unfortunately, they do. This letter from the Scots Chancellor, intimating Lauderdale's new authority and the coming delegation, expressly declares that your lordship must not be included in any discussions or negotiations. As outlaw, and forfeited by the Estates, they say, and excommunicated by their Kirk.'

'Dear God!' Montrose breathed. 'Do you mean to *agree* to this outrageous demand? This insult!'

Charles cleared his throat. 'My lord – it is a condition of the discussions. We, we deplore it. But if anything is to be achieved . . .'

'His Majesty greatly admires and respects your lordship,' Hyde put in quickly, soothingly. 'But he cannot reject the whole of Scotland for one man's position. In especial when, as is here proved, he is anxious to consult and lean on you, privately . . .'

'More than that,' Charles broke in, eagerly. 'To honour you, my lord. I intend to show my great gratitude for all that you have done for my father. And the the realms that are now, in name, mine. And to show my fullest trust in you. So I would confirm

288

you in all your offices and positions. All, my lord.'

'But secretly, Sire? Not openly.'

'Er ... yes. I fear, meantime, it must be so.'

'To what end? So that you may negotiate with Lauderdale and these others who come? You, their King? What can they offer you, which is not yours already? The Crown? It is yours. In Scotland. Allegiance? They cannot withhold it. Even Argyll. What, then? Power? Power – that is all they have. The power of the sword and the pulpit, meantime. And think you, Your Grace, that they will yield up that power to you? In any respect? If they send to you, here, it is because they would *use* you. A puppet for their own purposes. For Argyll's. The Campbell will not yield one inch of his power. He has paid too high a price for it! That I can assure you. Until he is forced to do so – by a sharper sword than his own!'

There was silence in that room for a space, as King and Chancellor digested that. Then the latter spoke, blowing out his cheeks.

'You speak as a soldier, my lord. His Majesty is in no position to use the sword. Therefore he must use other methods. The conference-table. Negotiation.'

'What is thus important to be negotiated?'

Charles answered. 'They offer that I shall be proclaimed King, formally, from every market cross in Scotland. Also in the assembled Parliament. They will consider my possible return to Scotland, and my coronation.'

'As they cannot deny you. And in return ...?'

'I am to accept the Covenant.'

'A-a-ah! Which Covenant, Sire? The Solemn League?'

'I do not precisely understand the difference, my lord.'

Montrose swung on Hyde. 'You do, Sir Edward – *you* must know! You cannot conceivably advise His Grace to adhere to the Solemn League and Covenant. And it can be only that they want. You – an Englishman!'

'It is only a form of words, sir. A foolish bigoted form of words. But as a basis for negotiation, we would consider it. To gain a great advantage. The *National* Covenant is none so grievous. We might settle for that.'

'But – Sir Edward! You are named a man of sharp wits. Have you taken leave of them? Forgive my words, Sire – but this is no occasion for mere polite exchange. Of course the *National* Covenant is none so grievous. I had a hand in drawing it up, and know. His Grace your father came to accept it. The terms merely provide for freedom of worship, in Scotland. What I fought for – and would still fight for. It is to be *assumed* that Your Grace would agree to that, anyway. With an Episcopalean father and a Catholic mother, none would expect otherwise. It is the elementary right of every man . . .'

'To be sure, my lord. I agree, most heartily.'

'Then it is not *that* which these come to negotiate. But the damnable Solemn League and Covenant. Argyll's Covenant. The object of which is not religious freedom but religious tyranny, with political power. To impose a narrow Presbyterianism on all, by law. And moreover, to impose it upon your English realm also!' He swung back on Hyde. 'Is that a basis for negotiation ?'

'What would *you* suggest, my lord ?'

'You said, Sire, a little past, that you would confirm me in my offices and positions ? Though in secret. By that do you mean as Captain-General of your Scottish forces, and Viceroy or Governor there ?'

'Yes, my lord – and more than that. I would have you to command all, Commander-in-Chief of *all* my forces whatsoever, by land and sea. And meantime to be my ambassador-at-large, to all the courts and rulers of Europe.'

Montrose bowed, but briefly. 'Your Grace is kind. But the last is significant, is it not ? Ambassador-at-large, meantime! You would have me, therefore, at *other* courts. Not your own! This is the secrecy again ? A kind of banishment, indeed! Meantime.'

Hyde all but choked, and Charles bit his lip.

'Good God – no! Never that, my lord. But, clearly, it would be a sign of my trust and favour. While yet you were not present at these negotiations . . .' The young voice tailed away.

'Precisely, Sire.' Montrose contrived a smile. 'Banishment is too harsh a word, I agree. Forgive me. Shall we say . . . extrusion ? Politic retirement elsewhere ? Think you that you would have any need for a commander-in-chief thereafter ? Or a Viceroy in Scotland. Having yielded your royal authority in advance ?'

The King swallowed, but did not answer.

'But you asked what *I* would advise, Sire. That is simple. Declare now these appointments and offices, publically. Inform Lauderdale and the negotiators that naturally your commander for Scotland must be present at any discussion of the Scottish situation. And throw your whole authority and will behind the raising of an army for me to take back to Scotland just so soon as possible, to place you in *power* there, not as a puppet for Argyll. Aye – and come to Scotland with me, Sire, so that you *need* no Viceroy! Play the King of Scots indeed. That is my advice.'

If that left Charles Stewart and his Chancellor at a loss for words, it also somewhat surprised James Graham himself. He had not entered this room intending to make any such declaration and appeal. It seemed that, somehow, his mind had been made up for him.

The King swallowed audibly. 'You . . . you would do that, my lord? Lead an invasion – and take me with you?' His young – old eyes sparkled.

'It is what must be done if you are to fulfil your destiny, Sire. And to avenge your father's death. For which I also have a duty, I think.'

Hyde coughed loudly. 'Heady talk, my lord – soldier's talk. But scarcely practical, I suggest. His Majesty does not wish to start his reign by invasion and bloodshed. When his subjects are extending the hand of friendship, willing to negotiate. It would be an unstatesmanlike step. And if it failed, could lose him his Crown indeed. For ever. Moreover, to endanger his royal life in such adventure . . .!' The Chancellor shook his head severely. 'I cannot commend such a programme. I suggest, Sire, that this audience has achieved as much as is possible, at this stage.'

'Mm.' Charles looked uncertain, but threw one of his rueful smiles at Montrose.

'I agree with Sir Edward,' that man said, courteously now. 'Enough has been said. And I seek your royal forbearance and pardon if I have spoken over freely, have chosen my words ill. I did not come here, indeed, intending to offer to take up the sword again. I had thought that I had laid it down. But Your Grace's situation, your kindness, and above all, Scotland's need, forced me to say what I did. I trust, and believe, that you – as well as your advisers – will consider it well. I will await the outcome. May I say, Sire, that it has been my great joy to meet you? And to render to you my allegiance. It is yours to command. Have I your royal permission to retire?'

'Why yes, my lord Marquis. You, you have given me much to think upon. I thank you for it. I . . . I find plain speaking, on occasion, to my taste, I think! We shall discuss further, to be sure.'

'I thank you.'

'My lord – this audience, I would remind you, was secret. Was and is,' Hyde put in quickly. 'And must remain so.'

The Graham ignored that, bowed to his liege lord, and left the room.

*   *   *

Back in the Wassenaer Hof on his way to the rooms Elizabeth had insisted on providing for him – and for Napier and Kinnoull as well, so that it might look less personal – Montrose was waylaid by the Princess Sophia, who drew him into the music-room which served more or less as a private parlour for the family.

'Marquis – you have seen Charles? The new King?' she demanded, eagerly. 'How think you of him? Is he not . . . exciting? A prince of princes! You would get along well with him, I vow!'

'I found his Grace friendly and likeable, Highness. As a young man, much to be admired. As a King, it is a little early to say.'

'Oh, he will make a splendid King, I am sure. Not stiff and proud, as kings usually are! His people will love him, when they come to know him, of that I am certain.'

'His Grace has made a good start, it seems – with his cousin!'

She blushed, prettily. 'He is a great improvement on most of the princes. I have met – that is all,' she asserted. 'And he dances divinely. As he skates. He rides well too – like a, a centaur. And plays tennis better than any I have seen. He is so tall and dashing . . .'

'Altogether a most estimable young man, Highness. He is going to have little trouble with his *feminine* subjects, at least! Or . . . is he?'

'You, too! My lord, that is unworthy of you, I swear! Everyone casts up at him that wretched trollope Lucy Walters. A heartless scheming minx who set out to seduce him . . .'

'Our poor wronged Charles! Sophie on her pet subject, again!' The Princess Elizabeth had come into the music-room from a chamber beyond. 'Or should it be that Sophie is *Charles's* pet subject?'

'At least it is not *you*, Eliza, whom Charles dances with, and takes riding and skating! Nor do I blame him . . . !'

'Hush, Sophie – what will my lord of Montrose think of you? He must have a strange enough opinion of this family, as it is, I do declare!'

'My opinion of the Bohemian royal family could scarcely be

higher, Highness,' James Graham assured, smiling. 'So much beauty, talent, vigour and kindness, in one household, is hardly to be credited.'

'You perhaps should keep such fine speeches for Louie. Or Mamma, my lord.'

'And you have not met our brother Charles Louis!' Sophie giggled.

'Sophie – restrain yourself!' her elder sister reproved. 'My lord – pay no heed. She has had her head turned by our saturnine cousin's recent attentions . . .'

'I have *not*! And he is not saturnine. He is very good-looking, in one way. You all call him ugly, copying Mamma, just because you are jealous. He is a lot better-looking than that dry old stick Descartes *you* dote on, and write endless screeds to! Pretending it is philosophy! As for Louie and her sighings and moonings . . . !'

'What of Louie?' Although, as always, slightly husky, the voice came clearly from the other room. 'I can hear very well Sophie.'

'Ha – the Princess Louise is here,' Montrose said. 'I must pay my respects.' Uncertain whether to be glad for the interruption, or otherwise, he moved over to the open doorway, and through.

She was standing at an easel, in an old paint-smudged smock, brushes and palate in hand. She did not turn as he entered the room.

'Princess – you are busy. Forgive me. I would not wish to interrupt. But I could not ignore you when I heard your voice.' It did not fail to occur to him that if she had heard her sister so clearly, she had heard him also, and could have come through had she so desired.

Almost as though she had read his thoughts, Eliza, behind him commented, 'Oh, Louie would *wish* you to interrupt her, I am sure! She merely would have you come to her, not she come to you, my lord!'

'As is but right and proper,' the man acceded mildly.

Louise spoke, still without turning her head from the painting. 'Had you any sisters, my lord? Or brothers, rather – since sisters would be more kindly to a brother, I think. *I* am blessed with mine, you will notice? They are a little trying at times – but much kinder when such as the Marquis of Montrose is not present.'

'That is unfair . . . !' Sophie exclaimed hotly. 'You cannot blame us if you are so, so difficult.'

293

'Highnesses!' Montrose protested. 'I seem to be the unwitting cause of a rift in the lute, a discord in this music-room! I had better retire, I think – since it seems that you treat each other more kindly when I am not here!'

'No. You have not yet told me how it went with King Charles. Did you agree? He told me that he thinks you the hero of the age. Those were his very words – the hero of the age.' Sophie nodded importantly, with something only she was able to declare.

'If you go before Mamma comes, we all will get the rough side of her tongue,' Eliza said. 'Shall we not, Louie?'

'Probably,' Louise agreed, shrugging slightly. 'But that is no concern of my lord's. He will wish to escape from this nest of idle chattering women, I think. As who would blame him? Or deny him?'

James Graham looked from her stiff, besmocked back to the other two, and shook his head gently. Then he moved over, closer to the easel. 'May I see what you paint, Highness?' he asked. 'I have no talent that way, myself – but I greatly admire those who have.'

'Lord Jamie – you call Mamma Elizabeth, when you think none hear you,' the irrepressible Sophie declared. 'Must you call us all Highness, all the time?'

He drew a hand over his mouth. 'If Your Highnesses prefer otherwise. In private.'

'We do – oh, we do. *You* do, Louie, I swear.'

'My lord of Montrose will do as he thinks best. He always does,' her sister said. But she turned round, at last, and her eyes rose to his.

Meeting her look, the man was strangely moved. The other two young women might not have been present, in those moments. There was a distinct and undeniable rapport and affinity between them, a clear mutual awareness and some sort of bond. It was an alarming and momentarily bewildering recognition for James Graham, bringing with it an immediate sense of both satisfaction and guilt, of pleasure and pain. This should not be, he was well aware. Yet there was delight in it …

Neither spoke, and it was Eliza who commented.

'His lordship may prefer to keep his distance. From some of us,' she said drily. 'He must find us something of a … confusion.' She had some uncanny knack of mind-reading, that eldest and least beautiful of the sisters.

The man withdrew his gaze, to transfer it to the canvas on the easel – although he was only partially aware of what he saw. It was the painter that preoccupied him, not the painting, mentally, emotionally and physically – that, and an awareness of a sense of betrayal. *His* betrayal of Elizabeth. In thus mentally embracing the daughter when it was the mother whom he loved. What had suddenly happened to him?

Long he peered at the picture, as though examining its every brush-mark. It was the portrait of an old wizened man peering regretfully into an empty tankard. Only the face was completed, the rest only sketched in. But that face was vividly alive, set in lines of experience and constant disappointment, rheumy eyes preoccupied with the obvious emptiness of what he held, and seeking in its dregs for all that the drinker had lost, or failed to find, in a long life. The thing was a clear allegory, but displaying extraordinary depth and understanding, sympathy, especially for a young woman and a princess, insight into character and emotion, and an ability to portray it surely and with vigour. That, of course, was what had allegedly sparked off her interest in himself, at their first meeting in Hamburg, her concern with character wherever it might be found. Not that James Graham consciously perceived all this in those moments, his eye looking inwards rather than outwards. He straightened up.

'A notable work. Great . . . compassion,' he said. 'There is feeling, deeply perceived, Louie. And displayed.' It was the first time he had used her Christian name, let alone the familiar Louie.

'Not deeply enough displayed,' she answered shortly. 'Not one tenth of what I would show, is there.'

'An old drunken sot's maudlin tears?' Sophie cried.

'That old man's tears are my own. And all the world's,' Montrose told her; and he heard the sharp intake of Louie's breath at his side.

'Then you should see her picture of *you*, Lord Jamie!' the younger sister asserted with a quick laugh.

'I heard, yes, that a portrait was being drawn. From memory. I was much flattered – and would be most interested to see it . . .'

'No!' Louise said forcefully. 'He is *not* to see it. I told you all . . .'

'Why not? It is not so bad as *all* that!'

'Because it reveals the artist more truly than the sitter!' Eliza said calmly.

'It is not to be shown, I say . . .'

There was a diversion as Queen Elizabeth swept in, her lovely face flushed from the cold air, hair disordered, eyes sparkling, magnificent in riding-habit and ostrich-feathered wide-brimmed hat.

'Arguing, as always, my nestlings!' she cried. 'And before my lord! On my oath, you are incorrigible! Heigho – I am late. I met my lord Earl of Crawford, new come from Paris and the Louvre. To see the King. A very gallant cavalier, I must say. Vehement. He would have swept even an old lady like myself out of my saddle, had I given him an inch of encouragement.'

'And you did not, Mamma?'

Elizabeth ignored her namesake. 'He is a major-general of your own, my Lord Jamie, he tells me?'

'Hardly of my own, Your Majesty.' Montrose bowed. 'His commission was direct from His late Grace, your brother. My-self, I would have used my lord's undoubted abilities . . . differently.'

'Aha – nicely put! I can just see it. And you two together. Sparks flying, when a fizzing rocket meets a deep-glowing fire! He said that he had gone from Scotland to Henrietta Maria as your ambassador. So I told him that I hoped he soldiered better than he played envoy, or Heaven help the Marquis and the King's cause! I do not think that he liked that.' Her laughter pealed out rich, musical, uninhibited.

Looking from her to her second daughter, James Graham knew a complex feeling, compounded of understanding, relief and sympathy. It was something of her mother in Louie which attracted him to her. But when Elizabeth herself came into the company, her daughters, indeed all others, might almost not be there. Louie had deep, banked-down fires, yes, and much that spoke quietly, directly to something in himself; but her mother was all of her plus so much more, the most alive person, without exception, whom it had ever been his joy and privilege to meet. And she loved him – the miracle of it, she loved him!

'I was admiring Louise's painting, Majesty,' he said, care-fully. 'So full of warmth and compassion, seeing below the surface. She sees that old man as *mankind*, I think. Whereas others can see only a drunken sot.' He glanced round, smiling, for Sophia – but she had slipped away, out of the room.

The Queen nodded. 'Kind,' she said. 'Louie has to put up with much raillery, I fear. She will the more cherish your . . . understanding.' And, as Louise turned away abruptly, at that, she shrugged, but cheerfully. 'Ah me – who would be a mother? Now – tell me, how did you fare with my nephew Charles? You are back sooner than I looked for you?'

'I found His Grace an attractive and interesting young man, Your Majesty. We spoke of many matters. And learned to know each other a little, I think.'

'But . . . ? But – you are disappointed in him?'

'Say that I perhaps had not appreciated how young he is. Nor how much he is under Hyde's thumb.'

'Ah! Ned Hyde? That was the trouble? Was he there? All the time?'

'Yes. I could not object to that, with so new a monarch. But his influence was too strong, too much that of the tutor, I fear.'

'He has been in charge of Charles for too long. A complacent little man. But with his uses, also. For he has countered Henrietta Maria's influence with her son, in some measure . . .'

'Has he, Mamma? What of Mistress Walters – Sophie's *bete noire*? And Charles's other ladies, then?'

Sophie came back, as though on the enunciation of her name, carrying something bulky.

'Oh, no!' That was Louise, hotly.

'But yes, Louie!' her sister cried, and turned round her burden, whipping off the cloth that covered it. She held up a painted canvas, the portrait of Montrose, for him to inspect.

'You are cruel! Heartless!' Louise exclaimed. And swinging round, she positively ran from the room.

'That was not kindly done, Sophie,' her mother said. 'But – the Lord Jamie would have to see it, some time.'

James Graham looked at the picture – and did not fail to recognise why its painter had not wished him to see it. Not that it was ill done, or a poor likeness – quite the reverse. It was in fact a very handsome portrait, pleasingly and naturally postured, attractively coloured, and unmistakably Montrose, in his most gallant stance, against a background of smoky war-clouds. Yet there was something wrong with it, something not true. And it did not demand any particular perception to recognise what it was. It was the subject's expression of sheer love and fervour. Not the fervour of battle or loyalty or enthusiasm, but simply and clearly that of a man's love for a woman, for the woman those eyes seemed to feast upon. It was extraordinary that mere paint could be made to express an emotion so frankly, vividly.

'I see,' he said, sighing a little. 'A most . . . telling picture.

Remarkable. Done by a most gifted hand. And mind. And done from memory, to be sure. Or, at least from . . .' he did not finish that.

'Done from *heart* rather than hand, I'd say!' Eliza observed.

'Yes. Well, take it away, Sophie,' the Queen said. 'Louie will not quickly forgive you for this. I think. Off with you.' She turned. 'And you too, Eliza, if you please. I have more important matters I wish to discuss with my lord. Matters of State.'

'Of *State*, Mamma ?' That young woman smiled. 'I will see to it, then, that you are not disturbed!'

'Do that, baggage!'

Montrose spoke. 'And will you be so good as to tell the Princess Louise that I admired her portrait ? And am both flattered . . . and unworthy. Tell her kindly, please.'

Eliza nodded. 'I understand,' she said. She looked back, from the doorway. 'We do not scratch at each other *all* the time,' she added, and went.

Alone, the man and woman eyed each other unspeaking for a long moment, and then came into each other's arms. Her hat fell off.

'Dear Jamie,' she murmured, against his lips. 'You are kind. What a tangle! How can you . . . put up with us all ?'

'I am deeply, humbly, grateful,' he said. 'For all.'

'Are you ? Are you ?' She drew her head back a little, to look at him. 'Can that be true ?'

'The simple truth, Elizabeth. I have had not so much of love in my life that I do not cherish it. When so generously given. By whomsoever.'

'By whomsoever! By mother and daughter! An old woman – and a young one!'

'Years have little to do with true love. Or with a great deal that is important in living. That at least I have learned.'

'Yes. But . . . you are sure ? In your own mind ? Louie has so much more to offer than have I.'

'Yes, I am sure.' He paused, only for a moment. 'To be honest, for a space I wondered. A little. Before you came. But whenever you entered I knew beyond all doubt. And rejoiced to know it.'

'I am glad, then, glad. Selfishly. Had it been otherwise, I do not think that I would have given you up so very readily. Without a fight. And when Elizabeth Stewart fights, I warn you . . . !'

He closed her lips on that threat.

Presently she detached herself. 'Now, to get back to our important matters of state! No, no – do not be greedy, Jamie. Time enough for that. You cannot trifle with kings and queens and look to escape your obligations to their game of kingcraft. What of Charles? I thought that I had primed him well. And he does admire you – there is no doubt of that. What went wrong? Can I help?'

'You could aid me to work on Charles's mind, my dear. To wean him from Hyde's tutorship, at least where Scotland is concerned.' He paused, drawing a breath. 'I offered to take an army back to Scotland to gain *his* throne for him. And asked him to come with me. I had to do it.'

In silence she searched his face, and a prolonged sigh escaped her. Then she nodded. 'Yes. Yes, for you, it had to be that, in the end. I tried to convince myself otherwise. To keep you here. But – I knew in my heart that it could not be. That you would go back to Scotland eventually, to hazard all. James Graham being James Graham. And, leave Elizabeth Stewart.'

'When *Charles* Stewart sits on his Scottish throne, Elizabeth Stewart will be as well in Scotland as in the Hague. And no exile, any more.'

She gazed away beyond him. 'True,' she said, at last. 'Jamie – what is to become of us? You and me? Can we ever . . . is it possible . . . ?'

'Anything is possible – if we are determined to have it so, my dear. Greater difficulties than this. It is in God's hands – but if we set *our* hands to it, and our hearts, we shall not fail. Here – or hereafter.'

'Very well.' Elizabeth nodded again. 'I accept that. From James Graham. I do not think that I would accept it from any other. I shall not doubt the future, then. But meantime, thank God, we have the present! Enough of this talk, my dear. Matters of State be damned! We have . . . each other.'

'With all my heart!' he said.

CHAPTER TWENTY-ONE

Once again, therefore, as so often before, it was a matter of waiting, for James Graham. But this waiting was different. Now, indeed, he almost welcomed the delay. For now he had Elizabeth and delight – even though it had to be a very discreet delight.

It was as well that he could feel this way, for in all truth his cause did not make much apparent headway that first half of 1649. Charles and his councillors maintained their attitude of official non-recognition, however ridiculous the consequences in a comparatively small city like the Hague. Everyone knew that the young King personally favoured the Graham, and only kept him at a distance for reasons of state. That they met, on occasion, at the Wassanaer Hof and elsewhere was inevitable and likewise well known. But the fiction was kept up.

The new representatives from Scotland in due course arrived to reinforce the objectionable Lauderdale – in theory to supersede him, Lanark their leader, now being in name at least the senior. For he was in fact now Duke of Hamilton. His brother, captured after Preston, had recently followed his erstwhile and ill-served master to an English scaffold, the heavy hand of General Cromwell – who now dominated an English Parliament which acknowledged no king and called the Kingdom a Commonwealth – unfaltering with the axe. Montrose had heartily disliked the man, and with reason – but he grieved and was shocked that he should have been slain so. He made a point of letting the former Lanark know of this – Elizabeth inviting one or two of the new Scots Engagers to dinner at the Wassanaer Hof and James Graham appearing thereat as an honoured guest. Nor did, or could, the Queen of Bohemia's other guests make protest; certainly they did not march out. This was typical of the crazy situation which prevailed at the Hague in the year 1649.

William Hamilton was a weaker but rather less arrogant and stupid edition of his brother, and was in fact considerably in awe of Montrose. In public he assiduously, if with evident embarrassment, avoided anything but a monosyllabic exchange with the Graham; but when, with Elizabeth's aid, the latter contrived it so that they might have a brief private conversation, the new Duke was a little more forthcoming. He admitted that the situation in Scotland was bad, that Argyll's rule was hateful, that they needed their King back on the throne, as a civil authority for all decent men to rally round, and to counter the overweening dominance and tyranny of the zealot ministers; but insisted that, with Argyll and the Kirk swaying them, the Estates were wholly set on the King adhering to the Solemn League and Covenant. Nothing else would do. As also, of course, Montrose's own exclusion. He, Hamilton, could not relax on these basic conditions one iota. He was nominally in charge of the negotiations; but he knew Argyll did not trust him. Lauderdale was still the Campbell's man, and in constant secret touch with Scotland. He was sorry, but there was nothing that he could do to ease the situation.

So the charade went on. The negotiations continued seemingly endlessly. Progress was made on a number of minor matters, and some not so minor – for instance a total break with Cromwell and the English Parliamentarians. But on the main issue of contention, that Charles must accept and sign the Solemn League and Covenant, with its essential corollary that Presbyterianism must be imposed on *all* the King's realms, there was no agreement.

So matters stood when, in May, still another deputation arrived from Scotland – and this time, no Engagers. They came direct from the Chancellor – which meant, from Argyll – and proved to be a much tougher and less discursive party. They had the immediate effect of tightening up the Scots position, cancelling much that had been accepted, and generally changing the atmosphere. They were led by the Earl of Cassillis, a sour and hardened West-country Presbyterian, nick-named The Solemn, and one of the actual framers of the Solemn League and Covenant. With him came Master Robert Baillie, one of the Kirk's most vociferous and active zealots, and kinsman of the unfortunate General William Baillie whom Montrose had humiliated so frequently in the field.

The new Commissioners made no attempt to conceal their contempt for Hamilton and his team, even for Lauderdale; and their annoyance – or Argyll's – that negotiations had dragged out thus long and not been satisfactorily concluded. They made it abundantly clear that they considered that they held the whiphand. All would start afresh – and would be dealt with expeditiously from now on. King Charles they treated almost as a cipher. They had not come to bargain, or indeed to negotiate at all. They had come to inform, to state, to demand. Charles had been duly proclaimed as King from the market crosses of Scotland, with trumpet and tuck of drum. In return, if that proclamation was to be followed by a coronation, he must accede to three demands. The Solemn League and Covenant must be subscribed, in total. All Acts of the Scottish Parliament, past, present and future, were to be homologated, and taken as binding on the King. All civil matters and questions must be referred to the said Parliament, hereafter – and all religious to the General Assembly. No matters of State should be decided without their consent. Nothing could be simpler.

They brought other word than that from Scotland. George Gordon, Marquis of Huntly, had been surprised and captured in Aberdeenshire, hurried south to Edinburgh and there executed out of hand – as an enemy of the State. His heir, the Viscount Aboyne, was somewhere in exile and said to be dying. The young Lord Lewis now led the Clan Gordon undisputed – and had come to terms with Argyll. A purge was proceeding in Scotland amongst all who were not wholly for the Solemn League and militant Presbyterianism; even many of the more moderate ministers were being deposed and driven from their parishes. There had been an abortive rising in the North, led by Mackenzie of Pluscarden, the diffident Earl of Seaforth's brother, but this had been put down with vigour by David Leslie, the usual executions following – though Seaforth himself had got out of Scotland in time.

It was all a grim development for Montrose and his cause. But it had its brighter side. The sheer arrogance and lack of all respect on the part of Cassillis and Baillie grievously offended young Charles and set his advisers by the ears. There was now really nothing to negotiate about; it was either complete surrender to the Commissioners, or nothing. Little was to be gained, therefore, by keeping Montrose out of sight any more. After another secret meeting at the Wassenaer Hof, where James Graham pointed out the obvious, and moreover that the news from Scotland had its hopeful side, since clearly Argyll was being forced to hold down the country by arms and terror, the King announced publicly that he was reappointing his illustrious and trusted friend, the Marquis of Montrose, Captain-General and commander-in-chief of all his forces, and that therefore he was entitled to, and must, take part in any further debates and negotiations in which matters military might be involved. Since arms were already in use in Scotland, and none could assert that they would not continue to be so, the Marquis must be present.

That set the cat amongst the pigeons with a vengeance. The Commissioners were faced with the choice of swallowing their condition against Montrose being at the conference-table, or of packing up and going home with nothing decided. They compromised. They declared that they could not accept the excommunicate and malignant James Graham in any degree as a negotiator; but that they would attend one more meeting with the King and his advisers, not to negotiate but to sum up what had been achieved, preparatory to their departure for Scotland.

A confrontation was at last to be effected.

*   *   *

And so Montrose finally crossed the threshold of the wing of the Binnenhoff Palace lent to His Britannic Majesty. He entered the heavily ornate conference-chamber, in an atmosphere of high tension, immediately behind King Charles, the Commissioners from Scotland, already present and seated, perforce rising to their feet at the monarch's arrival, however galling in that they seemed to be standing for the Captain-General also. Every eye was on James Graham, who came in with grave dignity but no sort of triumph or flourish – even when Charles, taking his throne-like chair at the head of the long table, waved him to the seat immediately on his right, first on that side of the board, hitherto always occupied by Sir Edward Hyde – who now sat one farther down. The message was clear – and something like a growl rose from the ranks of the Scots Commissioners. Though not from all the Scots present, for now the right-hand side of the table was furnished with certain other peers of Scotland, at Montrose's suggestion, the Earls of Crawford, Kinnoull, even Seaforth – who had arrived timeously at the Hague only the day before – and the Lords Napier and Sinclair.

A chair scraped back, and although John Kennedy, 6th Earl of Cassillis did not rise, he drew every eye. He was a stocky, heavy, greying man of middle years, square-faced, with bushy eyebrows and a lowering expression, dressed more like a divine than a great nobleman.

'Your Grace,' he rasped, in a nasal voice 'in the name of this Commission of the Estates, I do protest at the presence of James

Graham, so-called Marquis of Montrose, at this table, and in the company of honest men! He is here against the wishes, advice and consciences of those whose duty and concern it is to guide Your Grace on Scottish matters, an outlaw and renegade, forfeited for crimes unnumbered against the Scottish realm. No negotiation or dealing with him is permissible or possible. I demand that he be dismissed forthwith. In the name of the Commission of the Estates.'

The Reverend Robert Baillie, tall, shock-headed, urgent, hot-eyed, jumped to his feet with all the vigour of a much younger man. 'I further that demand. In the name of the General Assembly of the Kirk of Scotland. I say that I cannot sit at a table with a notorious sinner, excommunicated by the Kirk, a man justly cast out of the Church of God, upon whose head lies more innocent blood than on any other for many years, the most bloody murderer in our nation!' Trembling with his emotion, he pointed at Montrose.

There were gasps around the table at this passionate onslaught, and not all from the King's side, Hamilton especially looking highly uncomfortable. Charles turned to Montrose, dark brows raised – but that man looked straight in front of him, grave expression unchanged. He did not speak.

The young King cleared his throat. 'Master Baillie, I request that you use more temperate language in my royal presence,' he said. 'My lord Marquis is here on my authority, and it is not my desire that he should withdraw. So, I fear . . .' A slight pause, and that flashing smile, '. . . I fear that since you cannot sit at table with him, you will have to remain standing! Or, hm, leave us.'

There were some smothered chuckles at that, and Archie Napier, who had half risen to protest on his uncle's behalf, subsided, grinning.

Baillie, blinking those hot eyes, bit his lip and looked uncertain. Then, pushing back his chair a good yard from the table, he sat down thereon behind the backs of his colleagues. Into the uncomfortable silence, a thick but fruity voice spoke, coarse, spluttering a little, but strong. 'Sire – if the Marquis of Montrose is to be present, then there can be no further negotiation. For this is part of our remit – as was made fell clear before this. If it is your royal wish, then we must accept it, in this house.' The speaker rather underlined that word *this*. He was a burly, almost gross man, younger than the previous spokesmen, but florid, gone to fat, with double chin, thick sensuous lips and small shrewd pig-like eyes, John Maitland, 2nd Earl of Lauderdale, grandson of James VI and I's Chancellor Maitland, and great-grandson of Mary Queen of Scots' agile Secretary Maitland of Lethington. 'But we may at least detail and sum up what has already been discussed and accepted. And so we may not entirely waste our time – and Your Grace's.'

'I am still open to conviction, my lord, therefore to negotiation. If these talks must end without decision, then I call all to witness that it is not my wish or choosing. *I* will still negotiate.'

'How can you say that?' Cassillis – who had looked none too pleased at Lauderdale's apparent taking of the lead – demanded. 'When Your Grace has rejected all three of our main points – that you take the Covenant, homologate all Acts of Parliament, and in future act only with the agreement of the Estates and the General Assembly. Lacking acceptance of these terms, we must return to Scotland, nothing achieved. And Your Grace no nearer your throne!'

'Terms, my lord? Did I hear aright?' That was James Graham. 'Do you, an Earl of Scotland, present *terms* to *Ard Righ*, your liege lord?'

Cassillis's great fist banged down on the table. 'Sire – I'll no' bandy words with this, this felon! But, these are terms, yes. Not mine, but of the Estates of your Scottish realm. Either you accept them – or you do not ascend the throne.'

Charles seemed about to make hot retort, but a cough from Hyde caused him to pause, shrug and produce his rueful grin. 'But, my lord – what would you? I have agreed to sign your Covenant – the National one, not the other, which appears to me to interfere impossibly in the affairs of my other realm of England. I have agreed to consider all the Acts and edicts of the Parliaments which have sat in Scotland since the last accepted by my royal father. You cannot expect me to homologate them un-read? You have not brought them all with you, have you? But I would *wish* to approve them, if I may. And I have said that I will indeed consult with the Estates, as is right and proper, in all major matters of policy and law. The Assembly of the Kirk is another matter. For it is a private body with no civil authority. But I will say that I have no wish or intention to interfere with the governance of the Kirk – any more than it should interfere in the governance of the realm. I cannot see, my lord, wherein we are so far from agreement.'

'Then Your Grace's sight must be much impaired!' Cassillis snapped. 'No doubt through immaturity and ill-advice!' And he glared round the opposite side of the table. 'You canna cozen us with words, see you. The terms are clear – no' to be mistaken. Either you agree to them, without quibble or reserve – or you continue to bide here in exile!'

When the outraged murmur of the King's advisers sank away, Montrose spoke quietly. 'I think there is a third alternative, my Lord Cassillis.'

The Kennedy did not answer him, but he eyed him like a wary bull.

'His Grace may return to Scotland, his kingdom, under other auspices than your unmannerly ones, sir. And *take* what is his own, by right.'

There was silence at that. The two sides were now clearly in naked confrontation, all pretence dropped.

It was Lauderdale who spoke. 'Invasion, my lord of Montrose! Against his Grace's own people? We have had enough of bloodshed.'

'Have you, sir? I have not seen you risking *your* blood. On either side!'

'I am a man of peace, sir.'

'How fortunate you are! Whereas I am a man of blood, it seems? A murderer most vile, according to Master Baillie. Admittedly I have seen blood shed in the cause of His late Majesty. Even a little of my own. And am prepared to shed more, for His Grace here – all of my own, if need be. For I do believe, sir, that right, justice, freedom, truth, are more precious even than blood – mine own, or yours. But, Lord Lauderdale, since you are a proclaimed man of peace, you will not oppose His Grace's landing on the shores of his own ancient kingdom? Or urge others to do so. Thus you will suffer no blood-letting. Will you?'

Frowning, the other did not reply.

There was a general muttering round the table. Robert Baillie began to speak, recollected that he had declared that he could not, and subsided into frustrated silence.

The Reverend Alexander Jaffray spoke instead. 'If Your Highness listens to this evil man, this barbarian who has taken up the sword and will most undoubtedly perish by the sword, you will make your name hated in every corner of the realm,' he cried.

'Master Jaffray – you were at Philiphaugh, I believe,' Montrose said, conversationally. 'Urging on the godly work of slaughter. How many men, aye, and women and children also, did *you* slay, or urge to be slain that day? By the sword, the pike, the bullet, the cudgel, by drowning? Tell His Grace – for they would have been *his* subjects.'

'They were God's enemies, sirrah, whosoever subjects! Idolatrous savages. Catholic Erse and heathenish Highland scum! Do you dare name such in the same breath as God's elect people . . . ?'

'I do, sir – I do. Christ died for them, as much as for you. Will you, can you, deny that?'

'I am not here to justify the purposes of Almighty God to an excommunicate.'

'Very well. You have your answer, Sire. I say, send these stiff-necked and self-righteous persecutors of your Scottish subjects back to the man who sent them. Archibald Campbell, with the word that you will sign the *National* Covenant, deal well and faithfully with the decisions of Parliament and govern through it, and will allow freedom of worship for all whatsoever, be they Presbyterian, Episcopalean or Roman. And that you will come in person quickly thereafter, for your royal coronation, adequately supported. And that no subject, Argyll or other, will offer the King of Scots terms! Send that message, Sire – and that said, I see no need to detain these gentlemen further.'

Strangely enough it was Edward Hyde who protested. 'Sire – Your Majesty We . . . my lord of Montrose goes too fast. We are reasonable men. We must act as statesmen, not swordsmen! Especially when my lord Marquis of Argyll has shown that he would prefer so to act. He has held out a hand . . .'

'A hand that grasped £200,000 as price for his master, by God!' That was the Earl of Crawford.

'Sire – do not be distracted by these unhelpful interruptions,' the Chancellor urged. 'We must look at the situation as it is, not as we would wish it to be. Whatever is past, the Marquis of Argyll has extended a hand to Your Majesty. You can, I do conceive, meet two of his conditions. As for the Solemn League and Covenant, it is scarcely possible for you to sign it as it is at present worded, however much you might wish – since it would impose Presbyterian church-government on England. Which is, hm, unacceptable. But not only this, it would in consequence preclude all co-operation between Scots and English royalists, such as is vitally necessary. So I say, as a reasonable man, ask my lord of Argyll and the Estates to amend the wording thereof sufficiently for Your Majesty to sign it. None so difficult, surely. A word here and there – that is all.' Hyde put his plump fingers together, and beamed over them at all concerned, a civilised man triumphant. 'Thus all three conditions will be met, and all resolved. And the fourth matter for consideration will fall into its due and proper sequence . . .'

'Fourth matter, man ? What fourth matter ?'That was Cassillis.

'One which was not entrusted to your Commission – which would have been unsuitable, my lord,' the little man declared primly. 'Since it is a more personal matter. Sent direct from my lord Marquis to His Majesty. Through my humble self. My lord of Argyll, in token of his goodwill and honest and loyal intentions, suggests that his daughter, the Lady Anne Campbell, should be married to His Majesty.'

'Merciful . . . God!' Montrose got out, chokingly.

There was chaos around that table, on both sides, men exclaiming, shouting, thumping the board, jumping to their feet. King Charles sat back, watching, a curious expression on his saturnine features. He made no attempt to halt the uproar – although his Chancellor did, beating on the table with a roll of paper, his shocked voice rising to a squeak, totally without effect.

At length Montrose turned to the young monarch, his poise recovered. 'Sire – you will not control them now. Nor, I think, should wish to. I would advise that you rise and leave. The best way. At this juncture. *Your* dignity intact, at least. Better tactics for the future, anyway.'

Charles nodded, relievedly, got to his feet, and inclined his head towards the noisy company. Then he turned, and walked unhurriedly to the door. Montrose managed to reach and open it for him, in time. They passed through, and it shut behind them.

'Mary Mother of God!' the King – who was, of course, a good official Protestant – exclaimed. 'That was . . . an experience! Heaven preserve me from many such! Is that what Privy Councils are like in Scotland, my lord ?'

'Do not think too hardly of the Scots, Sire. These were scarcely representative. And at least they did not swallow the Campbell's insult to Your Grace, as Hyde seems to have done.'

Charles looked at him thoughtfully for a moment, and then changed the subject. 'You said, just then, something about better tactics for the future. What did you mean ?'

'I meant, Sire, that after this you cannot sit down again with these Commissioners. Even if they would. Not without seeming to surrender your position. You have given them *something* to take home with them – more I think than they should have. So, I humbly suggest that Your Grace should remove yourself.'

'Remove myself? I? Go away?'

'Yes. Go – before they do. Show that *you* clearly have had sufficient. Not that *they* have left you. Go, meantime, somewhere away from the Hague. And, if you will, seem to link your going with armed preparations. Such will well serve your cause, I am sure.'

'And *your*'s, my lord!'

'My cause is your own, Sire. I have no other.'

'Where could I go? To Paris? To my mother? Not that, I think!'

'Your sister and the Prince of Orange are gone to Breda, in Brabant, meantime. Could you not go there? Seem to concern yourself with shipping. Prince Rupert used Breda when he was recruiting ships and men. Busy yourself with that, Sire. Or, if you do not in truth, *seem* to. Nothing will more surely disturb these Commissioners. And Argyll.'

'Ned Hyde will not like it.'

'Hyde has had his chance. And what has it won Your Grace?'

'I . . . I will think on it, my lord. Yes – I believe you have the rights of it . . .'

CHAPTER TWENTY-TWO

James Graham rode through the mellow smiling Rhineland province of Utrecht in the golden late-August sunshine, with only Archie Napier for company, his mind something of a battle-ground for his all too demanding emotions. At long last the waiting, the uncertainty, the painful frustrations, seemed to be almost over. The action for which his whole nature craved was about to replace the years of delay and disappointment – even though it was not the scale of action he had visualised and there was still much of disappointment, foot-dragging, almost betrayal involved. And he was going to see Elizabeth again, after six weeks of absence. But that was as bitter-sweet as the rest.

The Queen of Bohemia and her family had been lent, for some summers, the small, old and semi-derelict royal castle of Rhenen, on the Nether Rhine, to escape to in the hot months when the dusty plains around the Hague baked, and where she could indulge in the active pursuits which she loved, hunting in the forests, hawking in the low hills, boating excursions on the great river. It was only a roosting-place, primitive, uncomfortable – but Elizabeth greatly enjoyed it, and was grateful to her niece's husband for letting her use it. Montrose had not been there previously.

They rode down to the town by the riverside, jingled through the narrow streets, and on up the circular roadway which climbed round and round the steep rocky bluff behind, past the outer and inner walls and gatehouses. At close range the castle looked a deal less romantic, with here and there decayed out-buildings, sagging roofs, broken masonry and fallen plaster. There were no guards at either gatehouse to challenge callers.

Clattering into the high central courtyard under the soaring towers where pigeons cooed and grass grew between the paving-stones, they found Princess Louise helping an elderly groom at one of the handles of the obviously deep draw-well in the centre. Looking up, at their arrival, she did not fail to look disconcerted and embarrassed, but there was no lack of eagerness in her glance – even though she replaced it by a frown and went on still more vigorously winding her handle. Archie gallantly leapt down and ran to relieve her at her labour, just as the brimming bucket came to the top. A row of already filled buckets stood nearby.

James Graham came to her, smiling, hands outstretched. 'How well you look, Louie. And how lovely!' He leant, to kiss both her flushed cheeks, a proceeding Napier eyed with a touch of envy. 'Rhenen agrees with you, to be sure. Even with all the water to hoist from the depths of the earth. How good to see you again.'

'And you, my lord. My *lords*.' She had excuse for sounding breathless. 'We believed you in Brussels.'

'We have come from there. The more happy to be here.'

'You will find Mamma gathering plums,' Louie said, looking away. 'There is an orchard. On a terrace – over that side. Hugo will show you.'

He was about to suggest that it would be better if she showed him herself, but thought better of it. 'Archie will be glad to aid you with the water, I am sure,' he said easily, and strolled off with the groom.

Through a pend below a corbelled tower, they came out on a sloping terrace grown with old and gnarled fruit-trees, and down the somewhat lessened incline people were working, filling baskets with the fat purple plums. Amongst the leafage Montrose could not identify individuals. Dismissing the guide, he wandered down amongst the trees. The noise of bees was here superseding the cooing of the doves.

He saw the Princess Eliza sitting on a stool, her back against a tree-trunk, eyes apparently closed, and, feeling disinclined for a verbal passage at arms just then, moved discreetly away. Then he heard an inconsequential, crooning singing – and his heart lifted to the voice. He made his way towards the sound.

Elizabeth was up a ladder, head amongst the branches, pulling fruit and putting the plums in a basket hung on an iron hook, humming a melody as she worked. The man bowed to her silken stockings.

'Your elevated Highness,' he observed, judicially, 'has a well-turned ankle!'

She looked down, wide-eyed. 'Jamie!' she cried. 'On my soul – Jamie Graham! Here's joy!' And she came down that ladder in a rush more illustrative of her physical fitness and agility than of her dignity.

But it was the clear and apparent duty of a gentleman to aid her in the business, if not actually to catch her bodily. Montrose did not neglect his responsibilities.

In each other's arms for a moment they clung tightly, before separating, with swift glances around. Dressed in oldest clothing, cheek smudged with green lichen from the tree, fingers stained with the fruit, eyes shining, she looked entirely ravishing nevertheless. He said as much.

'My dear, my dear!' she breathed, in not much more than a whisper, consciously or otherwise seeking not to draw attention to themselves a moment before they must, there amongst the serried, low-branched trees. 'How good, how splendid. And the better for being unexpected. In your letter of a week past you did not say . . . ? Are you finished at Brussels, then? Or is this but an interlude?' She shook her head. 'But – never heed. You are here – that is all that matters.'

'Agreed. After the stolid mynheers of the States-General, you can scarcely conceive how glorious a sight you make, Elizabeth, my love – smears and all! Yes, I have finished with Brussels at last, thank God – although less profitably than I had hoped. No more kicking my heels *there*, at least.'

'Good! Then you will be able to stay awhile? You deserve a diversion, a respite. I shall take you boar-hunting, Jamie – a change from boors! We shall sail the river, fish with spears – a new sport I have discovered – visit the monasteries where they make the wine . . .'

'Do not tempt me!' he broke in on her, pleading. 'Alas, I cannot stay. I am here only, to to . . .' He could not bring himself to use the phrase 'say goodbye'. 'Only two nights, my dear. Then I must be on my way.'

'Jamie – oh, no!' She clutched his arm. 'Not . . . not away? Going away!' She shook her head, decisively, as though she would not hear it. 'Do not tell me. Not now. Not this happy moment. Let us have this, at least . . .'

'Yes. Assuredly. With all my heart. We are not so rich in moments like these, you and I, to squander them! I . . .' He paused, and touched her elbow. 'But – we are discovered. Here comes Sophie . . .'

That evening, on a high balcony of the castle, with the air still warm, they sat looking out over the gleaming Rhine, and talked, while Eliza played gentle, wistful music on a lute in the room behind them, Louie whittled a block of wood into the shape of a monkey, with chisel and knife, and Henrietta, the youngest of the

312

family, played with a gangling puppy. Sophia had gone walking with Archie Napier.

'So – the States-General finally gave you the moneys? But less than you hoped?' Elizabeth said.

'Yes. After Charles let it be known that he was supporting my plans all seemed set fair, for the money. A loan, of course. But then, when from Breda he of a sudden announced his support for an immediate new expedition to Ireland, the States-General began to doubt again. As I could not blame them. He could not stage both ventures successfully, they said. But I wrote of that, to you, in June.'

'Yes, indeed. It was foolishness. The folly of a young man lacking experience. And badly advised – other than by yourself. *I* felt in part responsible, Jamie – since it was, no doubt, my son Rupert who sent to Charles urging that aid and reinforcement be sent. But – you put that right, did you not? You went to Breda, and changed Charles's mind?'

'It was not so much I who changed it, but Cromwell! Cromwell's successful expedition to Ireland changed all. With Ormonde easily defeated – as I feared he must be – there could be no further Irish adventure. But, although I brought Charles back to Brussels and the States-General, they had lost some of their confidence in my cause. Or, at least, the King's full commitment to it. So, I have got only one-third of what I hoped for.'

'I am sorry. In my relief that Rupert and Maurice were safe, I had not realised how much that foolish venture was costing *you*. But I did write to you not to place over much reliance in Charles, urged you to go to Breda earlier, not to let him long out of your sight and influence. He is a strange young man, my nephew, not wholly trustworthy . . .'

'Mamma!' Henrietta protested. 'How unkind.'

'Not unkind, stupid, but looking facts in the face. As one must, when men's whole lives are at stake. I like Charles very well. He is charming, attractive – too attractive. But devious. Perhaps he could not be otherwise with the mother and grandmother he had! Young, he swings too much according to the last advice he receives. Seems to wish to agree with all – yet deep down pursues unspoken ways all his own.'

'But he greatly admires my lord . . .'

'That does not change his nature. Or make his policies the more reliable.' Elizabeth turned back to Montrose. 'And now

313

he has gone to his mother, in France. I cannot think that pleased you, either!'

'No. Although I could by no means attempt to dissuade him. He will not persuade Queen Henrietta to a Scottish venture, nor to find money for it. He left Brussels for St. Germain before the States-General made its final decision.'

'And now?'

'Before we parted, he gave me all the *authority* I need. Nothing more was said as to me being commander-in-chief of his forces – but that is of no moment. I never sought it. I am Captain-General and Lieutenant-Governor of Scotland, with complete powers to act there as I think fit. In his royal name. I can now move, at last.'

'And the money?' That was Louise. 'Have you sufficient?' For your needs? To hire an Army?'

'No, nothing sufficient,' he admitted. 'Not with shipping to hire. Although I am hopeful, in that respect, of help from a Scots merchant of Gothenburg – a man of great wealth. I cannot take an army. Only an officer-corps – and mainly Scots, at that. But experienced veterans, such as I greatly need. I have this credit from the States-General – although it applies only within the Emperor's territories – and have already made arrangements in Brussels. Hurry will see to the enrolling there. I have sent to the Elector of Brandenburg for the moneys he has promised – through the kindness of your royal mother. Also to the Duke of Courland. I hope to collect more at Hamburg – where also I hope to hire shipping. Then I go to your kinsman the new King of Denmark, at Copenhagen, to try hold him to his father's word. Finally to Gothenburg, and the merchant Maclear.'

'That will take . . . some time?' Elizabeth said.

'Yes. And timing is of the essence, now. I cannot hope to be ready to sail while still this campaigning season lasts. But there may be advantage in that also – if only I can seize it. I know from experience that Argyll and his generals will never contemplate a winter campaign. They esteem it impossible, in a mountainous land like Scotland. So, I shall seek to land in Scotland when and where I am least expected, while it is still winter, God aiding me.'

'A winter crossing, by sea?' the Queen said. 'Is that practicable? Is it not dangerous?'

'Danger? There is danger in all that we do, in this matter. But it is practicable, shipmasters assure me.'

There was silence, then, save for the lute's liquid notes.

'Where will you make for? To land?' Louise asked.

'Where we will not be looked for. Where we may have time and peace to assemble, muster, send out messengers to the clans, without being attacked in the meantime. The Orkney Islands. It is almost the shortest voyage from the Skagerrack, with like to be little Scots shipping to spy us. And Orkney is a little world unto itself; yet close to the Scottish mainland. And the Earl of Morton, Kinnoull's uncle, is master there – and a good King's man. I will send Kinnoull, with a small token force, to Orkney beforehand. At once. From Hamburg, if I may get the ships. So that they have the autumn and most of the winter to prepare, gather and train local men, make ready to receive my main expedition. Even if Argyll learns of their arrival, he will not anticipate any large descent there, I think. And in winter. Then, without delay, we shall cross to Caithness – there is no lack of shipping in Orkney, small boats. And south, down through the Scottish Highlands.'

'And you are sanguine? Of course?' Elizabeth demanded, suddenly urgent. 'You seem, to a mere woman's mind, to be gambling in this. Heavily.'

'I am gambling, yes. War *is* a gamble. Things are not as I would have had them. But I must make the attempt. I have had to delay too long. If a blow is to be struck, it must be soon. While Charles is fresh on his throne. So that the Scots people can perceive a new start. While there is still hope in the land. The longer we wait, the more difficult the task.'

'I understand.' She sighed – and Elizabeth Stewart was not a great sigher. 'So you leave us . . . soon?'

'Two nights from now I have arranged to see Kinnoull and Hurry at the Hague. Then on to Hamburg. I am sorry, so very sorry – but time presses on me, and there is no avoiding my duty.'

Louise got up, and hurried away, wordless. The lute, and the puppy's grunts had it all to themselves.

*   *   *

Leave-taking was a sore business. All would have wished it to be got over as swiftly as possible, in the end. But the decencies had to be observed. Archie Napier was both a help and a nuisance, brisk, unemotional but all too present. To gain a few precious moments of privacy Elizabeth resorted to a device, transparent enough but effective, of suddenly recollecting a message she had for Montrose to deliver at the Hague, and taking him back with her to her own room to collect it, leaving the others in the court-yard.

Out of sight of them all, she turned to him. 'Jamie – this is damnable! I am like a stricken, doting girl – but I can scarcely control myself. This of goodbye – I do not think that I can face it.'

'Nor you alone. But we must, my dear. Must try to make it a memory to cherish, not a misery to be got over.'

'Ah – how noble! So sensible! So like a man!' she exclaimed. 'But – do you realise what this *is*, Jamie? This is *parting*! It may be the, the end. We may never see each other again.'

'Not the end, Elizabeth – never that. Our love cannot end. Now or ever. It is eternal. And we shall see each other again – of this I have no doubt.'

'But – oh God, you may be killed! You are thrusting yourself into dire danger.'

'Even so, we shall see each other again. Hereafter.'

'I wish that I had your faith. But that is not how I want to see you.' She clutched him. 'It is *you*, in the flesh. My Jamie Graham. Not some, some spirit!'

He held her close, but said nothing.

'Oh, I am weak, weak,' she mumbled into his shoulder. 'I am sorry. But I cannot bear the thought of living without you. Living and living . . . !'

'You will not be without me, ever. That I promise you. What-ever happens, my heart. Dear Elizabeth – we have taken each the other. Two human souls cannot do more. This parting is grievous. But only that. It is not a severance, an ending. I do not fear the future. It is ours.'

'Will you come back to me, Jamie?'

'Either that – or you will come to me,' he assured her, gravely.

She searched his face, as though to discern all the implications of his words. Then she nodded. 'I will come.'

'Then, then we need care for nothing. For what transpires. You and I. We hold it all. In our hearts. This leave-taking is but a step on our way together.'

'Yes,' she whispered. 'Yes. I will, I will hold to that.'

They clung to each other for a little, and then turned and went back to the others.

In the courtyard, Elizabeth spoke as nearly naturally as she could. 'At the Hague, Jamie, make time to go see Gerard Honthorst. The portrait of you that I commissioned is near

316

finished. He but needs a few brush-strokes for the features, the eyes. Give him that, of your precious time – on my royal command! It is a mite stern, I think – but I will hang it in my cabinet. And at least it will serve to frighten away the Brethren! Your Scots enemies, when they come plaguing me.'

'It shall be done, Madam. But I had rather the artist painted in a smile on me! I have had enough of sternness. As . . . in the other.' And he threw an understanding glance at Louise.

'Tell Honthorst so, then.'

Montrose said goodbye to the young women, Henrietta, Sophia, Eliza. Louise he gripped more tightly.

'The stout and constant heart,' he murmured, in her ear. 'It cannot be defeated. *You* will not be defeated. That I know.'

'And . . . you?'

'Both of us,' he said. And kissed her.

Then he turned to the Queen, straightening up his shoulders. 'I have a journey to make, Highness,' he said. 'Have I Your Majesty's permission to leave?'

Head high, she mustered a smile. 'You have, Jamie Graham. We will receive you to our royal presence . . . another day!' Almost gaily she said it.

'For that day I wait,' he answered, raised her hand to his lips, and bowed low.

Archie Napier flourished his feathered beaver, and held the horses while uncle mounted.

'God save the Queen!' Montrose said, from the saddle, and reining round spurred at once into a trot for the gatehouse arch – and dared not to look back.

PART THREE

CHAPTER TWENTY-THREE

As James Graham had watched Scotland recede from his sight forty-two long months before, so from the heaving bows of another Scandinavian ship he watched it loom again before him, grey and forbidding in the thin rain, on the 20th of March, 1650, a harsh barrier of rocks and cliffs ringed with the white water of great breaking seas, long, low-lying – for this was Orkney, not the mountainous mainland. And if his mood on that other occasion had been grim, sombre as the scene, now, despite the fact that this was what he had waited and longed and prayed for for so long, the return to his native land, his humour was little more cheerful. There was not much lift of the heart for Montrose at this homecoming, weeks later than he had intended.

It was as though almost everything conspired to depress him. Nothing had gone well in the six months since he had taken leave of Elizabeth at Rhenen. Admittedly Kinnoull had successfully managed to sail from Amsterdam for Orkney, via Copenhagen, at the end of August with an advance-party of eighty experienced mercenaries and 100 Danish volunteers, and after a fair voyage had landed without incident. But that was as far as the credit side stretched. At Kirkwall he had found his uncle, Robert Douglas, 8th Earl of Morton, gravely ill – and he had died in November. This was serious, for Morton's influence was paramount, as lord of the islands – and the new earl was only a youth. But this was only the beginning of misfortune; for Kinnoull himself had been suffering from recurring fevers contracted in the Low Countries, and possibly as a result of his transfer to the wet cold of the North, the younger man fell ill at Kirkwall only a few days later, with pleurisy, and followed his uncle to the grave before the end of the year. This grievous news had been brought to Montrose at Gothenburg by Sir James Douglas, Morton's brother, in January. He had other tidings to impart also. Word had not been long in reaching the South as to Kinnoull's landing, and General David Leslie had marched north, with a Covenant army. He had made no attempt at a crossing to Orkney – but the threat was there.

Nevertheless, Douglas was optimistic over the military situation. Leslie's army was not large, and had very much settled into winter quarters. The people of Scotland, by and large, were sickened with the Covenant regime and ready to rise, he assured. He promised 1,000 from Orkney itself, and they could be sure of 2,000 of Seaforth's Mackenzies when they landed on the mainland. Others also had sent promises. Montrose could reckon on 10,000 men from the North to face Leslie. Only arms, munitions, powder and shot, were in desperately short supply.

To aid in this situation Montrose had despatched a squadron of four old vessels from Gothenburg – all that he could hire – filled with guns, and munitions, and 1,200 men, mainly Danes and Netherlanders, with Scots officers. But a frightful gale had caught these vessels in the savage northern seas, and only the one ship had reached Orkney, with 200 men.

People began to say that God's hand was against Montrose.

But this was not the worst of James Graham's anxieties, sorrowful as he was for the lost men. As he braced himself against the thrumming rigging of the Swedish *Herderinnen* and watched the spires of St. Magnus's Cathedral grow out of the rain and scud, his real unease came from a letter in his pocket, a letter from Elizabeth delivered to him a day or two before he sailed from Bergen, on the 16th of March, with his shipload of veteran officers. The letter itself was a joy and a comfort – although it had an ominous postscript to the effect that the Queen was hearing ill rumours from St. Germain. But it had enclosed another letter, this indeed headed from St. Germain, and written on the 19th of September, from his new liege lord and monarch, sent via Rhenen. It was a friendly, even flattering letter. But there was a paragraph therein which, taken in conjunction with Elizabeth's postscript, hit James Graham like a body blow. It ran:

I entreat you to go on vigorously, and with your wonted courage and care, in the preservation of those trusts I have committed to you, and not to be startled with any reports you may hear, as if I were otherwise inclined to the Presbyterians than when I left you. I assure you I am upon the same principles I was, and depend as much as ever upon your undertakings and endeavours for my service, being fully resolved to assist and support you therein to the utter most of my power.

The thought of those words '. . . not to be startled with any reports you may hear . . .' and from that address and source, had remained like a leaden weight with Montrose ever since. Something was wrong, basically wrong, somewhere – he felt it in his bones. 'As if I were otherwise inclined to the Presbyterians than when I left you.' Could he trust young Charles Stewart? Elizabeth had said that he should not. And if not, what might be the consequences for this venture?

To counter the sudden fears and doubts which, if they affected him, must still more affect others once they became generally known, Montrose had composed and issued a Declaration before he sailed, a resounding manifesto announcing his intentions to overthrow the evil men who held Scotland in thrall and who had sold their monarch to his death, and were denying men freedom to worship God in their own chosen way. And he committed, advisedly King Charles II to this venture, which was being carried out in his royal name and authority. As a precaution against unnamed doubts, it was the best that he could do. Archie Napier and George Wishart, left behind at Hamburg to muster and send on reinforcements and munitions, would publish it abroad.

Hurry and Sir James Douglas had joined him in the *Herderinnen*'s bows, the latter a small middle-aged man wrapped in a cloak against the weather.

'Not long now, my lord,' Douglas said. 'By God's teeth, I'll not be sorry to set foot on dry land again! In yon storm, I feared we would never win to Pomona.'

'Pomona . . . ?'

'The name for the main island of Orkney. It will gain a new fame as the place where the great Marquis of Montrose returned to deliver his native land!'

'So be it we are kindly received!' Hurry put in. 'How do we know that Leslie has not crossed the Pentland Firth and is waiting for us?'

'There would have been warnings – beacons, smokes, boats out . . .'

'Nevertheless, we shall not sail blindly in,' Montrose decided. 'Have the shipmaster to lie off the harbour mouth a few cables' length, and send a boat in. Many Swedes and Norwegians trade here. Find out what transpires. There will be little suspicion of a single ship flying the Swedish flag.'

This precaution was carried out, and a group of Swedes rowed ashore. The others had not long to wait, however, before it was seen returning – and rather fuller of folk than when it went.

As he watched from the ship's side, Montrose, suddenly perceiving, straightened up – and the dark mood which had clothed him for a while dropped from him like a cast cloak. 'Pate!' he cried. 'Black Pate!' And he raised an arm, and shouted his delight and greetings.

Colonel Pate Graham of Inchbrakie was the first man up the rope-ladder to the deck, and unashamedly the two friends embraced each other in incoherent joy, while the onlookers grinned and chuckled their amusement – and also their relief. For, if Black Pate could thus sail out openly from Kirkwall, all must be well therein.

'Jamie, Jamie . . .!' was all that Inchbrakie could get out. 'At last, Jamie – at last . . .!'

'Pate – God be praised! Man – how good, how very good! *You*, here. To come to Orkney. This is a joy. A welcome home, indeed!'

'I came two weeks past. When I heard that Kinnoull expected you. To wait for you. You, you heard that he had died . . .?'

'Yes. A tragedy. A grievous loss. And Morton too. But you, Pate – you look well, your own sturdy black self! Worth a regiment, I swear! And Jean, your wife – she is well also? And your bairns? And, and mine?'

'Aye – all well. Yours with their grandsire, my lord of Southesk. At Kinnaird. James too, released this past year. Confined to Kinnaird, mind. They may not travel abroad or see any but their kin. But they are well . . .'

'Praise God for that!' Montrose recollected his duty. Two young men had climbed up after Pate, and were waiting. 'And these gentlemen . . .?'

'William Hay, my lord – new Earl of Kinnoull. And James Crichton, my lord Viscount Frendraught. Others await you ashore.'

'My lords, I rejoice to see you. In the King's name, I greet you.' He did not actually say that it was good to find Frendraught on the right side – for he had fought against him previously. 'This is a good augury. I thank you for your courtesy in coming to meet me . . .'

And so the *Herderinnen* drew in to the harbour of Kirkwall, in wind and rain, and James Graham set foot again on Scottish soil. Despite the weather a crowd had gathered, the Provost and

324

magistrates to the fore, and it was in something like a triumph, a canny, undemonstrative Scots triumph, that the Viceroy made his way through the narrowest streets in Europe to the Earl's Palace opposite St. Magnus's Cathedral, the splendid castellated pile started by Mary Queen of Scots' half-brother Robert Stewart, when first Bishop then Earl of Orkney. He had been Elizabeth's great-uncle – however much of a scoundrel.

Here men came flocking to greet the King's representative. But despite the welcome and enthusiasm, it did not take James Graham long to perceive that although Kinnoull's advance-party had been in Orkney for five months, the persons and personages who ought to have been flocking to the Royal Standard were neither present nor represented. Of the great lords, the two who had come out in the boat were in fact the only representatives – and these not of the most powerful. There were a number of Graham lairds, some old companions-in-arms like Ogilvy of Powrie, Hay of Delgatie, Drummond of Balloch and Major David Guthrie; also many local Orkney landowners. But of the men who could provide the necessary major reinforcements, there was no sign.

Montrose said as much to Black Pate when they could be alone together.

'Orkney is a long way north, James,' the other reminded. 'And Argyll's spies are everywhere. Watching especially those known to be your friends. I only won away by a stratagem. Airlie, Madderty, Fleming, Erskine and the rest are as good as prisoners in their own houses. They will rise – but only when you are a deal farther south than Kirkwall!'

The other nodded. 'I know well the danger and problems. For these. But I had hoped for others. Reay, chief of the Mackays – I had looked for him here. His lands are just across the Firth. Seaforth is still in Holland, I believe – but his brother, Mackenzie of Pluscarden, has shown that he is a better fighter. I thought to see *him*. And the Rosses? Where are they? Balnagown should be here. The Munroes? They took part in Pluscarden's rising. All these are North Country clans. I told Kinnoull to call them in. Where are they?'

Pate Graham had no answer to that.

Montrose found that he had, as command, a total of some 1,700 men – those whom Kinnoull had brought, the 200 survivors of the ill-fated second expeditionary force, those who had come with himself, plus the men raised locally in Orkney.

A highly unbalanced force, at that, with a great preponderance of mercenary officers, no cavalry, and the Orkneymen almost totally untrained.

Nevertheless it was a nucleus, an armed force, and James Graham was in no state to be over-critical, however far below expectations and requirements it fell. He set about the training and improving of it the very next day, with a will, marshalling it into cadres, at this stage heavily over-officered, which could rapidly be expanded into companies and regiments.

Cavalry was the big problem, as ever, for although Montrose had over £10,000 in cash, largely advanced by the gallant John Maclear in Gothenburg, set aside for the purchase or hiring of horseflesh, Orkney was not the place to do this, the short-legged ponies of the islands being quite unsuitable for military work. A round-up of gentlemen's horses in the area produced only some forty usable animals – his total cavalry meantime. His tactics, for some time ahead therefore, must be to operate where cavalry, enemy cavalry, could not function – however hindering this must be to his eventual campaign.

The third day after their arrival at Kirkwall, a courier landed from a fishing-boat come from the Scottish mainland, a royal courier, one Major Harry May. He had been on Montrose's trail, it seemed, for many weeks, having left the King in Jersey in mid-January. Hearing, at Copenhagen, that the Graham had sailed, he had taken passage in the first ship voyaging to Scotland, and landed at Aberdeen, thereafter making his way over-land to John o' Groats. Major May, an Englishman, was caustic in his observations on travel in Scotland in March.

Montrose, who at least had adequate, indeed spacious quarters in the Earl's Palace of Kirkwall, took the royal package, quite a bulky one, to open in a private room. It contained three bundles. The first, unwrapped, proved to be the splendid insignia and ribbon of the Order of the Garter, bestowed by a grateful monarch on his illustrious Viceroy as a mark of confidence and esteem. The recipient was appreciative, but considered the timing odd. Laying it aside, he opened the larger of the remaining packets, which contained a bundle of copies of correspondence, in what he believed to be the neat and spidery handwriting of Edward Hyde. The smaller packet was heavily sealed with the royal arms, and in Charles's own hand, dated the 12th of January, 1650, at Jersey.

As he scanned this, the man's face quickly set and grew grim, and the leaden weight which he had carried about with him since leaving Gothenburg kicked anew and violently. A groan of sheer pain escaped him.

Charles wrote in as friendly and flattering a fashion as ever, declaring how much pleasure it gave him to appoint his most valued and trusted servant to the Most Noble Order of the Garter, the highest honour he could pay him in present circumstances. But then he went on to announce that he had reopened negotiations with Argyll and the Estates, and to such good effects that a treaty was actually in preparation – which might make it possible to gain his Scottish kingdom without distressing bloodshed. And, more important still, could result in a Scots invasion over the border, to link up with the English royalists and so sweep Cromwell and the rebellious Parliamentarians from power, with a consequent restoration to his joint throne of the United Kingdom – which, after all, was his main objective. He, Charles, was most hopeful of this new initiative – as the enclosed documents would show – and was convinced that his Captain-General's venture in the North would greatly strengthen his hand in these new negotiations. He urged Montrose to proceed vigorously and firmly on his undertaking, doubting not that all his loyal and well-affected subjects in Scotland would cordially and effectually join him, to force any who were against an equitable treaty to reconsider. He ended:

> We will not, before or during the treaty, do anything contrary to the power and authority which we have given you by our commission, nor consent to anything that may bring the least degree of diminution to it; and if the said treaty should produce an agreement, we will, with our uttermost care, so provide for the honour and interest of yourself, and of all that shall engage with you, as shall let the whole world see the high esteem we have for you.

All this was most carefully and painstakingly written, as though from a copy. But the letter concluded with an obviously hurried scrawled afterthought, which urged Montrose not to take alarm at any reports or messages from others, and reiterating that he, Charles, would never consent to anything to his friend's prejudice.

Appalled, James Graham stared unseeing out of the window towards St. Magnus's brown-stone towers and spires. The folly of it, the sheer, devious-minded folly! To authorise and despatch an armed invasion – and then to enter into negotiations with those to be assaulted, without warning or consent, behind the invader's back! Especially with such as Argyll. It would, it *must*, be construed by all as sheer weakness, complete lack of confidence in the military attempt, an undermining of all Montrose's aims and authority, whatever Charles wrote about trust and esteem. How many would now risk all by rising to support the invasion, when a treaty was in the offing? And a treaty which, if agreed, could only mean one thing, Charles's signing of the Solemn League and Covenant. Argyll in his strong position – stronger now than ever – would never resile one inch from that basic demand. Which meant that there could be *no* co-operation with the English royalists, who would never draw sword to have Covenant-style Presbyterianism imposed upon them, as the Solemn League demanded. Once this got known, the military venture was as good as doomed. Perhaps it had been doomed from the outset . . . ?

When James Graham at length returned to the others, in the Great Hall, he had schooled himself and his features to calm inscrutability. Rather stiffly for him, however, he questioned Major May as to how much he knew of the new negotiations and proposed treaty, and how much bruited abroad it all was generally?

'Why, my lord, all know of it,' the other answered. 'It is no secret – indeed it was of a purpose published far and wide. His Majesty and his advisers believed it to be a notable step forward, proof that reason and good sense will prevail and that the sword is not the only way to solve the affairs of nations.'

All present were now listening intently, faces tense. Pate Graham began to speak, and then shut his mouth almost with a click.

Montrose went on, level-voiced. 'This notable step has been published abroad? So long ago as January? Then it will of a certainty have reached Scotland. Argyll will have seen to that. It will now be known far and wide.'

'It was spoken of in Aberdeen, yes.'

'It will be the less likely to inspire military fervour I think!'

There was an ominous growl from the listening group of senior officers. Many looked uncomfortable.

James Graham changed the subject. 'Coming north, sir, what did you learn of the enemy? Or perhaps we do not call them that, now ? Since the King is in negotiation with them ? Say then, the Covenant forces ? Do you know how they are said to be disposed ?'

'Yes, my lord Marquis – that is well-enough known also. The country is full of the talk of it. General Leslie has returned to Edinburgh, leaving Major-General Strachan in command in the North. Why is not said. Strachan has taken up a position at a place called the Ord of Caithness, some thirty-five miles south of Thurso. A strong place where the hills come down in great cliffs to the sea. I passed near by, in guise of a packman – all travellers must pass there, or climb the mountains. Also he garrisons the strong castles of Dunrobin, Skibo, Skelbo and Dornoch behind him, belonging, they say, to the Earl of Sutherland.'

'Yes, Sutherland was always hot for the Covenant. Have you any notion as to his numbers ? Strachan's, not the local Sutherland levies.'

'It is said that he has 3,000 foot, my lord, and 1,500 horse. Dragoons.'

Glances were exchanged all around that noble apartment. Fifteen hundred heavy cavalry. And *they* had forty !

Montrose, well aware of those glances, shrugged. 'He has all of the Northern Highlands to hold, with these. Most of it country of hills, bogs and torrents where dragoons are of little use. Is there any word of the clans ? The Northern clans. The Mackenzies in especial. Seaforth's people.'

'I heard that there was some fighting between Mackenzies and MacDonalds in the west, my lord. But I understand that this is nothing unusual amongst these savages.'

'I thank you for your informations, Major,' Montrose said bleakly. 'But when I desire your observations on the qualities of His Grace's Highland subjects, I will ask for it !' He turned away.

Later, as they watched the men training on the sandy links west of the town, Black Pate spoke out, though quietly. 'James – we are betrayed, are we not ? Struck in the back. By the young man we have taken up arms to seat on his throne ! Can we go on ?'

'Can we do other, Pate ? We have no choice, as I see it. These negotiations will achieve nothing for the King. He has no least idea of the men with whom he would deal. Even if there *is* a treaty, even if he signs the damnable Solemn League and is brought to Scotland, he will not rule. He will be kept a captive puppet, to do the Campbell's bidding. As much a prisoner as ever was his father. It was not for that I swore allegiance and service.'

'But we will be hamstrung, now. Who will join our attempt while the King sits at table with our opponents? Your second Charles is sending us to our deaths!'

Montrose drew a deep breath. 'It may not be so bad as that, Pate. It must sorely hamper us, yes. But it could also hamper Leslie and Strachan. They too will be less than eager for battle, in the circumstances, risking their skins for a cause which may already be won and lost. Leslie in especial – he is a soldier first and foremost; and no soldier likes to campaign with negotiations going on behind him.'

'So – you aim to fight? Despite all?'

'I see no other course. It is that – or returning to the Continent. We shall soon outstay our welcome in Orkney. Moreover, for any peace and good to come to Scotland, Argyll and his minions must be unseated and put down. Whatever Charles Stewart may think. Nothing else will serve. I am still Viceroy and Captain-General of Scotland. Charles himself orders me to press on vigorously – for he believes this will strengthen *his* hand at the conference-table – however much it weakens mine. I am a card to play, no more, no less, But he is still my liege lord and I have accepted his commission. We must go on with the venture.'

'With our hands tied. With not one-tenth of the numbers you looked for. And with none likely to rise in our favour.'

'Even so. But – we have faced like odds before, Pate. This is not like you ...?'

'No – God knows it is not for myself, James! It is for you I burn. After all, that you have done, suffered, sacrificed, all you *are* – betrayed again, thrown to the wolves, your counsel rejected. I wonder that you have any regard or loyalty left for the Stewarts!'

'Is my duty, and yours Pate, lessened because our High King makes mistakes? Trusts the wrong advisers? An oath of allegiance is more than a courtesy – at least, *I* deem it so. Especially that of an Earl of Scotland. I am bound by it, man.' He lightened his voice, shook his head. 'Besides, the situation is less ill, I think, than you fear. You know the Highland terrain as well as I do. If we can outfight, out-manoeuvre or outmarch Strachan at this Ord of Caithness, we have the whole of Highland Scotland before us, to cherish us. The Clan Donald Federation – will they not flock to me again? If only in hatred for the Campbells. Even though Colkitto is far away in Ireland. The Farquharsons, the Camerons, the Athollmen, the MacGregors – these care not for conference-tables and treaties, or even for King Charles, I think! But they will follow *me*, I do believe – especially to unseat Argyll, as they have done before. Even Gordon, if we get that far, will have reason to think again . . .'

'That insolent pup, the Lord Lewis, is now Marquis of Huntly, Cock o' the North, with his father and Aboyne dead. He will do nothing for love of you, James.'

'No. But for love of something else, perhaps. If he sees the tide flowing strongly enough. Did you know that he wrote to the new King, declaring himself to be his most loyal and devoted subject, as well as the most powerful, and requesting the Order of the Garter? The sheer, shameless arrogance of it! The Garter!' Montrose mustered a smile. 'I could offer him mine, in exchange for 1,000 Gordon horse!'

Pate Graham muttered something unrepeatable. 'We march, then?' he said.

'Yes. We march. But not just yet. First, I will send a strong advance-party across the Firth, to spy out the land. To settle the best landing-place. To try to rally local support – though I cannot hope for much from the Sinclairs, led by their oaf of an earl! To advance on Strachan – as near as may be without coming to blows. Test the situation. While the main force here completes training and marshalling. It had better be Hurry who goes – rather than yourself, Pate. He is Major-General, after all, and anxious to prove himself a good King's man! Also he is the most experienced soldier – although I know you love him not. Such a venture will suit him very well – for he is bold enough. I will give him a strong brigade – our best-trained 500. And we follow when he sends word.'

Inchbrakie part shrugged, part nodded. 'Perhaps you have the rights of it,' he acceded.

'Can you suggest better?'

'No-o-o . . .'

On the 12th of April Montrose and the main Royalist force of about 1,000 sailed across the stormy Pentland Firth in a fleet of fishing-boats, to land without incident near John o' Groats. Hurry had crossed here a week before and recommended it as landing-place. They were unlikely to be opposed, he reported. Caithness was a land unto itself, its Sinclair barons utterly uninterested in national affairs, from which they were so far removed, and concerned only with internecine feuding. Hurry himself had encountered no real difficulties, and had pressed on southwards, as commanded, his first opposition being at the Sinclair castle of Dunbeath, forty miles on, and ten miles north of the Ord, where the laird, Sir John, was a member of the Estates and had made a fortune as a merchant in the South. It was a strong place, and Hurry had by-passed it, proceeding on past Berriedale to the Ord. Here he had discovered that Major May had been wrong with his information. General Strachan was not here, but farther south, rumoured to be at Tain. It was the Earl of Sutherland who held the Ord – but at Hurry's appearance, he had relinquished his strong strategic position and retired southwards without fight. Fearing to put too great a distance between himself and his commander, Hurry had settled in at the Ord, fortifying the cliff-top position still further.

So Montrose marched westwards without delay along the very northern shore of the Scottish mainland, seventeen miles from John o' Groats to Thurso, the Caithness capital, a small grey town at the head of its bay. Here, still without opposition, he unfurled the Royal Standard in the market-place – and with it, the banner the Douglas ladies had made at Kirkwall showing the late King Charles with his head at a rather gruesome distance from his body, and beneath it the legend *Judge and Defend my Cause, Oh Lord*. This was a little embarrassing, but would probably do no harm. At the unfurling, he issued a proclamation, as Viceroy, summoning all loyal and true subjects of the King to come and make their allegiance. The Provost and not a few citizens came and did so – but no Sinclair lairds, the Earl of Caithness biding watchfully in his evil eagle's nest of a hold at Castle Girnigoe, twenty miles away, north of Wick. Montrose let him be.

One hundred or so Mackays from the west arrived next day; but Lord Reay himself was not with them. He sent his greetings, declared that he was gathering his strength, and would join the royal army as soon as he could – although he dared not too greatly denude his lands of fighting-men for fear of raiding Sinclairs and Gunns.

Montrose could not wait for him. He left Sir Harry Graham and 200 men at Thurso, to accept allegiances in his name, keep the Sinclairs preoccupied, and receive and marshal incoming reinforcements. Also to maintain a link with Orkney, where two more shiploads of arms and munitions were expected. Then he marched southwards through the desolate Caithness moors, to join Hurry.

Hurry met them near Dunbeath Castle, having left his advance-party at the Ord. His information was that the Earl of Sutherland had retired south as far as Tain, on the southern side of the Dornoch Firth – why, with his preponderance in numbers, was not clear. But there were rumours that Leslie was hurrying north again, from Edinburgh, with reinforcements, and had reached Brechin in Angus. Probably Strachan, at Tain, on the border of Ross and Sutherland, was waiting for him, and had called the Earl of Sutherland back, delaying encounter until the Covenant could be sure of winning. Hurry urged, therefore, that they marched upon him with all speed.

'Why should Strachan wait – if he has four or five times our numbers? He is no faint-heart.' Montrose shook his head. 'I see another possible reason. He wishes to entice us down into the flat coastal levels around the Dornoch Firth, where his cavalry will be able to operate most effectively. Hereabouts is no cavalry country – so he abandons it. He will know, to be sure, that we have no cavalry. He wants us down on those plains, for a wager!'

'But if we wait, he will be reinforced – with Leslie himself back to take command.'

'Even so, we shall not play his game. If Leslie was only at Brechin when last you heard, it will take him many days to reach the Dornoch Firth, with 150 miles of difficult country to cover, four great firths to win round. So we need not rush into Strachan's trap, I think.'

333

'You said before that time was of essence. What do we do, then? Kick our heels at the Ord ...?'

'We will give the Mackenzies a day or two more to join us. I have sent Pluscarden urgent couriers. And meanwhile we shall assault this castle of Dunbeath.'

That surprised them all, even Black Pate – for in the past Montrose had always made a point of not wasting time and effort on reducing powerful strongholds, for which he had not the necessary cannon and special techniques, preferring to leave them isolated. He explained.

'I do not mind leaving enemy castles behind me – when I am advancing, when my strategy ahead is clear in my mind. As it is not, here. I do not relish to have the enemy *both* in front and behind me – especially with a sea-coast on my flank. There is this fishertown here at the mouth of the Dunbeath River – Portormin – not large but sufficient for fishing-craft. A fleet of boats could sail up here from Tain. This enemy-held castle overlooking and guarding Portormin might tempt Strachan to send up a sea-borne force behind us. And if they landed here, they could cut our links with Thurso, with Sir Harry, with the Mackays, even with Orkney. That might matter little, soon – but not at this stage. We must have reinforcements. We shall assail Sir John Sinclair, gentlemen, while we wait for the Mackenzies.'

That they did, there on the slanting shelf above the high cliffs. Without artillery, and with small-arms fire more demonstrative than effective against thick stone walling, they could do little more than settle in around the landward side of the castle, beyond its ditch and drawbridge, shout demands for surrender and make other threatening noises, reinforced by the odd sniping shot at windows or glimpsed movement. But that very first evening, a local man, a Sinclair himself, connected to the former line of lairds, who had some grudge against the new Sir John of a different branch, came to the Viceroy, proclaiming himself a good King's man, and declaring that he could stop the water-supply of the castle. There *was* a draw-well in the courtyard, yes – but it was not a true well, tapping no subterranean spring. Its shaft went down to an underground burn – and the informant could show them where that burn *went* underground a mile or so inland, on the hillside. They could cut off the water without difficulty.

Rather foolishly loth to use such methods as he was, Montrose reminded himself that he was dealing with men who used the 'phrase Jesus and No Quarter!' as a slogan and did not fail to act up to those sentiments. He sent a party up the hill, with the renegade Sinclair, to damn and divert the stream.

Dunbeath Castle capitulated on the evening of the second day, without casualties on either side. Sir John Sinclair and his family Montrose treated courteously, saying that he would not turn them out of their home and would only install a garrison in the castle for as short a time as was necessary. That night he held a council-of-war in Sir John's hall, with the noise of great seas smashing themselves into spray on the rocks hundreds of feet below.

'There appear to be three courses open to us, gentlemen,' he summarised. 'We can go down into the level lands around the Dornoch Firth, and fight it out with Strachan who waits for us at Tain. We can bide here until the Mackenzies come – but they are a Highland force, not horsed either. There is, indeed, *no* cavalry to be obtained north of Inverness and the Great Glen, I fear. The Rosses and Munroes may raise a few horsemen – but unfortunately they are on the wrong side of Strachan, south of Tain, and we have no reason to believe that they will rise until we reach them. If then. The third course, as I see it, is to take to the heather, to make a great half-circuit inland to west and south across bog and mountain, and attempt to pass Strachan by altogether, heading south for the Great Glen and the mountain mass of Highland Scotland without coming to blows with the enemy at all. How think you, my friends?'

'I am against bog-hopping and goat-clambering about on hills!' Hurry, the professional soldier said, wrinkling a long nose in disgust at the thought. 'I say take our courage in our hands, and attack Strachan before Leslie can reach him. You, my lord, are notable for making the country fight for you – as I know to my cost! We need not assail the enemy on the ground of *their* choosing, which will suit their cavalry. There is marshland flanking the Dornach Firth estuary. If we could inveigle them into that, bog down their horses . . .'

'If I had Highlanders fighting for me, I would agree with that, Sir John. But I have none. Our army is made up of Orkneymen with no experience of war, and mercenary Netherlanders and Danes. Good troops but not used to fighting as the clansmen fight, light, half-naked, speedy, on only a handful of oatmeal. Would they serve the case in your marshland? For the same reason, I am doubtful of leading them inland over the mountains.'

'Yet we cannot bide here,' the new Earl of Kinnoull declared. 'This will gain us nothing. And Leslie will come up with his reinforcements.'

'It all depends on the Mackenzies, does it not?' Frendraught asked. 'These are Highlanders, such as we need in this pass. Two or three thousand of them. I say we *must* wait until they come up with us. They come from Kintail, do they not? Eighty, ninety miles to the west. They must be here soon.'

'If they come!' Pate Graham growled. 'We have waited for Seaforth's Mackenzies before this! His brother may be a better fighter – but little more reliable!'

'That is a risk I am aware of,' Montrose agreed. 'But he did rise last March – and has not dispersed his people. And there are the Mackays – fewer of them, but able fighters.'

'Do we wait here, then, for the Highlanders?' Hurry demanded. 'I say that is folly. We may wait for too long. And have Leslie to face. After your lordship's self, the best general in Scotland. Reinforced.'

There was a murmur of agreement around the table.

Frendraught spoke. 'You, my lord – what do *you* think? Why do you ask us? You are accepted as the greatest strategist in Europe. What do our opinions signify?'

'Much – they signify much,' James Graham reproved him. 'When men are asked to risk their lives, they should be consulted. No commander can consult all his ordinary soldiers. But his senior officers' views *must* weigh with him. But – if I *have* heard them all, here is what I would say. I agree, we should not linger here. I accept that our present troops are not such as could cross the trackless mountains at speed, with any great success – not yet. I recognise that Strachan should be defeated, if it is at all possible, before Leslie arrives. But I fear that we cannot hope to defeat him lacking the arrival of some of our Highland reinforcements, Mackenzies or Mackays. The Mackays would come from the north, behind us. The Mackenzies from the west, by Strathkannaird and Strathoykell, over the spine of North Scotland. Let us therefore put ourselves in a posture to meet the Mackenzies, and where the Mackays can reach us, and at the same time be able to try to manoeuvre Strachan into a battle-ground where his cavalry do not give him overwhelming advantage. Let us march south from the Ord, by Brora and Golspie, and then turn westwards from the coast, up the strath of the Fleet. We are there still a dozen miles north of Tain, as the crow flies, with the Dornoch Firth between. Safe from Strachan. Then we march up the valley of the Fleet to Lairg – say fifteen miles. There, if our scouts have not already found the Mackenzies for us, we turn south for Strathoykell. Wait for them there. And thereafter, with them, advance down the Oykell upon the Kyle of Sutherland, Dornoch and Tain. Take Strachan in flank, with a choice of battlegrounds. How say you?'

'How long would that take us?' Frendraught asked.

'Three days to Lairg, forced marching. From there to the Oykell, only six or seven miles.'

'You have forgotten Dunrobin, my lord,' Hurry said. 'Dunrobin Castle, the Earl of Sutherland's chiefest stronghold, stands in the way. At Golspie, before we reach the Fleet.'

'I have not forgotten Dunrobin. We can summon it to surrender – but it will be too strong for us to take. If it stands out against us, we must leave it behind, intact.'

The others accepted that. In the morning they would start out, making for Lairg and the Oykell – and pray that the Mackenzies were not long delayed.

*   *   *

On the 23rd of April they reached the Oykell, in a wild upland country of long heather ridges, deep wooded valleys and rushing peat-brown torrents, with still no sign of Clan Kenneth, the Mackenzies – or indeed of Clan Hugh, the Mackays. They waited for a day at Rosehall, near Inveroykell, where Glen Cassley came down from the north-west to join Strathoykell, all fretting now. None required to inform James Graham how bad this delay and seeming indecision was for the morale of their troops – although John Hurry did not fail to tell him so. Idling, dawdling, for a new invasion force, was the reverse of good tactics. Yet Montrose had no option, short of a premature battle for which he was hopelessly unfit, unready. Not 200 men had joined him since he had landed on the mainland of Scotland – where he had believed there would be thousands. He had few doubts, of course, as to why. King Charles's negotiations with Argyll had become known; a treaty was to be signed. This was no time to indulge in revolt – especially when it was obvious to all that Argyll held the upper hand. It could mean putting necks in a noose for nothing.

On the 24th one of Montrose's own couriers returned to them at Inveroykell, from the west. He brought news that Thomas

337

Mackenzie of Pluscarden was on the move, with 2,500 men. He had been dealing with an incursion of Macleods from the Isle of Lewis, in the Loch Broom and Braemore area, a perennial warfare. He intended to obey the vice-regal summons to join the Royal Standard, yes – but he had received a letter from his brother, the Earl of Seaforth in Holland, advising caution, as it was understood that King Charles was likely to command Montrose to lay down his arms and disband. Pluscarden, therefore, was not hastening as he might – despite urgings . . .

James Graham had to exercise all his well-tried restraint to prevent a furious outburst. But hold himself in he did.

'But Pluscarden is coming, you say?' he demanded of the Mackay courier. 'With his thousands. However slowly. He is following you up?'

'He comes, yes. Although whether he will fight, my lord, is another matter.'

'I see.' Montrose was actually trembling, so great was the grip he was exerting upon his temper and emotions. 'I see. Seaforth . . . and his brother! But – even if he will not draw the sword, 2,500 Mackenzie clansmen in battle array joining us may well have a notable effect upon Archibald Strachan! Who knows – it might serve . . . ?' He went pacing the greensward, and then came back. 'Where did you leave them? Coming up Strathkannaird? How far away?'

'He is not coming up Kannaird, lord. He comes by a different route. Which I have never trod, at all. So I came back by the way I knew – as I had gone. Mounted, moving fast. The Mackenzies march by secret mountain tracks, by high passes – but shorter, they say. From Braemore, by the Inverlael hills and the Glens Beg and Mor, to the Carron. Down Strathcarron to salt water. It cuts off twenty miles, they say . . .'

'Strathcarron? That is to the south of us. It joins this strath of Oykell miles to the eastwards, does it not? Ten miles down, at least? At the head of the Kyle of Sutherland, towards Tain!'

'Aye, lord. At Invercharron, below Invershin and Carbisdale. Where the Kyle narrows in. I know Strathcarron – although I have never crossed to it from the west, through the mountains.'

'And Pluscarden saves twenty miles of march, thus? Then, dear God – we must move down there, and quickly! Or he may get in *front* of us, meet Strachan before we do – which would be fatal. If he is reluctant to fight he might come to terms with Strachan. Before I could work on him.' Montrose, urgent now,

338

raised his voice. 'Pate! Pate – quickly! Inform all. We march. At once. With all speed . . .'

Fording the Oykell, which was running high, they marched without delay down the south bank of the river, by wooded hillside, bog and flooded haughland, scouts well ahead under Pate Graham. Nightfall found them some eight miles on, almost opposite Invershin, where the Shin came down from the Lairg. Here word reached them from Pate that he was at Invercharron, where the Carron joined the Oykell from the west, and there was no sign of the Mackenzies. There was a small village here, and the people declared that no large body of men had passed through recently. They did however report the presence of occasional small parties of Covenant horse, obviously scouting – but never more than a troop, less usually, at a time.

Montrose halted for the night opposite Invershin.

Next morning they were on the move again, south by east, down the strath, with the open water of the Kyle of Sutherland appearing before them, looking like a loch but actually an extension of the Dornoch Firth, when another galloper from Pate brought news that there was still no sign of the Mackenzies – and Inchbrakie had a picket out well up the Carron seeking contact. But there were two more positive items. A half-troop of cavalry was reported from the vicinity of Ardchronie two or three miles down the southern shore of the Kyle, from Invercharron; and a fisherman, who had rowed across the Kyle itself from the northern shore, was declaring that the Earl of Sutherland was on the march *northwards*, having ferried a large force over the Firth at the narrows near Edderton, Local talk, the fisherman said, was contradictory about Sutherland's movements after crossing. Some said that he was going to Dunrobin, his great castle near Golspie, which Montrose had summoned to surrender on his way south to the Oykell but had not waited to take; others that he was going to turn west, and march up the Fleet River, as Montrose himself had done, and so get behind the royalist force. All were agreed however that he was on the move northwards with a large force.

Montrose sought to puzzle this out. They were on the edge of Sutherland country – where it would be wise to assume that the Earl thereof was kept well informed of what went on in his domains, better informed than he himself was likely to be. Sutherland would know that Dunrobin was not being besieged – a fishing-boat slipping out of Dunrobin harbour could be at

Tain in a couple of hours. He would need no large force, therefore, to regain his castle. If he was moving north in strength, it must be either to cut the royalist communications with Caithness and Orkney, or to make the suggested encircling move behind them, up Fleet. In either case, it probably meant that Strachan was also moving, or preparing to move, from Tain. Almost certainly it would be a synchronised move, two-pronged. The chances were, then, that Strachan and his Covenant regulars were, or would be, marching towards them, directly up this south side of the Kyle, hoping to trap the royalist force from east and west in the tight valley of the Oykell. The half-troop of cavalry spotted could be his advance scouts.

There were the seeds of disaster in this situation.

But there were one or two considerations to be taken into account. Sutherland, if he was making a circling movement, must be given time to make it – so that Strachan would have to delay his much shorter cavalry advance to conform. Sutherland need not go all the way up to Lairg and down the Shin, of course; he could cut across the low hills which formed the barrier between the straths of Fleet and Oykell – if his people were tough enough. There was a rough route across. But he would still emerge on the wrong side of the Oykell – and it was running high, and the less easy to ford the farther down the strath. How soon would Sutherland be a menace, then? Pate did not say just *when* the enemy force had crossed the Firth – no doubt the fisherman did not know. But the probability was that it was early that day.

And, presumably, Sutherland was not just coming up the north side of the Kyle – the fisherman would have known *that*. The story was that he was going northwards, not westwards, in the meantime. From his ferry-landing it would be about ten miles up to Loch Fleet, at Skelbo. Then up that strath a short way, and over the hills for a dozen or more very rough miles. Say a thirty-mile circuit in all – more, if he went right up to Lairg. The chances were, then, that Strachan would allow Sutherland at least a whole day, possibly two, before he himself moved.

Had the Covenanters decided on action now, when they had been prepared to wait previously, because they had heard of the Mackenzies' approach? It could well be. If so, now it was a race. Could Pluscarden and his clansmen come down Strathcarron soon enough to reach the royalist force before they were trapped between Strachen and Sutherland?

It made a grim situation. If Montrose retired back up the Oykell to safety in the west, while he had time, he missed meeting the Mackenzies whose reinforcements he so vitally needed. And it was not merely a case of missing them; if Pluscarden, on his brother's advice, was so unenthusiastic about fighting as the Mackay courier suggested, he might well make his peace with Strachan when they met – and that would be the end of the Mackenzie aid. Montrose just could not contemplate that. On the other hand, if he moved down to Invercharron and waited there, as intended, and Pluscarden did not materialise, then the royalist foot was at the mercy of Strachan's dragoons, in that more open country.

He decided on a compromise. He would move down to where the strath *began* to widen, at the head of the Kyle, to some point where he had a prospect but still some way short of Invercharron, from whence he could quickly join the Mackenzies when they arrived, but which still left a line of retreat open to him. For a time, at least. Sutherland might block that line fairly soon.

It was a sorry tactical contretemps for the most renowned tactician in Europe.

They marched on eastwards, therefore, to the last major hill on their right, which represented almost the end of the range separating Strathoykell and Strathcarron, a steep and lofty bluff, rocky at summit and with birch-scrub at the foot, named, according to the Mackay, Greag Choineachan. At its south-east base was the small property of Carbisdale, where there was some clearing of the birch-scrub, a little tilled land, and a view down the strath. Here Montrose disposed his troops in a defensive situation, and as far as was possible, out of sight from the lower land. Then, with Hurry and a few other officers, he rode on down to Invercharron. There were no armed men to be seen, anywhere, Mackenzies or Covenanters.

At the Mill of Invercharron, where a ford crossed the Carron River just before it entered the Kyle, they found Pate Graham and his little group, hidden in the scrub. Pate was not happy.

'This is a poor place,' he declared. 'Poor for observing, poor for fighting in. I would be glad to see us out of it, James.'

'I also. But we have little choice. What is the present position, Pate?'

'There is not enough height here to see well, or far, over the firth-shore plain. And it is so covered in this birch-scrub that distant view is impossible. But there is a troop – possibly only half a troop – of dragoons over there. On those braes two miles down, where there are a scattering of croft-houses. They call it Upper Ardchronie. And I would think that they will know we are here, and are keeping watch on us. They do not greatly seek to hide themselves.'

'This is the same group you have watched for a while? Obviously a forward picket. You do not think that they have been reinforced?'

'Not that we have seen. Or heard of. I have sent out scouts. On foot, in disguise. But – with all that thick woodland a mile or so behind, who knows? That is Wester Fearn. A headland juts into the Kyle, there, with a deep bay behind, which we cannot see. All too low-lying for observation. Struie Hill behind you can see clearly enough. But Strachan could move up troops from Tain, by Edderton and the coast, completely hidden from us here by all that woodland at Western Fearn.'

'But your scouts have crept forwards? And have not reported any such movement?'

'No-o-o. They think that there is only this one troop between us and Edderton. The crofter folk here say the same. But – I do not like it.'

'What do you advise then, Pate?'

'I think I would retire. Not up Oykell again, where we could be cut off by Sutherland's force. But up this Carron, Hope to meet the Mackenzies the sooner. If ever we see them! But get away from these firth-side levels. There is danger here.'

'I know it. I would choose the same. But Mackay and others who know these parts, tell me that this Strathcarron quickly narrows into a high steep pass, at a place called Croick. No place for troops who are not mountaineers. We could be trapped in there. With our old Highland host it would have been child's play. But these Netherlanders and Orkneymen . . .! I dare not let them get cooped up in there, Pate.'

'Aye – that is true. James – where in God's name is Pluscarden and his people? They should have been here long since. Think you – think you they will fail us? That they delay, of a purpose?'

'I do not know. Would God I did! All I know is that I must have Highland reinforcements if I am going to fight in this country. All is based on that. I have no choice but to wait for the Mackenzies and the Mackays – if I may!'

So once again they settled to wait. That evening a newcomer was brought to Montrose, a loyalist Munro laird, of Achness, with half a dozen men. His report was not cheering. His own clan, and their neighbours, the Rosses, who had both risen for the King with Pluscarden the previous spring, had found Strachan and his dragoons, on their doorstep, too much for them. With word of King Charles talking peace, they had thought better of joining Montrose – indeed, they had joined Strachan, though not enthusiastically and under threat. Some like himself had objected – and if the lord Marquis made a strong move southwards into their country, they might well think again. But meantime they were on Strachan's side. He had no word about the Mackenzies and Pluscarden; he had understood them still to be far in the West. But as to the Covenant enemy, there was only the one troop of horse north of Tain, with Strachan also waiting. Waiting for Leslie.

Nine-tenths of warfare consisted of waiting, James Graham reminded himself and his colleagues.

They waited, then, strengthening their hill-side position with entrenchments below the Creag Choineachan, with the Culrain Burn in a steepish ravine to guard their flank. But in the early afternoon waiting abruptly ended. The, or a, troop of dragoons suddenly appeared, riding westwards, openly, out of the woodlands of Ardchronie, on over the levels towards them.

It was time now for decision, with the enemy riding straight for their present advanced position at the ford of Invercharron. Something had to be done about it. There were about fifty of them, and Montrose's horse numbered forty, not cavalry as such but mounted officers. Why the dragoons had decided to advance now, after delaying for so long, was anybody's guess – but it could well mean that Strachan's main body was coming up behind, at long last.

Hurry and his aide Major Lisle, a veteran cavalryman, were urgent now. These dragoons must be engaged and destroyed, before they got in amongst the unprotected infantry. Once let these loose on the unblooded Orkneymen, even fifty of them, and it would be massacre. The forty royalist horse were not so greatly outnumbered – and they were all gentlemen, officers and experienced. Pate agreed. A small victory now could have important results – apart from saving the infantry.

James Graham, faced with a united front, bowed to it, despite his own reluctance. Indeed, he had little option. To retire his

343

1,200 men in the face of fifty dragoons was barely thinkable in its results on morale. Whether the dragoons recognised this, or were in fact completely unaware of their danger, was not to be known. But they were heading straight for the fords across Carron in column of march.

'Very well,' Montrose acceded. 'We shall let them cross the river, so that they can be pinned against it thereafter. Sir John – you will take all our horse, save for a few officers remaining with me. I will lead a detachment of the foot, out of sight, north-abouts, down to the Carron, to hold the fords, so that no dragoons get back, and no reinforcements can reach them. The untried Orkneymen I shall leave here, on the higher ground, meantime. You must deal with the dragoons, thirty-five against fifty, as you think best.'

'Thank the Lord!' Hurry exclaimed. A bold commander of light cavalry, this was an encounter after his own heart. Dividing his thirty-five officers into two groups, one under Lisle the professional, they waited until the advancing dragoons had disappeared into the wooded hollow of the Carron, well over a mile eastwards, and then spurred off to do battle.

Montrose left Sir James Douglas, with Kinnoull, in charge of their own Orkneymen, and with Pate, Frendraught and Sir James's brother John, led the Continental mercenaries, to the number of about 400, down through the open woodland in a circling movement to the north, on the slopes parallel to the shore, at a steady trot, to reach the river below the fords and work up behind the dragoons.

Before they were half-way there they heard the clash of conflict. But as they ran, panting, amongst the birch-woods, Montrose jerked to Pate.

'Do you hear fighting?' he demanded. 'I hear a confusion. Beat of hooves. Shouting. But no clash of steel. Do you?'

'No. They may have broken and run. The dragoons. Hurry has surprised and broken them ? Already!'

'Unless it is Hurry who runs!' Frendraught put in.

'No – Hurry would not run, in this. He lacks not for courage . . .'

'If the dragoons are fleeing, we should be at the fords. Prevent them escaping . . .'

They ran the faster.

The scrub-birch denied prospects in most directions at this low level. But at one point, near a small headland, a clearing and

344

its thatched blackhouse suddenly revealed to them a group of about a dozen dragoons cantering on an opposite course about 300 yards farther up. These, though they could not help seeing the infantry, and some shook their drawn swords at them, made no attempt to ride them down or even to change course towards them. They rode on. And presently a group of five royalist officers, led by Drummond of Balloch, came dashing in pursuit, riding much faster. All passed out of sight in the trees.

'Save us – what sort of a ploy is that!' Pate panted.

'Poltroons!' Frendraught cried. 'Fleeing from half their number.'

Montrose did not share the Viscount's scorn. There was something wrong here. Those dragoons gave no impression of fleeing. Their cantering looked far more like an exercise. There had been no sign of the confusion of battle, no wounds, no helmets lost.

'I do not like it,' he said, as they ran on.

At the ford area there was no sign of fleeing cavalrymen. Montrose quickly placed his Continental infantry in a position to guard the crossings from either side. Down here, there were no distant views. He called Inchbrakie to him.

'Pate – take a couple of men and hurry up to the higher ground again. We can see nothing here. There is something amiss. These dragoons are neither fighting nor fleeing. I think they have been sent to keep our horse engaged, to bemuse us. A ruse. If so, there must be more enemy near by, to take advantage. I fear an attack in strength. We are as well here, at these fords, as anywhere. Meantime. But – the Orkneymen could be in danger. Hurry and the horse also. Off with you. Be my eyes. Get me information . . .'

It was not Pate who came racing down to them a few minutes thereafter, but the Earl of Kinnoull, gasping for breath.

'They are coming, James!' he exclaimed. 'Hundreds. They are upon us. Whole army! Plain filled with horse. They have us . . .!'

'Thank you, my lord,' Montrose said quietly. 'Regain your breath, pray. Then let us have it in order. Take your time, my friend.'

His calm stilled the incipient panic. Kinnoull managed to make it clear that soon after the fifty dragoons had crossed the fords, he and Douglas, up with the Orkneymen, had had their attention directed to movement away on the slopes to the south, their right front. Soon it was clear that a large infantry force was advancing down the braes that flanked the south side of Strathcarron. At first they were cheered, assuming that it was the Mackenzies at last – but they realised that they came from the wrong direction and had either cavalry support or many mounted officers, which the Mackay said the Mackenzies had not. Then it was seen that out from the same woodland of Ardchronie from which the dragoons had issued were coming large numbers of cavalry, troop upon troop, with banners . . .

'Heading for here ?' Montrose interrupted. 'These fords ?'

'Yes. Straight here. They cannot be far off now . . .'

Raising his voice, James Graham shouted to his officers to prepare all ranks to oppose a crossing of the river in strength from the east. Only a few to stand watch to the rear. Hide so far as possible . . .

They were barely settled into a defensive position when the first ranks of Strachan's horse came up fast through the trees making directly for the fords opposite the Mill of Invercharron. Unfortunately, some over-excited musketeer on their side fired his weapon before the horsemen were fully within range across the water – and then others followed suit. There was no wholesale decimation of the unsuspecting enemy, therefore. Even so, it was complete surprise. Clearly Strachan had never anticipated that the fords would be manned and held *after* his dragoon advance guard had crossed over. There was much confusion across the Carron, as new troops of horse cantered up to become involved with the first ones pressing back to be out of range.

Montrose passed urgent commands down his line to stop haphazard and wasteful shooting. Fire was to be disciplined, volleyed.

The fordable area was all within a compass of some 300 yards. The enemy appeared to know this, and presently four distinct crossings were attempted, simultaneously, at about seventy-yard intervals, with covering fire from Strachan's heavy dragoons equipped with muskets, to keep the opposition pinned down. But Montrose's Danish, German and Netherland mercenaries knew how to counter this, and zigzagging and bent double, moved into new positions without serious loss. They were able to halt all four crossing attempts.

The enemy withdrew in disorder into the trees again.

James Graham found one of Pate's men crouching at his side. 'Lord,' he said, 'Inchbrakie says to tell you that there is a clan

346

host, it may be 1,000, advancing frae the south. But a mile off. Munroes and Rosses, he jalouses. Stiffened wi' regular muske-teers and mounted officers, forbye. And there's cavalry – but, och, you've found them! Maybe six troops, Inchbrakie says. Aye – and General Hurry and his officers are right fully engaged, now, wi' thae dragoons. They've turned to fight, now.'

'Yes. I thank you. Tell me – is there another ford to this river? Higher?'

'Aye, lord – a mile up, nae mair. Naething downstream.'

'A pity!' Montrose turned. 'My lord of Kinnoull – take some five-score men, and this guide. To go guard another ford a mile up. At the run! But climb up into the woodland first, so that the enemy do not see where you go . . .' He stopped. 'Ah – dam-nation!'

Leaving a couple of troops of horse to face them across Carron, the main body of the Covenant cavalry was wheeling in column to their left, to spur off up the river-side.

'Too late! Strachan must know of the other fords. Do not go, my lord. You cannot outrun horse. We cannot stop them crossing, now.'

'Bravo, my lord Marquis!' Frendraught shouted from a little way off. 'The first joust is ours!'

Montrose muttered that this was no jousting, God help them! But he waved back, smiling encouragement on all. Then he called all but the regimental officers to him.

'Gentlemen – I am concerned for the Orkneymen. And for our horse. *This* is a fair defensive position – but our force is grievously scattered. Hay of Delgatie – I leave you in command here. My lords Kinnoull and Frendraught, and you, Powrie, and John Douglas – come with me.' He did not have to name young Menzies of Pitfodels, who was acting as standard-bearer, and never left the Captain-General's side. 'I shall join Sir James and the Orkneymen, seek to concentrate the horse, with them. And bring all down to the peninsula where this Carron joins the Kyle. It is low and marshy, and we will be protected on three sides by water. They will not overrun us there. Start moving your men, in stages, down-river, Delgatie, when I send you a runner. Is it understood?'

The six men went hurrying up through the open woodland, keeping a wary eye open for dragoons and ready to dive for cover at any moment. They saw no dragoons, but soon came on traces of a running fight. They found a riderless horse standing amongst bushes, and nearby the body of the cavalryman, Major Lisle, dead, shot through the head with a pistol-bullet. Near by a wounded Covenant trooper lay groaning in a pool of blood.

Frendraught caught the horse and brought it to Montrose. He mounted, to get to the Orkneymen the more swiftly, with Menzies of Pitfodels and the Royal Standard riding pillion behind him. He told the others to press on, and if they saw any of Hurry's group to tell them to rejoin the main force on the higher ground immediately. Then he spurred off.

He saw more bodies, and a stray horse or two, but paused for none. Then, half a mile short of the entrenchment area, his heart fell as he perceived a great body of men ahead of him. It was Sir James Douglas and the Orkneymen coming marching down.

'Dear God!' he groaned. 'The fools! The poor purblind fools . . .!'

But he mastered his anger in the interests of morale. Riding up, he called, 'Sir James – well met! But I must request you to turn your men about. The situation is much changed. About turn your men, and back to the prepared positions, if you please.'

'We were marching to your aid, my lord,' the Douglas explained. 'We heard of the assault at the fords.'

'Yes. I thank you. But – four troops of Covenant horse may be upon us at any moment. In column, like this, you could be cut to pieces in minutes. Quickly, now – have your men trot.'

As they hurried back towards the entrenchments, where they could at least have some hope of facing cavalry, Montrose racked his brain for the best way out of this tangle, this tactician's nightmare. He had intended to move the 800 Orkneymen downhill, to the north, to reach the low, marshy peninsula, to be sure – but it would have to be done properly, in an organised series of leap-frogging bounds, in say four companies, three giving covering fire while one ran forward, 200 yards at a time. And if possible with a group of horse to aid. This present straightforward marching in the open invited massacre. They would have to get back to the entrenchments, take up the defensive position they should never have left, and there organise the companies, meantime trying to round up what was left of Hurry's horse . . .

But it was not to be. A group of about a dozen horsed officers, one seriously wounded, did join them, all that was left of Lisle's party, under Major David Guthrie; of Hurry and the others they

348

had seen nothing for some time. Inchbrakie had met them and told them to report back at the entrenchments. Montrose mounted Pitfodels on the wounded man's horse.

A shout from the rear turned all heads. Covenant cavalry was appearing out of the scrub behind them, not a quarter-mile away. And in large numbers. This was not the remnants of the fifty dragoons. These were the first of the troops who had crossed the upper fords.

'Form schiltroms! Two hollow squares,' Montrose shouted to the Orkneymen. 'Front ranks kneeling, others standing. Quickly – two schiltroms.' They had practised this at Kirkwall – pray heaven they had not forgotten how. 'No fire before seventy yards. Front ranks to fire first. Then standing men, as they reload.'

In some fashion the 800 formed into two ragged squares. These were crofters and fishermen, in action for the first time, untrained infantry facing heavy regular cavalry. If they made a poor showing, who could blame them? Certainly not James Graham. He, for his part, now devoted himself to the dozen horsemen.

'Into a wedge behind me. Wedge-formation, gentlemen. Tight. Guthrie – Drummond – the horns of the V. Keep tight, my friends, and we shall drive through anything.' He raised his plumed hat, from under the Lion Rampant standard which Menzies held bravely above him. 'For God and King Charles!'

A cheer arose, faltering at first, but gaining in strength.

The Covenant horse had slowed their approach. There appeared to be two troops, of approximately 100 each. A bugle was blown, no doubt to bring the other two troops up to their aid. Then, still in two formations, they extended into line abreast, obviously preparing to charge. The trees, though scattered, open, hampered them somewhat.

'Sir James – control your fire,' Montrose warned. 'The first charge you should break. The second we will try to disperse. Then, one of your schiltroms to rise. Run 200 yards, while the other covers them. Towards the entrenchments. Then they will cover you. Leap-frogging. You have it? We must get back to the trenches.'

The Douglas raised his hand in acknowledgment at the same moment as the Covenant horse charged.

The Orkneymen's shooting was ragged and premature indeed, and much of it wasted. There was no clear distinction between the volleys. Some horses and riders fell and, as always in a charge tripped up others. But the charge was not halted. These were light dragoons, not heavy, equipped with large horse-pistols which they fired from the saddle, and then drew their sabres. The second troop let the first get half-way to the schiltroms before they followed on in similar style.

Montrose had to wait, or he would run into the Orkneymen's fire. But as this began to die away, he raised his sword high, slashed its point down towards the enemy, and dug in his spurs. Behind him, tight as men and horse could pack themselves, his wedge thundered after him.

He drove over at a tangent, behind the first troop and in front of the second. At this stage, his aim was not actual fighting, sword-play, but to break up the second charge. This rear-ward troop, he knew, were unlikely to fire their pistols meantime, for fear of hitting their comrades in front. Not all of his own people had pistols loaded and ready. Such as had followed their leader's example and fired them into the advancing line.

That first drive of the wedge was a complete success, in that it utterly broke up the second troop's rush. There was no real clash, for as the royalists drove slantwise across the dragoon's front, even though it was twelve to 100, the latter reined aside this way and that, the first rank confusing the rear, so that in only a few seconds the whole was in milling chaos, all forward impetus lost.

Without casualty, Montrose now sought to perform the most difficult of manoeuvres, to swing a racing wedge round upon itself in a restricted space for a charge in the reverse direction, and in tree-dotted terrain. It was less than successful, for most of his dozen were not trained cavalrymen, and though Guthrie and Drummond at the rear did their best to whip the others into formation again swiftly, precious moments were lost.

Montrose waiting, fretting, had a chance to look at the Orkneymen and groaned at what he saw. Utter confusion prevailed there. One schiltrom was already broken and in process of retiring – but the men streaming off in panic, throwing away their arms the better to run from the slashing sabres and trampling hooves. Obviously these would not halt, to form up again. The other formation, Douglas's own, was in better shape, still recognisable as a defensive unit, and most of the dragoons were leaving it alone, milling round after the fleeing men, to leave it to the second troop.

His wedge not quite so tightly marshalled this time, James

Graham drove forward again for the incoherent mass of troopers, the officers of which were now furiously seeking to re-form it. This time pistol-shots cracked out at them, and two of the wedge were hit, before they crashed into the enemy – but owing to the press of horseflesh, neither actually fell to the ground, carried along slumped in their saddles.

At the point of the wedge, sword slashing in figure-of-eight fashion left and right, James Graham bored through the Covenant horse. Men and beasts reared up before him, reined aside, swayed, ducked or went down, steel flashed before his eyes, shots whistled past him, men shouted and cursed, falling, flailing horses screamed high terror. Twice his own mount stumbled, all but throwing him. A buffet from behind, by his own Royal Standard, knocked off his hat as Menzies of Pitfodels reeled in his saddle from a sabre-slash. Then they were through, with only a scattering of troopers fleeing before them.

But now his wedge was in a sorry state. Only seven of them remained, and only four unwounded. Both Guthrie and Drummond, in the dangerous tail positions, were down. Pitfodels was obviously seriously wounded, the Lion Rampant leaning drunkenly.

The second troop of dragoons was dispersed meanwhile, and would take some time to reassemble. Douglas's schiltrom, though battered, was still a unit, the first troop's effectiveness largely dissipated in pursuing the fleeing Orkneymen of the other formation.

James Graham, shaking his long waving hair clear of his face, sought to wipe perspiration from his eyes and found it to be blood, from an unsuspected graze on his forehead.

'A smaller wedge, gentlemen,' he cried. 'We must save Douglas's schiltrom if we can. Pitfodels – can you sit your horse?'

'Yes-e-es,' that young man got out, through clenched teeth.

Montrose was urging his horse forward once more, towards the schiltrom, when he gained an unexpected reinforcement. It was Kinnoull, Frendraught and John Douglas, on captured horses, dashing up from the east – and even three men were welcome. But not their news. They shouted that two more troops of Covenant cavalry, with Strachan's own banner, were just behind.

By the time they reached the schiltrom, the new enemy was emerging from the trees to the east. In his heart James Graham

351

knew that this was the end. Nothing, no amount of improvising, of heroism, could save them now. The fresh cavalry would rally the earlier troopers, only dispersed, not defeated, the Strachan would know how to control them. It was only a question of time, brief time. Where was Hurry . . . ?

Nevertheless, he shouted his orders with assurance, even with his accustomed courtesy. 'Sir James – here is your brother John. Divide your men in two companies, if you please. John, take one. The leap-frogging move, 200-yard rushes. John's company first – you cover them. Four moves should make the entrenchments. We will try to protect you. My Lord Frendraught – take the Standard. Pitfodels is sore hurt . . .'

'I can . . . make do . . . my lord,' Menzies jerked, white-faced.

'Very well. A tight wedge, gentlemen. One more. Behind me. Out to the flank, here. Till we see how they will attack.'

Strachan was an experienced commander. No doubt told what had happened to the first two troops, he did not repeat their tactics. Instead of a long line-abreast charge, he sent two half-troops forward in column, at the trot, fully 200 yards apart, making but poor targets for a wedge attack. His main body he held back in the centre, and then moved it forward also, but pacing slowly.

Montrose knew well what that meant. Those dragoons in the centre would be heavies, equipped with muskets, not pistols. At that slow pace, when they got within range – and twice the range of the pistols, and more – they would be able to fire from the saddle, then throw away the muskets and charge with the sabre. Musket-fire, so much more accurate and lethal . . .

'The left-hand half-troop first,' he called, to his nine horsemen. 'We will try take them in flank. They'll mask us from musket-fire so. Sir James – those dragoons have muskets. More dangerous. You fire yours at 100 yards. Aim for their horses – larger targets. Then run. Controlled running. To your brother. You have it ?'

Without waiting for an answer, the gallant little party under the red and gold Lion Rampant rode out, half-left, towards the advancing enemy.

The fifty half-troop of Strachan's right was, of course, ready for them. This time there was no surprise. As, presently, Montrose swung his group round in a semicircle to drive straight at the centre of the column, the pistols cracked out. One horse and two riders went down. Then the column sought to open, divide, to let the wedge through. Montrose wrenched his mount's head round hard to the left, and managed to drive into the rear half of the troop, in pounding, slashing fury. He was aware of blood before his eyes, a red-faced man who seemed to yell soundlessly in his face, all teeth and spittle. He felt his horse check, as though to a heavy blow, but plunge on. He heard the rattle of musket-fire from all around, but remotely, only through a great ringing in his head. Then there was nobody in front of him, and he was almost swept out of the saddle by a birch-tree branch.

Turning, swaying, to look behind him, dizzy, he found that he had only four companions now. Menzies of Pitfodels was gone, and Frendraught had the Standard. Kinnoull was there, Ogilvy of Powrie and Sir William Johnston. As he stared, blinking away the blood from his eyes, his horse gently collapsed under him, and died. He managed to throw himself clear, but fell on his knees, sword spinning.

Frendraught and Ogilvy were down beside him in a trice, banner and all, helping him up, bringing back his sword. 'Up on my horse, James!' the Viscount cried.

But Ogilvy brought him a riderless beast, of which there were not a few standing around now, and aided him into the saddle.

The situation elsewhere on that curious battlefield was far from static. Sir James Douglas's truncated schiltrom had now broken before the main Covenant advance, and the men were streaming away westwards with the cavalry in pursuit. Whether they could ever be halted again, was doubtful. His brother's group had indeed formed up farther back, after a fashion. Down upon them bore hunted and hunters both.

There was little effective that Montrose could do – but he had to try. He had brought these Orkneymen here; he could not desert them now. His head was spinning, and coherent thought difficult. Without any very clear idea of what to do, other than to return to action, he led his direly reduced group back into the fray.

But before ever they could affect the issue, John Douglas's formation broke, and now the entire part-wooded slope was covered with fleeing foot chased by savage horsemen. There could be no possible rally. Kinnoull shouted as much at the Graham's back, while Frendraught urged him to save himself, and quickly, for the sake of the cause.

They had rather reckoned without Colonel Archibald Strachan, acting Major-General. As that stern religionist saw the collapse of the Lord's enemies' main force, he drew back a company of heavy dragoons from the general pursuit to turn to look for Montrose. The little party under the Lion Rampant was in the act of pulling round, preparatory to flight, when an unexpected volley of musket-fire from these dragoons crashed out, all directed at them.

The wonder was that any of the five men survived in that sudden hail of lead. Three of the five horses fell, including Montrose's new one, its rider's shoulder grazed by a shot. Kinnoull and Frendraught alone remained in their saddles, the latter slumped over, wounded in the thigh, the Standard dropping to the grass.

As Montrose picked himself up, reeling, Frendraught slid to the ground grimacing with pain.

'Take this beast, James,' he gasped, 'I, I am . . . done. Quick – flee! They come. For God's sake . . .!' And he pitched forward on top of the Lion Rampant.

James Graham, groaning, did not delay. He flung himself up into the vacated saddle, and kicked in his heels, spurring after Kinnoull who was already dashing off. A scatter of musket- and pistol-shots followed them as they plunged away northwards, but this time none found a mark.

Carbisdale was over, not so much a battle as a protracted folly and disaster.

CHAPTER TWENTY-FIVE

It was some time before, pounding along behind Kinnoull, James Graham was really aware of anything other than pain, grief, humiliation and the need to keep upright in his saddle and ahead of pursuit. He did know that they were pursued, though shots had soon ceased behind them. Fortunately they were heavy dragoons that were involved, and their own captured horses were light cavalry mounts, which gave them a slightly better turn of speed. But he knew not where they were, or where they were going.

Gradually however his mind cleared and his will reasserted itself. Gazing about him, he realised that they were heading north-westwards up Strathoykell; that Kinnoull, concerned only with flight, had ridden off directly back whence they had come, in automatic reaction, with the enemy to the south and east and the waters of the Kyle to the north. But up here, at any time, they might run into the Earl of Sutherland's force, marching down.

Forcing himself, with a major effort, to think ahead constructively, coherently, he decided that Sutherland would necessarily be advancing down this southern side of the Oykell, if he was there at all. Somehow, then, they must get across the estuary. He tried to recollect the lie of the land, observed two days before as they had headed south-eastwards. The Oykell, he was fairly sure, had not been fordable, or indeed swimmable, for the last many miles of his course, rushing in a deep channel. But soon after it opened into the tidal Kyle, the latter had narrowed suddenly, for a short distance, with a low headland of sorts reaching out towards the north shore. Just below Invershin, if he remembered rightly. If the tide was not at too strong an ebb, it might be possible to swim horses across there. Not more than half a mile ahead now . . .

He shouted to Kinnoull to pull away right-handed, down-hill, towards the waterside.

It was more thickly wooded here, and their progress was slowed. But that would apply also to their pursuers. And the cover was better. Down through the birches and alders they plunged, horses and riders whipped by the branches. At the mud-lined shore, as they reined left-handed along it, Kinnoull groaned, pointing. Two horsemen were there, flailing their mounts, riding in the same direction.

'Only two. And fleeing. Ours,' Montrose jerked, and slowed a little, to let them catch up.

They were two of Hurry's group, both Sinclairs – indeed almost the only Sinclairs they had been able to enroll; Sir Edward, a middle-aged Orkneyman, descendant of the St. Clair Earls of Orkney; and Major Alexander of Brims, a cadet of Caithness. They were obviously much heartened to find themselves in Montrose's company again. They too were trying to find a place to cross the Kyle. They were all that was left of Hurry's party, they panted, all the rest dead, wounded or captured, Hurry with them.

They came to the low marshy point Montrose had remembered, scarcely to be called a headland, but at least narrowing the Kyle to no more than 300 yards, just a little way above Invershin Castle on the northern shore. It was now or never. Dragoons were in sight behind them, but well out of musket-range. James Graham led the way, spurring his reluctant horse through the thick, black, half-tide mud and into the cold water.

There was only some 200 yard of actual swimming. Fortunately the tide was coming in, helping to neutralise the Oykell's current. Even so they were swept downstream quite some distance, strongly as the tired beasts strove, the riders half swimming alongside, urgent, desperate enough scarcely to notice the chill.

They dragged themselves out, over more mud, on to a green cattle-dotted meadow, closer to Invershin Castle, a small Sutherland hold, than was comfortable. Looking back, they saw that the first of the dragoons had reached the opposite shore, but had drawn up there, watching, as yet making no attempt to follow – no doubt hoping that no officer would arrive to order them to take to the water.

Shivering now in wet clothes, the four fugitives rode on north-westwards. The River Shin came in on their right almost immediately, from the Lairg area, and the Sinclairs were for turning up its valley, to get quickly away from this dangerous Strathoykell. But Montrose pointed out that it was a populous valley, and narrow, its people Sutherlands. They could not hope to traverse it without being seen, and the folk would be hostile. Better to ford Shin and continue up the north side of Oykell meantime, and take the next valley on the right, Glen Cassley, some seven or eight miles up. They knew it and its drove-road – it was the way they had come south to Inveroykell some days ago. It was a much wilder route, with little habitation – safer. They must try to cross the mountains north-westwards, to the Mackay country of Reay. If Lord Reay's 1,000 Mackays were indeed marching to join him, they would be as apt to come that way as the long way round by Thurso. If they could meet them . . .

There was still no sign of the Earl of Sutherland's force on the far side of the Oykell. The fact was actually worrying Montrose somewhat now. If Sutherland was not over there, where was he? Delayed, and coming down Shin behind them? Or Cassley in front?

They could see their troop of dragoons now riding parallel with their own progress on the far side of the river, keeping them in view. This was dangerous also. There just might possibly be somewhere that men and horses could cross, short of Inveroykell ford. And they could signal to allies on this side.

He put it to the others. Reluctant as he was, he thought that they should abandon the horses. They were too ken-speckle, would not blend into the background scene. And it was horsemen that the enemy would be on the look-out for. He proposed that they actually turned back a little way, on their beasts, as though they had changed their minds, and were going to flee up the Shin. The dragoons across the valley would see it. Then they would abandon their horses in the thickish wood they had passed half a mile back, and proceed thereafter, north-westwards again, on foot but on the higher ground meantime, as inconspicuously as possible, taking advantage of the cover. James Graham made this a suggestion, not an order. He conceived it proper no longer to command his fellow-fugitives.

None contraverted his proposals, however – little as they relished the thought of having to do their escaping on foot. Or of actually turning back, even for a short distance. But they did it – and had the satisfaction of seeing the dragoons across Oykell pause also, and then turn back.

In the wood of Altass, Montrose abandoned more than his horse. He took off his handsome black chased-steel breast-plate, and his wet coat with the star and ribbon of the Garter – which he had been wearing as visible sign of his authority as Viceroy –

and even his sword-belt and pistol. None of these would solve any problems for them now, where inconspicuousness might. They would undoubtedly require all their strength for the major walking and climbing ahead of them. Unfortunately they could none of them dispense with their heavy thigh-length riding-boots without alternative footwear, unsuitable as these were. Hiding all beneath tree-roots – as unlikely a depository for the insignia of the Garter as probably had yet been conceived – and leaving the horses hitched loosely, they turned westwards once more out of the wood, now making use of hollows, trees, out-cropping rock and all other cover, to hide their progress.

Montrose's shoulder had stiffened up, and his hair-line wound throbbed painfully, Kinnoull also was hurt, his ribs crushed by a fall from his horse, possibly even cracked. Neither of the Sinclairs appeared to be injured, but Sir Edward was the oldest of the party and hardly robust. They had not a morsel of food between them. But at least they were glad of the activity to generate warmth, to dry their clothing.

It was now late afternoon, and for the remainder of that day they made their way up Strathoykell's north bank, high above the river-side road, without incident. They saw much to-ing and fro-ing on the far side of the strath and just before dusk a mounted patrol came cantering down the road on their own side, from the west. But there was no searching of their braesides meantime; presumably it was believed that they had gone up Shin.

Darkness overtook them near the mouth of Glen Cassley; but, weary as they were, they dare not rest yet. They stumbled on a shepherd's cabin in the entrance of the glen, near the ford, where dogs barked vociferously in alarm. The others were for beating a hasty retreat, but Montrose demurred. This would make it clear to the inhabitants that fugitives had passed this way, he reasoned – and in the morning they would be able to tell enquiring dragoons and send them up the glen after them. Better to make use of the opportunity. He gave Major Sinclair some silver and asked him to go forward to the house, to declare that he was a fugitive from battle and had a wounded comrade, and seek to buy food and old clothing, plaids, anything to cover them. But to stress that they were proceeding up Oykell, after fording Cass-ley. Ask about the ford, and how far it was to the west coast, up Oykell. The Mackay had mentioned Elphin, up there. Ask about Elphin. So that, when questioned, the cottagers would be sure to send the hunt in that direction, not up Cassley.

Presently Alexander Sinclair came back. He had managed to procure two plaids and some rags of old clothing. But little food. The shepherd had been friendly enough, but his own meal-kist was sadly low, at the end of the winter, and he had no meat in the house. A couple of bannocks, a handful of oatmeal, and some cold boiled salmon from the river, was all that he could provide.

They shared these morsels, and pressed on up the glen, not crossing the ford.

Some three miles up, they halted from sheer exhaustion, and huddled together in the heather in the lee of a great outcrop. It had begun to rain and they spread the plaids over them. Despite wet, cold and discomfort, they all sank into sleep almost immediately.

They wakened chilled, cramped, hungry and depressed, to the grey misery of dawn, with cold, seeping mist hanging low over all, no vistas, no food. But at least they were still undiscovered, and unlikely to be spotted in the mist. The others prevailed on Montrose, as the most conspicuous, as well as the one most vitally important to avoid capture, to exchange his fine clothing for most of the shepherd's ragged contributions. As had been discovered on an earlier occasion, however, no matter how shabby the clothing, it could not make James Graham look other than distinguished, assured, characterful. His scalp wound was bleeding again, slightly, and he tore up part of his silken shirt to make a bandage.

They moved on.

Although they none of them felt in conversational mood, and the disaster and losses of yesterday were still rather too close for discussion, it was necessary to decide on their immediate aims. There were really only two choices of action. Either they should head north by east to try to reach Sir Harry Graham and his rearguard in the Thurso area; or north-westwards into the friendly Mackay country of Reay. The two Sinclairs preferred the former, as might be expected. Kinnoull the latter. Montrose tended to agree with Kinnoull. His reasoning was that Harry Graham was capable of doing all that could be done up in Caithness, maintaining the links with Orkney; yet he had no large force, and the Sinclairs, as a clan, would not rise before – so would be a deal less likely to do so now. Whereas Lord Reay and the Mackays were committed. And they were a much larger clan, dominating all the very north-west corner of the mainland. Even if, on their way there they missed the promised 1,000 men, in a

359

week or so on Reay they could muster another 1,000 and more. With such Montrose could wage a Highland campaign still, overcome the effects of yesterday's set-back, and be down in Atholl, threatening the Lowlands, in a month.

It was brave talking, on purpose – but not unrealistic. All had not been lost at Carbisdale. Indeed, taken in the context of the entire Scottish cause, it was only a preliminary minor skirmish gone wrong, a false start before the real campaign started, grievous as was the loss of officer-corps personnel and friends, and the sad sacrifice of the Orkneymen. But it was not with these latter that Montrose had hoped to win Scotland for the King. He did not put into words, however, the much more ominous background situation which was, in fact, the real cause of yesterday's defeat – the climate of opinion beginning to prevail in Scotland, caused by Charles's renewed sitting down with the Covenanters, and talk of a treaty which was stifling all enthusiasm for uprising against Argyll meantime, and had almost certainly made the Mackenzies drag their feet and fail him and caused the Munroes and Rosses to attach themselves to Strachen. If the Mackays chose to take the same line . . . !

Unfortunately for their decision, however, none of the fugitives really knew this wild country, save by repute. They had indeed come south down Glen Cassley earlier, but had never left the deep valley-floor. Two-thirds of the way up, they recollected, the side-glen of Muic struck off westwards. They would take that for the Reay country, by Assynt. But meantime they were on the wrong side of the Cassley – and the mist was so thick that they could not see more than fifty yards.

Montrose thought that he remembered crossing from the west to the east side of the glen, on the march down, at a ford fairly soon after Glen Muic came in. They must look out for that ford, therefore, and cross there.

They did not find it so soon as they anticipated. Indeed it was mid-afternoon, and still thick, cloying mist, before they were able to discover a spot where they might get across the rushing torrent – and it was not the place where they had forded before, all recognised.

However, about an hour later, they found a fairly large incoming stream on the left, and felt rather than saw that they were in the mouth of a widish tributary valley. It might be the Muic, or it might not; but at least it led off westwards in the direction they wanted to go. They decided to follow it up.

Soon they were climbing, but there was a track of sorts. They followed it for hour after hour, climbing all the time, and growing more certain that it was not Glen Muic. An early dusk found them, ravenous, weary and uncertain; and when their deteriorating track made a substantial fork, with nothing to indicate which was the major prong, they decided to halt for the night, in the hope that the mist would be gone by morning, and they might see approximately where they were and which was the route.

That was a grim night. This bare expanse of peat-hags was much colder than in the sheltered valley. Their hunger was now a pain, gnawing, and leaving them light-headed. Montrose barely slept at all, the pain in his head throbbing. And as the night progressed, a new anxiety came to him. For Sir Edward Sinclair, who had been noticeably silent all that day and tending to lag behind, was moaning and groaning and sometimes talking wildly, obviously not so much dreaming nightmares as in semi-conscious raving. Never a robust man, he was too old and unused to hard living and campaigning for this sort of thing. That he was going to hold them up on the morrow, to say the least of it, was most apparent.

The mist changed to rain, half sleet indeed at this high altitude, just before dawn. Huddled beneath the plaids, shivering, they waited for the light to grow. Sir Edward was quieter now, but sunk in a heavy lethargy. Montrose forced himself to talk, talk incessantly, cheerfully, about plans for the future, past campaigns, his experiences in Europe. Alexander Sinclair responded well, but Kinnoull, never a talkative young man, was as silent as Sir Edward, hunched, depressed. Hunger ate at their vitals like rats.

When eventually they realised that it would grow no lighter, there were still no distant prospects. The rain had to some extent washed away the mist, but itself formed driving curtains to screen the view. They appeared to be on a lofty peat-pocked plateau, a wilderness of black hags and old heather, with vague hill-sides looming around but no certainty. As far as the forking paths went, there was nothing at all to choose from.

Some discussion arose between Montrose and Alexander Sinclair as to which to take – or even whether possibly to go back down to Cassley – Kinnoull and Sir Edward evincing no interest. Montrose thought the left-hand track ought to be the more hopeful in that it should bring them to lower ground more quickly, more or less due westwards – for he was pretty sure that they were considerably north of Glen Muic and that therefore the vast and daunting mountain massif of the Ben More Assynt group must lie ahead north-westwards, though they could see nothing of it. Sinclair argued that if they bore to the right they would do better, that Ben More was not so near as all that, and that direction should allow them to pass south-westwards of it and its great neighbour Conival, to reach Inchnadamph and the head of Loch Assynt. And even if it did not, the more to the right they swung, the better, for it would bring them ever nearer to the head of Glen Cassley, which, he had heard, swung strongly westwards in its higher reaches. Indeed they ought never to have left Cassley, he declared.

'Then would you prefer that we turn back, down to Cassley glen again, Major?' James Graham asked. 'I am prepared to consider it.'

'No, not that. It might be dangerous to retrace our steps. We may be followed, run into a patrol. No, I say we should take this right-hand track. And if it leads us to upper Glen Cassley, so much the better. From there only a low ridge can separate it from upper Shin – four miles, no more. And we are on the road for Caithness.'

'You are still anxious to get to Caithness, then? You would rather that than go on the longer road to Reay?'

'To be sure – I would. And Sir Edward too, I warrant. Indeed, I doubt if he will survive the long evil tramp across these damnable mountains, my lord. We could get him through to Shin, though. Perhaps put him up in some shepherd's cabin, till he can win safely northwards.'

Montrose nodded. 'You may be right. Yet it is better for the cause that I make for the Mackays, as swiftly as may be,' he declared. He looked at the other two, painful brows wrinkled. They offered no guidance or help. 'See you, Major – I think that we should part company. You and my lord of Kinnoull take Sir Edward and make for the Upper Cassley and upper Shin. The quickest way to food and shelter. And I will press on for Assynt and Reay.'

'But . . . my lord! Alone, you would not survive! We cannot leave you . . .'

'I will do very well . . .'

'*I* do not intend to leave him,' Kinnoull announced thickly. 'I stay with James.' It was the first words he had spoken for long.

362

Montrose would, in fact, have preferred it otherwise, but could not say so. Kinnoull would more likely be a hindrance than a help, and in his present state not notable company either.

Sir Edward seemed to gain an accession of strength and interest at this prospect of Caithness and the shorter journey. No doubt he felt his own beloved Orkney to be suddenly nearer. They shook hands and parted there, then, taking a plaid and a share of the available money, all in a blatter of sleet that was almost snow, the Sinclairs eager to be off.

Unspeaking, the two peers of Scotland turned westwards.

*   *   *

There are more varieties of hell than one, undoubtedly, and grey, wet cold at a high altitude in peat-hag country can be as terrible a sort as any blazing of eternal fires. All that grievous day James Graham and William Hay forced their stumbling way approximately west by north, into a north-west sleet-laden wind, famished, in pain, all but frozen. The track took them for some miles – how far they could not calculate – and then, bringing them to a rushing peat-stained torrent, did not recommence, so far as they could discover, on the other side. Snow was beginning to lie and presumably covering what slight traces of track there might be, and there was no vantage-point to give them a prospect. They discovered a narrow deer-path heading in roughly the right direction; but it turned and twisted as such do, and after a while petered out. They could only keep facing into the icy wind, staggering and tripping onwards over a broken, savage, endless terrain of tall old heather, quaking peat-sumps, the semi-fossilised roots of huge ancient trees from a warmer era. outcropping rock and innumerable rushing burns. Their pace grew slower and slower. Kinnoull undoubtedly would have halted, laid down and given up, had not Montrose consistently urged him on.

James Graham, for the first time, began to contemplate dying in this empty, ferocious wilderness – he for whom the Highlands had always sounded a clarion-call.

It was mid-afternoon when, at last, there was a break in the weather, the sleet died away and the clouds began to lift – although the wind blew still harder and colder. Gradually colour, distance and dimension returned to the land – but what it revealed was utterly appalling.

They were in the centre of a great basin of the mountains, a sort of amphitheatre two or three miles wide, a place of bogs and moraines and low heather knolls by the hundred, with a small, lost, slate-grey loch over to their right. But it was not the immediate prospect which held their daunted gaze so much as the enormous mountain mass which reared up behind the lochan, seeming almost to overhang them, thousands of feet above, three great, snow-streaked towering peaks, all streaming, glistening rock-face, beetling precipice, white falling water and soaring pinnacles, vast, overpowering. With a groan, Kinnoull sank down in the heather and buried his face in his shivering hands.

Montrose drew a long, quivering breath, but sought to hold his voice steady. 'Look at that, Will,' he said. 'See – we know where we are now. Those giants – they can be none other than Ben More Assynt and Conival. I know not the name of the third. But – I was right.' His voice faltered. 'God help the Sinclairs – they, they must have walked straight into it! Though – perhaps their track swung away in time. It must lead somewhere. But, see you – if we are south of Ben More, then Loch Assynt and its low strath cannot be so far away. To the west. And Neil Macleod of Assynt served with me for a little, after Inverlochy. With one of Seaforth's companies. A King's man.'

Kinnoull did not respond, or even look up.

Montrose turned his gaze towards the south-west, where there was a major gap in the encircling barrier of the mountains, some three miles away.

'Yonder is our route, Will. Through that col. You can see that there are no great hills beyond. That *must* lead into the strath of Assynt, since it lies south-west of Ben More. Three more miles to the col. Then, say another three, and we shall be safe. Six miles, no more . . .'

The other raised his head. 'Then you go on, James – if you can. For I cannot.'

'You can, man – you can. And *must*! Together we can do it. We may well find food, a house, before then. Coming to lower ground. It is food that you need. A bite to eat and you will find your strength again. Chew on these heather-stems, as I have done – who knows, there may be good in it. Come.' He put a hand under the other's arm and hoisted him to his feet – although the effort almost toppled himself.

They lurched off in the new direction, arm-in-arm.

That col took an unconscionable time to draw any nearer. The ground, as they approached it, grew ever more waterlogged, with small lochans and peat-pools everywhere – typical West Sutherland landscape. Slithering, ploutering, circling, they dragged themselves on.

Montrose raised a croaking cheer at the first stunted Scots pine, a twisted, poor thing but significant, proof that they were coming down to the tree-level and therefore the possible haunts of men. But soon thereafter they had to wade one more of the countless rushing burns – and crossing this, William Hay slipped on the slimy stones of the bottom and fell his length in the icy water. Montrose managed to grab him before he was swept away and dragged him to the bank.

But now Kinnoull could not stand, much less walk. He had dislocated his hip, it seemed.

James Gordon had no choice. He could by no means carry his friend. They would both die if he was just to lie down beside the man, here. He must go on, try to bring the other help and food – although it was a grievous decision to leave him there. Dragging Kinnoull into the lee of a great outcrop and pulling heather to form a barrier around him, he wrapped the plaid round his soaking, shivering conpanion, promised aid, confided him to God's keeping, and pressed on.

The climb up to the col, although nothing steep nor long, taxed Montrose to the utmost. Darkness descended upon him in that defile, but he stumbled on. There could be no halting now. Weakened with hunger and exhaustion, if he let himself sink down – as his whole being craved – he might well never rise again.

That night had an unreality for him, an utterly unearthly quality beyond all description. Fortunately the floor of the defile contained a fairly well-defined track which carried him onwards, westwards – otherwise, most certainly, he could not long have continued in the darkness. As it was he continually tripped over obstacles – and when he fell it demanded all his will-power each time to rise once more. He lost all impression of time, or even of where he was, relatively. More and more his mind, his consciousness, was far elsewhere, mainly with Elizabeth whose love, warm understanding and support were more real to him than any present conditions. Other presences came to be with him also – Magdalen, young Johnnie, George Gordon, Magnus O'Cahan, Archie Napier – but always Elizabeth was at his elbow. She was his prime strength that night, of the will, where there was no strength of the body left.

More and more frequently he stumbled into trees, as time wore on, and somewhere on his left a rushing river kept him company, he was aware.

Daylight found him still moving forward, however slowly, unsteadily and in fits and starts, in fairly level immediate country with the great hills behind him. Hills remained all round, but they had drawn back and were no longer major mountains although, half-right, in the far distance, a strange jagged saw-tooth ridge soared, blocking all view to the north-west. He believed that he was, indeed, in Assynt, and that would be the great Quinag, of which he had heard – but he was so light-headed that he scarcely felt a lift of the heart in consequence.

Perhaps this was as well. For the reverse also applied, and when, an hour or two later, he saw some way off a low-browed, turf-roofed cabin and made therefor in a sort of dazed eagerness, his disappointment at finding it empty and abandoned was cushioned also. Although he avidly searched every corner and cranny of its peat-smoke-blackened interior for even a grain of meal, he discovered nothing.

Almost automatically now he lurched on.

Sometime that bright windy forenoon it penetrated to his consciousness that he had been aware of some factor for a while, something good, significant. With an effort of concentration he recognised that it was a scent, the scent of peat smoke, on the north-westerly wind. Forcing himself to clamber, partly on all-fours, up a heather-knoll by the track-side, and blinking weak tears from his eyes, he managed to distinguish another cot-house, just like the last one, a short distance half-right – only this one had a blue plume of smoke rising from the centre of its heather thatch. Gabbling aloud, he staggered crazily towards it.

A barking dog heralded his arrival, and an elderly man and woman came to the cavern of a door. But seeing his reeling, tottering state, they hurried forward to aid and support him. Between them they led, half-carried him into the warm, dark interior.

They set him on a bench by the peat fire in mid-floor. The man gave him a quaigh of fiery whisky to drink. Then the woman brought a wooden bowl of venison and oatmeal stew, ladled out of a large black pot which hung from an iron swee above the fire. He gulped it down, scarcely noticing that it burned his mouth, while they patted his shoulders and fussed over him, shaking their heads.

It came to him in his dizzy relief, elation and gratitude, that e was babbling to them in English, and that they were not nderstanding a word of him. He groped for the Gaelic words – 'hich he knew quite well, but which in his present state it took major effort to find and bring forth. He told them that he was Iontrose, the King's Viceroy; that he had suffered defeat at arbisdale on the Kyle of Sutherland; that the Earl of Kinnoull 'as lying injured some miles back beyond the pass – between it nd the lochan under Ben More and Conival – and desperately eeded help. A pony – had they a garron? To get Kinnoull?

Amidst exclamations of wonder and sympathy, the man de-lared that, alas, he had no garron. He was a shepherd, and it was lonely house. The nearest garrons would be down at Chalda, n the shore of the big loch, where Ardvreck had a farm – four iiles on. But his son, on the hill seeing to the sheep, would soon e back for his meal. Then he and his son would go find the ther lord . . .

Montrose was vaguely agitated that this was insufficient, that e must do better for Kinnoull than that. But his agitation was uted, lacked force. Indeed, he could scarcely remain upright n the bench. What with the warmth of the cabin, the whisky nd food in his stomach, on top of utter exhaustion, he could not eep his eyes open. Seeing it, the woman guided him to a pallet f sheepskins in a corner. He was asleep before even he was fully tretched thereon. The couple had to lift his booted legs up after im.

They had considerable difficulty in rousing him, an hour later. 'Lord,' the man was shouting in his ear, shaking him, 'wake ou! They are coming. The soldiers. A party of soldiers, what-ver. On horses. Coming from the road, from the west. Quickly - you must hide, lord.'

Somehow they got him off those sheepskins. The cabin was uilt on a slope, and the lower end of the single long chamber erved as byre for the cow, no partition separating beast from wners – though it had a different door, and the soil from the yre drained away down the slope beyond. The new season's asture was not yet sprouting, so the beast was still tethered in ts winter stall. At its head was a wooden trough, as manger, and nder this Montrose was pushed by his urgent hosts, with an rmful of bog-hay piled over him, the cow snuffing and puffing lose by.

They were only just in time. The barking of the dog, the thud

367

of hooves and the jingling of bits and bridles was overlaid by th
shouts of men. Then an authoritative voice, obviously an office
and within the house, spoke in English. He announced that h
came in the name of the Estates of the Realm, and was lookin
for fugitives, supporters of the excommunicate rebel and man o
blood Montrose, who had been defeated in the east. Man
fugitives were known to have scattered all over these hills, an
were to be hunted down like the ungodly vermin they were. Ha
any come here, or been seen in the vicinity?

The shepherd declared in the Gaelic that he was sorry but h
did not understand the gentleman's English.

The officer apparently had an interpreter, who translated i
all, adding a threat or two of his own as to the dire results o
lying or hiding aught.

Montrose, beneath his hay, could hear every word.

The shepherd said again that he was sorry, but he could no
help. His back was hurting him, from an old fall, and he had no
been out this day. But he had seen no strangers on the hi
yesterday or the day before.

The officer grunted, and demanded whisky. While it was bein
brought, he pointed out that anyone caught harbouring any o
the traitorous rebels would be hanged from his own rooftree. Bu
that any word of the man Montrose himself would gain the give
a rich reward, if he was captured. There was a price of no les
than £25,000 on the malignant's head, promised by the Marqui
of Argyll himself. A mighty fortune. So let them keep watch.

Translated, the shepherd assured that he would not fail t
watch well.

There was no actual search of the cabin – it was all open to th
soldier's gaze. One man did clump into the byre and thrust
bayonet into the heap of hay from which the shepherd had taker
the armful to cover the fugitive – but he did not squeeze up pas
the cow to prod below the manger.

Lying still, Montrose heard the military leave the cabin an
ride away.

The couple came for him presently, to assure him that all wa
clear, that the soldiers had ridden off eastwards, the way he ha
come. He could come out.

James Graham, although still light-headed, was in comman
of his senses again. He declared his undying gratitude, that h
would never forget the kindness and self-sacrificing Christia
charity for a stranger which he had received at the shieling o

Glaschyle. Pressing some money upon them, he would not hear of the woman removing the dirty bandage from his brow and dressing the wound. They had done more than sufficient. He was going, now. He had brought them into dire danger, just to save his own skin. God helping him, he would not let that happen again to innocent strangers. But if they could get food and aid to the Earl of Kinnoull, he would be eternally in their debt still further.

They urged him to stay, and sleep again; but though his every inch cried out to agree, he would not. The military might be back, or another patrol come.

At the cabin door he asked where was Ardvreck? They had mentioned the name in connection with the big loch. Loch Assynt? Macleod of Assynt had served under him once. He was a loyal King's man, and in a position to help him. They told him that the head of Loch Assynt was only two miles to the west, at Inchnadamph, and that the castle of Ardvreck was but two miles farther, on the north shore, easily seen. The soldiers had gone in the other direction, eastwards, so all should be well.

Drinking a coggie of milk, and with a bannock to sustain him on his way, James Graham set out again, with a thankful heart.

It did not take him long to discover, however, that he was still desperately weak and in no state for walking. Soon all was swimming before his eyes, and frequently he had to go down on hands and knees, head hanging, or he would have pitched prostrate. It seemed to take him hours to reach the Inchnadamph vicinity, with the wide spread of the six-mile-long Loch Assynt opening before him.

There were houses here, even a tiny turf-roofed chapel. Even though the dragoons were now presumably far to the east, Montrose decided not to risk calling here, but made a long, difficult and he hoped undetected circuit to the right, at about half a mile's distance, having to ford another quite major river in the process. In his present state it took him almost two hours, before he could proceed again along the track which followed the north shore of the loch.

It seemed, however, that all his sore hiding and skulking had been for nothing; for presently he heard shouting behind him, and turning, saw two men hurrying after him. They were Highlanders, dressed in ragged tartans and plaids. He waited for them, since he was in no condition to do anything else.

They proved to be a rough-looking pair, but were civil

enough, asking who he was and where he had come from, also where he was going – in the Gaelic of course. With his bandaged head and obviously Lowland style, they would have been fools not to guess that he was one of the fugitives from the battle; but he saw no need to inform them of anything else other than that he was a traveller seeking Macleod of Assynt and had unfortunately met with an accident. At mention of Macleod's name, the two men eyed each other, and one announced that they were in fact gillies of Macleod's and that they would take the gentleman to their master.

So they went on together – and perceiving their charge's faltering steps, the pair each took an arm and supported him on his way, for which he was grateful.

They had not far to go. Quite soon, rounding a bend of the loch-shore, they came into view of a low green promontory jutting into the water, at the tip of which rose starkly a tall, narrow tower-house, four storeys and a garret, typical with corbelling, crowstepped gabling and steep roofing, all within a small curtain-walled and loop-holed courtyard. A scattering of cot-houses surrounded the castle, amongst a patchwork of tiny, odd-shaped fields and peat-stacks. It looked a fairly primitive place to be the centre of a lairdship large as a southern county – but, in this mountainous wilderness, reassuring.

Watched with interest from every cabin door, they came to Ardvreck Castle. There, although the iron yett and great oaken door both stood open, Montrose was left at the threshold in care of one gillie while the other went to announce arrival. The visitor understood the reason for this seeming discourtesy in an innately courteous people; once a stranger had crossed a Highland threshold, the laws of hospitality came into force – and such visitor, unwelcome, might prove an embarrassment.

A young man, thick-set and with reddish hair and a straggle of thin beard, came back with the gillie. He was dressed in tartans little better than his servants', with a long calfskin waistcoat. He did not smile any welcome to his unannounced guest.

'So, you have found one of them!' he commented, in Gaelic. 'Where did you pick him up?'

'Assynt,' Montrose said, in English. 'I greet you. It is some time since we foregathered. I make so bold as to crave your hospitality for a little.'

At the speaker's manner and tone of voice, Macleod peered. 'Who are you?' he demanded. He was scarcely to be blamed, perhaps, for failing to recognise his former Captain-General in the gaunt, head-bandaged, peat-stained scarecrow before him.

'James Graham of Montrose – who else ? Though . . . scarce at my best, sir !'

'God Almighty !' Assynt gasped. 'Montrose! I . . . I did not know you. Mercy on us – yourself!'

The other nodded. He was leaning against the doorpost now.

'They . . . they have not caught you, then ? Och – dear God, and you're wounded, whatever !'

'A little. But more . . . weary.' Montrose closed his eyes, swaying.

'My lord – you are ill.' There was some concern now, in the other's voice. 'Come away in . . .' Belatedly, Macleod made his decision.

'Neil !' The single word halted him and turned him round – and opened James Graham's heavy-lidded eyes. A young woman was there, peering from behind, slight, not uncomely, but sharp-featured. She was looking at the visitor with no kindness.

'It is Montrose himself, Christian – the Marquis of Montrose. Wounded . . .'

'And hunted! With a price on his head,' the young woman added shortly.

'Lady Ardvreck ?' The Graham managed even a hint of a bow. 'Your servant, ma'am. A sore sight, to be sure. But . . . still the King's Viceroy !' It was faintly if significantly said. He clung to the doorpost still, for support.

'He must come in,' Macleod said, shaking his red head. 'It is necessary. He must come in, Christian. We cannot . . .' He left the rest unsaid.

Without a word she turned and hurried back into the house. Her husband took Montrose's arm and led him inside, after her.

Aided up the winding turnpike stair to the modest hall of the castle on the first floor, the visitor was set down at a long table, near the peat fire in the moulded stone fireplace. It was all not so very different from the shepherd's cabin, larger but with little of refinement or graciousness, and almost as dark, for the windows were small. But there was one notable difference here – there was little of welcome, and the food and drink given were offered at the hands of the master of the house, not the mistress. Christian Macleod stayed out of sight, her disapproval evident for all that.

But James Graham was in no condition to complain or reproach, hardly to notice. He did say that if his presence was awkward or an embarrassment, he would press on – to which Neil Macleod made no very outraged protest, though he did declare that his lordship must rest before thinking of so doing. Which was a self-evident fact, for twice during the meal James Graham slumped over the table two-thirds asleep, and had to be roused to eat more. Eventually the young man led him up a further and narrower flight of the turnpike stair to a bedchamber on the second floor. The guest collapsed on the bed, and scarcely heard his host say that he would send up hot water and dressings for washing and the wound. Montrose was deep asleep when an old woman arrived with these, and she had to perform her ministrations on a scarcely conscious patient.

*   *   *

Montrose slept the clock round twice, so that it was the evening of the next day before he wakened sufficiently to be aware of his situation. It was the arrival of another exhausted fugitive, carried in by gillies, to share his room, which roused him – none other than Sinclair of Brims. But the Major was in such a state of fatigue and exposure as to be quite incoherent and wandering in his mind, so that the other could get nothing out of him that night. More food came at the hands of the old woman, but of their host and his wife there was no sign. When Montrose asked to see the laird, he was told that himself was from home. He tried to get some nourishment down his companion's throat, but with scant success, and decided that it was best to leave him to sleep. No lamp was brought for them, and James Graham was glad enough to sink back into slumber himself, once more.

Next morning, Sinclair was tossing and turning in a fever. Montrose grew anxious for him. About noon Neil Macleod made an appearance. He vouchsafed no explanation for his absence, but declared that there were many parties of soldiers quartering all the surrounding valleys, and since some might well come to Ardvreck and search the house, it would be safer for his guests to be down in the vaulted basement cellars. These had dark wall-chambers in which they could hide, if need be. Montrose asked him if he preferred that he, at least, left the castle at once, patrols or none, so that no charge of harbouring the prime fugitive might fall upon him? But Macleod said no, so long as they were safe hidden in the cellarage. So down they went, supporting Sinclair between them.

It was dark, chill and miserable down in the semi-subterranean vault, with only a single narrow slit-window; but there were two mural garderobes in the thickness of the walling, which could be screened with piled peat and would provide hiding-place if need be. Macleod brought down their bedding from aloft, blankets on heaped deerskins, and provided them with ample to eat and drink. It was far from comfortable – but compared with what they had been through, it was not to be complained about.

Macleod seemed less than anxious for converse with his uninvited visitors, but Montrose detained him to speak of the future. They must leave just so soon as Sinclair was fit to travel. He had been heading for the Reay country, and hoping to meet the Lord Reay and a large force of Mackays. But now that the word of the Carbisdale defeat had spread over the countryside, Reay would almost certainly have turned back – and moreover might well be disinclined for further adventuring meantime, until he saw larger backing for the King's cause. As who would blame him? Therefore he, Montrose, now believed that he should make for Caithness, *en route* for Orkney, where he was expecting considerable reinforcements of men and arms at any time. Would Ardvreck aid him to get to Thurso, where Sir Harry Graham and the royalist rearguard was based?

Macleod's expression was hard to distinguish in the gloom; but he sounded anything but enthusiastic.

'It would be difficult, my lord,' he said. 'With all these soldiers scouring the hills. Dangerous. You would likely be captured.'

'Is it not more dangerous to remain here? And bring down trouble upon yourself? Besides, *you* must know secret ways through the mountains, the passes and glens. I swear that you could guide us, my friend, so that we could outwit all these Lowland soldiery – you, in your own Highlands?'

'It is not so easy. For me to get away, see you. It is a bad time. Time for the spring sowing. For the beasts to be got out on to the hill pastures. A busy time, whatever. I am a poor man, my lord Marquis – no great noble. I have to earn my bread . . .'

James Graham sought to keep the contempt out of his voice. 'You shall be richly rewarded for your services, Ardvreck, never fear. And for what I ask of you. You will lose nothing by guiding us to Thurso, providing garrons for us to ride. A week of your time would be well spent so.'

The other, edging towards the door, muttered something

about being unable to leave Ardvreck meantime. Personal matters, his lordship would understand. Perhaps later . . .

'Then send a gillie with us. Two garrons, a gillie and some food. That is all we need. That at least you can do? And for that service, Ardvreck, I will give you a note-of-hand for whatsoever sum you require. Make it sufficiently large, man. Argyll is not the only one in Scotland who can offer rich rewards!'

Macleod had the grace at least to cough, almost to choke, make some sort of protesting disclaimer, and hurry out, slamming the cellar-door after him.

That evening Major Sinclair's fever abated, and he became lucid though very weak. Broken-voiced he informed that there had been disaster, that Sir Edward would be dead by now. They had progressed fairly well for some time after parting from Montrose and Kinnoull. But the snowstorm seemed to sap all the remaining strength out of the older man. They had had to take shelter for the night in a cranny of the rocks, and the next morning Sir Edward had refused to rise. He, Brims, had forcibly dragged him on – but quite soon the other had collapsed, taken some sort of seizure, lost consciousness. He had no option but to leave him there, with the plaid around him, and struggle on. But when the blizzard cleared he had found himself amongst mighty mountains, and he realised that he was far from where he had expected to be, far to the west obviously. Rather than turn back, he had pressed on westwards, making for this Assynt area. For how long he wandered amongst those hellish mountains he knew not. Two days and nights, or three? Then barking dogs had found him, and two men after them, Highlanders, gillies, who had brought him here. They were indeed Macleod's men, and had been searching the hills for fugitives.

'You were fortunate indeed, my friend. They might have been soldiers, dragoons. There are many searching, it seems.'

'Aye, no doubt.' Sinclair did not sound very convinced of his good fortune. 'Can they give us no light in here?' he demanded querulously. 'It is black as a whale's belly!'

'Ardvreck advises against it. He says light would shine out, under the door and through the window-slit. Let it be known that there were occupants of this vault. It could be a wise precaution.'

'Perhaps. My lord – do you trust Ardvreck?'

Montrose took time to answer that. 'I would not wish to say that I did not, Major,' he declared at length, carefully. 'He is our host. We eat his bread. He undoubtedly endangers himself and his house by harbouring us. It would ill become me to say that I mistrusted him.'

'*I* am not so nice, my lord Marquis! I do *not* trust the man. Admittedly, I do not know him. But those gillies of his, who found me, were scarcely friendly. They may have saved me from wandering to my death – but they treated me with scant kindness. I believe that they were more pleased at finding me than saving me! They were searching for fugitives, yes – but my notion is that they were not doing so out of love for our cause.'

'Gillies' behaviour does not matter, Major. It is their master who counts.'

'And their master is married on a daughter of Munro of Lemlair! The Munroes who failed to rise for you – and took the wrong side at Carbisdale.'

'Is she a Munro, then? That I did not know.' Montrose sounded very thoughtful. 'Certainly I do not think that she approves of our being here. She did not want me brought in – and I have not once set eyes on her, since. But . . . Macleod served with me once. I can surely trust one of my own officers . . .'

'Not your's, my lord – Seaforth's, you said. And Seaforth has also failed you, ere this. What happened to his brother, Pluscarden, and the Mackenzies? Where are they?'

There was a long silence in that dark vault.

'Perhaps there is something in what you say,' Montrose said at length. 'At least it would be wise to take precautions. If we may. To tell the truth, some such fears have been at the back of my own mind. I put them from me as unworthy. But – you may have the rights of it. Tomorrow, I think, if you are fit to travel, we shall leave this house. Patrols or none.'

'Aye – that would be best. I will travel, yes. On a garron if I may, on foot if I must. I am not done yet!' the younger man declared, determination in his voice. 'It is Caithness for me.' He paused. 'What of my Lord Kinnoull?'

'I had to leave him – as you left Sir Edward. He put out his hip, falling in a river. But I asked the shepherd who befriended me to go to his aid. With his son. Their dog would find him. They were good folk, most kind – they would not fail to go for him, I am sure. Tomorrow we will ride back that way, see how he fares . . .'

So, next morning, when the old woman brought them their breakfast porridge and milk, Montrose asked to see Ardvreck. She came back presently to say that himself would come when he could, but was unable to do so just then. In a little small while . . .

They waited – but the little while dragged noticeably. Sinclair, though still weak, declared himself fit for the road. Now they were impatient to be gone. At length, courtesy towards their hosts gave way to urgency. They opened the cellar door and entered the short dark passage without.

This also had a massive door – and it was locked.

They stared at each other in the half dark, shaken. It *could* be for their own security, to prevent anyone straying into the basement and discovering them. But to be locked in, unwarned, was ominous.

They knocked on the heavy door, without result. Then they banged and shouted. There was no response. Appalled, they went back to the vault.

Some time later, listening intently, they heard the key turn in the outer door. In a moment they were out in the arched stone lobby. It was the old woman again.

'Himself has been out. But he will see your honours now,' she informed. 'Come, you.'

They followed her up the stairs and into the hall.

Their host was indeed there, with his wife. But also four men, three wearing steel breastplates and helmets. The fourth wore a black, wide-brimmed, Puritan-type hat, with a black cavalry cloak. He bowed, very briefly.

'You are James Graham, sometimes styled Marquis of Montrose?' he said crisply. 'I am Major-General Holbourn, representing the Estates of this Realm. You are my prisoner, sir.'

There was a long silence. Then Montrose bowed. 'At your service, General. You have had to come a long way for this . . . audience. My apologies! Have you breakfasted? I am sure Lady Ardvreck will accommodate you. At *my* charges, of course.'

The other frowned. 'I have not come for dalliance, sir. My instructions are to take you to General Strachan. At once. We ride, sir.'

'Very well. I am at your disposal. But my friend here, Major Sinclair of Brims, is sick. Suffering from exposure. He is in no state to travel . . .'

'He will travel,' Holbourn interrupted shortly.

Inclining his head, Montrose turned to Macleod and his wife. Haggard, clad still in the ragged clothing obtained from the shepherd in Glen Cassley, his bearing and presence nevertheless

376

dominated the scene. 'Ardvreck – you have chosen your bargain,' he said mildly. 'May it sustain you hereafter. We all have to make our choice, and then live with it. Ma'am – I thank you for your hospitality, and regret that you were troubled by my presence. I shall not forget Ardvreck in Assynt!'

With a sort of choking groan, Neil Macleod turned and all but ran from his own hall.

Holbourn signed to his lieutenants. 'Enough,' he said. 'Bring the prisoners out.' And he also made for the door.

'But, sir – you go? So soon?' Christian Macleod asked, urgently.

'We do, Mistress. My orders are to bring the malignant James Graham before General Strachan at Tain, without delay. We will be on our way.'

'But . . . the money, sir? The reward . . . ?' That was almost a wail.

'Do you think that I carry £25,000 Scots about on my person, woman? You will get it, never fear. The meal you shall have from Tain. The money you must await, from my lord Marquis of Argyll. A good day to you.'

James Graham shook his head. 'Campbell gold, ma'am. I fear – I fear that you must labour further ere ever you see it!' There was only sorrow in his voice.

CHAPTER TWENTY-SIX

Outside the castle's little courtyard they tied Montrose's wrists together with rope, and were mounting him on one of the cavalry horses, Sinclair on another, when General Holbourn intervened.

'Not so,' he commanded. 'That broken-down shelt over there. That will serve an excommunicate traitor very well!' He pointed to a miserable ancient grey garron of Macleod's, all bones and sores, standing drooping in the infield – used, no doubt, for carrying in the peats. 'Give Macleod a pound for it – and he will be overpaid!'

'It will delay us, sir . . .'

'We shall see that it does not!'

Throwing some old rags of plaiding over the poor beast's back, with a looped rope for stirrups, the troopers mounted their chief prisoner thereon, and tied his ankles together, under the brute's sagging belly, with more rope. Sinclair they allowed to ride normally on a cavalry charger. Thus, with an escort of a full troop of light dragoons, they left Ardvreck Castle and turned eastwards along Loch Assynt, on the long road to destiny. Not one of the Ardvreck cottagers turned out to watch them go.

Holbourn was accurate when he said that they would not allow the short-legged, aged garron to hold them up. One trooper led it on a rope from in front, and another behind beat it about the croup when it flagged. Spaced well behind the jingling leaders, and as far ahead of the main troop, the sorry creature was hustled along, faster than it had moved for many a year. On its swaying back its rider knew a real sympathy, and indeed protested at the rope's-end floggings from the rear, not a few of which came perilously near to striking himself.

It made a weary journey – but James Graham reminded himself that it was a deal less taxing than had been his journey westwards. Anyway, his mind was scarcely there at all, but far hence, concerned with matters infinitely more important to himself than this pettily spiteful progress. As they passed near the shieling of Glaschyle, however, he did return to the present for a little, to wonder whether William Hay of Kinnoull lay therein. But he did no more than merely glance towards the cabin, for fear of seeming to take too great an interest. The dog barked at them passing, but no figures appeared at the open doorway.

It was nearly fifty miles of savage country to Tain, with only a drove-road pitted with bogs, climbing over high passes and fording innumerable rushing torrents – which, oddly enough, the broad-hooved, short-legged garron crossed a deal better than did the Lowland cavalry mounts. The going became very slow, and Montrose's beast, in consequence, managed well enough. They went by Lochs Awe and Borralin and over the watershed, the very roof of Scotland, to join the upper east-flowing Oykell again, stopping for the night at Rosehall, in the mouth of Glen Cassley, within a mile of the spot where the clothing Montrose was wearing had come from. Wrists and ankles still tied, he was thrown into a cow-byre under strong guard – where the beasts and the hay kept him a deal warmer than he had been in Ardvreck vault. Sinclair was bestowed elsewhere. They seemed determined to keep the two prisoners separate, and to heap the contumely on James Graham the excommunicate.

Next day was wet, thin chill rain with mist low on the hills. So that the scene of the battle – if that it could be called – was mercifully blotted out across the Kyle as they passed Carbisdale. For Holbourn held, for some reason, to this north side of the firth. It made a grim day's riding, and Montrose was beginning to feel light-headed again, partly with the swaying of his saddleless mount's awkward gait. An early dusk found them at the Skibo peninsula, at the ferry-haven opposite Edderton of Tain – but the tide was out and the flat ferry scows needed for transporting cavalry could not ply. They put up for the night at Skibo Castle near by.

There an odd incident took place. Montrose was once again deposited in mean quarters, but to his surprise presently was brought out, his bonds untied, and he was led into the castle proper, indeed upstairs to its hall. There he found Holbourn and his officers seated at table with their hostess, an old, fierce dame, bent and thin, but with a lively eye. It was, of course, a Sutherland house, and Lady Skibo no friend of Montrose's cause. Her son, of the name of Gray, was out with the Earl's force. But she rose, nevertheless, from her seat at the head of the table, as he was led in – which caused some shuffling discomfort amongst her guests, who ought to have risen with her, in common courtesy, but dared not when their commander remained determinedly seated and scowling. The two troopers who had brought the prisoner up thrust him into a chair at the foot of the table, where Holbourn indicated, and stood guard behind him.

'No, sir – not there!' old Lady Skibo exclaimed, in a voice cracked but stern. 'Up here. Have ye no understanding, man?' It was to Holbourn she spoke.

'He will do very well there, Mistress. Too well. Let him be, I say.'

'Let him be, *you* say! You'll no' order me in *my* house, soldier! My lord Marquis – I dinna care overmuch for your policies, but I ken how the King's Captain-General should be treated in a decent house. Come up here, to my side, if you please.'

'Nonsense, woman! The man is an excommunicate felon! He stays where he is – or returns to his cell.' Holbourn glared, as Montrose rose from his seat. 'Sit down!' he roared.

'*You* give orders in Skibo, scum?' the old lady screamed. And reaching forward she picked up the steaming leg of mutton from its ashet and brought it down in splattering fury on the head of the astounded Major-General, covering him with its juices. Two more skelps she got in, left and right, with her odd weapon, before she slapped it down again on its plate.

There was a silence of utter consternation in that hall as, purple with rage and humiliation, Holbourn lurched to his feet, mouth open, wiping his face.

Montrose it was who spoke. 'Lady Skibo – may I congratulate you on your notable courtesy? And judgment. The Major-General, as a soldier, I am sure will commend your aim! And your mutton smells delicious!'

'God damn you, you old bitch! God damn you!' Holbourn spluttered. 'As Christ's my witness, you'll pay for this ...!'

'Dinna blaspheme in my house, soldier!' their hostess cried. 'This is a God-fearing house, and I'll have no swearing! Sit down and take your meat like a decent body – or leave my table. Come you, Marquis – up here by my side. I kenned your mother ...'

Holbourn, gasping for words and breath both, stormed from the room. But at the door he turned, and pointed a shaking finger, first at the troopers and then at Montrose.

'Get that man out of here and down to his kennel, fools!' he shouted. And to his officers, 'All of you – leave this house. D'you hear – leave this house.'

So, despite the violent protests of Lady Skibo, James Graham was urgently hustled away below again, to bread and water. But man is nourished not by bread alone. His spirits took a distinct upwards turn, that night.

On the morrow they came across the ferry to Tain, where Holbourn got rid of his objectionable prisoner – not to Strachan as he expected but to General David Leslie himself, who had arrived at last and sent Strachan south personally with the glad news of his own victory.

Montrose was brought before the commander-in-chief in the handsome Tolbooth of the royal burgh of Tain. These two had been not unfriendly once, but after the vile excesses and butchery of Philiphaugh, James Graham retained no respect for the man, however able a soldier. They greeted each other stiffly, before a battery of officers and black-robed ministers, the latter not backward in voicing their hatred for the impious excommunicate renegade who had sold himself to the Devil, and glee at his apprehension.

When he could make himself heard above the divine chorus, Leslie spoke levelly but uneasily, scarcely glancing at his scarecrow of a prisoner.

'James Graham, sometime Earl and Marquis of Montrose, you have been taken in arms against the Estates of the Realm of Scotland. You had previously been outlawed and forfeited by the said Estates, and condemned to death. Also excommunicated by the Kirk of Scotland in Assembly. Therefore it is my duty to conduct you to your deserved end and execution. Not to trial, for you have been tried already and no further debate is necessary. You are to die.'

There was a shout of approval from the clerical committee which the Covenant imposed upon its commanders.

Montrose inclined his head. 'We are all to die, General. Even you. Even these reverend gentlemen. It is all a matter of when, of timing. Personally I have not found my living, of late, of such delight that I cannot bear to leave it. Here, at Tain, is as good a place to die as any, I think.'

'Not so. You go to Edinburgh for your execution, sir.'

'A pity. So long and weary a journey, for nothing, is it not? For us all. Why not exert your undoubted authority, General, as commander-in-chief – on which may I congratulate you? As on the 50,000 merks reward and the gold chain you received for your slaughter at Philiphaugh! Execute me here and save much trouble. After all, a renowned ancestor of your own, betrayed at Tain, would have sought the same felicity, I am sure – instead of being dragged all the way south to Berwick to be hanged, drawn and quartered by English Edward.' He referred to Nigel Bruce, the hero-king's brother, captured here along with the Queen and others, also on the way to Orkney. For the General was a son of of Patrick Leslie, first Lord Lindores, whose mother had been daughter of Robert Stewart, Earl of Orkney, half-brother of Mary Queen of Scots – and therefore descended from the Bruce.

Leslie frowned. 'No, sir. My orders are explicit. You are to be carried to Edinburgh, there to meet your deserved fate.'

'A pity. However – if needs must. I hope, in that case, that you may provide me – at my own charges, I hasten to say – with some rather cleaner wear than this, for the journey. And allow me to shave. Also to ride something more fit for the road than Ard-vreck's broken garron, which has all but died under me. It deserves execution a deal less than I do! One of General Holbourn's . . . economies.'

'No, sir. None of these. Major-General Holbourn was acting strictly to his orders. As I must do. These are the Lord Chancellor's commands, in the name of the Estates. You will travel to Edinburgh in the fullest indignity of your state as an ex-communicate traitor. There will be no remission of severity.'

'I am here, General, in the name and on the written authority of His Grace the King of Scots, Charles Stewart. In whose name you also must hold your commission. But mine is by his own hand. How then can I be a traitor to Scotland, excommunicate or otherwise ?'

'Silence!' the other cried, looking unhappy. 'I am not here to answer your questions. We march tomorrow.' He turned to an officer. 'Remove the prisoner . . .'

Leslie made an early start in the morning, with a large company, clerical and lay. Montrose found that he had indeed been allotted a new mount – but it was the seediest nag they had been able to find in Tain, a gaunt and pathetic bag of bones. The same old plaiding still served for saddle, though, since it was raining again, the prisoner was allowed to drape part of the smelly tartan about his shoulders. Wrists and ankles bound as before, he was led fore and aft by troopers. He had merely exchanged gaolers and escort.

They rode by Alness and the Cromarty Firth to Dingwall, and turned up Strathpeffer to Brahan Castle, a thirty-five-mile journey. At Dingwall a sizeable town, a picket spurred ahead to warn the magistrates and people to turn out, and as they entered the crowded streets a herald and trumpeter rode before the entourage chanting 'Here comes James Graham, a traitor to his country.' Over and over again this monotonous proclamation was made – but there was no corresponding raillery or outcry from the watching throng. It was Munro and Ross country, but for all that only silence greeted the procession, save for the occasional God bless you and cry of pity or shame.

Brahan Castle was Seaforth's eastern seat – but the Earl was still prudently on the Continent, and his brother Pluscarden no more in evidence here than he had been at Strathcarron. The Covenanters made very free with the Mackenzie's house and gear; but, as hitherto, Montrose was confined in the poorest quarters. Not that he cared. He had other matters to preoccupy his mind. Moreover, he grew to be on quite good terms with the common soldiers who were his immediate guards, and fared rather better than his captors intended.

Next day, by Beauly they came to Inverness, round the firth. Here again the Provost and magistrates were summoned to watch the parade, and the herald made his repeated proclamation. But here Provost Forbes of Culloden, a laird of some standing in his own right, chose to interpret Leslie's orders in his own way. He had tables of meats and drink laid out at the Mercat Cross, for all to partake, guards and prisoners – and noting Montrose's bound condition, he brought forward refreshments for him with his own hands. Leslie, taken by surprise, could not forbid it without an unedifying scene – and Forbes was an influential man.

'My lord,' the Provost said, bowing to the principal prisoner, 'I am sorry for your circumstances.'

Montrose smiled. 'I thank you, sir, for your kindness. I am no less sorry for being the object of your pity.'

Two of the town's ministers had come up, to stand behind the Provost – and whether because of the other's example, or otherwise, these did not rail upon and castigate the prisoner as others of their kind had done. Leslie sent an officer to announce, belatedly, that there must be no intercourse with the Estates' prisoner. Provost, ministers and captive eyed each other gravely, thoughtfully, for a little, and then turned away.

At Inverness a quite large group of prisoners from Carbisdale had already been assembled – and in fact were gathered here at the Cross to join Leslie's train, and also partaking of the provender. Amongst them James Graham was both glad and sorry to see many friends, some of whom he had feared dead, including Sir John Hurry, Sir James Douglas and Graham of Balgowan. His captors would not allow him to speak with these, of course, but at least they could exchange signals. He noted that Frendraught was not amongst them, and wondered. They were almost all bandaged, one way or another, witness to the fact that, however small the numbers involved, Carbisdale had been no cheaply won victory.

The enlarged cavalcade spent the night at Castle Stewart, near Nairn, a house of the Earl of Moray. Montrose had hoped to be quartered with the other prisoners, but he was still kept segregated – just as he must still ride the sorry nag, in rags, while the others wore their own clothes and rode cavalry chargers. In the towns of Nairn and Forres and Elgin some citizens duly turned out to jeer and mock, notably clergy, as Argyll had sent orders to be done – but very few in relation to the population; and no stones and filth was thrown, as was also the Campbell's instructions. On the contrary, there were many cries of sympathy and goodwill – which the captive acknowledged with the same quiet courtesy as he did the raillery.

They came to Keith, in upland Banffshire, on the Saturday night, the 8th of May, and the ministers with them insisted on a halt for the Sabbbath. In the morning Montrose must attend divine worship in the parish church, after a night spent in an open field. But this was no ordinary service, for he was permitted no change to decent clothing, and led, still bound with ropes, not to a pew amongst the other worshippers, but to a stool-of-repentance set apart and in front of all. And there he was preached at, at length and with vituperative vigour, by Master William Kininmonth, on the texts of 1st Samuel 15, verses 32–35; and 2nd Kings 18 at verse 17, the first concerned with the hewing to pieces of Agag and the fullest slaughter of the Amalekites, with an amplitude of gory details and assurances of eternal damnation. So overcome was the preacher with his religious fervour over the working out of the first text, that he had to pause, tears streaming down his cheeks, preparatory to launching on the second. Into the brief blessed silence, James Graham himself spoke – to the shocked offence of the godly.

'Rail on, Rabshakeh!' he observed, and swivelled round on his stool, to turn his back on the pulpit. The congregation did not know whether to be more distressed by the raising of a nonministerial voice in church, or by the fact that this excommunicate miscreant knew his Old Testament sufficiently well to cap the text thus appositely.

The endless journey was resumed next day.

They were now moving through the country over which Montrose had campaigned with such success and frequency. His captors sought to make the most of it, organising demonstrations and scenes, the herald who announced the approach of the dis- credited traitor being so employed almost continuously. Down through the centre of Aberdeenshire they went, avoiding the hill country to the west where Gordons or Farquharsons might just conceivably have attempted a rescue. At Pitcaple Castle, in the valley of the Urie, they spent the night of the 13th of May, and here destiny was almost cheated. For Leslie of Pitcaple had been King's man enough to serve in Hamilton's ill-fated Engagement attempt, and moreover his wife was in fact a far-out kinswoman of Montrose's own. In her husband's absence the lady played a subtle game, not on the face of it objecting to James Graham's treatment and segregation but instead feasting and wining Leslie and his officers in especially lavish fashion. And not only the officers, for she sent down to Montrose's immediate guards a sufficiency of whisky to put them all into a state of temulent beatitude and caring very little what happened to their prisoner. Around midnight, Lady Pitcaple herself came down to the castle vaults – to find her kinsman the only waking inmate. She told him that if he followed her, she could bring him to an under- ground passage, opening from a contiguous vault, which would bring him out beyond the courtyard's curtain-wall. She could not untie his bonds, but he ought to be able to hobble down to the river-side and get away.

Warmly he thanked her – and refused. 'Whether or not I escaped thus, in my person,' he said, 'I would never escape in my mind or my conscience. And I have reached such stage where my peace of mind is worth more than all else to me. Too many already have suffered and died, on my account. Kin of my own in especial. You are that. There would be no mercy for you. Being a woman would not save you from Argyll's spleen. More- over, your husband is already in bad odour with the Covenan- ters, over the Engagement trouble. My escape from his house could put a halter round his neck. I thank you – but no.'

Nothing the lady could say would shake his resolution. Weeping, she left.

For some reason Leslie avoided the city of Aberdeen thereafter, although it had no reason to love Montrose. They marched south by Kintore, Banchory on the Dee, and the Slug Road to Stonehaven, and so into the Mearns. And there, despite consistently rigorous treatment, Leslie showed a trace of humanity by turning eastwards at Brechin, down the River South Esk, and halting for a night at Kinnaird Castle, beside Old Montrose. Perhaps his objective was not all altruistic but partly to display to this Graham district the low estate to which his wickedness had brought James Graham, and the hopelessness of any betterment for him. And perhaps to underline, to the Earl of Southesk, the difficult position he was in through having such a son-in-law. But at least, though still held close captive, the prisoner was able to see his two younger children again, bitter-sweet as was this experience. And in an awkward and cryptic interview with Southesk, attended by guards, he heard something of his wife's last days and death – although he did not learn much thereby, for his father-in-law had never been of a forthcoming nature, or eloquent, especially towards the man whom he held to have encompassed the ruin of his daughter. But young Robert, now aged eleven, and Jean, aged six, were well and sturdy, and seemingly happy enough with their grandfather. Jamie now Earl of Kincardine, was safely out of the country, on his way to the Netherlands – where undoubtedly Elizabeth would look after him. With this Montrose had to be content.

Being led away from Kinnaird the following morning constituted the hardest trial of the entire grim journey.

Riding through the fair land of Angus, they stopped for the next night at the Durham house of Grange of Monifeith, between Arbroath and Dundee. Here again only an old lady was in charge – and of the same calibre as the Ladies Skibo and Pitcaple. Strangely enough she chose the same methods as the latter to display her resentment at the treatment of James Graham, managing to get the guard drunk once more, this time on strong ale and brandy. She came to the prisoner in the night, with women's clothing of her own for him to don – and after whispered argument he agreed to make the escape attempt. He told himself that she was no relative of his, and old enough surely to be free from even Campbell reprisals – at which, when he mentioned it, she snorted vigorously. Also, the laird, her son, was a confirmed Covenanter and member of the Estates. Unfortunately, however, the attempt came to naught, for it was a bright moonlight night, and one of the guard was not only a total abstainer from strong drink but evidently a restless noctambulist. At any rate, he was outside on the prowl, and observing what was seemingly two women emerging furtively from the back quarters, he went to investigate. In his wrist-bound state, and unarmed, Montrose could neither run nor fight and it was all over, amidst much outcry, in a few seconds. Thereafter the guard was changed, and neither befuddled miscreants, officer-in-charge, prisoner nor aged hostess, left in any doubts as to the weight of General Leslie's wrath.

It could be assumed that no similar opportunities for escape would be allowed to occur.

The city of Dundee, despite its sufferings in Montrose's campaigns, received the prisoner kindly, almost warmly, to Leslie's embarrassment, the magistrates insisting on greeting him with wine and refreshments at the Cross, and the streets thronged with quiet, respectful and sympathetic crowds. At sight of his rags, decent clothing was hastily produced, and his captors, not desiring to damn themselves as viciously heartless in the eyes of this consistently Covenanting city, did not refuse permission for the prisoner to change into it. He was still kept bound, however, and though the old grey nag had died under him, another equally decrepit mount had been found.

It was with real gratitude that James Graham left Dundee, dressed in a good black suit of broadcloth and, with head held higher, he faced the hostile Fife across Tay, and the still more hostile Edinburgh's smoke across Forth. A journey, any journey, was what a man made of it. This one had enriched him as much, perhaps, as any he had made.

CHAPTER TWENTY-SEVEN

Leslie had sent messengers ahead, and when the coastal vessel bearing Montrose and the other officer prisoners arrived at Leith on the Saturday afternoon of the 18th of May, 1650, there was no lack of preparations to receive it. A great crowd was present at the dockside, and Provost Sir James Stewart of Coltness and the magistrates of Edinburgh had come down in force to take charge of the captives, with the Town Guard – the same which had escorted James Graham on many another occasion. There was a certain amount of confusion at the harbour, for on the same tide a still larger vessel than Leslie's coaster from Dysart had sailed in, from Holland, bearing no less than King Charles's personal envoy Sir William Fleming, with messages, oddly enough, both for his Captain-General and for the latter's enemies Argyll and the Estates. When Fleming learned that the reception was staged not for himself but for a captive Montrose, he was somewhat put out, especially when he perceived the sort of reception it was, and that he was not to be allowed to present the King's letter to this recipient. His information that it was, amongst other things, King Charles's command to the Captain-General to lay down his arms and disband his forces on agreed and honourable terms, was greeted with considerable hooting and rudery.

Montrose himself, on disembarking, was left in no doubts that from now on nothing would be left to chance. The Provost and Council ceremoniously greeted Leslie and his staff but studiously ignored the prisoners. Not so certain ministers, cheer-leaders and rabble-rousers, commissioned to lead the populace in abuse and contumely, who, at a given signal, raised a great shouting, pointing and jeering at the traitor James Graham, slayer of the innocent, friend of Papists, sold to the Devil, excommunicate and man of blood. The good folk of Leith did not rise to the occasion, however, being always suspicious of orders from Edinburgh anyway, but watched in silence. The eggers-on grew the more hysterical.

The prisoners were not left alone while the Provost collogued with Leslie. The Town Guard roughly marshalled all save Montrose into a column for the two-mile march up to the Capital from the firth-shore – the craft they had sailed in from Fife had had no accommodation for horses and only Leslie's and one or two other mounts had been shipped over. An old heavy cart-horse had been found for Montrose himself, without saddle or bridle, and on this he was placed, tied as before with ropes, with a scullion-boy to lead it. They waited for a considerable time while Leslie, and also the doubtful Fleming, partook of the Provost's refreshment. Then at last the march to Edinburgh began, the herald chanting his monotonous announcement before, the other prisoners shuffling along on foot.

They entered the city by the Water Gate, at the east and bottom end of the Canongate, near Holyroodhouse and the Abbey. Here a new deputation awaited the entourage, consisting now of the city's law officers plus the public hangman. Provost Stewart and the magistrates had apparently played their part, and like Leslie drew aside, while the minions of justice took over.

First of all a lengthy proclamation of the Estates was read out, declaring that since James Graham had already been tried, found guilty of treason, forfeited and excommunicated, there was no need for, nor could there be, further trial. Only the manner of carrying out the sentence of death had had to be decided, and this was now pronounced. The foresworn traitor and renegade, as well as forfeiting all rights, estates, properties, titles and life, had also forfeited the right to die in any seemly fashion appropriate to his former rank and style. He was to be conducted to the Tolbooth of Edinburgh, there to be lodged in the lowest common cell. From thence, in due course, he was to be taken to the town gibbet to be hanged as a common malefactor, not executed on the block like a more worthy rebel. But he was not to escape the axe altogether, for after being hanged his head was to be hewn from off his trunk and placed on a spike above the said Tolbooth; and each of his limbs were likewise to be severed from his body and sent to be displayed in prominent places in the towns of Glasgow, Stirling, Perth and Aberdeen, there to remain for all time coming. What remained of the trunk was to be thrown, unburied, into the felons' pit on the Burgh-muir of Edinburgh. If, however, in God's great mercy, he was to publicly and fully repent of all his wicked misdeeds and shameful treasons and murders and heresies, his excommunication might be withdrawn, and his limbless, headless trunk permitted to be buried in that Greyfriars kirkyard where he had once been first to sign the noble National Covenant which he had so basely and impiously betrayed. In all this process it was hoped, instructed and commanded that the citizens of Edinburgh as representing all whom James Graham had maltreated, shamed and caused to suffer, would display their hatred and revulsion against the said traitor, with every means at their disposal. This was the sentence of the Committee of the Estates of Scotland, given on the 17th day of May, the year of Our Gracious Lord 1650. God save the King!

The reader handed this impressive document to Montrose to scan, that he might verify the writing, signatures, seals and all relevant details, but he shook his head.

'I thank you, sir – no,' he said. ' I have heard it very well, and am sure that you read it accurately. My only concern is that His Grace, my master and yours, whose royal commission I bear, should be thus dishonoured by being invoked in so sorry a matter.'

The hangman, who had his open flat cart with him, drawn by four horses, was now motioned forward. He untied the principal captive's bonds – but only to lead him to the cart, to tie him thereon again, an arm stretched out and bound on either side to the vehicle.

'Why this, friend ?' James Graham asked.

'Orders,' the man muttered, uneasily. 'Sae you'll no' can ward off whit's thrown at you, man.'

'Ah, I see. All is thought of.'

The other snatched off Montrose's old Highland bonnet, which he had worn for so long. 'Orders, tae. You're to be uncovered, see you. And I'm no'.' And he tapped the red bonnet he wore himself.

'You are welcome, indeed.'

So the final short stage of a long journey was commenced, up the Canongate's cobbles, between the tall grey gabled lands and tenements where Scotland's aristocracy had their town-houses amongst the teeming warrens, pig-sties and poultry-sheds of lesser folk. The narrow street was packed, and Montrose braced himself on his cart to face the hail of filth and missiles recommended by authority of State and Church. Yet, strangely, none was forthcoming. At a snail's pace, in complete silence save for the clop-clop of the horses' hooves, the creaking of the cart and the shuffling of feet behind, the procession made its way up the crowded climbing thoroughfare, with scarcely room for it to pass – and whatever men and women thought, not a hand or a voice was raised.

Just the hint of a smile played about James Graham's unwashed, unshaven and wasted, but still supremely handsome, features, as he thought of the day he had ridden up this same street with Johnnie Kilpont, straight from London and King Charles I's rejection, and decided that though he loved Scotland he did not love Edinburgh. He might be seeing Kilpont again soon now – and they could compare impressions! Seeing others too, perhaps, who had gone on ahead – his own eager Johnnie, and poor lost Magdalen, lost no longer, God being good. Aye, and Archie Napier the father, Magnus O'Cahan, Will Rollo, Tom Ogilvy, Nat Gordon. All the best of his friends had gone on already – a blessed thought. Save only Elizabeth – and Black Pate Graham. George Gordon, now – he would rejoice to see George again, George, who had chosen in the end to die for him against his own father, and died a clean death in battle, as consequence . . .

It was by chance that, as his mind dwelt on George, Lord Gordon, whom he had loved, his head-high glance lighted on dark eyes that stared on him from quite close by. Eyes gazed at him, of course, from every window of the teeming lands, rich and poor, nobles and burghers and common folk, and he returned none of the stares. But these eyes were different, seeming to bore into him, filled with venom, hate – the eyes of George Gordon's own sister, the Lady Jean, now married to the young Earl of Haddington. With a group of richly dressed personages she was standing on a stone balcony projecting from one of the windows of the Earl of Moray's townhouse. Because of the projection, and the narrowness of the street, they were only a few feet from the cart, though slightly higher. As Montrose approached, the young Countess suddenly laughed shrilly, a shocking, hysterical sound in the prevalent hush. Then leaning forward, she spat directly in James Graham's face.

He was unable to wipe away the spittle. He did not even turn his face away. Instead he eyed her wonderingly. The Gordons had always been a strange, unpredictable family, George much the best of them – and she had seen her father led to be executed here in Edinburgh, and might well somehow blame himself as partly responsible.

He did not answer her – but someone in the throng below

answered for him, in justice or otherwise. 'You painted whore!' a woman's voice yelled. 'Yoursel' it is should be in the cairt, paying for your adulteries, you!'

There was a low rumble of agreement from the crowd, and then the silence resumed.

James Graham had scarcely heard that last. For, standing next to Jean Gordon on the balcony he had suddenly recognised an exquisite young man to be none other than another Archibald Campbell, Lord Lorne, Argyll's son – and the recognition reminded him that one of his guards had told him a day or two before that his great enemy's heir was being wed that week to the Earl of Moray's daughter. This, then, would be the wedding-party at Moray House, still celebrating. Immediately, as he trundled past, his glance swept the others on the balcony – and there, sure enough, half hidden behind the others, typically, he caught a glimpse of two hooded foxy eyes, one of them squint, under reddish brows, beside the pale cadaverous features of Johnston of Warriston, now Lord Warriston of Session no less. For a timeless moment James Graham and Archibald Campbell eyed each other in eloquent if wordless communion. Then *MacCailean Mor* turned abruptly away, knuckles to mouth, and pushing Warriston aside got back through the window, and flung the shutter to behind him. Montrose continued on his creaking way.

And now his small smile was, although no broader, assured, content, almost triumphant. For, in a way, he had won. Won his last long and personal battle. Only he and the Campbell knew it – but who else did it concern? That brief exchange proclaimed him the victor, beyond all manner of doubt, an old score settled at last. The rest he could face untroubled – and indeed the sooner the better.

It took a long time to win up the steep mile of Canongate and High Street, past the Canongate Tolbooth, the Netherbow Port and the scores of noblemen's lodgings, where faces peered or peeped from behind glass, curtains or shutters. At the Mercat Cross beside St. Giles, James Graham was paraded round the high gibbet erected for him – and recalled, with even a trace of wry amusement, how the Earl of Rothes had said to him one day, on this very spot, 'Watch you – or you'll no' be at rest till you are lifted up above the rest o' us on three fathoms o' a rope!' He would perhaps have the opportunity to congratulate Rothes on that curious prophecy quite shortly now.

They untied him then and flung him into the filthy, dark, semi-subterranean vault of the city's Tolbooth – from which, by the smells and atmosphere, the usual occupants – thieves, pickpockets and harlots – had only just been removed to make room for him. From the Estates' declaration he had expected to be incarcerated with these felons – and knew not whether to be glad or sorry. He had been denied anyone to talk with, although surrounded by people, for two weeks. He still had a few coins, and instructed the hangman to put hand into his pocket to take them, as was the custom and very wise precaution.

He sank down upon the dirty straw of a corner, and closed his eyes – for he was in fact very tired. It had been a long and trying day – it had taken over two hours to come up from the Water Gate, and the city bells were now ringing for seven o'clock.

He had barely sat down, however, when lamps were brought to light up the sordid scene – and he understood why the cell had been cleared of its former occupants, when a group of black-robed divines and a deputation from the Estates was ushered in. Montrose recognised some of them, including Master James Guthrie, minister of the High Kirk at Stirling, one of the most prominent of the Covenanting party, who appeared to be in charge. These did not greet the prisoner as a person, but set about their business without delay or preamble, Master Guthrie launching into a lengthy prayer which his companions punctuated with frequent Amens, evidently to encourage rather than to bring to a halt. Though it was not in fact so much a prayer as a vigorous reminder to Almighty God of the full scale and enormity of the sins of the wretched miscreant and ruthless assassin here before Him, a catalogue of accusation in the form of a demand for suitable divine vengeance. When at length this came to a close, one of the clerks of the Estates stepped forward and declared that he was sent and empowered to examine the prisoner on sundry matters, a dull and mumbling lawyer who peered at a paper in the poor light the while. Quickly having enough of this, Montrose interrupted.

'Forgive me, sir – but I fear that I am in no state to give due and proper heed to your remarks. I am somewhat weary with the compliments you and yours have already put upon me this day. I shall be a better listener on another occasion, I promise you. I request that you, and your reverend friends, do me the honour to leave, for this night.'

The clerk puffed, indignant. 'How, how dare you! You, a

condemned prisoner! I come here with the authority of the Estates of Parliament.'

'The Estates of Parliament have no authority, sir, save from the King's Grace. I serve the King, and the King only. I hold his royal commission as his personal representative and Viceroy. Until His Grace supersedes that commission, I decline to accept any lesser authority. I can do no less, without reducing His Grace's position. *Has* King Charles superseded my commission, sir? I understand that letters from him, to myself as also to the Estates, arrived this afternoon.'

The lawyer hesitated, and conferred in a whisper with one of his fellows, while the ministers muttered angrily. Then he cleared his throat. 'The King and the Estates are now come to full agreement,' he declared. 'Your commissions and authority are no longer of any effect.'

'My commission and authority was given me directly by the King. Likewise termination of that authority must also come to me from the King. Have you brought me His Grace's letter, addressed to me?'

'That is unnecessary.'

'It is entirely necessary. Until I have read the signed and sealed writings of King Charles relieving me of my offices and responsibilities, which he put upon me, as King of Scots, I am still Viceroy and Captain-General. You will return and tell the Committee of Estates so, sir. And inform that, as such, I require to appear before them, in the King's royal name. Now, go, if you please. All of you. The day has proved something tedious. I am now going to sleep.'

And, strangely, they went, his authority – whether Charles Stewart had revoked it, or not – sufficiently evident and effective or that, at least.

*   *   *

The morrow was the Lord's Day and James Graham knew well what this was likely to involve. It meant another grim day to live through, for the Kirk would never allow his hanging on a Sunday. He had now reached the stage of wishing it all over, and a day's remission was no cause for satisfaction.

He was not dragged to church, as on the previous Sabbath, but the day's carefully arranged programme was by no means delayed till after the period of public worship. Ministers would no doubt declare his infamy and shame from every city pulpit, but sufficient others were found to repair to the Tolbooth at an early hour, before even the guard had breakfasted, to harangue the prisoner and leave him in no doubt that this was not to be a day of rest for him. Master Guthrie was back again, with the Reverends Robert Traill and Mungo Law and others, set on convincing Montrose that he was the most depraved and abandoned of God's creation, unworthy almost to be so-called – yet the Almighty's mercy, as shown forth by his true Body on earth, the Kirk of Scotland, was such that a contrite and detailed repentance might even yet result in his obtaining the grace of a Christian burial, and his soul's journey towards the terrible judgment-seat might be started at least without the complete and assured eternal damnation involved in dying excommunicate.

James Graham heard them out, thanked them for their concern for his immortal soul, but reminded that he, like them, had been journeying towards judgment all his days, and that he did not see that any last-moment recantations were likely to deceive the all-seeing Father – a Popish doctrine which he was surprised to find his Presbyterian friends clinging to. Moreover he had chosen to make this last stage of his journey uncomplaining and at peace with himself. He was a great sinner undoubtedly, but his sins had not been against the King, the Kirk or the people of Scotland, but against the good God Himself; therefore the matter of repentance was between him and his Maker and Saviour, none other. He therefore wished them all a good day – and sought leave to make his peace with God in private.

Loud were the rejections of this shameful arrogance and indeed blasphemous insult to the Almighty and to Christ's Kirk. *They* were the interpreters of God's laws and commands, not a forsworn, blood-drenched excommunicate. They and only they had the power to grant him Christian burial and lift damnation from his perjured soul. How dare he contemplate his last journey to the gibbet unforgiven by Holy Kirk? If yesterday's progress on the hangman's cart was shame, how much more appalling would be the final unrepentant journey to hell's eternal flames?

Gravely he informed the clerics that, though he was sorry to disappoint them, he had found yesterday's journey quite the most honourable and satisfying he had ever made, with God's loving presence in fact nearer to him than he had been privileged to know previously. But – perhaps they did not worship the same God?

395

At this ultimate profanity, the divines left him, shocked to the core, and it was the turn of the secular arm. This was represented by members of the Committee of the Estates, led by Warriston and the Provost Sir James Stewart of Coltness again – who was at pains to point out that though the final arrangements for the execution were *his* responsibility, as chief magistrate, the rigorous terms as to the cutting up and disposal of the body were wholly the Committee's.

Montrose sympathised.

Warriston, that hot-eyed fanatic, though seeming older as well as more richly clad, was as tense and perfervid as ever. When the prisoner asked kindly after the Marquis of Argyll, whom he thought had not looked well yesterday, the other swallowed convulsively, his prominent Adam's-apple leaping about as though of independent life, and forthwith launched into a tirade. He declared, amidst a positive spray of saliva which his hearer found distressing, that he, James Graham, was about to suffer the well-merited end of all who betrayed their Creator, their nation, their Church and their fellow-men. That he was a man whose savagery against the State was equalled only by the viciousness of his private life, as was well known. That he had not only signed but helped to word the Covenant – and then had taken up arm against it, and moreover employed heathen Irish barbarians to terrorise Scotland and spill oceans of his own compatriots' blood.

When the speaker had to pause for very panted breath, Montrose shook his head. 'If I was even half of what you call me, my Lord Warriston, I would deserve all that your busy Committee have planned for me. But you, as one of this realm's judges, are surely bound by the common rules of evidence and proof? What evidence do you have that I ever spoke or acted against the National Covenant which I signed? You have none, for I did not do so. As for the so-called Solemn League and Covenant, this I had no part in, nor could have, since it is a shameful denial of the liberties of free men. That I oppose, yes – and will go on opposing so long as there is breath in my body. Which is not like to be long, I thank God! That I led Irish troops, amongst others, I agree and rejoice in, for they were better fighters than any they opposed, and were, moreover, as much subjects of the King for whom they and I fought as were the Scots rebels they so soundly beat. As for their religion, I am no Papist any more than you are, sir – but did General Leslie refuse to fight alongside

General Cromwell's Ironsides because they were not Presbyterians? Or did you refuse to employ General Middleton because he is an Episcopalian? That a man's religion is his own is something else that I will gladly die for, yours, mine, or the Irish. As to shedding Scottish blood, this I swear by all that I hold holy – and in my present position, you will agree, I should not so swear lightly – that I grieved sorely for every drop that was shed, and sought with all my power to avoid anything such . . .'

'Liar!' Warriston shouted. 'Liar!'

He shrugged. 'Would *you* lie when you are to die the next day? And, tell me also – how much good Scots blood was shed after Philiphaugh? And by whom? You sir, I heard, demanded the death penalty on many friends of mine.'

'They were traitors, all traitors. And deserved death.'

'Traitors to whom? Not to their King. So, my lord of Session, Scots blood may be shed, so be it that it is the blood of those who oppose Archibald Campbell and Archibald Johnston! Not others. Is that the Court of Session's justice in 1650?'

'It is the Estates of Scotland that condemns you. Not me. Nor the Court of Session.'

'Ah, yes. The Estates. They condemn me? Sitting as a court?'

'They did. And most rightly.'

'My lord – you are a judge. And I a magistrate. So that we know something of court procedure. Can you tell me how I could be condemned by any court of justice before which I have not appeared? To which no evidence of defence has been given, or sought? Hang me by all means, and the sooner the better for my comfort. But do not cloak your murder under the names of trial or sentence. Or anything other than hatred. Be honest, at least!'

All but frothing at the lips, Warriston rushed out of the cell, and in some confusion the others followed him.

Only then was James Graham allowed his breakfast of oatmeal. His request for water to wash and a razor to shave were, as usual, refused. The officer of the Town Guard, a drunken boorish individual named Weir, leeringly explained that the prisoner might choose to cut his throat with the razor and so cheat the hangman.

All that day Montrose was harassed by relays of ministers, parliamentarians and officials of the law. Never for a moment was he left alone, for when there were no deputations, Major Weir filled the cell with his minions of the Guard and led them in mockery and witticisms. These the prisoner was largely able to ignore, drawing into himself. But it had got around that he disliked tobacco smoke, and most evidently the authorities had seized on this, for the Guard were supplied with unlimited quantities of the weed, with the fumes of which they filled his vault and took delight in puffing in their captive's face. Strangely enough he found this pettiness, of all his trials, the sorest to bear.

It made an endless day. But the evening brought slight relief, for the obnoxious Weir went off duty and was replaced by an older lieutenant of less vicious disposition, who cleared the soldiers out of the cell and actually left Montrose with a lamp, so that he could read the small pocket Bible which had never left his person throughout all his wanderings, and had provided an unfailing source of solace and strength. It did not fail him now.

Later that night the new officer returned, bearing a bundle of clothing, including a quite handsome suit of black and silver, red silken hose and good buckled shoes, with a scarlet cloak laced with gold filigree, also a broad-brimmed black beaver hat with silver cord.

'Ladies gave this in for your lordship,' the lieutenant said. 'They gave no names, but wished you very well, and God-speed.'

'That was kind, indeed.' It would probably be the Napiers, from Merchiston not far away, his niece and his nephew's wife. 'And kind of *you*, my friend, to let me have them. Others would not. I should be sorry if you were to suffer for your actions. Major Weir would not approve, I think.'

'I care not for Weir. He was too drunk to give me any instructions. Besides, I take my orders from the Provost, Sir James Stewart. And he is not a hard man.' He cleared his throat. 'I, I have been through the pockets, my lord. That I had to do, see you. There was a razor. I took it out. Orders. But there is some money. Paper. A quill and ink-horn. I had no orders against such.'

'I am greatly in your debt, sir. These will make so much of difference. Also I thank you for leaving me in peace. And for the lamp. God will reward you one day, if I cannot.'

'I want no reward, lord. I mind well your lordship, in happier days. I am for the King, as are most folk. But what can we do ?'

'Your time will come, friend. But – I will pray that you do not suffer for what you have permitted.'

'I heard the Provost saying that you are to be taken before the Estates tomorrow. Your lordship will require to be decently dressed for that. If I am questioned, I will say that I believed it is for that the clothes were fetched. As, belike, it is.'

'The Estates . . . ? This is strange, is it not ? The Estates *sent* me their declaration and sentence. They were finished with me. What more is there to say, or do ? Save hang me.'

'I know not, my lord. But I heard Sir James say something of a letter from the King, just come. It may be – I do not know – that it might be that you are yet to be saved. Reprieved.'

'No, no, my friend. Not that, I assure you. King Campbell rules Scotland still, not King Charles. And the Campbell will not permit any reprieve for *me*, whatever the King's letters may say. That I know well. What the Estates wish of me, other than my speedy end, I do not know. But . . . it means that I will have another grievous day to face. I had hoped for quicker . . . release.'

The lieutenant bit his lip and turned away. At the cell door he paused. 'My lord,' he said hesitantly, 'I'd have you know – many feel for you. Many wish you well. The folk – they are not for this. They know you the King's friend. But . . .' Shrugging, he left the rest unsaid, and Montrose was alone again.

Now, of course, his mind was in a turmoil, much less settled and resigned than heretofore. He believed what he had said about Argyll's implacable resolution to have him dead, and the unlikelihood of any repreive; but he would have been more than human not to have grasped at even this slender straw of hope, however much he told himself not to. And the kindness represented in the bringing of these clothes, and the officer's words, although uplifting his heart, unsettled him. He had steeled himself to accept harshness and savagery; but benevolence, humanity, was another matter, tending to upset. He was scarcely used to it.

The pen and ink was a great comfort, with the lamp. He could write now. Whether letters would be allowed to go out from here, he did not know – but he could try it. He wrote a long letter to Elizabeth, commending his son James to her care, making lighter of his position than the facts warranted, and avoiding any criticism of her nephew Charles. He wrote also, less fully, to his own nephew Archie Napier, again carefully avoiding anything which could be of aid to his enemies, if read – as these letters almost certainly would be. Then, since sleep seemed far away, he tried to compose and discipline his disturbed mind from going over and over the faint possibilities of reprieve, by setting down the poem, or some of it, which he had been turning over in his mind these last days. It was not far from morning before he extinguished the lamp.

The new day brought back Major Weir and renewed harsh conditions. Mocking comment was made on the fine clothes the prisoner now had – but there was no attempt to make him divest himself. No doubt Weir assumed they had been officially ordered and provided for the day's programme. In mid forenoon officers arrived to conduct the captive over to Parliament House, a short distance. The lieutenant had evidently been right, and the Committee of the Estates had had cause to think again.

Wrists still tied with rope, he was put into an ante-room with a guard, and left there for a full hour, wondering. Then he was led into the same Parliament Hall where he had appeared as accused prisoner before this, the last time with King Charles I himself a silent observer. He found himself in the presence of about a dozen men, most of whom he knew well, former colleagues on the Tables and other committees. The Chancellor, the Earl of Loudoun, occupied the chair, so that it was presumably a sitting of the official Committee of the Estates. Of the Chancellor's chief, Argyll, there was no sign – although that strange man might be lurking and peeping from behind any door. Warriston was there, in the capacity of secretary, the Earls of Cassillis and Eglinton, the Lords Balmerino and Balfour of Burleigh, and others. Some way apart sat a group of ministers. By their own Assembly's decision they could not take part in Estates business – but they could watch and scowl. There was not a remotely friendly glance in that chamber.

James Graham bowed briefly, and spoke before any other had time to do so.

'I give you a good morning, my lords and gentlemen,' he said equably, assuredly. 'I am glad to see your faces. At last. And not before time, I think you will agree. You, my Lord Chancellor, have much to make clear to me, the King's Lieutenant, have you not?'

'Silence!' Loudoun banged on his table. 'The prisoner will speak only when spoken to. Only in answer to questions. Remove the man's hat.'

'In this Parliament Hall of our realm, my lord, you cannot prevent me speaking. Apart from His Grace's royal commission which I hold, I am an Earl of Scotland, of somewhat more ancient vintage than any here! I belong to this place, of right, as my fathers have done before me. Had you wished for my silence, you should not have brought me *here*.'

'Watch your insolent tongue, traitor!' Loudoun turned to Warriston. 'Proceed.'

Clearing throat nervously, that uneasy individual began to read from a lengthy paper, with none of the fire and vigour with which he had once read the National Covenant. It was dry, wordy, lawyer's stuff, and it took some time before Montrose perceived what was the gist of it. Presently it became evident however that it was a pronunciamento to the effect that the King had written to his Scots Parliament on the 8th day of May declaring that on the 2nd he had signed a treaty with his loyal Scots commissioners at Breda, by which he agreed to accept the Solemn League and Covenant and all its provisions, and to disband all armed forces mustered against the said Scottish Estates. Further His Majesty had commanded his former Captain-General and Viceroy, James Graham, to lay down his arms. If the said James Graham did so, without further hostile acts against the Estates, then His Majesty recommended him and his men to the mercy of his loyal Estates, and suggested that he and they, if they so wished, should be permitted to leave the country.

With some shuffling of papers, Warriston, pausing, glanced towards Loudoun. There was complete silence in the great chamber.

'However,' he went on, picking his words more carefully now, 'on the 12th day of May there was a further letter from His Majesty, in which he disclaimed all responsibility for the actions of the said James Graham, and declared that the previous letter, of the 8th of May, was not to be delivered and read, or if it had been so, it was to be countermanded. The result therefore of His Majesty's correspondence and wishes is that the prisoner James Graham no longer holds any commission soever of the King's Grace, and that any recommendations to mercy are withdrawn. The authority of the Committee of the Estates, therefore, to pronounce and enforce sentence, is clear and unchallengeable.'

Listening, Montrose groaned in his spirit for Charles Stewart – but also did some quick calculations, and thought that he understood. The Treaty of Breda had been signed on the 2nd of May, and the King had written a letter on the 5th ordering a disbandment of forces and acquainting the Estates that this was done. Then on the 8th he had apparently written another letter to the Estates, which was not here quoted, the one now countermanded. This, no doubt, was the one Sir William Fleming had brought to Leith, with one for himself which he had not been allowed to see. Probably it contained instructions for his, Montrose's safety and good treatment. It had to be nullified therefore, countermanded, if this execution was not to be an obvious and illegal spurning of the King's commands and wishes. Therefore this alleged letter of the 12th of May was either a forgery or had been doctored. The former more likely, for this was only the 20th of May, and this document had been worked upon for at the very least a day before. Given favourable conditions, it would have been just about right for Fleming to reach Leith on the 18th, leaving Breda on the 8th. But for a letter written on the 12th to be here before the 19th was all but impossible.

So he recognised now why he had been brought here this morning. The King's letters brought by Fleming had changed the legalities of the situation as far as the parliamentary forfeiture, trial in absence and condemnation were concerned. Therefore a seeming new condemnation and sentence had to be put through, in a hurry, which did not appear to conflict with the royal wishes – since the Treaty of Breda accepted Charles as the lawful monarch and would bring him to Scotland shortly. That almost certain forgery had been necessary to contrive it would be a small enough matter for Campbell government, and could be blamed on other hands later. It explained the delay in carrying out the death sentence – and undoubtedly implied that such delay would not last much longer.

John Campbell of Loudoun took up the attack. He was a poor speaker, and had nothing new to say. He merely reiterated all the old assertions about betraying Covenant, Kirk and country, soaking the land in blood at the hands of Irish savages, and the imperative need for Scotland to be rid of such a scourge once and for all. God had brought James Graham to a just punishment. Before receiving sentence had the prisoner anything to say?

Clearly Warriston had passed on Montrose's observations as to the invalidity of a court which condemned a captive unheard and without defence. He knew well that the sentence would be the same, and that this was a formality to give it a more lawful flavour. After all he had answered to his inquisitors in his cell, there was really nothing worth adding. But he had to exercise his right to speak.

He did so restrainedly, declaring that since the Estates had now accepted the King's authority, he looked on this Committee as sitting in the monarch's name and so was content to appear bareheaded as though His Grace was indeed present. He averred that all he had done was done in the name and with the authority of the King. The National Covenant he was still faithful to. As for the Solemn League, he had never had hand in it, for which he thanked his Maker, for it was nothing but a shame and a distress to both kingdoms. As for military matters he admitted that disorders could not entirely be prevented in any army, but that anything such that he learned of amongst his troops he had punished severely, and that instead of indicting him for spilling Scots blood they should rather thank him for preserving many thousands of lives, as had ever been his close concern. Lastly, he had come back to Scotland the last month on their King's direct command, in order to accelerate agreement in instilling an urgency into the situation – whereby this Treaty of Breda had in fact been brought to a speedier conclusion. He sought therefore to be judged by the laws of God, of nature and of nations, and moreover the laws of this land. And if they decided against him, he appealed with more confidence to the righteous Judge of all the world, who one day must be both *their* judge and his own.

They heard him in silence, although the ministers coughed and muttered.

Then, without comment, Loudoun ordered him to his knees to hear sentence in an appropriate posture. When James Graham remained standing, the guards were ordered to bring him to the floor, which they did easily enough by kicking him behind the knees and then holding him down.

Thereafter, Warriston read the same detailed sentence as to hanging, beheading, quartering and displaying, without Christian burial, exactly as it had been pronounced at the Water Gate. The charade over, the Chancellor curtly ordered the prisoner's removal back to his cell, and sentence to be carried out the next day at two o'clock in the afternoon. God save the King!

Before the words were fully out, the Committee-members were rising to leave.

* * *

That night, his last in this present state, even though he was not left alone as on the previous evening, James Graham, at peace in his mind again, with all uncertainty past, was able to finish the poem he had started, amidst the bickerings and jeers of his guards, and wrote also a sort of grim little prayer as counterblast to their persistent raillery, his lips curving to a small smile as he penned it.

> *Let them bestow on every airt a limb,*
> *Then open all my veins that I may swim*
> *To Thee, my Maker, in that crimson lake;*
> *Then place my parboiled head upon a stake,*
> *Scatter my ashes, strew them in the air –*
> *Lord! Since Thou knowest where all these atoms are,*
> *I'm hopeful Thou'lt recover once my dust,*
> *And confident Thou'lt raise me with the just.*

He even read this out to his drunken crew, when he could gain silence – and did achieve an abashed hush for a little thereafter. And in it told himself that this was scarcely the note on which to end his earthly compositions. So he set down again these extra lines, which he had made up long before and still saw no reason to refute, as a sort of postscript:

> *He either fears his fate too much,*
> *Or his deserts are small,*
> *That dares not put it to the touch,*
> *To gain or lose it all.*

He blessed the kind thought of his anonymous benefactors who had brought him the pen, ink and paper.

When the last of the guard had staggered through to the guardroom, he arranged his clothes decently for the morrow, extinguished the lamp, and lay down on his straw. Unlike the night before with its questions and errant hopes, he fell asleep almost as soon as he closed his eyes, and slept as peacefully as a child.

To awaken knowingly to one's last morning on earth is by any standards an experience of some profundity, conducive to a sharpening of the perceptions and a discarding of the superficial and the frivolous, even though a sense of relief may be a major reaction. Nevertheless, James Graham took particular care with his toilet on this occasion, in so far as he might. He was still denied the use of a razor, but he obtained cold water to wash his person thoroughly. He dusted his clothing as best he could, sought to sponge off stains, wiped his shoes clean with straw, and combed his hair and beard.

The ministers were back at him from an early hour, and though he requested that his last hours might be private, they would have none of it, determined up to the last moment to effect the saving of his soul. He did ask if he might be permitted to say goodbye to any of his friends who might be available, and would so honour him, but this was refused.

It made an interminable forenoon.

At length the Provost arrived, with the bailies and official execution party, which included Warriston but none of the other principals. Sir James Stewart was uncomfortable, almost apologetic. When the prisoner was ready, they would proceed. There was no hurry. If the godly ministers required longer . . . ?

'No, sir – let us be on our way,' Montrose told him. 'I have been too long a-dying, as it is. If the reverend gentlemen have not been able to recover my soul by now, we must needs just leave it to our Maker! Proceed, Sir James.' And he raised his bound hands to put on his beaver.

Promptly Major Weir snatched it off his head, with a curse, much disarranging his hair in the process. 'You'll no' need that!' he declared.

'True, sir. I thank you for reminding me.' James Graham took his comb from a pocket, with difficulty, and ran it two-handedly through his fine, long, wavy hair, to restore its neatness.

Breathing hard, Warriston protested. 'Man – in your state you would be better taking care for your immortal soul than for your worthless body and appearance, combing the hairs of your head!'

'My lord, my head is still mine own. Tonight, when it shall be yours, treat it as you will.' He finished the combing, and bowed to the Provost.

So at last Montrose finally left Edinburgh's Tolbooth and emerged into the packed High Street. A sudden silence at the sight of him was broken by a resounding roll of drums from massed soldiery drawn up to line both sides of the street.

'Military honours also!' he remarked, to the Provost.

'A precaution, just,' Sir James, a humourless man, corrected. 'That all remember that the guard is sufficient strong. To prevent any attempt at rescue.'

'A rescue? Here? Soldiers? Am I still a terror to them, then?' The prisoner smiled. 'I think, aye I think even my *ghost* will haunt them! After you, Provost.'

They had only a short distance to walk to the scaffold and gibbet beside the Mercat Cross, where the hangman awaited them. James Graham greeted him, as he mounted to the first platform, almost as an old friend.

'A good day to you. To us both. Our meeting again has been unduly delayed. Through no will of mine, I assure you. Ah – who have we here?'

Since now the Kirk had washed its hands of him, at last, and no friends were permitted to be with the rejected excommunicate, a young boy had been deputed to act as final ministrant, and to take down on a paper any last-moment confession or statement – a nice touch. The youngster had in his hands, as well as paper, pen and ink horn, a leather-bound book and a roll of parchment. Also a small length of rope. Taking this in at a glance, Montrose looked to where the Reverends Robert Traill and Mungo Law stood, at the far side of the gallows-platform, at their most severe, as though what followed was nothing to do with them, thank God. He bowed.

'Too young to be contaminated?' he enquired interestedly.

They answered nothing.

He turned back to the boy. 'Your name, young man? Since you are to help me thus, on my way. And what have you there, with the Bible?'

'No Bible, sir,' the lad answered clearly. 'It is for, for him.' And he nodded towards the hangman. 'And my name is Robert Gordon, sir.'

'Ha – Gordon! Here is a joyful omen. I knew another Gordon lad, not unlike yourself, once. And loved him well. It may be that I shall see him very shortly now. I thank you for your attendance, Robert Gordon.'

'I have to write down what you say, sir.'

'Ah, yes. I know that it is customary to address a speech to the company on such occasions. Though, to tell truth, I am something weary of words, lad.'

'No, sir – not to the company, sir. It is not allowed. Only to me – that I may write it down.'

'You say so, Robert? A strange provision. But as well, perhaps. For I have no great deal to say. And you will not be so rushed, in setting it forth.'

Clearing his throat, the hangman stepped forward. 'First of all sir – there's this. As commanded.' He took the book, the scroll and the rope from the boy, and tied the two items together at either end of the rope. James Graham noted that the man's hands were trembling – and hoped that they would not tremble too greatly for efficiency hereafter. He also perceived that the book was a copy of his own *Life and Memoirs* by George Wishart, and the parchment was the declaration of his sentence of hanging and quartering. By the rope, the hangman hung these around his neck.

'Why, friend, this is a most kindly thought,' he commented. 'My vanity, perhaps? But I am as glad to have one as the other by me, my life and my death conveniently to hand!'

'Speak now,' the other grunted. 'But quietly, see you. No' to the folk. They dinna want a disturbance.'

'Of course. A disturbance would be unseemly.' Montrose looked a little doubtfully at the waiting dark-eyed boy. He seemed an unlikely recipient for a man's last expressed thoughts. It would be Warriston's strange and twisted mind which had thought of that, for a certainty. Warriston was watching now, from just below the front of the scaffold. There was no sign of Argyll, as usual, a modest man who ever preferred the background.

Montrose turned to the Provost and group of bailies who waited on the scaffold behind him, well apart from the two ministers, and spoke conversationally.

'I am sorry if this matter of my end is something scandalous for any good Christian, my friends. Who knows the rights and wrongs of it? For my own sins, I acknowledge it to be just before God. For my public acts, I see it . . . otherwise.' He paused, thinking of the busy scribe. 'I forgive those who have brought it about. I forgive them also, if less heartily than I should, for their oppression of the poor, and their perversion of judgment and justice in this kingdom. If God forgives sins, which I do believe, who am I to do otherwise? Indeed, who am I to say anything, at this juncture? Save that what I have done, in Scotland, was done on the commands of my sovereign, and yours. I acknowledge nothing other than to fear God and honour the King.'

There was some clearing of throats amongst those near enough to hear, at this bringing in of the King – which undoubtedly was the last thing that was wanted. Although Montrose had not lifted up his voice, he spoke clearly and slowly, and the crowd, even though unable to hear, maintained an extraordinary hush, so that a barking dog somewhere in one of the flanking closes, made all the competing sound.

James Graham looked down at Warriston, who certainly could hear him. 'Some would have me to blame the late King – the same men who *sold* the late King. God forbid! He, if as some say he lived a saint, did die a martyr. I pray God that I may make as fair an end as he did. As for His Majesty now living, I die his servant. And say to you that never any people, I believe, might be more happy in a king. I pray that he be so dealt with as not to be betrayed, as his father was.'

Warriston was gesticulating at the hangman – who, however, looked at the Provost. That man gave no sign.

'It is enough,' the prisoner said, turning back to the boy. 'Overmuch perhaps, Robert? I have no more to say, save that I desire your prayers. I leave my soul to God, my service to my prince, my goodwill to my friends, and my name and charity to you all.'

The dog barked and barked, an irrelevant, weary sound.

Montrose turned to the hangman. 'Now, my friend, play your part. My hands are pinioned – but you will find some small further moneys in my pocket.'

The man gestured to him to climb the few steps higher, to the little platform, only large enough for two, where the noose dangled from the thirty-foot-high gibbet.

Bowing right, left and then to the executioner, he climbed the final ladder unhurriedly but firmly. At the top he made way for the man mounting behind him.

'There is little room up here,' he mentioned smilingly, as he perceived the tears streaming down the hangman's cheeks.

It had been a dull cloudy day, with a chill wind off the sea, but as he stood there waiting, while the other put the noose around his neck and adjusted the knot in place, a brilliant golden shaft of sunlight struck down to irradiate the ancient grey street, its cobblestones and soaring tenements. He had never loved this towering city, but in the sudden illumination of light and colour and shadow, he seemed to see it differently, a place of two faces, two characters, ever at war with itself, cold yet seeking warmth, harsh yet wistfully lovely, steeped in blood yet somehow eternally innocent – like the nation for which it was the capital, self-torn to its enduring hurt.

'God have mercy on this afflicted land!' he said aloud,

chokingly – and the man at his back pushed, and launched him from the platform.

A great gulping sigh arose and swept the crowd like a tide that ebbed and flowed, as the rope jerked taut, and James Graham left Edinburgh gladly for a better place.

POSTSCRIPT

Charles II made a bad bargain. When he arrived in Scotland a month after Montrose's execution, even though he signed the Solemn League and Covenant on landing, it was to threats, humiliation, religious brow-beating – six sermons a day – the cynical exploitation by the Covenanting leadership, though the common people greeted him warmly. Cromwell promptly invaded Scotland with 16,000 of his new Model Army, and Charles was hastily packed off to the North as embarrassment, being forced to denounce his father's blood-guiltiness, as sop. Cromwell defeated David Leslie at Dunbar, largely because of clerical intervention, with great slaughter. Charles became a fugitive in his own kingdom, and the victor took up residence in the same Moray House in Edinburgh's Canongate where Argyll had watched Montrose pass on the hangman's cart. The Campbell played a double game, ferrying between Edinburgh and the skulking King in the North; and on New Year's Day, 1651 he actually placed the crown on Charles's head at Scone – but made it abundantly clear that he could take it off again equally well. But Cromwell was more than a match for both of them, out-manoeuvring Argyll and eventually defeating Charles at Worcester. The young King was smuggled back to Holland and nine more years of exile.

After Cromwell's death in 1658 both kingdoms quickly rejected his Protectorate. The Restoration followed, and Charles at last returned to his two thrones. But not to his ancient kingdom of Scotland. Never again would he set foot in that hated land.

In July 1661 the Scots Parliament revoked all sentences on the great Marquis of Montrose. A solemn procession was organised to collect all available portions of his body, to bring them to lie in state in the Abbey of Holyrood, till the parts might come in from farther afield. On the 11th of May next year Edinburgh went *en fete*. The greatest state funeral ever staged carried the remains of James Graham for final burial in St. Giles. The castle cannon thundered, the crowds cheered, fourteen earls carried the splendid coffin, the insignia of the Garter on top – with a clutch of Graham lairds, including Pate Graham of Inchbrakie to see that they did it properly – and twelve other peers bore the pall, including the Lords Madderty and Frendraught who had both survived. And in the same Edinburgh Castle where the cannon belched, Archibald Campbell, Marquis of Argyll, lay prisoner, listening. He was executed for treason a few days later, at the same spot on which James Graham had died, and his head fixed upon the spike which had borne his enemy's. The same court as condemned Argyll did as much for Johnston of Warriston, and he was hanged at the Cross in July the same year.

David Leslie, victor of Philiphaugh, was created Lord Newark by Charles, in August, with a pension for life.

Nigel Tranter

The first of two enthralling novels about
THE MARQUIS OF MONTROSE

The Young Montrose

**James Graham
— the brilliant young Marquis of Montrose**

One man alone could not change the course of history. But James
Graham was determined to try. A gallant soldier, talented leader and
compelling personality, his fame has echoed down the centuries. For
the young Marquis of Montrose was to give his utmost in the service of
his beloved monarch.

After his great Robert the Bruce trilogy, Nigel Tranter embarks on the
first part of the fascinating story of Montrose.

Robert The Bruce

BOOK 1: THE STEPS TO THE EMPTY THRONE

The Heroic story of Robert the Bruce and the turbulent struggle for an Independent Scotland

The year is 1296 and Edward Plantagenet, King of England, is determined to hammer the rebellious Scots into submission. Bruce, despite internal clashes with that headstrong figure, William Wallace, and his fierce love for his antagonist's god-daughter, gives himself the task of uniting the Scots against the invaders from the South.

And so begins this deadly struggle for national survival – with battle-scarred Scotland as the prize.

BOOK 2: THE PATH OF THE HERO KING

Robert the Bruce – his rise from the ashes of defeat to the glowing triumph of Bannockburn

At the opening of this stirring novel, the reader meets Bruce as a man broken in every way except in spirit. He has been excommunicated and is a fugitive from the English. With the exception of his wife, nobody has any faith in him and his vision of freedom. Indeed the war-weary Scots seem long past caring.

But from this desperate situation and in the face of apparently unbearable setbacks where he loses all but his life, Robert the Bruce rises and finally faces the English at the historic battle of Bannockburn.

BOOK 3: THE PRICE OF THE KING'S PEACE

Robert the Bruce – his passionate struggle for Scotland's freedom continued

Bannockburn was far from the end for Robert the Bruce and Scotland: not even the beginning of the end – only the end of the beginning. There remained fourteen years of struggle, savagery, heroism and treachery before the English could be brought to sit at a peace-table and to acknowledge Bruce as a sovereign king.

This superb novel charts these years, revealing the splendid flowering of Bruce's character – now a real king, reunited with his wife Elizabeth and determined to continue the fight for an independent Scotland, sustained by a passionate love for his land and people.

THE ROBERT THE BRUCE TRILOGY

Acclaimed by the critics:

"Very readable ... the author weaves his way authoritatively through the highways and byways of this bloodthirsty period, and paints some life-like portraits of top people of the time"

DAILY TELEGRAPH

"Mr Tranter writes with knowledge and feeling"

THE SCOTSMAN

"Nigel Tranter's gift of storytelling is aided in this superb tale by a wealth of historical incident and colour"

DARLINGTON EVENING DESPATCH

"Nigel Tranter is no dry-as-dust historian, but his wide-ranging tremendous story is not all blood and fire. It has humour, colour and beauty and unexpected tenderness. It is a novel to remember"

MANCHESTER EVENING NEWS

"It's all stirring stuff"

GLASGOW EVENING TIMES

"... this is historical novel writing at its best ... a book of consistently high standard of literary artistry ... a very fine work indeed"

CORK EXAMINER

"Absorbing ... a notable achievement"

THE SCOTSMAN

"It is a rich and complex web that Mr. Tranter has woven ... a rattling good yarn"

ABERDEEN PRESS AND JOURNAL

"A fine achievement, displaying a high standard of professional craftsmanship and wide research"

SCOTLAND'S MAGAZINE

CORONET BOOKS

ALSO BY NIGEL TRANTER,
AND AVAILABLE IN CORONET—

The Robert the Bruce Trilogy

☐ 15098 X	The Steps to the Empty Throne	95p
☐ 16222 8	The Path of the Hero King	95p
☐ 16324 0	The Price of the King's Peace	95p
☐ 16466 2	Black Douglas	£1.25
☐ 18768 9	The Clansman	40p
☐ 18767 0	Gold for Prince Charlie	40p
☐ 21237 3	The Wallace	£1.25
☐ 16213 9	Montrose: The Young Montrose	50p

'Nigel Tranter captures the spirit of the times and with an absorbing attention to detail.' *Yorkshire Evening Post*